Praise for *Before I Die*

'I don't care how old you are. This book will not leave you'
New York Times

'A book that will make you happy to be alive' *Heat*

'This is an affecting and brave novel. Tessa is such a rich character . . .
For everyone, it is a reminder to value the people that matter, seize the
moment, wish with courage, adventure with relish' *Guardian*

'Extraordinary' *Sunday Times*

'A sad and beautiful book' *Irish Times*

Praise for *You Against Me*

'I loved it . . . beautifully written with a painful but penetrating
awareness' Jill Murphy, *TheBookbag.co.uk*

'A tale of love across the social divide . . . a triumph' *Observer*

'Blows other novels out of the water' *Sugar*

'An intense and arresting love story'
Natasha Harding, *The Sun*

'A thrilling, high stakes novel of love across the barricades . . .
gripping' Julia Eccleshare, *LoveReading.co.uk*

'A rich, sensitive, highly accomplished novel'
Robert Dunbar, *Books for Keeps*

Jenny Downham trained as an actor and worked in alternative theatre before starting to write. Her first novel, *Before I Die*, is an international bestseller. It won the Branford Boase Award for most promising debut, the Australian Silver Inky Award for best international novel and was shortlisted for the Guardian's Children's Fiction Prize. Jenny lives in London.

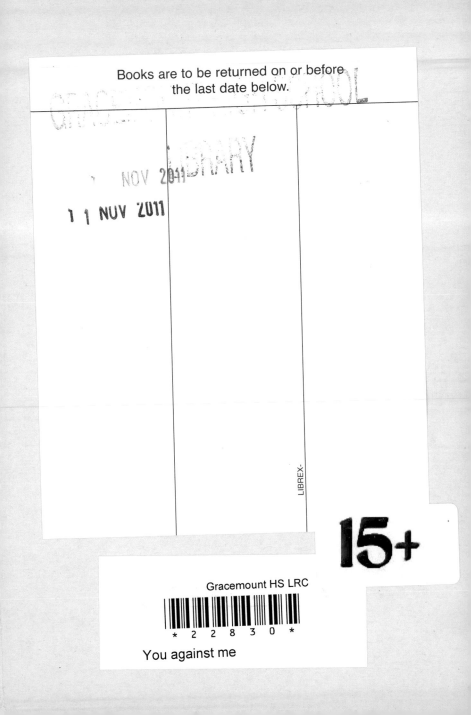

Books are to be returned on or before
the last date below.

NOV 2011

1 1 NOV 2011

15+

Also by Jenny Downham:

Before I Die

you
against
me

jenny downham

David Fickling Books

YOU AGAINST ME
A DAVID FICKLING BOOK 978 1 849 92048 3

First published in Great Britain by David Fickling Books,
a division of Random House Children's Books
A Random House Group Company

Hardback edition published 2010
This edition published 2011

1 3 5 7 9 10 8 6 4 2

The Random House Group Limited supports the Forest Stewardship
Council (FSC), the leading international forest certification
organization. All our titles that are printed on Greenpeace-approved
FSC-certified paper carry the FSC logo. Our paper procurement
policy can be found at www.randomhouse.co.uk/environment.

Mixed Sources
Product group from well-managed
forests and other controlled sources
www.fsc.org Cert no. TT-COC-002139
© 1996 Forest Stewardship Council

Set in Frutiger Light

DAVID FICKLING BOOKS
31 Beaumont Street, Oxford, OX1 2NP

www.**randomhouse**.co.uk
www.**totallyrandombooks**.co.uk

Addresses for companies within The Random House Group Limited
can be found at: www.randomhouse.co.uk/offices.htm

THE RANDOM HOUSE GROUP Limited Reg. No. 954009

A CIP catalogue record for this book is available from the British Library.

Printed and bound in Great Britain by CPI Bookmarque, Croydon, CR0 4TD

For HJD and AKD

One

Mikey couldn't believe his life.

Here was the milk on the counter in front of him. Here was Ajay, hand out expectantly. And here was Mikey, scrabbling for coins among the old receipts and bits of tissue in his jacket pocket. A woman in the queue behind him shuffled her feet. Behind her, a bloke coughed impatiently.

Anger stirred Mikey's gut. 'Sorry,' he mumbled. 'I'll have to leave it.'

Ajay shook his head. 'Take the milk and pay me tomorrow, it's all right. And here, take some chocolate for your sisters.'

'No. You're OK.'

'Don't be daft, take it.' Ajay put a couple of Kit Kats in the carrier bag with the milk. 'And have a good day, yeah?'

Mikey doubted it. He hadn't had one of those for weeks. Still, he managed a quick nod of thanks, grabbed the bag and legged it.

Outside, the rain was still going, a fine mist falling into light from the fluorescent strip above the door. He breathed in deep, trying to smell the sea, but the air smelled of fridges – something to do with the fans blowing warm from the shop behind him. He yanked up his hood and crossed the road back to the estate.

When he got back to the flat, Holly was sitting on the carpet in front of the TV, eating Cookie Crisps from the packet. Karyn had stopped crying and was kneeling behind her, quietly brushing her sister's hair.

Mikey looked her up and down. 'You feeling better?'

'A bit.'

'So, you want to tell me what happened?'

Karyn shrugged. 'I tried to go out. I got as far as the front door.'

'Well, that's something.'

She rolled her eyes. 'Crack open the champagne.'

'It's a start.'

'No, Mikey, it's the end. Holly needed milk for cereal and I couldn't even manage that.'

'Well, I've got some now, so you want a cup of tea?'

He went to the kitchen and filled the kettle. He opened the curtains, then the window. The rain was slowing down and it smelled fresh out there now. He could hear a child crying. A woman shouting. A door slammed three times. *Bang. Bang. Bang.*

Holly came in and dumped the cereal box on the counter. Mikey waggled the collar of her pyjama top. 'Why aren't you dressed for school?'

'Because I'm not going.'

'Yeah, you are.'

She collapsed backwards against the fridge, her head flung

10

up towards the ceiling. 'I can't go to school, it's the bail hearing!'

He frowned at her. How the hell did she know about that? 'Listen, Holly, if you promise to go and get dressed, I'll give you a Kit Kat.'

'Is it two or four sticks?'

'Four.'

He rummaged in the carrier bag, pulled out one of the bars and dangled it at her. 'And can you wake Mum up?'

Holly looked up, surprised. 'Really?'

'Yeah.' If this wasn't an emergency, he didn't know what was.

Holly shook her head as if the idea was crazy, grabbed the Kit Kat and ran away up the stairs.

Mum thought the police would help Karyn, that was the trouble. After taking Karyn to the station and reporting what had happened, Mum had stepped back, probably telling herself she'd done her bit. But the police were crap. They'd asked Karyn loads of personal questions, even though she was upset. Then the cop who brought her home frowned at the mess, like she was judging the whole family. Mum thought that was normal, but Mikey had bitten his tongue in frustration, tasted blood in his mouth, the rust and the thickness of it.

Later, when the cop went, Mikey got the address out of Karyn and told Jacko to bring the car. Jacko brought the lads with him too, but when they got to the bastard's house they were too late – Tom Parker had been arrested hours ago and forensics were already scouring the place.

For nearly two weeks Mikey had tried to swallow the anger. But how did he stop his stomach tilting every time Karyn cried? How did he watch Holly stroking Karyn's arm, squeezing her shoulder, giving little wet taps to her face, like she was a radio that needed tuning or a TV that had gone wrong?

Mum's solution was to hide herself away. But an eight-year-old comforting a fifteen-year-old meant the world was upside down. And something had to be done about it.

He made the tea and took it through, put it on the table in front of Karyn. She'd made a nest for herself on the sofa. She kept doing that – covering herself with cushions, blankets, jumpers.

Mikey went over and sat on the edge. 'How you feeling now?' With the light behind her she looked so sad.

'He's probably out already,' she said. 'Just walking about having a nice time.'

'He won't be allowed anywhere near you. He won't be allowed to text you or talk to you or anything. He'll probably be tagged, so he can't go out after dark.'

She nodded, but she didn't look sure. 'There's this girl at school,' she said. 'Last term she had seven boyfriends and everyone said she was a slag.'

This again. 'You're not a slag, Karyn.'

'And there's a boy in my tutor group and he had ten girlfriends. You know what they call him?'

Mikey shook his head.

'A player.'

'Well, they're wrong.'

'So what's the word for someone like him?'

12

'I don't know.'

She sighed, lay back on the sofa and stared at the ceiling. 'I watched this programme on TV,' she said. 'What happened to me happens to loads of girls. Loads and loads.'

Mikey looked at his nails. They were all ragged. Did he bite them? When did he start doing that?

'Most girls don't report it, because hardly any boys get done for it. Something like six in a hundred. That's not very many, is it?'

Mikey shook his head again, bit his lip.

'When I opened the door just now, there were some kids down in the courtyard and they all looked at me. If I go back to school, everyone will stare at me too.' She lowered her eyes and he felt the shame wash off her in waves. 'They'll look at me as if I deserved it. Tom Parker invited me to his house and I went, so how can anything be his fault?' She pushed a handful of hair from her face. 'That doesn't even make any sense.'

He wanted her to stop talking. He felt a rising panic that if she didn't stop right now, she was going to go on and on for ever. Maybe she'd even talk about the night it happened. He couldn't bear to listen to that again.

'I'm going to get him for you,' he said. It came out loud and sounded very certain.

'You are?'

'Yeah.'

It was strange how words meant something when they came out of your mouth. Inside your head they were safe and silent, but once they were outside, people grabbed hold of them.

She sat up. 'What are you going to do?'

'I'm going to go to his house and smash his head in.'

Karyn pressed the flat of her hand against her forehead as if the thought of it gave her a headache. 'You'll never get away with it.'

But Mikey could tell by the sudden glow in her eyes that she wanted him to do this for her. He hadn't done it and he should have done it. And if he did it, then she could stop hurting.

There was a bloke on the estate no one messed with. He'd got his son's moped back when some kids nicked it. He knew people who knew people. That was the kind of man everyone admired. If you tried to hurt him, you'd bounce off. Mikey had never battered anyone before, but the thought of that bloke made him feel stronger. He stood up, certain of his plan. He'd go alone this time, take gloves and wear a hoodie. If he didn't leave fingerprints, he'd get away with it.

He went to the kitchen and dragged the tool box out from under the sink. Just holding the spanner made him feel better – there was something about how heavy it was, how definite it felt to hold it in his hand. The feelings went into the object. He felt positively cheerful as he put on his jacket, rammed the spanner into his pocket and did up his zip.

Karyn looked at him, her eyes shining. 'You're seriously going to get him?'

'Yep.'

'And you're seriously going to hurt him?'

'I said so, didn't I?'

And that's when Mum staggered in, fag in hand, shielding her eyes like everything was too bright.

Holly was jumping up and down behind her. 'Look!' she cried. 'Mum's awake. She's actually downstairs.'

'Reporting for duty,' Mum said.

It was like watching someone come up from a dive. She had to remember who she was, that she really did live here, that today was the bail hearing and this family really did need to get their act together.

Holly cleared a place for her on the sofa, then sat on her lap and rubbed noses with her. 'Do I have to go to school? Can I spend the day with you instead?'

'Course you can.'

'No!' Mikey said. 'Karyn's cop's coming round, remember?'

Mum frowned. 'Is she, why?'

'Because that's what she does.'

'I don't want her to come any more,' Karyn said. 'She asks stupid questions.'

'Well, she's coming anyway,' Mikey snapped, 'so Holly can't be here, can she? You want a cop to notice she's not in school?'

Light dawned on his mother's face. She looked around the lounge and over to the kitchen. Both rooms were a mess – the table covered in junk, unwashed plates and saucepans in the sink.

'You've got about an hour,' Mikey told her.

She glared at him. 'You think I don't know that?'

Holly put the TV back on at top volume and music crashed around them.

'Turn it off,' Mikey yelled. It would send their mum back to bed. But Holly ignored him so he unplugged it.

Mum rubbed her face over and over. 'Make me a coffee, Mikey.'

Make it yourself, he thought. But still, he switched the kettle back on and rinsed out a mug.

'After this smoke I'll wash up,' Mum said. She took another puff on her cigarette, then looked right at him in that way she sometimes did, as if she could see right inside him. 'You look tired.'

'Looking after you lot, that's why.'

'Where were you last night?'

'Out and about.'

'Were you with that new girlfriend? Sarah, is it?'

'Sienna.'

'That was the last one.'

'No, that was Shannon.'

Holly laughed long and loud. 'You're so *bad*, Mikey!'

In his pocket the spanner hummed. He handed Mum her coffee. 'I have to go now.'

'Go where?'

'I've got business.'

She scowled at him. 'I don't want you looking for trouble.'

She was a bit clever like that. You thought she was hung-over and wouldn't notice stuff, but she often did.

'I mean it,' she said. 'Keep your nose out. We don't need any more hassle.'

But all he said was, 'I'm going.'

'What about Holly? She can't walk to school on her own.'

'Then you'll have to take her. That's what parents are for, isn't it?'

She shook her head at him. 'You know what's wrong with you, Mikey?'

'No, Mum, but I bet you're about to tell me.'

She took up her fag, knocked off the ash and took a last deep drag, blowing the smoke right at him. 'You're not as tough as you think you are.'

Two

Down the stairs, two at a time. Past graffiti walls – AIMEE IS A SLAPPER, LAUREN SUCKS FOR FREE, CALL TOBY IF YOU WANT HOT SEX – and out the main doors into the street. Mikey swung a left, avoiding the take-away wrappers and beer cans strewn round the bus shelter, dodging two old blokes with their shopping trolleys taking up all the room on the pavement, and started to run. Away from the estate, past the crowd of kids outside Ajay's with their breakfasts of crisps and Coke, past the butcher's and the card shop, towards the high street.

The sky was flat and grey. The air smelled of diesel and fish. He ran through the market. The stalls were going up, the crazy colours of the fruit and vegetables all chucked together. The usual group of lads hung about on the benches. He ran past a girl with a pram, a woman counting her change outside Lidl, an old man with a walking stick, an old woman clutching his arm, both tiny and hunched.

He was going to keep running until he got there. He was going to mash Tom Parker. Tom Parker would never grow old.

At the traffic lights, a bloke leaned out of his car window and whistled at a girl. 'Smile for me, baby.'

The girl gave the bloke the finger, then saw Mikey and waved. 'Hiya, Mikey.'

He jogged on the spot as she crossed the road towards him. 'Hey, Sienna. I can't talk now.'

She pressed herself close, gave him a quick kiss. 'You're all sweaty.'

'I was running.'

'Away from me?'

He shrugged as if that was too complicated to understand. 'I need to go.'

She crossed her arms and frowned at him. 'Will I see you later?'

It was like the world got bigger or louder or something, pressing in on him and asking for stuff. He looked right at her, tried to feel what he'd felt only a minute earlier when he saw her waving, some sort of warmth.

'Meet me at work,' he said. 'I don't mind.'

'You don't mind? Well, thanks very much!' She wrapped her arms around herself, didn't even look back at him as she walked away.

He wasn't good for her. He wasn't actually sure he'd ever be good for anyone. He couldn't be bothered most of the time. Girls asked too many questions, and they always expected you to know how they were feeling, and he was always getting it wrong.

He'd lost minutes now, lost momentum. He started running again. Away from the high street, following the curve of Lower

Road. Groups of kids walked slowly in the same direction – a gathering, a building up. Karyn should be with them. He ran in the road to avoid them, past the teachers' car park, past the gates.

He stalled when he saw some of Karyn's mates on the bridge, four of them huddled together looking down at the water. One of them spotted him and nudged the others and they all turned round.

He was supposed to stop, he knew that. He was supposed to go over and tell them how Karyn was, to pass on her thanks for the notes and little presents they kept sending. But he knew what would happen if he did – they'd ask questions. Like, *When will she see us?* And, *Why won't she answer our texts?* Like, *When's the trial?* And, *Do you think she'll ever come back to school?* And he'd have to tell them that he didn't know, that nothing had changed since the last time they'd asked.

He snapped on a smile and waved. 'Can't stop.'

Dodging cars, faster now, over the junction, past the station and up the Norwich Road. One foot in front of the other like a warrior. He thought of Karyn as he ran. He was the only brother she had and it was his job to take care of her. He'd never felt that before, the terrible responsibility of it. He felt adult, male, purposeful. He could do this, he really could. It'd be easy. He checked his pocket for the spanner. It was still there. It felt right and good.

His legs burned now. He could taste salt on his tongue, like the sea got caught in the air on this side of town. It was fresher here, wilder. There was more space for things. Here was Wratton Drive,

Acacia Walk and Wilbur Place. Even the names were different, the trees taller.

He slowed to a jog. Here was the lane, like something from a country magazine. Here was the gated entrance. And behind it, the house with its lawn and windows, its shine and curtains and space. There was even a Jag XJ sparkling in the driveway.

Mikey heaved himself over the gate and walked in a straight line up the gravel drive. Things would never be the same after he knocked on the door. He knew it like it was written down and stamped with a seal. He was going to mash Tom Parker and watch him leak all over the doorstep.

The knocker was brass, a lion with a bushy mane and golden eyes. He banged it hard, three times. He wanted them to know he meant business.

Nothing. Nobody came.

There was a kind of hush instead, like everything suddenly shut up and was listening, like all the objects in the posh house took a breath and held it in. He touched the wall to steady himself, then knocked again.

A girl opened the door. She was wearing a skirt and T-shirt. Bare legs, bare arms.

She said, 'Yes?'

He wasn't expecting a girl. A girl the same age as Karyn. He could hardly look at her.

'Are you with the caterers?' she said.

'What?'

'Are you here to do the food?'

Maybe he didn't have the right house. He checked the door for a number, but there wasn't one. He looked inside the hallway, as if that would give him a clue. It was huge, all wooden floor and fancy rugs. There was a table, a bench, an umbrella stand, a place for boots and shoes.

The girl said, 'Shall I get my mum?'

He looked at her again – the little skirt she was wearing, the blues and purples of her T-shirt, the way she had her hair in a pony-tail that swung.

He said, 'Are you Tom Parker's sister?'

'Yeah.'

'Is he here?'

She narrowed her eyes. 'No.'

The sound of a dog barking inside the house. It stopped. Silence.

'Where is he then?'

She stepped out, pulled the door shut behind her and leaned against it. 'Are you a friend of his?'

'Yeah.'

'Then you know where he is.'

He fingered the spanner in his pocket. 'Well, I know the bail hearing's today. I just wondered when he'd be home.'

'We don't know.'

Seconds went past, minutes maybe. For the first time he noticed a raw-looking scar running from the corner of her mouth down her chin. She saw him looking and stared right back. He knew about girls and she felt bad about that scar.

He smiled. 'So, what's your name then?'

She blushed, but didn't look away. 'My dad put a message on Tom's Facebook page to tell his friends what was happening.'

Mikey shrugged. 'I haven't checked my computer for days.'

'Do you know him from college?'

'Yeah.'

'I haven't seen you before.'

He thought of the college in town where he'd gone to ask about catering courses once, and held her gaze. 'Well, I'm so busy studying, I don't get time to socialize. I don't want to mess up my exams.'

She obviously fell for it because her face softened. 'Tell me about it. Mine start in May and I've hardly done any work.'

That was ages away, why was she worrying? But talking about it changed something in her. She leaned towards him a fraction, as if she'd decided to trust him. 'Listen,' she said, 'we're having a party later.'

A party? Because her brother was out on bail?

'Come if you like. Tom could do with friends around him tonight.'

But before he could tell her what he thought of that, a woman came round the corner of the house, waving crisply at them. 'At last,' she called. 'I was beginning to panic.'

The girl shot him a look of apology. 'She thinks you're the caterer.'

The woman came up, swinging a clipboard and looking at Mikey. 'You're with Amazing Grazing, yes?'

The girl sighed. 'No, Mum. He's not.'

23

'Oh, who are you then? Are you the marquee man?'

He was supposed to answer. He was supposed to say no, but all he could think was that she would realize at once, that she wouldn't be fooled like her daughter. She would call the dog, security guards, the police.

'He's one of Tom's friends, Mum.'

'Oh, I see. Well, Tom's not due until later.'

'I told him that.'

The woman turned to her. 'It's all right, love. Why don't you get back to your revision?'

The girl gave Mikey a quick smile, then went back through the door and shut it behind her. He was left with the mother.

'I hope you don't mind,' she said. 'We really are very busy.'

He hated her. That she didn't know him at all, that she dismissed him so easily.

'Come back for the party. All Tom's friends are welcome.' She walked briskly away clutching her clipboard, her bony arse barely moving. No meat to her, no swing.

He stood there for a minute, wondering if it was all a joke.

He looked at the driveway, at the trees lining the fence, at the electric gate – so different from the estate, the noise of people living close together. Where were the cars, the yelling, the doors slamming, the sound of other people's lives?

In his jacket pocket, the spanner hurt his ribs. He smiled as he walked round the Jag twice. Karyn said the bastard's car was snazzy. Here it was – yellow as a canary and so clean it reflected the sky in its windows.

It was easy, like running a pen across paper, and so satisfying to know how expensive it would be to fix. He let the spanner find a route, let it zigzag across the door, scratch a dented path across the wheel trim and over the bonnet – like a tin you could open if you cut all the way round, then ripped off the lid. The only thing missing was blood.

He'd come back for that later.

Three

There's a way of slicing the skin from an orange that means none of the bitter white stuff gets left on the fruit. Mikey didn't use to know this. Dex had taught him. It was hypnotic, seeing if he could peel the whole thing without the skin breaking once, coils of bright orange trailing to the floor. He liked his fingers being sticky. He liked knowing that when he'd peeled the whole lot, Dex was going to show him how to make a brandy glaze.

There was peace at the pub. Routine. Jacko poured peas and sweetcorn into saucepans of hot water. Dex scrubbed potatoes by the back door, his bare feet in the rain. Mikey had sorted the salad bar like he did every morning – prawn cocktail, egg mimosa, coleslaw. They were OK, the three of them. Everything was as it should be. It was easy to forget the world outside.

'You two boys are quiet today,' Dex said. 'You got girl trouble again?'

Mikey shook his head. 'Not the kind you mean.'

'I have,' Jacko said. 'I can't get one.'

'Sienna's got a sister,' Mikey said.

'What's she like?'

'Dunno, never met her.'

'How long you been seeing Sienna?'

'Two weeks.'

Jacko laughed. 'Well, introduce me to her sister quick, 'cos that's a world record for you.'

Dex waved the peeler at him. 'If I had daughters, you two would terrify me.'

'It's Mikey you want to be scared of,' Jacko said. 'He can get any girl he wants, I swear it. Hey, Mikey, tell Dex about your first time.'

'With Sienna?'

'No, your *very* first time.'

Mikey grinned. 'I'm not telling him that.'

'She went down on him,' Jacko said. 'Met her in a bar, never even knew her name and she went down on him.'

Dex tutted. 'That stuff's private. You shouldn't be talking about things like that.'

'Can you believe it?' Jacko said. 'That any girl would do that?'

'I can't believe half the things you two get up to,' Dex said.

Mikey wondered what Dex would think if he knew about Sienna crying into her pillow the night before. How he hadn't wanted to kiss her, how he couldn't be bothered to undress her, how he'd almost changed his mind about the whole thing and then crept home in the middle of the night.

He stared at Dex for a bit, trying to work him out. He had a shaved head and a mad French accent and he looked like he'd thump you if you eyed him wrong, but Mikey had never heard him raise his voice, never seen him lose his temper. He had tattoos on his hands that he did himself with a pin and a bottle of ink – I LOVE SUE spread across his knuckles. He did stuff for her too – fantastic grub after hours, presents when it wasn't her birthday. He even wrote her a song once. Jacko said he was a doormat. But maybe that was love?

The door swung open and Sue stood there. She folded her arms and looked the three of them up and down. 'I need a cleaner. Someone chucked up in the bogs last night.'

'You're looking at chefs, mon amour,' Dex told her, without looking up from his peeling.

She snorted, took a step in and tapped Mikey on the shoulder. 'You'll do.'

Mikey shook his head at her. 'I'm about to make a flan.'

'It's a pub, not a Gordon bloody Ramsay restaurant. You're here to pot-wash, and you're here to clean the toilets if that's what I want you to do. Come on, we open in twenty minutes.'

He took the plastic apron she offered and tied it over his jeans. He followed her through the bar to the cleaning cupboard. She handed him a mop, a bucket, a bottle of bleach, then led him to the toilets. 'And make sure you wash your hands after.'

As he threw buckets of hot water and bleach into the bogs, Mikey felt a heaviness settle over him. It was all right if he was in the kitchen, or out with Jacko. Even with a girl it went away a bit. But these last two weeks, whenever he was at home or just by himself, it crashed back. As he washed down the walls with a mop, he thought about where he'd be in a year, two, five. He counted out ages. In five years Karyn would be twenty. Holly would be thirteen. His mum would be forty-two. He'd be twenty-three. He shrugged the numbers away in irritation. It was the kind of calculation kids did. Go too far with numbers like that and you ended up dead.

He tried not to breathe in the stink as he swilled the mop under the tap. He tried to remember that one day he'd be worth more than this. He'd live in London, maybe get a place in Tottenham, where his mum grew up. He'd have a chef's job and earn tons of cash. He'd get season tickets for Spurs and invite Holly to all the home games. He tried to believe it as he put everything back in the cleaning cupboard and washed his hands with soap from the dispenser.

He needed a fag. Surely Sue wouldn't moan at him for that? The bogs were sparkling. Outside, it was raining hard, a sudden rush dumping from the sky. He liked it. It matched his mood.

He stared at the cars parked by the harbour wall, their windows steamed up, the people inside waiting for the pub to get its act together and serve them lunch.

The door swung open and Jacko came and lit up a fag next to him. Together they watched a girl walk past, hands in her pockets, shoulders shrugged against the rain. Jacko sucked his teeth. 'I love the way every single one of them is different.'

He was always coming out with mad stuff. It was comforting. With your oldest friend you should be free to say what was on your mind.

'Bail today,' Mikey said.

Jacko nodded. 'I saw your mum in the pub last night. She reckoned he'll definitely get it this time.'

'The cops made some deal with his lawyer, that's why. Soon he'll be running about like he did nothing wrong.'

'What're you going to do?'

'Dunno. Got to do something though. Karyn says she's never leaving the flat again.'

Jacko looked at Mikey long and hard. 'You serious?'

'I told her he wouldn't be allowed near her, but it made no difference.'

'Bastard!'

Mikey nodded, knew Jacko would understand. 'I went by his house again. I wanted to get him, but he wasn't there.'

'You went solo?'

'I got mad. I had to do something.' Mikey threw his fag end into a puddle, listened to it hiss. 'Anyway, you were at work.'

'I'd drop everything.' Jacko slapped Mikey's back with the flat of his hand. 'You should know that.'

Mikey told him the whole story then – the spanner, the journey to the house, the party to celebrate getting bail. It was good standing there talking about it. It warmed Mikey up.

'They've got caterers and everything. I met his mum and sister and they thought I was a mate of his, even invited me to the fucking thing.'

Jacko whistled. 'Man, that's mental!'

'Imagine telling Karyn that. Imagine how that'll make her feel.'

'Don't tell her, it's too harsh.' Jacko chucked his rollie stub into the puddle at their feet. Two soggy cigarette butts floating together like a couple of boats.

A plan began to form in the silence. It was a crazy plan, and Mikey tried to push it away, but it kept building. He thought of home, told himself he should have a kick-about in the courtyard with Holly to make up for not taking her to school, told himself he had to get some shopping in case Mum forgot. But the plan wouldn't go away. His family would have to manage – he couldn't look after them all the time. 'You busy tonight?'

A slow smile dawned on Jacko's face. 'We're going to crash the party?'

'I promised Karyn I'd get him. Why not get him on the night he least expects it?'

'You want me to call backup?'

He meant Woody, Sean, Mark – the lads they'd gone to school with, the ones they'd fought side-by-side with through years of playground scraps and teen battles over territory. They still met up for regular games of pool and a pint, but all of them had moved on. Woody was married now, even had a kid on the way. Sean and Mark were apprentice brickies. The night Karyn came back from the police station, they'd been solid when Jacko called them. None of them would forget the anger they shared that night, but it wasn't fair to ask them again. Karyn was *his* sister, this was *his* fight.

'We'll get noticed if we go team-handy.'

Jacko nodded. Mikey could see him running over the basics in his head – tactics and plans for intel kicking in. In school fights,

31

Jacko had been strategy king. His hours on the Xbox proved useful in the real world.

Sue came out then and tapped at her watch.

'There'll be loads of people there,' Jacko said as they followed her back through the bar. 'But we'll have darkness as cover.' He held the door to the kitchen open. Dex had the radio tuned in to his usual country station, where the songs were always about divorce and heartache and preachers. He waved the peeling knife at them.

'My boys!' he said.

Jacko leaned in to Mikey. 'You want me to drive?'

'You're up for it?'

'Course! I'm here for you, man. I'll do whatever you need.'

Mikey smiled. It was the first time anything had gone right for days.

Four

Ellie Parker sat on the patio steps and waved her arms like antennae at the sun. It was strange, because as she did this, the whole garden fell suddenly silent. She held her breath because she didn't want to spoil it, it was so beautiful. For a moment, it was as if she was controlling the universe. Then the catering woman clunked past carrying a stack of boxes, and her mother came up with her clipboard and said, 'Thank goodness that rain's stopped.'

Ellie tugged a leaf from the bay tree and broke it in half, smelled it, then ripped it to shreds. She scattered the sharp pieces over the steps. She ripped another and another, their green turning bruised and ruined in her hands.

Her mother sat next to her and leaned in close. 'Stop worrying, love. Your brother's safely in the car on his way home.'

'What if the police change their minds?'

'It's been through Crown Court. There's no going back.'

'What if they suddenly get new information?'

Mum shook her head, smiling confidently. 'Dad's got everything under control and we're going to get through this, you wait and see.'

Ellie wanted to believe her, but sometimes when she closed her eyes she saw things that felt impossible to get through. She saw Tom taken in for questioning, pale and scared as they led him away. She saw the van parked in the driveway with SCIENTIFIC SERVICES written on the side, and the scene-of-crime officers in their black clothes walking out of the house with Tom's laptop, his bed sheets and duvet in plastic bags. Then there were the lads in the car who watched everything from the lane, so you just knew it would be all over town by morning. She saw the officer put a padlock and tape on Tom's door and heard him say, 'Don't tamper with it, please, this room is a crime scene now.' And Dad said, 'Surely we have rights in our own home?' Mum sat on the stairs and wept. Tears washed into her mouth.

Ellie concentrated on trying to calm the nerves in her belly. It was as if something was stuck there and needed to come out. She looked around the garden at the empty tables and stacks of chairs, at the boxes of lanterns waiting to be hung, at the ladder leaning against the fence, and she wished more than anything that it could be just the four of them tonight – back in their old house, miles from here, with a takeaway and a DVD.

Mum nudged her, as if reading her thoughts. 'It'll be fine, Ellie, really it will. We're getting our Tom back. Let's try and be happy today.'

Ellie nodded, but couldn't quite look her in the eye. 'Mum, can I tell you something?'

Her mother's smile died at the corners, her whole body stiffened. 'You can talk to me about anything, you know that.'

'Karyn McKenzie's not taking her exams. In fact, she's left school.'

They sat in awkward silence for a minute. Ellie gnawed on her lip. She should have kept quiet, but it was hard holding on to so many things. Sometimes the smaller ones slipped out.

'I had a friend,' her mother said, 'who got attacked by two men and dragged into a car. She didn't make it up, it really happened. It was terrible and brutal, but she used it as a turning point and changed everything about her life.'

'What's that supposed to mean?'

'It means,' her mother said, standing up and brushing non-existent fluff from her trousers, 'that you make your own luck. Now I'm going to talk to the marquee man. If you hear the car, shout for me. I want to be there when he arrives. And if you're stuck for something to do, put some balloons up.'

Sometimes Ellie imagined Karyn McKenzie as monstrous – cloaked and hooded and laughing maniacally as she clawed Tom down into a sulphurous pit. In real life she knew she was tall and skinny with long dark hair and she lived on a housing estate across town. She fancied Tom, had done for ages apparently. She was clearly desperate for him to notice her that Saturday night, with her red-hot nail varnish, purple lipstick and flaming orange mini-skirt stretched tight around her thighs. At school she had a reputation for being good at Art and pretty much crap at everything else. It did seem crazy to give up your exams though – even a few

GCSEs could lead to college and maybe a career of some kind. If you gave up in Year Eleven, then the whole thing slid away from you for ever.

A girl walked by carrying two silver tea trays. She was Ellie's age, maybe a bit older, dressed in a black skirt and white shirt. She stopped in front of Ellie, said, 'You're the sister, right?' She leaned forward conspiratorially. 'What's it like then? Must be weird for you.' She was wearing a lot of make-up.

Ellie said, 'Haven't you got work to do, or something?' Then she stood up and walked round the side of the house to the driveway.

Sometimes it felt physical, as if walls were moving slowly towards her. Sometimes it felt psychological, a strange panic in her brain, which meant if she had to live in this nightmare for one more minute she'd self-combust. The only way she knew to deal with it was to switch off and think of something else, which was becoming increasingly difficult. Walking away was a whole lot easier. She didn't go far because she didn't have a coat on, just up the gravel drive to the electric gate. She pressed the button, waited for it to slide open and stepped through. The lane was churned to mud and patched with dirty puddles, the first few daffodils trembled on the grass verge. The gate shut behind her.

This was the lane she watched from her window every night, wondering when Tom would come home. *Trust me*, his letter said. She'd wanted the words to take off from the page and circle the sky. Bold, neon words swooping low over town, skimming shops and houses before sweeping up the coast road to hang permanently above the sea. *Trust me*. And everyone would read the words and have faith. The court case would be dropped and they'd all go back to normal.

But faith was hard to hold on to. After twelve whole days and nights, Ellie was unravelling. She couldn't sit, couldn't stand, found it difficult to concentrate on anything. The day was moving quickly, every minute hurtling forwards; even the hours she'd spent doing revision had rushed by.

A cloud passed the sun then, and darkness came skimming down the lane, creating a dark pool of shadow at her feet. A dog barked from some neighbour's garden and almost immediately the cloud shifted and the world glared so brightly that she had to shield her eyes. When she could see again, her dad's car was cornering the lane. And, like a magic trick, Tom's face was at the window, grinning at her.

Ellie whooped. She couldn't help it, it came bursting out of her as the car drew near.

'He's here!' she yelled, and her mum must've been close by, because she came running round the side of the house waving her clipboard.

'Open the gate, Ellie, let them in!'

Here he was, like the Pope, stepping out of the car and into the garden. Mum ran to him, laughing, and he opened his arms to her. They swayed together for a moment as if they were dancing. Ellie was surprised at how tender it was.

She felt strangely shy of him as he looked over their mother's shoulder and smiled at her, as if she'd become an adult in the last fortnight and this was her house and he was the guest. He looked different – thinner maybe.

Ellie said, 'They let you out then?'

He laughed as he ambled over. 'The police wanted to keep me, it's true, but I told them I missed my sister.' He put an arm round her and squeezed her for a moment. 'You OK?'

She smiled. 'I am now.'

His eyes slid back to the car, to Mum heaving his rucksack out of the boot, to Dad unloading the suitcase. It was the case he'd taken skiing. Strange to think it had been in an aeroplane and all the way to the Alps as well as to the young offenders' unit in Norwich.

Dad wheeled it towards them. 'Take a look over there, Tom, at what your sister's done.'

Ellie felt embarrassed as her dad pointed out the banner strung along the fence. It had taken her three afternoons, but it seemed a bit cheesy now. She'd painted the four of them under a rainbow with a giant heart around them. At the top, she'd created a family coat of arms with the motto TOM PARKER IS INNOCENT. But the whole thing was beginning to rip at the corners where she'd tacked it to the fence. It looked more like a tatty old bed sheet than something she once cared about.

'Took her hours,' Dad said, and he gave Ellie a smile. It was the first time he'd looked directly at her for days.

Tom gave her a nudge. 'It's sweet, Ellie, thanks.'

Mum came up with Tom's jacket in her arms, stroking it, smoothing it flat. 'There's a bit of a surprise round the back too,' she said.

'What kind of surprise?' Tom looked suspicious and Ellie felt her pulse race. This hadn't been her idea and she knew Tom might hate it.

'Let's get it over with,' she said, and she led him round the side of house.

A marquee had blossomed on the lawn. The tables inside were lit with heaters, their chairs neatly placed around them. Plates, glasses and cutlery were stacked on a trestle table. This was where the food was going, and already the waitresses were laying out tablecloths and napkins. Up in the walnut tree, Chinese lanterns gently swung, and on every available fence post, strings of balloons tugged in the breeze.

Ellie watched Tom taking it all in. 'It's a party,' she said.

He ran a hand through his hair. 'I gathered that.'

'You don't like it, do you?' She spun round to her parents. 'I told you he wouldn't like it. Didn't I say?'

Her father's face darkened with annoyance. 'Shall we let Tom decide if he likes it or not, Eleanor?'

Mum put her hand on Tom's arm. 'Would you rather have no fuss?'

'You've gone to loads of trouble,' Tom said. 'But what if I hadn't got bail?'

Mum did a sort of punctured laugh. 'Your father refused to entertain that possibility.'

'Never a doubt,' Dad said breezily. 'I booked the caterers days ago, that's how certain I was.' He reached over and patted Tom on the back. 'So, what do you reckon? Pleased with it?'

'It's fine.' Tom took another look around. 'You never know, it may even be fun.'

'Good, well done.' Dad beamed at him. 'We've invited everyone who matters. We need to show the world you've got nothing to hide.' He gestured to the suitcase. 'I'll take this upstairs, then I've got a few calls to make. You relax, Tom. You're home and safe now.'

Mum laid her hand flat against Tom's cheek. 'I'll take your jacket in, and check how things are going with the caterers.'

It was weird how they kept explaining themselves – they'd been doing it since Tom got arrested. *I'm just popping into the office. I'm going upstairs to see if I can grab some sleep. We'll be with the lawyer for a while.* It was as if they thought they'd disappear if they didn't say where they were.

'What are you two going to do?' Mum said.

Tom smiled. 'We'll find something.'

Five

The spare room was pink with flocked wallpaper. Ellie and her mum hadn't been able to do anything about that, but they'd got Tom a new mattress and changed the curtains. They'd put the portable TV up on a wall bracket and spread DVDs and books along the shelf.

Tom stood in the doorway and shook his head at it. 'I feel like a guest.'

It was gloomy inside and Ellie snapped on the light. 'Didn't Dad tell you?'

'Probably.' Tom crossed to the bed and sat down, smoothed the duvet with his hands. 'I don't listen to half the stuff he says.'

'Well, he tried to get the police to take the lock off your bedroom door, but everything seems to take so long. It's all new though, the duvet and everything. Me and Mum went shopping.'

'I always think of Gran when I see this room,' he said. 'All those pills she had and how crazy she was.' He looked about, wrinkled his nose. 'It still smells of her in here.'

'We put the commode in the loft, so it shouldn't. Open the window.'

'Does she know about me?' He shot Ellie a glance. 'Or is it too shameful?'

'She barely knows her own name. I think they're waiting to see the outcome before they tell her anything.'

'The outcome? Christ, you sound like Dad.' He reached into his pocket and found his cigarettes, walked to the window and opened it.

Ellie watched him light a cigarette and pull smoke hard into his lungs. It was like fingers down chalkboards or forks over plates. The desperation of it. She wanted to cover her ears, look away. But instead, she sat and watched him inhale and exhale three more times. Finally, he turned to her.

'I'm sorry, Ellie. I shouldn't take it out on you.'

'It's OK.'

'Dad's driving me nuts. He fired the lawyer who mucked up my first bail application and got some top-notch bloke instead. He doesn't trust him though, talks to him as if he's a kid fresh out of law school.'

'He wants the best for you.'

Tom smiled grimly at her. 'It's embarrassing.'

'It'll be over soon.'

'You think? According to the top-notch guy, it's only just begun.'

He blew the last smoke out into the garden, then tossed the butt after it. 'You want to do something exciting?'

'OK.'

'Good. Wait there.'

He wasn't gone long, came back with the hair clippers and planted them in her hand. 'Cut it all off.'

She was stunned. 'All of it?'

'Short back and sides. I don't want it long any more.'

'I don't know how to use them. I've never done it before.'

'It's easy, like cutting grass.'

He set up a chair in the corner of the room by the mirror, then spread newspaper on the floor.

'Will you be angry if I get it wrong?'

Tom ripped off his T-shirt. 'Promise I won't. Anyway, I've got no choice. The nearest barber is in the high street, and my bail conditions don't let me anywhere near it.'

He straddled the chair and Ellie stood behind him, wielding the clippers. Their eyes met in the mirror.

She said, 'This is the most dangerous thing anyone's ever asked me to do.'

He laughed. 'Then you've led a very sheltered life.'

But it had taken Tom ages to grow his hair. It was what defined him, how people described him. *Tom – you know, the boy with all that blond hair.* That he wanted it gone was scary. That he'd chosen her to do it, that the bedroom door was shut, that it was private – these were the things that made it feel dangerous.

'Honestly, Tom, I don't think I can. What if I take off too much and you end up a skinhead?'

'Please, Ellie, before I change my mind.'

She held up a long strand of hair, but hesitated with the clippers. 'You might change your mind? What if you do?'

'I'm kidding. Just do it.'

Handful after handful fell to the floor and onto her bare feet. It drifted beyond the newspaper, driven by the breeze from the window, and piled up in the corner like a nest. His face changed as the hair fell. His eyes looked bigger, his ears appeared, the back of his neck became vulnerable. It was as if she was exposing him.

'You look younger,' was all she said when he asked why she looked sad. And when he wanted to know what was sad about being young, she told him that actually she was glad to be cutting his hair because she'd always been jealous of how good he looked with it long . . .

'I want your metabolism too,' she said. 'You get to eat whatever you want and look like a stick, but I eat one chocolate and I turn to pudge. How come you get all the luck?'

He shook his head. 'You don't even know, do you?'

'Know what?'

'How pretty you are. Everyone says so.'

'Everyone?'

'You know what my mate Freddie calls you?'

She shook her head, slightly afraid.

'Mermaid, that's what.'

'That's not even a compliment. Mermaids just sit about on rocks all day.'

He laughed. 'They're not easy, that's the point. No one gets to shag a mermaid because they don't let you.'

Ellie thought it was more to do with the fact that they had nothing below the waist but a tail, but maybe she was wrong about that, so she didn't say anything. Instead, she turned the attention back to him, because despite everything, she loved him and he needed to know that. As she clipped the hair round his ears, she quietly recited a list of all the nice things he'd ever done for her.

It included everything, from drawing pictures for her to colour in (which was years ago), through starting school (when he let her hang out with him in the playground, even though she was two years younger *and* a girl). Right up to the holiday in Kenya when the dog tried to bite her a second time and he stood in the way (which was the most heroic thing anyone had ever done for her).

'Before we moved house,' she said, 'whenever my friends came round, you'd always hang out for a bit and talk to us. If we ever saw you in town, you'd wave or come over and chat, like you were genuinely interested. No one else's brother ever bothered. I've always been proud of you for that.'

He smiled up at her. 'You say the sweetest things.'

'Well, you *do* the sweetest things. You made that speech at my sixteenth birthday saying how I was the best sister in the world, remember? And when I did that stupid leaving concert at school, you clapped loudest even though I was total rubbish and forgot all my words.'

Tom laughed as she reminded him of these things. It was great. Everything pulled together. He told the story of the summer they'd gone camping in southern France and the site was dull, dull, dull.

The swimming pool was shut and the entertainment was rubbish and the only good things were the pâtisserie and the kites they'd bought from the shop.

'We found that hill,' he said, 'you know the one? We flew the kites from the top and when we got bored we rolled all the way down and ran back up again.'

Ellie was amazed he remembered. She could have cut his hair for hours then. She loved how cosy it was together in the spare room, how she could hear the vague sounds of people setting up the party, their voices low and far away. It gave her courage. 'Can we talk about what happened that night?'

He swung round on the chair to look at her. 'Really? Can't I just have a break?'

Ellie lowered her eyes. 'There are things I don't understand.'

He frowned at her. 'Have you been talking to anyone?'

'Not really.' Ellie had a drifting sensation, as if this conversation was surrounded by smoke. 'I haven't been back to school yet.'

There was silence as they looked at each other. 'If I go down, Ellie, it'll be the end of everything for me.'

'I know.'

'There are guys in there . . .' His voice trailed off and he shook his head as if he'd seen the most unspeakable things. 'It was the longest two weeks of my life.'

There was something in his eyes. Their dark shine reminded her of the autumn he broke his arm, how he sat on the football field and howled with fury, because he had to miss the whole season and he'd only just made the team. She looked away.

'There,' she said. 'I've finished.' She stroked her hands over his hair, smoothing flyaway strands. 'It's cute.'

'Cute?' He rubbed his own hand over his head. 'That wasn't quite what I had in mind.'

'What did you want to look like?'

'Innocent.' He smiled at her in the mirror. 'Inoffensive and above suspicion.'

She sat on his bed and watched him dust the hair from his shoulders with his T-shirt. He sprayed deodorant under his arms, splashed aftershave onto his hands, rubbed them together then smoothed his palms across his face.

'Will I have to go to court and answer questions?' she asked. 'Or will they just read out my statement?'

He ignored her, pulled on his new stripy T-shirt. She'd chosen it for him with Mum last week and it still had the label on. He ripped it off and passed it to her. 'Recycling,' he said.

She put it in her pocket. 'Did you hear me?'

He fiddled with his shirt, straightening it in the mirror. 'You were the only other person here the whole time, which makes you the primary witness. You'll definitely have to go to court.'

Her stomach gripped. 'They can't make me say anything.'

'They can't make you say anything if you didn't *see* anything.'

She nodded. She felt a mixture of pity and fear as she looked at him, because the thought of what she should or shouldn't say made her feel scared. She'd been worrying about it for two weeks. It had been so bad one day that she'd fantasized that a nuclear bomb had gone off and she was the only person left alive. In the fantasy, she'd wandered about opening and closing doors, stirring up dust, picking things up and putting them down. It had been so peaceful.

She gnawed at her lip again. 'When the police interviewed me, I told them I went straight upstairs to bed when you brought everyone back.'

'Well, that's fine then.'

She blushed at the memory of scrambling up from the sofa in her slippers and pyjamas. Karyn and her mate Stacey glittered, surrounded by boys, fresh from the pub. They smiled down at her, told her she should stay and talk to them. But she knew by the look on her brother's face that he wanted her safe upstairs, and she felt such an idiot making an excuse about having a headache.

'The other thing I told them,' Ellie said, 'was I looked out of my window later and saw everyone outside.'

Tom turned from the mirror and blinked at her. 'I didn't know that.'

'I just said everyone looked like they were having a good time and you and Karyn had your arms round each other.'

'What did you say that for?'

'Because the police need to know she fancied you. Was that wrong?'

'It's OK,' he said. 'There's no need to get upset. It's me they're going to grill, not you.'

'She was flirting with you all night though.' Ellie curled her fists tight and pinched her thumbnails into her palms. 'I bet when you went into the bedroom to get the sleeping bag, she just pulled you down on top of her, didn't she?'

Tom winced. 'It's not something I'm proud of, Ellie, but yeah, that's pretty much what happened.'

She nodded. 'I thought so.'

He pushed the chair back under the desk. 'You reckon we can stop talking about this now? A sad little shag with a crazy girl is a bit humiliating to discuss with my sister. Maybe we should go downstairs and see if they need any help.'

He wrapped the newspaper into a parcel and put it in the bin. Ellie picked up the handful of hair from the corner and did the same. She was an idiot. It was horrible for him to be reminded of that night when he was supposed to be feeling safe with his family.

'Are you going to dress up?' he said. 'Team Parker and all that? Best foot forward.'

He was trying to make her laugh. This was how their father would speak.

'All hands on deck,' she said, because she wanted to give him something back.

He patted her quickly on the head. 'Don't forget.'

Another expression from their father. *Don't forget who you are.*

Don't forget whose side you're on.

Six

They parked the car by the river and walked up the lane to the house, Jacko still feeding Mikey last-minute bits of information from Tom Parker's Facebook page. Jacko had checked it out on the computer at work and now they both knew the bastard liked golf and sleeping and that all the friends on his page were girls.

'His favourite celebrity's Vin Diesel,' Jacko said, 'though I don't think we need to let that worry us, because he also likes *Where's Wally?*' He snapped his fingers, laughing. 'We're gonna take him easy!'

But at the gate, even Jacko was silenced. They stood open-mouthed, taking it in. The house was lit up like Christmas, with fairy lights strung in the trees and torches with real flames staked along the path.

Jacko whistled. 'Man, they've gone to town!'

'They've got no shame. I told you.'

The place seemed even bigger than before. There must be at least five bedrooms and the lawn wrapped itself round the whole house. There were flowers that showed up their colours even in the dark, like flowers from a shop stuck in the earth. The windows seemed bigger too, all glaring with light. They obviously didn't worry about heating bills, could just chuck cash away, probably had radiators at full blast and doors open and everything on stand-by all night long. There was a confidence to it that Mikey admired and hated at the same time – how come some people had so much? How come some kids got this for free?

'You think they'll suss we don't belong?' he said.

Jacko screwed up his forehead and looked offended. 'We belong everywhere.'

'What about the scratched-up Jag? You think they'll know it was me?'

'Nah, plenty of people hate the guy. Just keep the spanner out of sight.' Jacko drew in a last chestful of smoke before chucking his fag on the gravel. 'Right, remember what we said? First one to see him sends the other a text, then we reconvene for phase two.'

Mikey checked his mobile. He supposed it was some kind of plan.

Jacko went first, straight through the front door and inside like he knew the place. Mikey made his way round the side, following a trickle of guests just arriving. Round the back of the house, the garden opened up. It felt different from the front, almost tropical, with heaters belching out hot air and the grass still wet from the rain.

There were masses of people – adults as well as kids standing in groups on the lawn, others sitting at tables in a marquee with drinks and plates of food. Mikey was stunned by the effort that had gone into this.

He grabbed a beer from a woman with a tray and knocked half of it back. He wondered if anyone from school would recognize him. It'd been two years since he left and these kids were the ones who went on to college, so it was unlikely. He took another gulp of beer and tried to concentrate. *Find Tom Parker*, that was the plan. *Tell Jacko when he had.*

There was a group of boys sitting at one of the tables, there were more queuing for food, another group swigging beer over by the fence. They all had that posh look Mikey was expecting to find, but none matched the pixellated photo Jacko had shown him in the car.

He walked round the garden once, a whole circuit. Music pumped out from speakers, the leaves on the trees shivered, the grass thumped under his feet. He hated all these people in their smart clothes, with their wine and champagne. He thought of his sisters at home – Holly drawing crazy pictures with colours like mud and grey. Karyn trying to make dinner with no food in the house. Mum asleep. These people didn't care about his family at all. They were here to support Tom Parker. In fact, they were probably laughing at Karyn. Whispering about her, nudging each other. It was unforgivable.

A girl wobbled by on very high heels. She was drunk, he could see that.

'Hey,' he said, 'I'm looking for Tom Parker. You know him?'

She stopped and smiled. Her eyes were dark and drawn round the edge in blue. 'Who are you?'

He couldn't stumble at the first hurdle. 'Joe.' He had to be someone other than himself and he knew he'd never see her again.

'You're very good-looking.'

'So, do you know where Tom is?'

She waved her arm in the vague direction of the house. 'Somewhere. How do you know him?'

'College.' Second time today and it was beginning to sound true.

She leaned in to him as if she had a secret. 'You want to kiss me?'

'Not really.'

She laughed, puckered her lips and moved in closer. 'I bet you do.'

He looked about, but no one was taking any notice. He could pick her up and carry her off. He could drag her behind the marquee where it was dark and do whatever he liked to her. He could say she wanted it, that she asked for it.

'Come on,' the girl said. 'Kiss me then.'

Was this how trashed Karyn was that night?

He nudged her off. 'I don't want to.'

She looked insulted. 'Don't you like me?'

He gave her a peck on the cheek to shut her up. Her skin tasted expensive. He told her he'd see her later, though he'd run if he saw her coming. He waved her off and fumbled for his phone. He couldn't do this. He shouldn't be here. This was the stupidest idea he'd ever had.

Just as he was texting him, Jacko appeared. 'Target located,' he said.

'What?'

Jacko nodded at a tall boy loping across the grass towards a group of men. 'I've been tailing him for five minutes. It's definitely him.'

Tom Parker looked like a tosser – shirt and tie, schoolboy hair, shaking hands with all the adults. Looking at him made Mikey want to puke, made the knot in his gut tighten.

'Let's get him.'

But before he could move, Jacko caught him, said, 'Whoa! That's *not* the plan.'

'Bollocks to the plan!' Mikey tried to shake him off. 'Let go of me. I'm sick of this.'

'You whack him now, you'll get arrested,' Jacko hissed. 'How's that going to help Karyn?'

Mikey shoved him off. 'It's gonna help me!'

A woman walked past and looked curiously at them. 'Hello,' she said. 'Everything all right?'

'Perfect,' Jacko said, putting his arm round Mikey and reining him in. 'We were just saying what a lovely evening for a bail bash.'

The woman moved away, frowning slightly.

Mikey shrugged Jacko off again. 'I hate this place.'

'I know, I know.'

'I hate him too. Look at him – surrounded by suits and still untouchable. He's getting away with everything!'

Jacko sighed, opened his coat, pulled out a bottle and passed it to Mikey. 'I also located the drinks cabinet. I think you'll find this twenty-five-year-old malt whisky will clear your mind.'

Mikey took three long gulps. It flamed in his throat, warmed his belly. It was good to sink inside the feeling that somehow this was all going to work out. He took another gulp, and another.

Jacko smiled. 'Better?'

Mikey nodded. He was thinking of his mum with her morning Valium. For the first time he understood why she talked about taking the edge off the terror.

'He's the centre of attention,' Jacko said, 'so we need to stay calm and move on to phase two.' He winked. 'You get to do what you're best at, Mikey, and talk to girls. We need tactical intelligence – does he do martial arts? Is he left or right-handed? Has he got brothers and are they here? The usual stuff. I'll keep a visual and gather data as I tail him. We both need to suss out the best location for phase three – preferably somewhere dark and quiet with good escape routes.' He checked his watch. 'We'll reconvene on this position in an hour.'

Mikey felt momentarily dizzy. He rubbed his eyes. It would be great to pretend this was an ordinary night, that they'd crashed some random party, that he was here on the pull.

Jacko pressed the whisky bottle on him. 'Keep this, it's doing you good. Think of the Vikings, Mikey. Free booze. Posh birds. We're here to plunder.'

Mikey shook his head as Jacko walked backwards away from him. 'The Vikings?'

'Yep. And don't worry, the face-to-face thing's gonna happen. We'll perforate him at the end, when it's quiet.' He tapped a finger to his head. 'Stay frosty.'

Mikey took another swig of whisky and watched the clouds. Soon it would rain again. A downpour would be good – wet people rushing back to cars, the whole party ruined. Tom Parker would be left alone. An easy target.

Mikey scanned the lawn, looking for him, but he'd gone now, the circle of men broken up. There was the drunk girl again, moving slowly along the fence, staring at her own feet. She wouldn't be any help.

But there – who was that? On the bench, underneath that tree. Lanterns swayed above her, people everywhere, and her simply sitting there, the one still point. Mikey put the whisky in his pocket, plucked two beers from a waitress and smiled. He knew this girl. She'd opened the door to him earlier. She was Tom Parker's sister.

Seven

When he got to the bench, she looked up, but didn't smile.

'Mind if I sit down?' he said.

She shrugged, as if she didn't care either way, and slid along to make room. He put the beers on the bench between them. 'One of these is for you.'

'No thanks.' Her voice was softer than he remembered.

He took out his tobacco and rolled a thin one, offered it across. 'Smoke?'

She shook her head.

'So,' he said, 'not in a party mood then?'

'Not particularly.'

'Missing revision?'

He meant it as a joke, but she didn't get it. 'It's not that, it's just, I never expected it to be so . . .'

She let the sentence drop.

A group of girls cheered as some Lady Gaga song suddenly blared from the speakers outside the marquee. They started dancing, singing along to the words and pointing their fingers at the sky. A couple of boys stood watching and one of the girls wiggled her arse at them. Adults stood about on the grass, leaning towards each other in deep conversation. It was like there were two parties happening at once.

'Your brother knows a lot of people,' he said.

She sighed. 'Never underestimate the power of curiosity.'

'Are any of your friends here?'

'I didn't invite anyone.'

'You invited me.'

'Apart from you.'

She slid a fraction further away to show her utter lack of interest. He smiled. This would be a breeze.

'Where's your boyfriend then? Is he here?'

She frowned. 'Who?'

'Just thought you'd be with someone. Looking like you do.'

'No.'

Mikey inhaled, exhaled. He knew it was up to him to say something else, but most girls would've laughed when he mentioned a boyfriend, would've been flattered. Now everything that came into his head sounded fake. He sat and smoked and tried to work out what to do next.

It was solved for him – her phone rang and she stood up to fish it out of her pocket. 'Tom, yeah, I did text you,' she said. 'Because I couldn't see you anywhere, that's why. This is madness. Do you even know half these people?' She glanced back at Mikey only briefly before walking off down the slope. When she got to the fence, she opened a gate he hadn't even known was there and disappeared through it. Now what did he do?

Across the grass, Jacko was talking to some bloke in a suit and tie. He was taking his responsibilities seriously by the look of it – nodding and smiling, asking questions, gathering information. Mikey felt his throat tighten. That Jacko would do this for him when it wasn't even his fight – it was like having a brother.

He stood up, determined. He was going to walk across the grass and go through that gate and make Tom Parker's sister talk.

As he crossed the lawn, he realized how massive this garden was. Holly would love to live in a place like this – so big she could have her own frigging football pitch. Beyond the fence was the river, so that gate must be a private entrance to it. He imagined him and Holly running down this slope to their boat, jumping in whenever they wanted and getting the hell out of this town.

The lights from the party didn't reach the river, but he could still see the girl through the gate. She was off the phone now, standing there gazing across the water. A train was moving slowly along the tracks on the other side of the river. Its lights splashed the grass at her feet, her face lit up for a second and then went dark again. He'd envy this party if he was on that train – the marquee, the music, the enormity of the place. Funny how things could seem better from far away.

Before he even got through the gate she said, 'You shouldn't sneak up on people in the dark.'

'I wasn't.'

'Yeah, you were.'

59

He shut the gate behind him. 'What's so interesting through here anyway?'

'Nothing.' She waved her hand at the water. 'It's a river. There was a train and now it's gone.' She turned to him. 'As you can see, it's totally fascinating.'

'You should be careful,' he said, 'wandering about on your own.'

She didn't even blink. 'Is that supposed to be funny?'

Her eyes burned with something. Anger? Sadness? He had to look away. Karyn had eyes that deep. He swigged the last of his beer and chucked the empty bottle at the river. They both watched it – a dark missile, arcing against the sky before splashing into the water. Somewhere not far away, a duck called in alarm and then everything went quiet again.

Now what should he do? He wasn't going to look at her again, that was for sure. He didn't want to get to know her in that way, didn't need bridges between them. He tried to remember the plan. He had to believe he'd come to this party for something. He was supposed to be getting information out of her, that was it. But before he could think of anything to ask, she nudged his arm and pointed across the water to the field beyond.

'See the horses?' she said. He hadn't even noticed them – three of them beyond the railway line, marooned together under a tree. 'Keep watching them. Watch by their feet.'

It made his eyes go funny to stare into the darkness. The field became dark blue and thunderous as he watched, although as he kept looking, the colours got less dense and the edge of his vision became ragged with grey. Then, from below the tree, a shadow moved, hesitated, moved again. A fox, low and sleek, stood exposed on the grass, one paw raised, before gathering itself and vanishing diagonally across the field.

'See that?' she said.

'Yeah.'

She sighed, as if she was satisfied it existed now he'd seen it too. He glanced at her briefly, even though he'd told himself he wouldn't. He noticed her scar again. She saw him looking, ran her tongue along it. 'A dog bit me.'

'Serious?'

She nodded. 'I was on holiday and it came running out of the woods and jumped at my face. They thought it had rabies, but it didn't.'

'Rabies?'

'We were in Kenya.'

The closest he'd got to Africa was Dex teaching him how to roast goat meat with garlic.

She peered at him. 'Have you got any scars?'

Imagine she's some girl in a pub, he thought, and make something up. It helped not to look. 'I got shot once,' he told her, 'but it's on my arse.'

She laughed for the first time and he felt ridiculously pleased with himself. 'Some guy shot me five times at point blank range. You want to see?'

She shook her head, still smiling. 'You were running away if he shot you in the arse. Which makes you a coward.'

Now that wasn't an ordinary line – too quick-witted. Again, he felt confused. He wondered about this girl. She wasn't even drunk, not remotely, and there was loads of booze at the house. He decided to get back to the point.

'Tell me about your brother,' he said. 'Tell me two things about him.'

'I thought you knew him.'

'He's a friend of a friend really.'

She turned to him, frowning. 'Why don't we talk about you instead? Why don't you tell me two things about yourself?'

If he had to give something away to get something back, then he would. 'My special skills are cooking and kissing.'

She half smiled. 'How do you know you're good at them?'

'I practise. What about you?'

'I'll swap cooking for swimming.'

'And keep the other one?'

She looked at her feet, shy now. 'Maybe.'

'You like swimming? What's your favourite stroke?'

'Front crawl.'

He wanted to ask if she did competitions and stuff, if she'd ever won anything. He wanted to ask if she was genuinely good at kissing and did she want to prove it? But he wasn't supposed to be chatting her up. He needed to concentrate and steer the conversation to something useful.

'So, does your brother like swimming?'

She hesitated a moment too long. 'I'd rather not talk about him, if that's OK with you.'

Well, that shut him up.

He didn't say anything else. Girls liked the sound of their own voices and she'd probably speak again in a minute. But he wasn't going to. He wanted her to feel as stupid as he did.

While he waited, he looked at the way the river puckered in the breeze, dead leaves swirling on its surface. If he lived here, he'd be at this river all the time. He'd teach Holly stuff about it – the names of things and how to catch fish. He'd have to learn it himself first, of course, but that would be easy – he'd have a personal trainer, like people who joined a gym.

'What are you thinking about?'

Her voice startled him. But this was a good question. It meant she fancied him. 'I was thinking about you.'

'Yeah, right.'

'Serious. I think you're gorgeous.'

She sighed. 'Do you even want to have a proper conversation?'

He'd promised himself he wouldn't, but he looked right at her again. 'I was thinking about the river.'

'What about it?'

'I like the way it's moving, how it never stops.'

She thought about that for a minute, then said, 'Everything's moving really. The forward momentum of the earth is sixty-seven thousand miles an hour and the rotation is nearly two thousand miles an hour. We're also spinning around the centre of the Milky Way at some rate I forget.' She grinned at him. 'I've been revising Physics. You probably think I'm a total geek.'

He shook his head. 'Why don't we feel it then?'

'That we're moving?'

'Yeah. If we're spinning about so fast, how come we're not dizzy?'

'Because our perspective doesn't extend beyond our fixed surroundings.'

'What?'

'We only notice movement if it relates to what's right in front of us. In a plane above the clouds you don't notice speed because there's nothing to compare it with, but on the ground as you take off, you can feel you're going fast.'

He didn't know what to say. Keeping quiet was probably best. He didn't want her to know that he'd never been on a plane or that he didn't quite understand what she was talking about.

'Are you doing any sciences?' she asked.

He wasn't sure cooking would count, but he went for it anyway, told her he was doing an NVQ, with two days a week work experience attached. He didn't know if such a course even existed, but it sounded cool. And because he wanted to impress her more, he took the bottle of whisky from his jacket pocket and held it out. 'Look what I've got.'

'Where did you get that?'

'My mate. You want some?'

She shook her head, but he unstoppered it anyway, tipped the bottle back and took a long slug. Before he'd had time to swallow, she reached over and grabbed it from him. Whisky spilled down his chin and onto his jacket. He wiped his mouth, laughing. 'You said no.'

She smiled prettily. 'I changed my mind.'

He didn't know what would happen next and he didn't know what he'd do when it happened. He watched her sip. She grimaced as she swallowed, then passed the bottle back.

'Listen,' she said. 'I should probably go back. They might wonder where I am.'

'I'll come with you.'

'If you like.'

It was only as they went through the gate that he realized he hadn't found out anything useful about her brother at all.

'So,' she said as they walked back up the slope. 'How does your mate know Tom?'

She stopped walking and smiled. He knew she'd seen him falter. She leaned in to him, whispered, 'You better get your story straight, because here he comes.'

Tom Parker came walking down the slope towards them. He was thinner close up, and looked younger. He had big blue eyes, like he wouldn't hurt anyone. But Mikey knew his secret.

Tom smiled at his sister. 'All right, Ellie?'

So that was her name.

He said, 'Found someone to talk to in the end?'

She shrugged. 'Whatever.'

'Don't be like that. I've been looking for you for ages. Where have you been?'

Ah, it was thrilling how close he was. He had designer stubble, a sore place at the side of his mouth, a spattering of freckles across his nose. If they were alone, Mikey would reach into his pocket for the spanner. He'd yank it high and slam it down on the bastard's skull.

Tom frowned at the whisky in Mikey's hand. 'Where did you get that?' He leaned right in and grabbed the bottle from him.

Mikey shot a glance at Ellie. She was smiling, or rather trying not to laugh. 'Leave it, Tom. He didn't know it was Dad's.'

Tom waved it at them. 'You know how much this is worth? Two hundred quid a bottle. I'm sorry, but this is definitely not for public consumption.'

Mikey wanted to say something funny, but couldn't think of anything.

Tom turned to Ellie. 'Who *is* this?'

She hesitated. Mikey could hardly breathe, waiting for what she'd say. Finally, 'He's with me.'

Mikey liked that. All the tension coiled out of him, knowing she was on his side.

A boy came running up, pulled on Tom's sleeve. Mikey saw he was desperate for something. 'Your dad's freaking out,' the boy puffed. 'Some bloke's been asking questions about you and your dad thinks he's a journalist.'

'Where's the bloke now?' Mikey asked. He couldn't help himself, knew this kid was talking about Jacko.

The boy shook his head. 'Dunno. We chased him, but he got away.'

Maybe the relief showed on Mikey's face, because Tom narrowed his eyes at him suspiciously. 'If this is anything to do with you, you're in big trouble.' Then he spun off with the boy across the garden.

Ellie said, 'My brother's a bit wired tonight. Sorry.'

'Yeah.'

'He's had a hard time.'

'He should drink some of that whisky, help him relax.'

She didn't say anything to that, but she eyed him steadily for a moment. He didn't know what that meant.

'I should go and see if they're OK,' she said. 'If my dad's freaking out, the party's pretty much over.'

It was a disaster. Not only was she walking away, but Jacko had been chased out, which meant Tom Parker was going to escape a kicking for the second time.

'Nice to meet you,' she said.

He had to stop her. 'Give me your mobile number.'

She turned round. 'Why?'

Because he was supposed to be gathering intelligence. Because she was the best source. Because he could see the same anger simmering in her that he had in him and he wanted to know why. But what he said was, 'I'd like to see you again.'

She frowned. Maybe she didn't like him. They'd been laughing and it had seemed like it was going well, but maybe he'd read it wrong. The signs were probably different with girls like her. He kicked the dirt with his foot. She was making it difficult. She was making it seem real.

She pulled her phone from her pocket. 'You give me yours instead.'

He reeled it off. It wasn't what he wanted, but she shook her head when he asked for hers again. 'I might change my mind in the morning.'

He gave her his best grin. 'Why would you change your mind?'

She shrugged. 'You can't rely on anything.'

She looked sad for a minute and he thought he had to do something quickly. 'I'd like to get to know you better,' he said. 'No kidding.'

'Then maybe I'll call you.'

He watched her walk back up to the house, all the doors open, all the windows blazing with light.

Eight

Ellie had followed all the rules of invisibility. She wasn't wearing make-up, not even mascara. She'd taken out her earrings, removed her necklace and tied her hair up neatly with an elastic. Her grey skirt was regulation length and her white shirt was buttoned to the top. She had no perfume on.

A yell from downstairs made her jump. 'Hurry up, Ellie, we leave in five minutes!'

Maybe it would be all right. She gave herself a final look in the bathroom mirror, then opened the door and went downstairs.

Her mother clapped her hands to her face. 'Oh, love, you look perfect.'

Dad and Tom looked up from their breakfasts and took it all in, from the flat-heeled shoes to the thick black tights.

'Very smart,' Dad said.

Tom waved his fork in agreement, 'Looking studious, kid.'

Ellie pulled on her cardigan and did the buttons up slowly. 'You know everyone's going to stare at me?'

Her mum gave her a doleful look, but didn't say anything.

Tom said, 'I wish I was doing something normal today.'

'Well, why don't you go instead of me?'

He pulled a face at her. 'Very subtle, thanks.'

Ellie sighed, poured herself a juice and took a sip. Her mum stood at the end of the dining table wielding serving tongs. The platter in front of her was loaded with fried egg, sausage, bacon and mushrooms and next to it was a basket of croissants and pastries.

'Anyone for any more?' she said, and she snapped the tongs at the men like crocodile jaws.

Ellie frowned. 'Why have you made all this food?'

'Your mother's feeding us up,' Dad said. 'We've got a conference with the barrister this morning.' He had a notebook and pen in front of him, scribbled something down, then turned to Tom. 'We need to get together a record of your academic achievements – everything you were involved in at school, everything at college. Clubs, prizes, that kind of thing. Extra-curricular activities will go down well.'

Ellie reached for a croissant and spread it with butter. It was hardly a low-fat breakfast, but if she thought of herself as a soldier going into battle, then the calories were justified.

Dad continued to scribble things down in his notebook. 'The golf club tournament would count,' he said. 'You got through to the semi-final in that, didn't you, Tom?'

'Quarter-finals.'

'Oh, well, that's still something.'

It was like a war conference with maps and strategies. Ever

since the arrest it had been the same, as if Tom had been diagnosed with some rare and terrible illness and they all had to concentrate on finding a cure. Nothing else was important.

Ellie dolloped a great heap of strawberry jam on the side of her plate, then broke off pieces of buttery croissant and dunked them in.

'Hurry up, love.' Her mum passed her a napkin. 'You don't want to be late on your first day back.'

Soon she'd be out there in the world, being driven down the lane to the main road, past the station, across the junction and into town. She'd managed to bunk Monday and Tuesday by claiming she had study leave, but then Dad had bothered to check the school's website, so that wouldn't wash any more. She tried to get out of it one last time. 'Please, Mum, I don't actually feel that well . . .'

Her dad shot her a glance. 'School's statutory, Ellie.'

'Not if you're Karyn McKenzie.'

A name so hot it made Tom blush. So hot her dad yanked his glasses off and waved them at her. 'You've got nothing to be ashamed of, Eleanor, and that girl most certainly has, which is why she's skulking at home. Now you go to school and you show everyone that.'

'Like a sacrifice?'

'No, like someone who's done nothing wrong.'

'It's going to be horrible, with people taking sides.'

'Well, then you'll find out who your real friends are.'

He was referring to whoever had caused hundreds of pounds'

71

worth of damage to Tom's car by scratching it up. He was also referring to the various people who hadn't bothered showing up to the party. He'd gone on about their lame excuses for days – too much traffic on a Friday, no babysitter, too far to come from London, not enough notice. He hadn't confronted any of it, said it was too upsetting to deal with. But now he wanted his daughter to go out and tackle the world.

'You're living your life vicariously through me,' Ellie told him.

'Good word!' he said, pushing his glasses on with a smile and looking back down at his notebook. 'Probably worth two marks in GCSE English.'

She turned to her mother. 'Please, Mum.'

'No, I agree with Dad. You've been stuck indoors for days and there's no need for you to incarcerate yourself.'

Good word. How many points was that worth?

They'd obviously talked about it together and there was no dividing them. Ellie could see it in their eyes. Something premeditated and determined. She wiped her hands on the napkin and left the rest of the croissant on her plate.

'Well,' she said, 'I better go then. I hope you two have a fabulous time with the barrister.'

She got a sad smile from her mum for that. 'Come on,' she said, 'let's get you out of here.'

As the car turned out of the lane into the main road, Ellie opened the window. There was a spring tang in the air, sunlight bouncing off everything. Primroses sprouted at the roundabout and in baskets at the bus stop. She liked this journey, down the side of the park, past the church. It was almost possible to believe she was going somewhere lovely and that good things might happen.

But the only good thing that had happened for days was meeting the gatecrasher. Ellie shut her eyes to remember him – his lazy smile, his swagger. She'd been angry all night about the stupid party, about getting into trouble for cutting Tom's hair. Anger had made her confident, so when the boy came up to her, she hadn't blushed or stumbled over her words, hadn't minded about her scar. Standing in the half-light by the river, she felt as if new things were possible.

What was it Tom said this morning on the landing? *Be vigilant*.

But being so suspicious of everyone took all your words away. Now it was spreading to actions. Twice she'd written the gate-crasher a text. Twice she'd deleted it without sending.

'Do you know,' she told her mum, 'even in my dreams I'm careful.'

'What I *do* know is that I'm going to be late to see Tom and Dad off if I go round the one-way system.'

'Aren't you going with them?'

'I'm not needed, apparently.'

'What will you do all day?'

She shrugged. 'Usual things – tidy up, think about dinner. I might go over to Gran's and do a bit more clearing out.'

'I'll come. You've been asking me to help clear the cottage for weeks. We could go to the beach after. It'll be fun.'

'Nice try, but you're going to school. Can I drop you here? Are you all right to walk the last bit?'

She pulled over on the near side of the river. Ellie watched the water for a minute. It was dark and barely moving. Maybe she could dive in and turn into the mermaid Tom had talked about. She could splash about until it was time to go home, surrounded by ducks and soggy bread.

'Lunch money,' Mum said, and handed over ten pounds. 'And there's enough for a coffee after school with your friends. I'm sure Dad will understand if you don't come straight home and revise today.'

'I'm sure he won't.'

'Come on, love, don't be so hard on him. He wants you to do well in your exams, but he understands you need time for your mates too.'

Ellie wanted to explain that she had no mates, that fitting in at new school was more complex than her mum could ever imagine, that having your brother accused of sexual assault was not going to make it easier. But she also wanted to keep the hope alive in her mother's eyes.

'Well, if I'm late back,' she said brightly, 'you'll know where I am.'

She opened the door. She had to walk along the side of the river to meet the bridge. The school was on the other side – three low-level buildings, all glass and angles. There was the playground, washed with light, the high tangle of voices as kids walked towards it from every direction.

'You think everyone's going to stare?' she said.

'Of course not. But if they do, tell a teacher.'

'You think assembly will be cancelled, so I can be hot-seated in front of the whole school?'

'Oh, love, I know this is hard, but you have to be brave. Do it for Tom, sweetheart. Keep thinking of him.'

She leaned across and kissed Ellie on the forehead. Maybe it shone silver, like the one the good witch gave Dorothy in *The Wizard of Oz*.

Ellie could do with that kind of magic.

Nine

'Mikey, you awake?'

Holly stood in the doorway of his bedroom. He moaned softly, hoped it sounded like sleep. But she didn't go away.

'Mikey?' She climbed onto the bed and lay down.

There hadn't been a morning for weeks when he hadn't woken up to some kind of crisis. He took a deep breath. 'What's up?'

'Mum's gone again.'

He struggled to sit up, rubbed his eyes. 'Did she sleep in her bed?'

'No.'

'Did you look downstairs and out on the balcony?'

Holly nodded, curled her hand into his. 'And I knocked next door.'

'And they haven't seen her?'

'No.'

He sighed. He knew his mum was struggling with all this Karyn stuff, but it was only four weeks since the last time she'd done a bunk. He should have guessed last night, when she'd told him she was going to the pub for a quick one. Well, the quick one had obviously turned into something a hell of a lot longer, which meant she could be anywhere. With anyone. He fumbled for his mobile, but the only missed calls were from Jacko and Sienna. He scrolled through the contacts.

'Don't worry,' he said. 'We'll call her, shall we?'

Holly snuggled closer to listen. The phone rang four times, then the message clicked in. Their mother's voice apologizing for not being available.

'Maybe she's dead,' Holly said, her voice quivering.

'She's not.'

'She might be. You don't know.'

'I know everything, and she's not dead, OK?'

He left a message, told her to ring and *let me know where you are and when you're coming back*. Told her to *do it soon, please*.

'That should do it,' Holly said, like he could sort the world out that easily.

He turned to her, could just make out the shine of her eyes on the pillow beside him. 'In five minutes,' he said, 'we'll get up. Until then, you're only allowed to think about nice things.'

'OK.' She craned her head to see the clock. 'Can I think about football?'

'Yes.'

'I'll do the alphabet game. I'm going to start with Ossie Ardiles, then Dimitar Berbatov, then Clemence, then Defoe.'

'Great. Can you do it inside your head though?'

She lay there, her whole body flexing with thought. He could

77

almost hear the calculations. And while she did that, he listened to his messages. Sienna sounding sulky: *What happened to you last night? You wanna come round and make it up to me, 'cos I know it's your morning off?* Jacko sounding urgent: *New plan! Let me know when you're awake and I'll come and pick you up.*

Mikey sank back into the pillow and wondered if his life could actually get any worse – Karyn assaulted, the bloke who did it still unpunished, Mum missing and now pressure from women and mates. He closed his eyes and tried to distract himself by thinking about London. He'd work in a hotel. He'd wear a full set of chef's whites and have proper equipment – ramekin dishes, loose-based flan tins and specialist knives. He'd probably have other things too, things he didn't even know existed.

Holly got stuck. He could feel it in her body, as if breathing was suddenly difficult to do. She turned to him. 'Maybe Mum got hit by a car.'

'She didn't.'

'Or she went in a boat and it sank.'

'She didn't do that either.'

'Or a plane fell on her head.'

He told her to stop talking rubbish and get ready for school, she was already late. Then he took his phone to the bathroom and tried Mum again. Still no answer. He texted Jacko. He texted Sienna. Same message to both: *Totally up for it.* Whichever one got back to him first, that's what he'd do. Runnings with Jacko. Between the sheets with Sienna. Let fate decide. He was sick of being in charge.

He stared in the mirror as he pissed. He looked angry. He washed his face with cold water, then brushed his teeth. The toothpaste had nearly run out and he added that to the list in his head.

When he came out of the bathroom, Holly was on the landing eating a packet of crisps. She was still in her pyjamas.

'What are you doing?'

'My clothes are in the bedroom and Karyn won't let me in. I knocked, but she won't answer.' Holly stuffed another crisp in her mouth. 'She's probably dead too.'

'Oh for God's sake!' Mikey rapped on the door.

He checked the time. School started at nine, which meant they only had five minutes to get there. They wrote your name down in a book if you were late.

He turned to Holly. 'How much do you need the stuff that's in there?'

'A lot.'

He did a comedy knock to cheer himself up. *Tappity tap, tap, tap*. Then a police knock. *Wham, wham*, with a closed fist. He tried to sound like he meant it, but Karyn wasn't shifting.

'You could kick it down,' Holly said. 'You're allowed to do that in emergencies.'

He smiled at her. She smiled back. He'd forgotten how beautiful her smile was and because he didn't want it to fade, he tried *Open sesame* and *Abracadabra!* from the stories she liked. Then he pretended to be a wolf who could blow the door down.

'*Let me in, let me in, by the hair on my chinny chin chin.*'

It kept Holly smiling. But it made no difference to Karyn.

He leaned in, breathing on the paintwork. 'Please, Karyn, talk to me.'

He told her he was her big brother and she should trust him, that he'd do anything to help her if only she'd open the door.

Holly hopped from one foot to the other and gave him the thumbs-up as Karyn dragged a chair from under the handle. It was hot in the room and stuffy. Karyn slung herself on the bottom bunk, face down, her head hidden in pillows. She still had her tracksuit on. She'd been wearing it for days, had obviously started sleeping in it as well.

Holly marched straight over. 'Why did you lock me out?' She nudged at her sister with a bare foot. 'It's my room too. Just because something bad happened to you doesn't mean you can do what you like.'

Karyn rolled over. She looked startled, like someone blinking into light after hours shut in the dark. 'What did you just say?'

Mikey intervened. 'All right, all right! Holly, get your stuff and go and get dressed.'

Holly gave Karyn a final shove, then picked up two school shirts from a pile of dirty washing on the floor and sniffed them. 'They're smelly.'

Mikey grabbed them from her and sniffed them too, checked them for dirt and passed the cleanest one back. He added washing powder to the list in his head.

Holly walked really slowly to the door, where she stopped, her hand on the door handle.

'Get dressed, Holly!'

He knew she hated him shouting, but it made her speed up. She stuck her tongue out, slammed the door, thumped all the way down the hallway to the bathroom and slammed that door for good measure.

Mikey pulled a chair up next to the bed and sat down. 'So, what's up?'

Karyn looked at him, her face smeary with tears. 'Mum's gone.'

'Yeah, I'm sorry.'

'It's me, isn't it? I'm freaking her out.'

'You know what she's like – it doesn't take much to frighten her off.'

'It's definitely me. She's been drinking more since this happened, have you noticed? And sleeping loads.'

Behind her, through the window, he could see grass, litter, other flats. Weird to think that people with other lives were still under their duvets, pressing the snooze buttons on their alarm clocks and snuggling under for a few more minutes' escape.

Karyn ran a hand across her face, wiping away fresh tears. 'I'm trying to help as much as I used to, but I can't seem to hold it together. Holly wanted her hair plaited just now and my hands were shaking so much, I couldn't do it. How lame is that? I only shut her out so she didn't see me upset.'

He checked his phone. No messages. Maybe he'd go round to Sienna's anyway. She was always up for it.

'You don't want to listen to me, do you?' Karyn said.

'I don't mind.'

'You're bored, I know you are.' She pulled her knees up and hugged them. 'Sometimes, I wonder if you even believe me.'

'I'm going to get him for you, aren't I?'

'So you keep saying. Whacking him doesn't prove anything though.'

'It proves he can't mess with us.'

Holly came back in and sat on the rug. 'What's going on?'

Mikey turned to her. 'Holly, what the hell are you wearing?'

'The other stuff was stinky.'

'You can't wear your Tottenham kit to school.'

'School's shut. They just said so on TV.'

He laughed. Holly laughed with him.

Karyn stared at him with dark eyes. 'If you beat him up, you're going to get in trouble. How does that help anyone?'

He gave her a look that was supposed to tell her she shouldn't be talking about this in front of Holly. An eight-year-old would never keep her mouth shut. He was angry now, could feel it building inside him.

Holly blinked up at him, puzzled. 'What are you talking about?'

'Nothing. It doesn't matter.'

'But I want to know.'

'Please,' Mikey said, 'go and get dressed properly.' He rubbed the back of his neck. He was beginning to get a headache. 'I tell you what, if you're dressed in school uniform and back here in five minutes, I'll play footie with you in the courtyard later.'

'That's a bribe.'

'Yep.'

She scowled at him. 'Well, it's not big enough.'

'Maybe she should stay here,' Karyn said. 'That'd be easier for you.'

He wasn't sure if she was being sarcastic or not. Maybe she just didn't want to be alone.

'I don't mind,' Holly said. 'I can do drawing if I stay here. And we can play football.'

Mikey sat with it for a moment. They had to keep being normal, didn't they? Holly had missed loads of school recently. If they didn't keep up some kind of routine, wouldn't everything collapse?

'No,' he said, 'this is how it's going to be. Holly's going to get dressed in proper clothes. I'm going to see if there's anything in the kitchen to eat. Holly and Karyn are going to have breakfast, then I'm taking Holly to school and we'll put our names in the late book. Karyn will stay here and do tidying and sort food out for dinner, so when Holly gets home there will be something to eat.'

Karyn shook her head. 'She can't go to school if there's no one to collect her.'

It took a beat to sink in. Mum usually collected Holly, but Mum had gone. Karyn couldn't go out, so that left him. His shift finished at nine, so unless he blagged time off, it was impossible.

He went and sat on the toilet for a while to think about it. He took ages, hoping it would somehow all be sorted by the time he'd finished.

He thought of the bloke they'd seen on TV the night before, sent off to Iraq at eighteen – running about in all that heat with snipers aiming at his head. What had Karyn said? *Now there's somebody brave*. But the poor bastard had been shaking in front of the camera, and the look in his eyes was mad – something like terror, something like shame. Was that brave?

Mikey took a wad of toilet paper and wiped himself. Things usually seemed easier after a dump, like the world got put back in the right order.

The texts arrived when he was washing his hands. Jacko saying he'd meet him outside at ten. Sienna saying she'd expect him in half an hour. Mikey leaned over the sink and closed his eyes. By the time he'd taken Holly to school, he'd be late for both of them. It felt like spinning plates, keeping everyone happy, not letting anything fall.

He texted Sienna back, *Course*. He texted Jacko, *11.00 @ Sienna's*.

Holly was on the landing again when he came out of the bathroom. She had her school uniform and coat on, her book bag slung over one shoulder. She'd even made an attempt to plait her own hair.

'Don't worry,' he said. 'You don't have to go.'

'But I want to.'

'You can stay here with Karyn.'

'But we're doing scrap art today and that's my favourite.'

'Well, I can't take you now, I've just got busy. Anyway, you've been wanting to stay at home since you woke up.'

'No I haven't.'

He squatted down next to her and she looked back at him, her eyes all teary. 'What's going on?'

84

'I thought you'd be here too. I thought it was your day off. I don't want to be on my own with Karyn.' She stuck her thumb in her mouth and looked down at her feet. 'She makes me feel watery.'

Mikey felt his stomach grip again. He put both hands on her shoulders and made her look at him. 'School started half an hour ago, Holly. We'd get into real trouble if I took you in now. They'd tell me off and they'd tell Mum off. There's no one to pick you up either, so we'd all get told off twice. Then they'd send some nosy woman round to ask us all questions. And you know what that means, don't you?'

Holly nodded, her eyes wide with the thought of children's homes. It worked every time.

She followed him down the stairs and sat on the carpet in the hallway. In the lounge, the TV was blaring. At least Karyn had managed to get out of the bedroom.

Mikey sat on the bottom stair to put his trainers on. 'If Mum comes back, tell her to text me.'

'Will she come back soon?'

'Maybe.' It was the closest to the truth he could manage.

'What if she doesn't?'

'Well, then you get to watch TV all day with Karyn. Tell her you get to choose half the programmes, OK?'

'You tell her.'

But he didn't want to go in there in case she tried to stop him leaving. If he was going to fit Sienna in before hooking up with Jacko, he had to go now.

He kissed the top of Holly's head. 'I'll be back later with some shopping. I'll get us some nice things.'

'What if a bus hits you?'

'It won't.'

'But what if it does?' She looked at him with serious eyes. 'Please don't go.'

But he had to. It was only fair. He pulled on his jacket, did up his zip and smacked his chest like a gorilla. It usually made her laugh, but not today.

Ten

'Karyn McKenzie's a slut and everyone knows it.'

Ellie didn't know this girl, or any of the other kids who sidled up to her in the playground and stood around in small groups listening in.

'She started having sex in Year Eight,' the girl said. 'She bragged about that for weeks. And remember the rumour about her and that boy from college?'

Ellie nodded. Karyn was a liar who came from a crazy family. She got wasted and slept with Tom, then changed her mind in the morning. Ellie wished she'd come back to school days ago. She'd never been so popular.

'I heard she's gone really weird,' another girl said, 'all agora-phobic or alcoholic or something.'

'It's guilt,' the first girl said. 'If you turn up uninvited to a boy's house dressed like a ho, it's not a total surprise when he jumps you, is it?'

A couple of boys laughed. One of them patted Ellie on the back as if they'd been mates for years. 'So, did your brother get charged twice?'

'Um, sorry, what do you mean?'

'She's only fifteen, yeah?' He leaned close, grinning. 'Did he get charged once 'cos she's too young, and twice 'cos he never bothered asking if she wanted it?'

But before she could tell him to piss off, Rebecca and Lucy from her tutor group ran over. Lucy took her hand. 'You came back!'

'Yeah.'

'We didn't think you would.'

They asked question after question – *Were you in the house when it happened? Is it true you spoke to Karyn in the morning? Did she tell you she was going to the police?*

Ellie tried to stay calm. She felt as if she'd been running up stairs, or as if she'd suddenly become asthmatic. It was one thing listening to other people talk, but she didn't want to go into details herself.

'I'm not allowed to discuss it, sorry.'

Rebecca looked disappointed. 'We won't tell.'

She grabbed at the best excuse she could think of. 'The police said I shouldn't.'

Lucy put an arm round Ellie's shoulder. 'We're all friends.'

Ellie cast a quick look round. A boy gave her a wave as their eyes met, a boy next to him shook his head as if he was disappointed. A girl sucked her teeth, leaned back and said, 'Ellie Parker, you're so up your own arse.'

Laughter rippled through the crowd as Ellie moved away.

Maybe this was what it was like to be famous – not knowing

what was real and what was fake, just grinning and trying to let everything wash over you.

She walked the playground to kill time, head down, eyes on her shoes, one step at a time. Soon this would be over, soon the bell would go and she would be in her tutor room and there would be teachers and work to do. In a few days the great gossip machine would move on. She simply had to get through it until then.

It was difficult to get to the doors when the bell went. A boy brushed her arm, whispered, 'Your brother's a paedo.'

Another said, 'How's your brother?' And when Ellie told him Tom was fine, he said, 'Shame.'

Three girls who would never acknowledge her any other day came up.

'How's Tom managing?' they asked, all soft-voiced and concerned, as if he had many wives.

'Um, he's OK.'

'Tell him we're thinking of him. Tell him Lily, Alice and Caitlin send their love.'

'OK, thanks. I'll tell him.'

A strained stillness enveloped the tutor room as she went in, and all eyes turned to her as she made her way to her place. Conor Lockhead, the class prat, came straight over and sat on the edge of her desk.

'Hey,' he said. 'Is it true your brother raped a girl?'

Ellie chose to ignore him and slunk into her seat.

'Is he in prison?' Conor said.

'No.'

'So, he didn't do it?'

'He didn't do it.'

'Is he back at college?'

'He's not allowed back yet.'

Conor looked confused. 'I thought you said he didn't do it.'

'He didn't. Listen, I'm not supposed to talk about it.'

She got out a pen and paper and kept her eyes firmly fixed on them. She began to doodle a tree with many sprouting heads, all teeth and snarl. She wished she had a friend, someone to sit next to, keeping her safe.

Mr Donal came in, coughing, saw Ellie and smiled. 'Welcome back.'

And that's all he said. He had a stack of sheets with him, handed them out swiftly, and soon they were all occupied with filling in questionnaires on their progress reports. Excellent plan. Total silence. No talking allowed. No moving, or standing, or going to the toilet, or walking past and shoving secret elbows into Ellie's back. But it only lasted fifteen minutes, then the bell went for period one.

First to approach her in Maths was Danny, six foot tall and the only boy she'd ever kissed. He'd asked her for the last dance at the Christmas party and they hadn't spoken since. She blushed every time she saw him and today was no exception.

He said, 'Sorry to hear about your brother.'

'Thanks.'

'Has he got a court date?'

She shook her head, knew it made her look sullen, but she

couldn't speak, could barely look at him. This hadn't been her idea of the next conversation they'd have.

'Well, best of luck with it all.'

He walked away and it was like passing a baton, because before she'd even stopped blushing, a friend of Karyn's strode up.

'You're the talk of the school,' she said.

'Me, or my brother?'

'Well, since he's not here, I guess I mean you.'

Ellie stared down at her Maths book, prayed for the teacher to hurry up and tried to concentrate on saying very little.

The girl leaned forward. 'Karyn won't see anyone, she's locked herself in her flat and never goes out. You tell your brother that.'

'I'm not allowed to talk about this.'

The girl ignored her. 'We text her, but she won't see us. None of us. Not even Stacey.'

'I'm sorry, but I have nothing to say.'

'Do you feel guilty?'

Heat crept from Ellie's neck to her face. 'Why would I?'

'Well, if I was the only other person in a house when someone got raped, I'd feel pretty guilty.'

It was a total relief when Ms Farish arrived and the lesson began. On her worksheet, Ellie wrote out formulae. In her head, she tried to remember, like a series of photos, the sequence of things – Karyn and Stacey and three boys turned up at the house with Tom. It was Saturday night and Mum and Dad were away. Ellie went upstairs. Later, she looked out of her window and saw Tom and Karyn with their arms round each other. Even later, she saw them kiss on the landing outside her bedroom door. She watched Tom's hand creep down Karyn's back. She watched Karyn lift one of her strappy heels from the floor and press herself closer to him. No one knew Ellie saw that kiss, no one in the world. If Tom liked Karyn, and she liked him back, why would he hurt her? Why would he take something when Karyn was going to give it for free?

English followed Maths and was the last lesson before break. Kids who hadn't seen her yet either insisted on asking questions, or kept quiet and shot daggers with their eyes. Maybe when everyone had seen her once and decided what their response was, they'd get back to what they usually did and ignore her.

At break, the corridor wasn't as bad as she'd imagined. No one pushed her, no one thumped her or slammed her against the lockers. When she went to the toilet, the only other girl in there merely grinned and said, 'Hi.'

Ellie started to relax. It wasn't so bad. Far worse to be Karyn – stuck in her flat avoiding everyone. She probably wished she hadn't started all this, and that Tom was her boyfriend instead of her enemy.

So when Ellie saw Stacey and her mate sitting on a bench under the trees, she knew what she had to do. She felt brave and certain as she walked up and stood in front of them. They both stared up at her in total disbelief. But it was too late now.

She said, 'How's Karyn?'

Stacey shook her head slowly. 'Are you talking to me?'

'I was wondering how Karyn was.'

'Piss off.'

'I met you when you came round my house that night, do you remember? I know you're her friend and I didn't want to ignore you – it felt important.'

'Important?' Stacey's lips curled as if something tasted bad in her mouth.

'Yes.' Ellie knew she was blushing, hated how hot she felt. 'Someone told me she's not leaving her flat any more.'

Stacey stood up and took a step towards Ellie. She had thin lips and pale skin. Her eyes were brown. Ellie had never known any of these things about her before. 'If I got nut-job texts from your brother, I'd be too scared to go out.'

'He's not allowed to text her.'

'I'm talking *before*, when she told him she was going to the cops.'

Ellie shook her head. She had no clue what Stacey was talking about. 'How is she *now*? That's what I'm asking.'

Stacey took another step forward. 'She won't leave the flat, she won't see her friends, she won't come to school. She's having a total breakdown. Satisfied?'

'I'm sorry.'

'Why, what did you do?'

'Nothing. I'm sorry, that's all. Could you please tell her I'm sorry?'

'You think she gives a crap how you feel?'

Ellie could feel humiliation burning her face, down her neck to her chest. Even her fingers burned with shame. She turned away.

But Stacey grabbed her sleeve. 'Don't walk away from me!'

Ellie yanked her arm free and tried to push past them, but Stacey and her mate separated and came round on either side of her, backing her towards the fence. It was a perfect manoeuvre, like something rehearsed. They stood in front of Ellie, blocking her way. She tried to stare them out, but it was difficult to focus – the playground appeared to tilt behind them.

Stacey said, 'Why did you tell the cops you never saw anything?'

'Because I didn't.'

'How can that be true?'

Both girls looked her up and down. Ellie tried to push past, but they pushed her back. She stumbled, nearly fell.

Stacey said, 'Where were you all night?'

'Asleep.'

The mate said, 'Yeah, course you were.'

People were beginning to notice. Three boys standing further along the fence were clocking it all. One of them yelled, 'Cat fight.'

No, Ellie didn't want this. With people looking she'd have to do something, say something. She'd look stupid if she didn't defend herself. Or guilty.

She tried to break free again. 'Let me go.'

Stacey shoved her back. 'Or what? What you gonna do, bitch? You gonna rape me?'

She was blaring it out. The boys jogged over. Stacey's eyes glittered as she turned to them. 'She was threatening me, did you get that?'

Ellie felt a shift in her belly as more kids came running up. *What's going on? What's it about?* Acid churned in her stomach.

'Let me go.'

'Why should I?'

'Because I haven't done anything to you.'

'You're his lying sister, aren't you?'

And that's when Ellie felt anger, like liquid rising. 'And what are you, Stacey? What's the name for someone who dumps their best friend so they can go home with a boy?'

'I didn't dump her, I left her with your brother. How was I to know he was a rapist?'

'Why would he rape her when she was gagging for it?'

'Because he's a paedo perve, like the rest of his family.' Stacey rolled her eyes, playing to the audience. 'Your mum shag a dog, or something?'

'Yeah, course she did.' Ellie folded her arms at her. 'What else do you know?'

'I know you're a bitch.'

'You said that one already.'

'And a slapper.'

'Very original.' Ellie took a step nearer. Her brain felt pure, thoughts came hot and simple. 'At least I'm not fat.'

Stacey looked down at herself. 'I'm not fat.'

'You keep telling yourself that.'

Somebody laughed and Ellie felt a stab of pleasure. Stacey ran her tongue across her lips.

'Come on,' Ellie said, 'you must be able to think of something else to say about me. You can't be as dim as you look.'

'You're the one who's dim.'

'How?'

''Cos you're a nerd. Look at you, in your crap tights and shoes.'

Stacey had bronze foundation on her face. It stopped at the point where her chin met her neck, so there was a line. She had a spattering of spots across her forehead and around her nose. She was sweating.

Ellie shrugged. 'I can always change my clothes – what're you going to do about your face?'

Again, a ripple of laughter.

Blood thundered in her ears. 'Don't feel bad, Stacey. I'm sure your zits don't look obvious in the dark.'

The crowd whistled approval. Ellie was vaguely aware of someone trying to muscle nearer and someone else shoving them back. 'Don't stop them, man.'

Ellie slagged off Stacey's fake tan, her pudgy knees, her plastic earrings. The crowd laughed. And if they were laughing at Stacey, then they weren't laughing at her.

Every curse she'd ever heard any girl yell at any other came hurtling out of her mouth. If she said them first, then Stacey couldn't use them. Like a poison-pen letter – pass it on or die. She told Stacey she should sue her parents, warned her she wouldn't piss in her ear if her brain was on fire. And the crowd cheered her on.

It felt like spewing. You chuck up and the stink is out of you. You leave it somewhere else and you can walk away clean.

But Stacey couldn't stand it. She grabbed Ellie's ponytail and yanked it hard. Ellie put her hands to her head to protect herself, and Stacey slapped her. It jolted Ellie's neck, pain seared into her cheek.

'How'd you like that?' Stacey hissed, her face twisted, spit on her lips. 'You want some more?'

She pulled Ellie's hair again, slapped her a second time. Something rattled in Ellie's head, as if her brain had loosened. All her words were lost. No! No! She wouldn't win this. All the things Stacey couldn't say were spilling onto her head.

And then a miracle. 'Teacher!'

The crowd legged it, the teacher came bowling in. 'Break it up!' he yelled. 'Stacey Clarke, what the hell are you doing?'

And Stacey said, 'Me? It's not me! This girl's crazy!'

But she let go.

Ellie struggled free, her hand to her scalp, to her cheek. She opened one eye to Mr Morris, her History teacher.

He said, 'You OK?'

Her brain felt hot, the world seemed to have got brighter, like an over-developed photo. She said, 'Yeah.'

'Good, because you're both coming with me.'

He sat Ellie in reception, gave her a sheet of A4 and a pen. 'Write a statement,' he said. 'Exactly what happened, from the very beginning. I'll be back.'

He took Stacey with him. She scowled at Ellie over her shoulder as she was led away.

Ellie stared at the sheet for a moment. It swung from cream to white, through shades of eggshell blue to grey. Ellie wondered briefly if she had concussion. Maybe Stacey had given her brain damage.

She wrote her name on the top of the sheet and underlined it. The ink was blue.

Then she looked at the secretaries, two of them busy on their computers, completely ignoring her. Out in the foyer, a pale boy sat on a bench, his coat on his lap. Beyond the doors, the playground had emptied out, excitement over, classes resumed.

She should be in Art. It was the one thing she'd been looking forward to.

She looked back down at the paper. It reminded her of the police station, of the two detectives behind the desk. Good cop, bad cop. All the questions they'd asked. *Where were you? No, where exactly? Who was your brother with? What time was this? All we need is the truth, Ellie.*

Well, the truth was that she had *nothing further to add*. She scrawled this in big letters across the clean page, then she stood up and walked out of the office. One of the secretaries glanced up and looked straight back down. Ellie was evidently too much hassle for her. The boy in the foyer winced as she walked by. Maybe she should whack him, give him a reason to be afraid. What would happen to her then? How bad could she get?

She walked across the empty playground, her shoes scuffing the tarmac. She unzipped her coat, raked her hair until it was wild, undid her top shirt button and rolled her skirt high, so the breeze swirled her thighs. Everything seemed more than it usually did – the earth lit with sun so bright, a single seagull circling low over the river.

She stood on the bridge. She was different from earlier. The rush of badness was thrilling, like something had found a voice. She felt alive. Not a mermaid. Not someone who combed their hair all day and sat on a frigging rock. She mentally torched that image, watched all the scales catch fire and shimmer silver before sinking beneath the water.

She'd emerge as Phoenix from the X-Men movie – the one with the red eyes, so angry that she's off the scale, able to destroy the universe with the power of her mind.

And if she was Phoenix, then anything could happen next.

Eleven

They got dressed side by side. There was something medical about it, like they'd both just been checked over by a doctor. Mikey finished first and sat on the edge of the bed watching Sienna pull her shoes on. When she was done, she sat down next to him.

'What are you thinking?' she asked.

He was thinking about giraffes. He'd watched a pair of them shagging in a zoo once. The male was really desperate, scrabbling up high on his ridiculous legs. He kept sliding down and the female kept moving away, munching on a twig as if she hadn't even noticed. He'd thought sex would be like that – some girl gritting her teeth and him just getting on with it. And sometimes it was.

He wondered what Sienna would do if he didn't say anything, how long she'd last. He stole a look at her. Her hair was messy and her eye make-up was smudged. It was like looking at a stranger. *Who are you?* he thought. *Who have I just spent the last hour with?*

In the end she grabbed hold of his T-shirt and gave it a tug. 'Don't you fancy me any more?'

'I'm meeting a mate.'

'It's your morning off.'

He tapped his nose. 'We've got runnings.'

'What does that mean?'

She reached out to stroke him, but he shook her off and went over to the window. He looked down at the road below, willing Jacko to hurry up.

'So you shag me and then run away?'

Anger prickled under his skin. Why were women on at him all the time?

She folded her arms at him. 'I think you're pathetic.'

He sighed, checked his phone for messages. Two texts. He hadn't heard them arrive – must've been when he was in the middle of things with Sienna. One from Jacko saying he was outside and the other from an unknown number. He opened it up.

Still want to get to know me better?

Whoa! He absolutely wasn't expecting that!

'Who is it?' Sienna moved to see, but Mikey held the phone away from her.

He texted, *Does this mean u like me?*

'Serious,' Sienna said. 'Who's it from?'

She got up and tried to grab the phone from him, but he held it higher. 'It's private, all right?'

She flung herself back on the bed and pulled the duvet over her face.

'I told you I couldn't be with you all day,' he said.

A reply. *Ur ok.*

He grinned, texted back, *Only ok?*

He put the phone away. Days had passed and nothing – he'd almost stopped thinking she was real. He leaned over and patted Sienna through the duvet.

'Got to go.'

She yanked the duvet from her face and glared at him. He grabbed his tobacco and lighter from the table and held his hand out.

'Come on, let's have a smoke outside before I go.'

Jacko was down in the road sitting on the roof of his car. He gave them the thumbs-up as they appeared at the door.

Mikey leaned over the railing. 'Be with you in a minute, just having a smoke.'

'Have a good time up there?'

Sienna scowled. 'You gonna let him talk like that?'

'He doesn't mean it badly.'

Jacko chuckled as he slid off the roof, opened the door of his car and got out a duster. He rubbed lovingly at the windscreen, then bent down to do the same to the mirrors.

'Look at him,' Sienna said. 'All he thinks about is sex and cars.'

'He's a bloke.'

'He looks at me funny.'

'He fancies you.'

Mikey thought that'd make her feel better, but it didn't seem to. She frowned at him. 'Will I see you later?'

'I can't.'

'We could go out.'

'I've got work, then I've got to get shopping.'

'I'll come with you.'

'No.'

'I'll come to the flat later – you can introduce me to your sister.'

'She doesn't want to see anyone.'

Sienna glowered at him. 'Have you even asked her? She might like a visitor.'

'She's got plenty of mates who are up for the job if she does.'

'Why won't you let me help you? You don't have to do this all by yourself, you know.'

But he did. Karyn and Holly belonged to him and he belonged to them. He was the only brother they had.

'I don't think this is working,' Sienna said. 'I don't actually understand the point of you.'

Good call.

Sometimes Mikey fantasized about drowning – pretending to at least. Leaving his jacket and phone on some beach and swimming away. He could be anyone. He could start again. Do it better next time. He chucked his fag on the ground and stamped it out.

'I'm off.'

'You're walking away?'

He nodded, kept his mouth shut.

'If you go now, it's over. I mean it, don't bother calling me again.'

He didn't look back.

Twelve

'A text from his sister?' Jacko laughed so hard he nearly crashed the car. 'Oh man, you kill me. You genuinely can get any girl you want!'

'It doesn't mean anything.'

'Of course it does. Hey, let's stick her in the boot of the car and send her brother a ransom note!'

Mikey shook his head, smiling. 'What are you talking about? We're not going to kidnap her.'

'Listen, man, listen. Here's what happens after that. The brother climbs into his Jag XJ to come and find her, but in his rage he forgets he's got the supercharged version and goes roaring too fast at some corner. *Wham!* He hits a tree. Instant decapitation. Bits of his brain spattered all over the road.' Jacko slapped the steering wheel. 'That, my friend, is one beautiful revenge.'

They elaborated on the story as they drove through town, both of them doubled up with laughter as it got more and more ridiculous. They rammed Tom Parker's dead head on a stick and paraded it down the high street, leaving his bereaved family to scrape the rest of him off the tarmac. Grateful townspeople lined the streets. Flags were waved in their honour, pub doors were flung open, girls threw knickers and phone numbers.

'It'd be so cool!' Jacko howled, his eyes watering. 'We'll take the hottest girls to the Prince of Bengal – best table and free rogan josh and poppadoms all night!'

'Enough, enough!' Mikey laughed. 'Curry and love don't mix, you know that. Come on, man, we have to stop this. We've got to get serious and think what to do.'

It was beautiful weather for March, the window was down, his elbow was stuck out in the wind. They passed a group of cyclists – tourists from the bike-hire place, probably cycling along to look at the lighthouse, or maybe further round the coast to the crazy golf and slot machines. It had been Mikey's favourite outing as a kid – he and Karyn used to save up two pences until they had enough to make it worth getting the bus out there for the afternoon. Afterwards they bought ice cream and sat on the beach.

So, how could meeting Ellie Parker help Karyn? She'd be able to tell him stuff about her brother, where to find him alone, what his routines were. She didn't know who Mikey was. She fancied him. That was a lot in his favour.

Maybe he could meet her more than once, use all that charm Jacko was always telling him he had. He'd do it properly, really romance her. Then, when she was completely under his spell and he'd got all the information he needed, he'd dump her.

Nobody needed to know. He wouldn't tell Karyn or Mum. He'd make sure Ellie never found out who he was.

'Pull in after the lights,' Mikey said. 'Then turn round at the garage.'

'What's going on? I thought we were doing a recce of the golf club.'

'It'll have to wait.'

'I'm telling you, Tom Parker's a golf freak. We just need to check out CCTV and escape routes and we're laughing.' Jacko swung an imaginary club high above his head. 'We'll kill him on the green with a five iron.'

'I need to go back.'

'Back where?'

'I'm going to meet his sister.'

Jacko frowned. 'We're *really* going to kidnap her?'

'*We're* not going to do anything. *I'm* going to chat her up and get information out of her.'

Jacko lit a fag as they waited for the lights to change at the junction. 'You go anywhere near that girl with your dick, Mikey, and hell is going to suck you under.'

'I'm not going to shag her, I'm going to find stuff out.'

Jacko shook his head. 'You won't be able to help yourself.'

Mikey ignored him, texted, *When?*

The reply came flying back, *Now.*

'That's a bad sign,' Jacko said.

Mikey texted, *Where?*

Again, the text came straight back: *Cemetery.*

Jacko frowned. 'It's a stitch-up. She knows who you are.'

'No way. How could she?'

'I'm coming with you.'

'No, she'll freak if she sees two of us.'

Anyway, the cemetery was fine, nobody would be there, no chance of being seen. She might not know who he was, but plenty of people round this part of town did. It only took one person to say something careless and she'd never open up.

Jacko riffed on about rubbish all the way there, told him that when Tom Parker had his way with Karyn he'd broken every rule in the book, which meant his blood relations were tainted by evil. Complained that he could have had a lie-in if he'd known Mikey was going to abandon him. Grumbled that his mother had offered to cook him a slap-up breakfast and he'd turned it down. Told him they should have contacted Woody, Sean and Mark, because Mikey would never dare duck out of a co-op mission.

By the time he'd pulled the car in to the side of the road near the church and put on the hazards, he was in a right sulk. 'Just so you know,' Jacko said, 'I have a very bad feeling about this.'

'I'm getting that. But trust me, I know what I'm doing.'

'If you were capable of getting information out of this girl, you'd have done it already.' Jacko checked his watch. 'I'll give you an hour. That café we passed – I'll wait for you there.'

'You're gonna wait?' Mikey leaned back and peered at Jacko. His work shirt was hanging over his jeans like always, his jacket, with its strange checked pattern, looked as geeky as ever and the expression on his face was only a fraction away from grumpy. But he was a true mate. Mikey wanted to give him something, but apart from a rollie, he didn't know what.

'I appreciate that,' he said. It was all he could think of.

Jacko smiled reluctantly. 'Go on, get out the car. I want my breakfast.'

It felt like a loophole in time opened up as Mikey walked through the wooden gate and into the churchyard. The lemon light seeping over the grass made him feel slightly sick, but this was a good plan.

It was an amazing plan, in fact.

Thirteen

She heard him before she saw him. The click of the gate, the swish of shoes through grass. She opened her eyes, dazed for a moment by the sun's glare. He was wearing jeans and a white T-shirt, a battered leather jacket. He walked towards her, grinning, side-bent, hands in pockets, maybe shy.

He said, 'You're here.'

'Looks like it.'

'I wasn't sure you would be.'

'Me either.'

She tried to sound casual, as if arranging to meet boys in a churchyard was the sort of thing she did every day, but her heart was speeding and her voice sounded young and high. As he stood there looking down at her, she tried to breathe slowly, tried not to blush.

He looked as if he was trying to work something out. Then he said, 'It's good to see you, Ellie.'

He'd remembered her name. That meant he liked her.

'You want to sit down?' She tapped the space next to her on the bench.

He sat on his hands, leaned forward and looked around at the bleached stones and the lopsided graves. He didn't say anything and she liked that, that he was thinking about things, admiring the place. They were the only living ones here. It was exciting. The wind moved slowly through the grass, the sun made patterns on the graves.

'I didn't think you were ever going to text,' he said.

She shuffled her shoes on the grass, squashing it flat.

'I decided if you didn't text me by tomorrow, I was going to come round your house.'

She shot him a glance. 'Seriously?'

'Yeah. I wanted to see you.'

He felt absolutely present sitting there looking at her. And that made her feel absolutely present too, as if she'd been hazy before, or only half seen.

And then his phone rang. It startled them both. He fished it out of his pocket and checked who it was. 'Sorry,' he said. 'I should take this.'

He walked off a little way, but she could still hear him. She wondered if he knew that. He listened for a minute, then he said, 'Calm down. It's OK, it'll be OK.'

That's how boys often sounded when they were talking to girls – as if they were in charge, as if they knew best. Maybe he had a girlfriend.

He said, 'It's probably some religious nut, or someone selling dusters. Don't open it and they'll go away.' He looked over at Ellie. She stared at her shoes and pretended not to be listening. How long was he going to give them? She had all day. All night too, in fact.

He said, 'Well, I expect she'll come out when she gets hungry and at least you get to choose what's on TV. Listen, I'll call you later. I can't think about this now.' He ended the call, rolled his eyes. 'Sisters.'

Well, that was good. Not a girlfriend at least. 'How many have you got?'

He stuffed the phone back into his pocket and looked around. He didn't answer. He appeared not to have heard.

She stood up suddenly. 'You want to do something?'

'Like what?'

'I know a place we could go.'

She didn't wait for a reply, just walked away from him and headed down the slope. She didn't even turn to see if he was following. The grass was longer here and smelled damp from the river. It was as if the boundaries of the town got smudged and everything became wilder.

He jogged up behind her. 'Where are you taking me?'

'Trust me.'

She didn't know why she'd said that, but it sounded cool, as if she knew exactly what would happen next. She felt as if she'd been given a break from the real her – as if she could reinvent herself with this boy, say anything, be anyone.

She led him up a track, towards a cluster of oaks and beeches. They grew close together, their branches cutting the sky. The path became tangled and thin.

'Are you sure about this?' he said.

'Through here.'

She picked a daffodil and twirled it. She picked another and threaded it in her hair. A bird flew from a branch and startled her. She watched it flap away until it disappeared against the pale sky, her breath coming quick and shallow.

The spaces between the trees began to stretch. Sunshine danced again through the branches. The mud path turned to grass as they came out of shadow and into a glade that sloped gently down to the river. On the other side were fields and above them a faultless sky.

'Is this it?' he said.

'Yeah.'

She sat on the grass and looked down at the river. He sat next to her. She wondered if he was disappointed, if he'd been expecting a fairground or something.

'I didn't even know you could get to the river this way,' he said.

'It's pretty.'

It was. And it was slightly warmer away from the trees. Sitting here with him reminded her of the night of the party, looking across the train track together. She wondered if he was thinking that too, but she didn't ask him in case he said no.

'I used to come here a lot,' she said, 'when we first moved from London.'

'You used to live in London? My mum's from there.' He blinked at her as if he couldn't believe it. 'Why would you ever move?'

'My gran and granddad lived round here and they got sick. My mum wanted to be closer to them and the timing suited my dad. He works in property and house prices in London were sky-high, so he sold our house, changed jobs, then bought a house twice as big here when the prices fell. He often does stuff like that. I can never work out if it's clever or not.'

'Sounds pretty clever to me.'

'We had to leave all our friends behind and then my granddad died as soon as we got here and my gran freaked out and had to go into a nursing home. It all seemed a waste of time after that. My dad was the only happy one.'

There was something solid about the way he listened to her. It encouraged her to ask the question that had been troubling her for days.

'Why did you knock on the door and pretend to know my brother?'

It seemed to surprise him, because he actually blushed. 'What makes you think I was pretending?'

She laughed. 'Something to do with you not recognizing each other?'

He pulled up a handful of grass and chucked it towards the river as if he wanted to feed the water. He pulled up another handful and laid it next to him. 'I don't know him, you're right, but there was a rumour going round that he was having a party and I wanted to blag an invite, that's all.'

She was relieved. It was such a simple answer. If he was lying, surely he'd think of something more complicated.

'I don't mind,' she said. 'I thought it was funny. But you do realize I don't even know your name?'

Again, he blushed.

'Is it Rumpelstiltskin?'

'What?'

'From the story. You know, the one about that little bloke who gets the queen to guess his name?'

He shook his head – obviously didn't know what she was talking about. She felt foolish suddenly. Other girls didn't talk about this crap. She should have kept her mouth shut.

She took off her shoes and wiggled her toes on the grass, but stopped when she saw he was looking at her and covered them with her hands. She thought of Stacey and her mate, of all the girls at school, who if they saw her now would be amazed that she'd walked out and texted a boy and brought him to her secret place. It made her feel strong thinking of them.

She took off her coat and flung it on the grass, stood up, unzipped her skirt and let it fall to her feet.

'What are you doing?' he said quietly.

'Taking off my clothes.'

'Why are you doing that?'

She took off her cardigan and tights, but left her underwear and shirt on. She tried not to think about her fat thighs, but was really glad she'd shaved her legs the night before.

She turned to him. 'You fancy a swim?'

He looked astonished. 'In the river?'

'Why not?'

'It'll be freezing!'

'Are you scared?'

'No, I just haven't got swimming stuff.'

She waved a hand at herself. 'Neither have I.'

He frowned, pulled his jeans down an inch, as if he was checking to see if, by a miracle, he had swimming trunks on. She saw the top of his boxer shorts. There was very fine hair at the bottom of his belly, gathering to shadow. He caught her looking, and to stop herself blushing, she said, 'I dare you.'

He stared back at her for a moment, and then he laughed.

'Well,' he said. 'If you're going to dare me.'

He kicked off his trainers, pulled off his jacket and unbuckled his jeans. Ellie couldn't look, didn't want to melt. She turned away and walked down the slope towards the water. The grass ran out near the edge, turned to mud pocked with gravel. It sucked at her toes.

She doubted herself now. She'd done this loads of times before, but it looked dark in the water today and so murky that anything could be hiding. There were weeds at the edge and rushes gripping the side of the bank. But she couldn't show him she was afraid. She needed to keep being interesting to hold his attention.

She didn't even look as she jumped. She knew if she did, she wouldn't be able to do it. Instead, she screwed her eyes shut and leaped into the air. The cold shock of the water was crazy. It was like falling from a plane, plummeting somewhere so alien-cold that ice might gather on her outstretched arms.

'What's it like?' he called. He was hugging himself on the riverbank. He looked old-fashioned standing there in his underwear.

She couldn't answer. She had to keep moving it was so cold. She swam breast stroke to the opposite bank, then front crawl on the turn. She loved that feeling – swimming without thinking, celebrating the water like she owned it. She enjoyed the rhythm and discipline of it. When she'd been a member of the swimming club, she'd swum forty lengths every morning and come out feeling brain-washed, clean, alert.

'Coming in,' he shouted. He sounded as if he was trying to convince himself. It made her smile. She recognized that male bravado from Tom, convincing yourself at the same time as you convinced everyone else. Her dad did it with maps.

He tucked in his knees and jumped like she had. He yelled, all arms and legs, and a splash so big she had to turn her face away. When she looked back he'd disappeared beneath the water. She watched the bubbles and waited.

He came up gasping for air. 'God, it's cold.' He looked as if he was crying as water clung to his eyelashes and dripped down his cheeks.

'Feels good though, eh?'

'It's freezing!'

She swam to him, smiling. 'Can't you handle it?'

He splashed her. She splashed him back. He tried to dunk her, but he didn't know she was fast and could get away from him easily. She let him almost catch her, then sank beneath the surface, came up behind him and dunked him first. She swam away laughing. She floated on her back and looked at the sky. She hoped she looked thin and in control. The way her lungs stretched and accommodated made her feel like an athlete.

She grabbed hold of a low branch and watched him swim up to her. He grabbed hold of it too and they hung there together. When they didn't move, the river lay smooth, the water cloudy and dark.

'What happens if you drink it?' he said.

'You die.'

He looked startled. 'Serious?'

She grinned. 'No, it's Grade B, which is pretty clean. About three miles further along it spreads out into creeks and goes through the salt marshes. You wouldn't want to swim in it there.'

'Why not?'

'It's tidal by then, so you never know what the depth is. There's loads of sinking mud too.'

'I like how you know things,' he said, and he looked right at her.

'You do?'

'I like a lot about you, in fact.'

It sounded like such a line, she laughed.

'Your lips are blue,' he said.

He reached across and touched her mouth with his finger as if he could brush the cold away. And it was astonishing the things her body did in response – her heart racing, the crazy adrenalin rush. She wanted to kiss his finger. Or lick it. She wanted him to put it in her mouth.

'You don't exactly look warm yourself,' she whispered.

'Maybe we should get out then.'

But neither of them moved.

He leaned towards her. His eyes were brown flecked with dark

117

gold. He kissed her very gently. His hand touched her cheek as if she was infinitely precious.

After a while, he pulled back and said, 'I really think we should get out. You're shivering like mad.'

She buried her nose and mouth in the curve of his neck and kissed him once there to say goodbye. Then the two of them clambered up the side of the riverbank and raced to the spot where they'd left their clothes.

She grabbed her tights to use as a towel; he did the same with his T-shirt. They hopped about, teeth chattering, rubbing themselves dry.

'Run,' he said. 'Come on, we need to get warm.'

He grabbed her hand and pulled her along the grass. At the trees she wheeled him round and made them skip back. They took it in turns with instructions. Up and down the riverbank – jumping one way, hopping back, pogo-ing, aeroplane impressions (wings, plus engine sounds), before sinking ragged and laughing onto the grass.

'That,' he said, 'has only *just* begun to warm me up. I swear I've never been so cold in my life.'

'You should try the sea next,' she laughed. 'And I don't mean the sea anywhere tame, I mean the wild sea. My gran's got this cottage over by the bay and there's a great beach there. It's got amazing waves, really ferocious. I'll take you one day if you like.'

'Promise?'

'Course.'

And they both smiled, like they knew something, and his hand reached hers and clasped it tight, like being chosen and taken care of.

And that's when his phone rang again.

Don't answer it, she thought. *Stay here with me*. But he let go of her hand, leaned over for his jacket and fumbled in the pocket for his phone. When he saw who it was he stood up and walked a few steps down the slope.

'Again?' he said. It was a different voice from the one he'd used earlier. It had an edge of fear to it. 'What did you open it for? I told you not to. Why would you do that?'

He flicked Ellie a look.

'Is it your sister?' she mouthed.

He nodded, took a couple more steps down the slope. 'All right, calm down, they've gone now. No, I'm not telling you off. Listen, Holly, this is what I'm going to do. I'm going to come and see you, OK? I'll get Jacko to give me a lift and I'll be with you in twenty minutes. No, babe, I can't stay, I've got to go to work, but I'll bring you a treat. What would you like me to bring?'

Ellie pulled her clothes towards her. She managed to unbutton her wet shirt and swap it for her cardigan and coat without him seeing as he said goodbye to his sister. He immediately made another call and arranged to meet his friend at the cemetery gate in ten minutes.

That was it then. Day over. She'd known it was too good to last.

He slid his phone shut and walked back up the slope. 'Sorry,' he said.

'That sounded difficult.'

119

'My sister's upset. She's only eight and some people knocked on the door and she opened it and scared herself.'

'Wasn't your mum there?'

'She had to pop out.'

'Who were the people?'

'Um, no one, just random people. Anyway, I have to go.'

Ellie scrambled quickly into her skirt as if she'd been thinking the very same thing. Across the grass, he pulled on his jeans and socks and trainers. The moment when they'd kissed felt like a lifetime ago.

'Where do you work?' she said.

'In a pub. It's not in town, so you wouldn't know it. It's one of the touristy places down by the harbour.'

She kept quiet, hoping he'd invite her for lunch after he'd sorted his sister out. She could sit at the bar and chat to him, order a sandwich. She'd like that. But he didn't ask. In fact, he didn't say anything and his whole face closed down as if he never would again.

They walked back in silence. Her shoes were too big without her tights and slapped loudly on the path. Her wet underwear felt clammy and rubbed the inside of her thighs and under her arms. She trailed her wet shirt and tights from one hand, letting them scrape the ground, letting them gather dust and leaves and twigs. She didn't care. She wanted to collect stuff – secret smells and things from the path. She'd examine them when she got home and maybe what happened in the water might seem real.

But where the path came to the slope, and where the slope led them back to the graveyard and the bench, he stalled. He turned to her very seriously.

'I like you,' he said.

He made it sound as if she was bound to disagree with him. She nodded. His face said he was telling her something very important.

He said, 'I mean it. Whatever happens, you have to believe that.'

'That sounds a bit dramatic.'

He looked at his mobile again. 'I've gotta go.'

They walked together through the graveyard and out through the wooden gate. It was still way too early for school to finish and there was no one around. He seemed nervous standing out on the street. Didn't he want to be seen with her in public? Maybe she was too ugly. Or maybe he did have a girlfriend and what happened on the phone wasn't anything to do with his sister.

'Well, I'll say goodbye here then,' he said.

She needed to get back to the main road too, so even though he obviously didn't want to, they walked together towards the junction. He walked slightly in front of her, head down, hands in pockets.

When the car pulled up, he didn't even notice.

'That bloke in the car's waving,' she told him. 'Is that your friend?'

The car stopped right beside them. The window opened and the driver leaned over. 'Hey, man,' he said, 'jump in.'

Ellie stood awkwardly on the pavement as he got into the car. She wasn't sure what to do next. Would he ask her if she wanted a lift? If he did, should she say yes? Or should she make some cool excuse and walk away as if she too had somewhere to be?

The other boy grinned, said, 'Sorry to steal him away.'

It sounded as if the gatecrasher was hers, as if they were a couple, as if she had rights.

She smiled. 'That's OK.'

They both looked at her then, but she didn't feel seen. It was as if they looked only at the outside – her clothes, her ridiculous shoes. The gatecrasher's eyes seemed covered in some glaze that made him different from how he'd been at the river.

'Well,' she said, 'see you around.'

He nodded, barely looked at her as the car pulled away.

Fourteen

Mikey sat on the edge of the sofa and tried to look normal. He stared at the carpet, then at the cop's flat black shoes. He crossed his fingers and tried to think of something other than now, other than here. But the only things that came into his head were to do with this woman. What if she opened cupboards and searched around? Was she allowed to do that? Everything he'd shoved away that morning would fall on the floor at her feet – the dirty clothes and unwashed plates, the bottles and ashtrays and empty crisp packets. Things had got slightly out of control since Karyn stopped pulling her weight. What if this woman went upstairs and found Mum in her bed with the worst hangover of the year so far? Cops hunted for clues everywhere, didn't they? Like sniffer dogs.

'So,' she said, 'it's a shame Karyn doesn't want to come down and join us.'

'Yeah, she's not feeling well.'

He looked up and their eyes met. He knew he was blushing, knew she saw it happen. She glanced at her watch.

'Do you think Mum will be much longer? Would you mind ringing her one more time?'

He should have thought more carefully before he said she'd popped to the shops. He should've come up with some story that involved her visiting a sick relative miles away. Ireland would've been safe. It took a whole day to get back from there.

'Perhaps if she doesn't answer this time, you could leave a message and ask her to call you back?'

He hated the sound of Mum's messaging service. He'd rung it loads over the last few days, and every time she sounded very far away and absolutely like she didn't give a shit. When she'd reappeared last night, he'd told her how pissed off that made him – to be left in charge with no idea where she was or if she was safe. She cried. She told him sorry. Same old story.

'Hey, Mum, it's me. Karyn's policewoman's here and wants to talk to us, remember? We're sitting waiting for you, so can you hurry up?' He slid the phone shut and forced a smile. 'You could talk to me instead. I mean, if she doesn't come back before you have to go. I can just pass it all on when I see her.'

The cop nodded. 'There are some things I'd like to talk with you about, Mikey, but I also hoped to see Mum and Karyn. I wanted to explain to the whole family why I asked social services to get involved.'

'You scared the hell out of Holly turning up like that last week.'

'Yes, she opened the door and got upset. I'm sorry about that, but we did have an appointment, and Mum was aware of it. Didn't she mention that to you?'

124

No, she bloody didn't, and he couldn't believe she'd managed to hide it. Maybe that was why she'd gone on a bender. She must've got freaked out by the cop grassing them up.

'I've been working with Karyn for a while now, Mikey, and as I'm sure you're aware, she often refuses to talk to me. She's quite suspicious of the police, I think, and won't let me put her in touch with other services, like counselling or a rape crisis centre.'

Mikey flinched at that word, hated it.

'Over the weeks I've known her, I've begun to realize that perhaps there might be deeper issues within the family that are preventing her from moving forwards.'

'Like what?'

'It's complex, Mikey, but to give you an example, I've noticed that Mum's often asleep during the day, which means Karyn is alone a lot of the time. I've also noticed that Karyn takes on a lot of the care for her sister and feels obliged to help out with various domestic tasks such as cooking and cleaning that perhaps shouldn't be her responsibility right now.'

'She's always done that stuff. She likes it.'

'Maybe, but at the moment, it doesn't feel as if she has much choice in the matter. So, I contacted social services to help me get a better picture of the family.'

'You say Karyn's suspicious of you, but you've made it worse. Spying on the rest of us isn't going to make her trust you, is it?'

'I have a duty to report things that are troubling, Mikey, and, to be frank, there are things in this family that I find concerning.'

'Like my mum having a kip during the day?'

'Not only that. Holly too.'

'Holly? What are you worried about her for? She's fine.'

'She's often not in school, Mikey, and when I contacted her teacher, I was told that when Holly does turn up, she's often late, or else she's collected late at the end of the day. Apparently she's not had a book bag or PE kit with her for weeks now.'

'You're supposed to be here for Karyn. Why do you care about Holly forgetting her PE kit?'

'I *am* here for Karyn, but I have to look at her situation in context. An eight-year-old not going to school rings alarm bells, Mikey.'

She liked nosing around is what she meant. Karyn should've kept her cop on a tighter leash, been nice to her, chatted her up, distracted her from the rest of them.

'Is Holly in school today?'

The questions were starting. He had to concentrate.

'Yeah, I took her.'

'Well, that's great. Is it usually you who takes her?'

'It used to be Karyn, but now me and Mum take it in turns.'

Maybe if he promised to get Holly to school on time every day, this woman would get social services off their backs. He hated her being here, like some kind of bright needle in the lounge. If he got her on his side, if he made her think he was brilliant at everything, then maybe she'd go away and take all her nosy mates with her.

'So,' she said, 'Mum's picking Holly up later, is she?'

'Yeah.' He took a deep breath. 'Listen, would you like a cup of tea?'

She smiled across at him. 'That'd be lovely, thank you. Milk, no sugar, please.'

Well, that was a relief, since they didn't actually have any sugar. He went round the corner to the kitchen, put the kettle on and swilled the last dregs of milk around the bottom of the carton. He gave it a sniff. It was just about OK.

He watched her as he waited for the water to boil, caught her eyeing up the cards and magazines Karyn had got from her mates, checking out the curtains and TV, making sure the DVDs weren't all triple Xs.

The tea went well – the right colour and the milk didn't do that disgusting floating thing. He took it through and put it on the table in front of her, then sat back down.

'Thank you,' she said. She took a sip and smiled. 'Very nice.'

He nodded, wondered if he should tell her he was training to be a chef, but decided not to. It was probably best not to offer information. He'd only get himself in trouble.

They sat in silence for a minute as she drank her tea. It went on a bit long. Was he supposed to do something now, or say something? Was she expecting a biscuit? He felt the panic creep back. What if she asked for one? *Could I have a biscuit please, Mikey?* Like a test. Weren't children supposed to have nice things to eat in their homes? What if having no biscuits made her suspicious and she asked to look in the kitchen? There was half a packet of out-of-date frankfurters in the fridge, and that was it. There was no bread, no milk either now, no tins of stuff, nothing in the freezer except ice. They'd be shafted if she checked.

127

His heart began to pound again. Sitting there, with her glasses and her polite cup of tea, she reminded him of all the reasons he'd hated school.

'You know,' he said, 'Holly's really clever. It's not like if she misses a few lessons she's going to mess everything up, because she's the cleverest of the lot of us. She's always reading and drawing and running about.'

'I'm sure Holly's very bright, but she also needs to go to school every day. Do you know how many days unauthorized absence she's had this term?'

She'd spoken to the teacher already, so this was a trick. He shook his head and waited for her to tell him.

'Her average attendance is currently below sixty per cent. That means she's absent for at least four out of every ten days.'

'I know what sixty per cent means.'

'Of course, I'm sorry.' She put the tea down. 'The last two times I scheduled an appointment to see Karyn, nobody answered the door. When social services came round with me last week, they'd made an appointment with your mother, and Holly answered the door and told us she had no idea where Mum was. We were obviously concerned about that.'

He leaned back and folded his arms. It was like doing one of Holly's jigsaws, trying to work out where the right answers were.

'Maybe Mum went for a walk?'

That sounded healthy at least, but she sat there frowning at him.

'Holly had a tummy ache,' he said. 'I remember now, that's

why she missed school. Maybe Mum went to the chemist to get medicine. Karyn was here, so Holly wasn't alone. She probably said she didn't know where Mum was to make everything sound more exciting. She loves making up stories. It's a sign of intelligence.'

'Where were you that day, Mikey, if you don't mind me asking?'

His mind tripped to Ellie at the river, the challenge in her eyes as she dared him to jump. Her see-through shirt, the lace of her bra.

'I was at work.'

Having a job was bound to be a point in his favour.

She took another sip of tea, glanced at her watch again. 'OK, it doesn't look as if Mum's going to turn up, so maybe we should reschedule. But before I go, Mikey, I wanted to ask your advice. I'd like to get your view on Karyn, and how you think I could support her more. Is there anything you think she needs that she's not getting at the moment?'

What was he supposed to say to that? *Compensation*? *Revenge*? *Tom Parker dead*?

'I dunno, it's just going on so long, isn't it? She told me the other day she wished she'd never bothered reporting him. The thought of going to court really freaks her out, you know.'

'I know, and I can help her with that, Mikey. I can liaise with the school on her behalf, I can talk to her GP if she wants me to, I can bring her up to date on all news relating to the case and help her prepare for court. It won't be an easy ride, Mikey. But I'm here for her, believe me.'

'She won't leave the flat either, did you know that? She says she

129

doesn't want to bump into him, so she's stuck in all the time.'

'He's not allowed anywhere near this flat, or in the centre of town, or near the school. I've told Karyn that.'

'His mates could still get her.'

'That would also be breaking his bail conditions. If anyone intimidates Karyn or passes on any messages from Tom to her, then you must let me know.'

'And what happens when it's over? You'll dump her, won't you? After the court case, we'll never see you again.'

'That's why it's important I put Karyn in touch with services that can help her now and will continue to help her. If you can persuade her to look at some of the leaflets I've given her, that would be great. It might take a burden from your shoulders too, Mikey, you never know.' She put her cup down. 'How's Holly managing the situation with Karyn? Is she aware of what happened to her? Do you talk about it together?'

Mikey shook his head. 'She's a kid. She wouldn't understand.'

'Does she ever ask why Karyn isn't going to school any more, or wonder why her sister's upset?'

'Karyn's in Year Eleven, so was about to leave school anyway, and Holly thinks she's sad because a boy dumped her.'

'That's what you've told her?'

'Kind of.'

She nodded. 'And what about you? It must be very tough being the older brother of a girl in this situation.'

He wondered what she wanted to hear. Was he supposed to want vengeance, or was it best to tell her that he was leaving the whole thing well alone? He remembered what Mum had said once and went with that.

'I'm letting you lot deal with it.'

She nodded. He'd got that right at least.

'And we will deal with it, Mikey. I know the police ask a lot of questions and those questions can be upsetting for Karyn, but they need to get their facts straight. You know that, don't you? It's very personal stuff, very difficult to deal with. It's hard for all of you.'

He shrugged. How could this woman understand? No one would ever speak to her the way the cops spoke to Karyn, asking her if she'd slept with Tom before or if she usually got so drunk at parties. Women like her had been to university and knew all the right things to say. They had parents who came in pairs and grew up expecting the same for their own kids.

Mikey looked right at her for a second. For some strange reason, he imagined her eating an ice cream – strawberry and vanilla in some sunny back garden.

She smiled at him. 'You said earlier that you have a job.'

'I'm training to be a chef.'

'Good for you.' She was obviously impressed. 'Do you work full-time?'

He made it sound brilliant. He was practically head chef in this little story and the pub couldn't function without him. He described dishes he'd never made – coq au vin, cassoulet, chou-croute garnie and a classic Russian coulibiac. No, he told her, he had no intention of leaving Norfolk. Yes, he said, the pub was sending him to college soon to do his NVQ. Yes, that would mean more hours, but he was completely up for it. He was a hard worker. He had a focused mind. He didn't mention London and his dream that Karyn would get over this quickly so he'd be free to go there.

He finished with a flourish, told her he was bound to be promoted before the end of the year, then sat back on the sofa with his best grin.

But she didn't smile back. In fact, she was frowning again.

'That worries me, Mikey. That amount of responsibility and all those hours. I know your mum's not well and I know how hard the situation with Karyn must be. It might be worth considering if there's anyone else who can help you out for a while. A relative or family friend perhaps?'

'No,' he said, 'there's no one.'

Why wasn't he getting this right? And what did she mean about Mum not being well? How much did she know?

He imagined her going back to the police station and telling all her cop mates that he wasn't coping, then popping over to social services and telling them too. They'd all be tutting and fussing and making suggestions as to how he could do better in his sad little life.

'Listen,' he said. 'We can manage this. We'll make Holly go to school every day. It's not too much. We can do that, she likes school, so it'll be easy.'

'There's more to it than that, Mikey.'

'Like what?'

He'd offer her anything, promise everything.

She told him what social services would be looking for: Holly needed to be at school by nine o'clock every day and she needed her PE kit and book bag with her. She mustn't be smelly or dirty or tired and she must have had breakfast. Mum needed to call social services to see if they could offer support. Karyn needed to keep her appointments.

'I can help her, Mikey. It's my job to help her, but I can't do my job if she won't talk to me. If you could encourage her to trust me a bit more, that'd be great.'

She wanted him to call if he was worried about anything or wanted to talk, or if he thought of something Karyn might need. She gave him a little card with her direct number on it. It even had her name – Gillian.

He agreed to it all. It was a chance to believe everything could be better simply by saying it out loud.

In return she said she'd contact social services and tell them she'd spoken to him and that the family were perhaps managing better than she'd thought. She'd ask them to speak to Holly's school about getting her into some club that didn't finish until six o'clock, and maybe they could even investigate the possibility of a family support worker, whatever that was.

He promised that Mum would call her. He told her he understood that Karyn not meeting appointments was worrying and he'd do his best to persuade her to keep them. They nodded at each other. It was agreed. It was like beginning something new, starting over.

She began to put her coat on. 'It's fantastic you're working, Mikey.'

He smiled without meaning to. 'Yeah, I like cooking, it's cool. Have you ever been to the Queen's Head? It's one of the pubs by the harbour.'

'I don't know it,' she said. 'But maybe I'll try and get there one day.'

'It's all you can eat for a tenner. That's pretty good, eh? After my shifts end, I even get stuff for free.'

He hesitated. He meant the meal he got after work, the bits of meat and stuffing balls and chipolatas, all piled high. But he wondered if by saying it out loud, she'd know about the crisps he stuffed in his jacket for the girls, the peanuts and pork scratchings for Mum. She was a cop, wasn't she? She had a nose for crime.

'The boss is pleased with me,' he blustered. 'She says I'm a natural.'

'I'm sure you are.'

She stood up and hoisted her bag onto her shoulder. 'Well, I'll be off, Mikey, but remember, I think Mum should call social services today if possible.'

'I'll get her to do it.'

She nodded. 'Good.'

He'd survived. She smiled as she left, even said she looked forward to seeing him again.

As soon as the door was shut he yelled up to Karyn and she came out of her room and stood at the top of the stairs, wrapped in her duvet.

'She's gone,' he told her. 'I handled it.'

'What did she say?'

'That you should keep your frigging appointments. You know, if you hadn't pissed her off, she'd never have grassed us up. She's only trying to help. Considering she's a cop, she's OK.'

'She keeps wanting to talk about how I'm feeling and I want to forget it.'

'Maybe she actually cares. You ever thought of that?'

Karyn walked down the stairs, trailing the duvet behind her. When she got to the bottom step she held out her arms for a hug. He put his arms round her and they stood there together for a minute.

'There's some stuff we need to do,' he said.

She leaned back and looked at him. She looked paler than yesterday, and shorter. 'What stuff?'

'First, we've got to sober Mum up. Actually, *you've* got to sober her up, 'cos I've got to go to work. She has to phone social services and tell them why she bunked off the other day, get some shopping in, then collect Holly. Get her to call me as soon as she's properly awake and don't let her go to school if she's still hung-over – they'll be watching for that. Your cop rang the school as well, can you believe it?'

'Stop calling her *my* cop.'

'If Mum hasn't had a bath and isn't completely sober, you'll have to sort Holly out.'

Karyn shrank away from him. 'I'm not leaving the flat.'

'You don't have to. Ring one of your friends and get them to pick her up.'

'I'm not talking to people.'

135

'For God's sake, Karyn! It's just a few phone calls.'

He wanted to hit her. He wanted to slam the door and walk away. Couldn't she see that her mates needed something to do? Day after day they rang the doorbell to ask how she was. Giving them a job might make everyone feel better. But if he got into an argument about it now, he'd be even later for work than he was already. And if he walked off, Karyn'd go straight back to bed and she and Mum would sleep the whole day through.

He put his hands on Karyn's shoulders and looked into her eyes. He felt like a hypnotist.

'We're in this together,' he said, 'and you have to do something to help. Make Mum strong coffee, get her to drink loads of water, go in and talk to her, don't take any crap. We can't be late to collect Holly today. Do you understand?'

She nodded, but her eyes were full of tears.

'You're very brave,' he told her. 'Don't worry, it's all going to work out fine.'

Fifteen

Tom stopped the car before the bridge, switched the engine off and turned to Ellie.

'I'm not allowed any closer than this,' he said.

She looked down at her lap, at her fingers gripping the strap of her bag.

He said, 'I had a word with James and Freddie. They've got brothers at the school, and they'll be straight in there if anyone gives you trouble today.'

Random boys acting as bodyguards would only get her noticed more. What she really needed was for everyone to stop taking any notice of her whatsoever, then her life could go back to how it used to be.

'I'm sorry Dad gave you grief,' Tom said. 'He came down way too hard.'

It was true, he had. On and on about the shame she'd brought on the family by fighting in public, and the disappointment she'd caused by running away and not taking responsibility for her own behaviour, blah, blah. He'd only let her have two days and the weekend off, and was forcing her back already. This morning, he'd leaned over the breakfast table and said, 'I hope you realize how tough this is for your brother.'

Tom had been sweet, stepping in and saying it was tough for her too, that she'd been defending his reputation and the kids at school sounded like total losers. But even Dad's golden boy hadn't been able to blag her any more days off.

And now she had to get out of the car and walk over the bridge. She had to go through the gate on the other side and cross the empty playground, then through the main door and report to reception. From there she would be escorted into Spanish by Mr Spalding, the learning mentor. It had all been planned by her father on the phone, including the late arrival. She was allowed to miss registration, assembly and the busy morning corridors. She was officially a troubled child.

'You want my advice?' Tom said. He twisted in his seat to look at her properly. 'Keep your head down, stay focused on revision and exams and stay out of trouble. When you disappear for hours and refuse to say where you are, Mum and Dad are bound to go crazy.'

She shook her head at him. 'I didn't tell them where I was because I didn't want to lie.'

'But you haven't told me either and we normally share stuff like that.'

But the gatecrasher was her secret. She'd had five texts from him since the river and the latest one said, *When can I see you?* She wasn't going to tell anyone that.

'I hung around town.'

'So, why's that such a secret?'

'Dad hates me doing nothing. He probably expects me to go to the library and revise when I bunk off and Mum always takes his side. I didn't want the lecture, that's all.'

Tom nodded sympathetically. 'Yeah, yeah, they're ridiculous.'

There was a moment's silence, then she said, 'Would you phone in sick for me?'

'What?'

'Can you phone the school and pretend to be Dad?'

'No! He'll go round the bend if he finds out.'

'Please, Tom. I can't face it.'

She held her hand to her belly. It was going weird again, as if it was wrecked inside and small things were fluttering about. She thought she must have clutched it in her sleep too, because she'd woken up with the shape of a button from her pyjamas imprinted on her palm.

'What will you do all day?' Tom asked.

'I don't know, hang out with you?' She gave him a pleading smile. 'If I get home at the normal time, they're never going to know.'

He gazed at her for a second, then nodded. 'Don't tell them I did this.'

As he dialled, she watched his face and thought how weird it was that by sheer fluke of birth, she was his sister. *Sister, sister*. She said the word silently in her head and tried to make sense of it.

'Good morning,' Tom said. 'I'm ringing on behalf of my

daughter, Eleanor Parker, in Year Eleven. Just to let you know, she has a migraine and won't be in today.' He nodded as he listened to the response. 'Yes, yes, of course I'll tell her that. Thank you very much.' He snapped his phone shut and smiled. 'The receptionist hopes you get better soon.'

Ellie laughed. She couldn't help it. One simple phone call and she had a free day ahead of her.

'There's another trick,' Tom said as he started the ignition. 'You could try this one tomorrow. You go in for registration, leave before your first class and spend the morning in town, then go back for afternoon registration and bunk straight out again. I did it loads when I was at school and no one ever found out.'

She shook her head at him, amazed. 'I never knew that about you.'

They pulled away from the bridge, down Lower Road, past the newsagent's and Lidl and swung a right at the post office, then a sharp left. Space opened up quickly – fields, trees, hedgerows. Ellie opened the window. The verge was rich with wild flowers and swaying grass. She stuck her hand out and let the wind play with her fingers. Across the field a bird flew very fast in a straight line, then swooped down to the earth. This was great. Her and Tom off on an adventure. Like old times.

As they got nearer to the coast, the sun began to look hazy and far away. Ellie knew it was something to do with the weight of the atmosphere at sea level. *Advection*, it was called, or *sea mist*. By the time they pulled into the car park at the harbour, it had substance to it and was hanging damp and heavy above them.

They parked by the sea wall. Ellie had been to the harbour before, when it was busy with tourists – kids with crabbing lines and buckets, whole families trailing down through the car park to the beach. But today was a weekday and the weather was so dull now that the line between sky and sea was lost and the edges of the boats in the dock were blurred. Apart from a bloke fishing on the end of the jetty, the place was deserted. Even the souvenir shop had its hatches down.

'So,' Ellie said. 'What are we doing here then?'

Tom shrugged. 'I like the boats. I'm not allowed into town and I've got a curfew, but I can come here whenever I want.'

It was as if she heard it for the first time – what this meant to him, how hard this was. And she'd been all wrapped up in herself.

'I've been here every day since they let me out. And you know what I do when I get here?' He did a magician's *Duh-da!* and pulled a tin from his pocket.

'What is it?'

He took out a small chunk of something wrapped in cellophane and danced it in front of his nose. 'I'm trusting you with this, Ellie.' He sniffed it. 'Shame it's only Rocky.'

'Rocky?'

'Moroccan. It's a bit mild, but it's all I could get hold of.'

She knew he'd tried dope before – he'd been smoking it the night he brought everyone back. In the morning she'd buried the joint ends in the garden so their parents wouldn't find out. But this whole chunk – soft and dark as fudge – was something else completely.

She watched him lick the seam of a cigarette and strip the damp paper away. He didn't even bother checking outside as he emptied the tobacco into a giant Rizla and began to carefully heat the dope over his lighter.

'Watch and learn,' he said.

The car filled with sweet fumes. Ellie wondered if the smell would cling to her hair; if, when she got home, her dad would sniff and say, 'Are you on drugs now, Eleanor?'

Two women walked past in matching blue windcheaters and backpacks. They looked determined, solid. Ellie envied them.

'Should you be doing this?' she said. 'I mean, what if the police give you a drugs test or something?'

Tom sighed. 'I have to have something to look forward to.'

He crumbled the dope on top of the tobacco, then picked up the whole thing and rolled it with such infinite care it was mesmerizing. He twisted one end, then laid it on his knee while he tore off a small piece of cardboard from the Rizla packet and rolled it into a tube, which he stuck in the other end.

'What's that for?'

'A roach. It's to stop your lip burning.'

Her lip? Was he expecting her to have some?

He lit the joint, inhaled hard and closed his eyes to exhale. 'Every morning I look forward to this.' He took several more drags, and just as she thought she'd got away with it, that he was going to keep it all for himself, he said, 'So, now you're officially hanging with your big brother, are you going to have a few draws?'

'I don't know.'

'You won't even feel it. Just a little rush.'

It felt awkward in her hand, as if it was a prop from a game. She had a sudden memory of her and Tom rolling leaves from a bush in the garden into a sheet of A4 and setting it alight. They must've been about six and eight years old and pretending to smoke cigars.

She shot him a look. This was her brother. He always had been, always would be. She took a small drag and swilled the smoke around her mouth.

'Take it right down,' he said. 'Don't waste it.'

She tried to drag the smoke from her mouth into her lungs, but her throat tensed and she sent it straight back up again in a spluttering cough.

Tom laughed. 'You're such a rookie. Come on, you're not going to get stoned, you'll feel warm and a bit happy. Don't give up so easily.'

Under his instruction, she took a deeper drag and tried to pull the smoke right down. Her lungs burned, her brain swung sideways and the smoke came hacking out again.

Tom took the joint from her then, and inhaled ridiculously deeply, as if showing her how to do it properly. He blew the smoke out towards the windscreen. It bounced straight back at them in a pungent cloud.

He smiled dreamily at her. 'You've joined the dark side of the force now. You know that, don't you?'

She slunk down in her seat, embarrassed. She'd never in her whole life bunked school, smoked dope or kissed a boy whose name she didn't know, and yet in the last few days, she'd done all

143

these things. This was what it must be like to have control of your own life. This is what it would be like at university – she'd do whatever she wanted, whenever she wanted. No questions asked. No surveillance. Maybe she'd even get into smoking. It was quite nice after the initial rush.

Tom looked happier than she'd seen him for days, sitting there with a joint in his hand. She smiled at him. He was her brother. They were bound.

'Tom?'

'Mmm?'

'Did you like Karyn McKenzie once?'

He turned to her, surprised. 'Do we have to talk about this?'

'I know you hate her now, but before all this happened, did you like her?'

Tom opened his window, stretched his arm out and flexed his fingers. 'She's a slut.'

'So, why did you invite her round?'

'I didn't – she followed me home.'

'But you gave her a lift from the pub. You stood in the garden with your arm round her.'

'You want this to be a love story?'

'I just want to know.'

He sighed. 'You saw what she was wearing. You think I should go to jail for saying yes when she offered herself to me on a plate?'

'Did you send her threatening texts when she said she was going to the police?'

He looked at her sharply. 'Who told you that?'

144

'Is that why they didn't give you bail straight away? Dad said it was the rubbish lawyer, but it wasn't, was it?'

Tom licked the edge of his mouth with his tongue. 'When you saw her the next morning, when she came downstairs and you were in the kitchen, what did she say to you?'

This again. She hated this. This was like the police station. 'I already told you: she asked me for some orange juice and directions back into town.'

He nodded. 'Exactly. She didn't look hassled or anything, did she? She wasn't crying and she didn't say anything about being attacked, did she? She drank a glass of juice and left the house and went home. She didn't even bother going to the cops for hours.' He tossed the joint end out of the car and shut his window. He put the Rizla packet and the dope back in the tin. 'I sent her texts because she was about to stitch me up.'

This is what grief is like, Ellie thought. It had a shape in her mouth like an O.

'If I said I didn't want to be your witness, what would you do?'

He looked genuinely alarmed. 'You can't bail out on me!'

'I'm scared of going to court.'

'We're all fucking scared!'

'But they'll ask me questions and what if I get it wrong?'

'How hard can it be? Just say you don't know anything.'

'I did tell you Karyn was only fifteen though.'

'And I didn't hear you.'

'We had a whole conversation about it on the landing.'

'So now you want me to go to jail because I'm hard of hearing?'

145

She turned to him, her cheeks burning. 'How do you know she wanted you? How do you *really* know? She was so drunk she couldn't even walk.'

He leaned towards her, his face only centimetres from hers. He spoke very quietly. 'If you pull out, the cops will think I'm guilty.'

She shook her head, heart thumping. 'They won't.'

'They'll haul you down the station and ask you tons of questions. Then they'll get a witness order and force you to court, whether you want to go or not. They'll put you in the witness box and cross-examine you for hours. They'll think it's really suspicious that my own sister can't be bothered to defend me.'

Ellie blinked. She knew what would happen next. He'd withdraw all the warmth and replace it with coldness. It would be brutal, like the sun going in and sheet ice covering the sky. It had always been this way with Tom.

'I'm sorry,' she said.

He shook his head. 'It's ironic, I actually thought you were old enough to hang out with. But you're worse than Dad.'

She'd ruined it between them now and it had been so perfect.

'Get out of the car.'

'Here?'

'I'm meeting Freddie.'

'Can you take me home first?'

'Mum's there. You want her to know you're not in school?'

'So, what will I do all day?'

'I don't know, it was your idea to bunk. Why are you going on at me all the time? There's a bus back into town.'

146

So, she was stuck, the same as last week. Only then she'd had her anger and the river and the gatecrasher, and today she was dizzy from the dope and was being dumped in the middle of the harbour in a mist.

She closed her eyes, tried to get back to the anger. She wanted something to hold on to.

'Do you have any money?' she said.

He sighed, reached into his pocket and pulled out some coins, counted out five pounds and handed them to her. 'You've got to trust me, Ellie.' His face was still and his voice was very certain. 'I mean it.'

And then she got out of the car.

Sixteen

'Simple things have great weight,' Dex said as he laid out butter, milk and flour on the work surface in front of Mikey. 'You ever think how these three ingredients make a basic white sauce, but once you have that, you can make so many other things? Mornay, for instance, or soubise.'

This was what Mikey liked about cooking – you started with something simple and you added another simple thing to it and you ended up with something new and complicated. *Alchemy*, Dex called it, which was something to do with magic if you were French.

Dex had asked him to make a béchamel sauce for the lasagne. It was Mikey's favourite meal – all that pasta and cheese, and he knew Dex rated his sauce. He'd even swapped jobs with him and was now scrubbing out baking trays at the sink.

'I made lasagne for my mum once,' he told Dex. 'You should have seen her face.'

'She was proud?'

'She was gobsmacked. She didn't know I could do stuff like that.'

'You have a gift, Mikey. It's what I'm always saying.'

Mikey put butter in a pan and watched it soften, shifted it about with a wooden spoon for a bit, then sieved in an equal weight of flour and stirred. It formed into a greasy ball, slippery and hot in the pan. He added hot milk, slowly moistening the roux with it.

It was great not to have to worry about anything else but what was happening on the stove. Mikey knew that a good roux should be stiff and pull away from the sides of the pan, that an onion stuck with clove added flavour to the milk. Simple things he'd discovered.

'I think one day you will be a saucier,' Dex said. 'You know this is the highest position of the station cooks?'

'No, I don't want to make sauces all the time. I want to be a sous-chef, in charge of the whole meal from beginning to end.'

'Well, you must work hard then. You must practise and listen well and when the time comes, the food will tell you what your specialism is.'

Mikey laughed, because the idea of food telling him anything was amazing and ridiculous all at once. Dex chuckled too. It was great standing there together laughing.

Jacko came in then. He was carrying a pile of salad boxes and gave them both a puzzled look. 'What's going on?'

'Mikey is perfecting the art of the roux,' Dex said, and he waved the dishwashing brush at Jacko like a wand. 'He is whisking and whisking and ignoring the ache in his hand.'

'Well, it's really busy out there, you know.'

'We know,' Dex laughed, 'which is why we are hiding in here.'

Jacko banged the boxes down. 'So, am I supposed to chop these lettuces all by myself?'

All morning Jacko had been edgy and Mikey knew it was his fault. He'd been late for work every day last week and Jacko had covered for him. Today, he'd even lent him the car. Mikey had thanked him, promised him a game of pool and a pint after their shift, but maybe that wasn't enough.

'Come and have a go, Jacko,' he said. 'This needs attention for a while. You do the whisking, I'll do the lettuce if you like.'

'No, ta.'

'You might love it.'

'Why would I? I don't want to be a chef.'

Dex frowned. 'What finer ambition is there?'

'Plenty. There's a whole world out there.'

'And yet you're still here, the longest-serving kitchen assistant we ever had.'

Mikey watched Jacko stumble for words. He knew he'd gone to the job centre loads of times in an effort to get away from the pub. He hated peeling and chopping vegetables, said the smell of cooking got under his skin. But all he'd been offered was a job stacking shelves, and the woman at the job centre had said there was competition even for that. Mikey felt sorry for Jacko suddenly, and upset to see him blushing.

'Maybe you'll meet a girl,' Mikey said, 'and she'll look after you.'

It was meant to be kind. It was meant to make Jacko smile, so that everything could be all right between them again, but the look Jacko shot him said he hadn't taken it that way.

'Talking about yourself, Mikey?'

'What are you on about?'

''Cos you always meet plenty of girls, don't you?'

Mikey stopped whisking. 'What's that supposed to mean?'

Jacko stepped back, hands raised as if Mikey was about to shoot him with the whisk. 'Just saying we had a plan, remember?'

'Yeah, I know.'

'And you asked me to help you. But then you let a girl get in the way.'

'It's not quite that simple, is it?'

Jacko shrugged. 'She didn't tell you anything useful and now you've let another five days go by. She's not the solution, Mikey. It seems pretty simple to me.'

'I was busy last week.' Mikey spoke very slowly, so Jacko would remember his mum had been AWOL and he'd had to cope with Holly and Karyn alone. 'And I had a meeting this morning, remember? Or maybe you think I should've gone round his house before the meeting and kicked his face off in front of his parents?'

'Maybe you should.'

'Are you nuts?'

'Boys, boys!' Dex said. 'Look, now you've brought the boss in with your noise.'

Sue stood there, arms folded, looking the three of them up and down. 'I need a waiter.'

'And every day I tell you, you're looking at chefs,' Dex told her.

'Actually,' she said, 'I am looking at one chef, one kitchen assistant and one dishwasher.' She took a step in and tapped Mikey on

151

the shoulder. 'And I think you know which of those three you are.'

Mikey shook his head at her. 'I'll be a rubbish waiter.'

'You'll get tips.'

'I'll drop stuff.'

'I've got a shirt that'll fit you and those trousers will have to do.'

'But I'm in the middle of making a sauce.'

'I'll do you a trade. You do some waiting and I'll turn a blind eye to your time-keeping.'

Jacko laughed as Mikey snatched the shirt and went off to change in the toilets. Sue hovered outside the door waiting for him, then took him into the bar and got him a name badge.

'You're called Tyler today,' she told him.

There were loads of people in the bar area – tourists disappointed with the weather and holed up in caravans and chalets; this would be their day's main event. One couple had wet hair from the mist, sitting together like a pair of seals, sleek heads bent over the menu. Such ordinary clean lives. It made Mikey feel entirely crap.

He wondered about his mum, whether she was awake yet, if Karyn had managed to sober her up, if Holly was enjoying school. He envied his little sister suddenly – all that glitter and finger paint and sitting about with your mates.

Sue took him with her as she went to greet a family loitering in the doorway. 'Table for four, is it? Follow me, please.'

She led them to the back of the eating area – mum, dad, a couple of kids. Mikey trailed behind. He wondered what it would be like to be their son, their big boy, coming out with them for his lunch. But the fantasy only lasted until they'd sat down, when Sue turned to him and said, 'I'm only going to say this once, so listen up.'

She gave them the speech about how they should help themselves from the starter bar, then go up to the carvery to get their main course and veg. 'Tyler will look after you,' she told them. 'He'll get you drinks and desserts and anything else you need.'

Mikey stood there watching them settle themselves down. They completely ignored him. The little kids fought over the free pencils and drawing booklet, the woman folded their wet coats onto the backs of their chairs and the bloke kept checking his mobile. Mikey smiled at the woman, wanted her to see he knew what an idiot her husband was. He didn't want to be there, it was obvious. The woman smiled back. 'What's at the starter bar?' she said.

The bloke picked up his menu and scanned it, like maybe he could answer the question, but Mikey jumped in first. 'There's different salads, melon, or hot soup.'

'What flavour?' the woman said.

'I'll find out.'

The bloke looked up. 'Shouldn't you know?'

He didn't notice his wife smiling at Mikey as if she was sorry. *She knows he's a git*, Mikey thought, *and she wants us all to forgive him*. He recognized the look from his mother's face. She wore it whenever she got pissed and started getting nostalgic about some old boyfriend. Mikey wished he could gob in the soup. And that would just be for starters.

Back in the kitchen he envied Jacko, sweating now from the

ovens, turning the parsnips off their baking tray, emptying steaming piles of peas into bowls. Dex was sprinkling cheese over the finished lasagne. It was familiar in here.

'How's the real world?' Jacko asked.

'Full of tossers.'

'Could have told you that.'

Which was a small moment of warmth.

Maybe Mikey had been imagining the bad vibes, maybe everything was still OK between them. Just to check, he said, 'I'm going to get the bastard, you know. I promised Karyn and I haven't given up on it.'

Jacko shrugged. 'You need to hurry up, that's all I'm saying, or it'll never be done.'

He made it sound as if he was in charge, as if Mikey hadn't spent days churning all the details round in his head.

'All right,' Mikey said, 'what about Saturday?'

Jacko nodded. 'I'm up for that.'

'We both get a half day. We'll do the golf-club thing.'

They high-fived to seal the deal. Mates again.

Seventeen

Ellie sat on the harbour wall watching the boats bob up and down and listening to the rigging wires sing. She was cold and bored, because although the tide was going out and revealing the beach, nothing else was happening. The bloke fishing on the end of the jetty hadn't caught a single thing in the last ten minutes, the sun wasn't coming out and the mist wasn't clearing.

The odd thing about it was that somewhere up there, the weather was fine. The sun was simply trapped behind a cobwebbed sky. Only a mile or two down the coast, the day was probably blazing. Perhaps Tom was enjoying a sunny game of golf with Freddie, or sitting in the clubhouse with a pint of cold cider in his hand.

She was still furious with him for leaving her in the middle of nowhere with only a fiver. There wasn't a bus for hours and maybe he'd known that. He'd definitely known there was no way she was going to tell their parents he'd dumped her, because she'd get a massive bollocking for bunking school if she did.

She'd start walking back into town in a minute. It couldn't be more than three miles and she thought she remembered the way. She'd wander round the shops, or maybe go to the library until school was out, then go to the gate and see if any of the girls in her year wanted to hang out. It was about time she had some friends. Maybe she'd even tell them about the river and the gate-crasher to make herself seem more interesting. They might not believe her of course, because no one believed her when she said she'd kissed Danny at the Christmas party. Sometimes she even wondered herself if any of the good things that happened to her were true, because they seemed fleeting compared to the bad things.

Even her amazing plan had gone wrong. She'd thought of it almost as soon as Tom had dumped her, and had immediately put it into action – the gatecrasher had said he worked in a pub by the harbour; well, then she would find him and spend the rest of the day sitting at the bar chatting to him.

The first pub she tried was the White Horse and it was full of old men clutching pints. They turned round en masse to stare at her when she opened the door, and although she managed to stutter that she was looking for someone who worked there, they all laughed at her, because the man behind the bar was about a hundred years old and was the only employee.

In the Earl of Mowbray, she was braver, even made it to the bar to ask if a boy worked there. She described him – dark, tall, about eighteen. The barman gave her a lewd smile and said, 'Won't I do, darling?'

She blushed furiously, and again she was laughed at.

'What's his name then, love?' the barman said as she made her way back to the door. And Ellie realized that she still didn't know, and the whole enterprise suddenly seemed ridiculous and humiliating. She'd wanted to walk in and see his smile, to sit down with him and have a drink. She'd imagined he'd give her a lift home, that they'd arrange to meet later. This day had seemed such a gift, but it was turning out to be worse than school.

She stood up to collect her bag, but was distracted by a sudden movement down on the jetty. The fisherman was unhooking his rod from its tripod and he must've caught something big, because the whole line was bending. Ellie leaned right over the harbour wall to see better.

And there, through the mist and cloud, a fish shimmered silver against the sky before crashing at the man's feet. He bent down and grabbed it round the neck before it could slip back into the water. With his other hand he reached blindly down next to him and brought up a large stone.

Ellie leaned forward. He was going to kill it. Weren't you supposed to chuck them back in?

The man lifted the stone above his head and, without even hesitating, smashed it down so hard that the fish's head caved in. Even from where Ellie was standing, she could see its brains ooze onto the jetty.

She was stunned. One minute the fish had been thrashing and wild, gasping in air. And now it was dead. For the first time, the man looked up and noticed her.

'Mackerel,' he shouted.

Like knowing its name made a difference. She pretended she hadn't heard because she didn't want to have a conversation with a psychopathic fish-killer. She kept an eye on him while he put the fish in a bucket, then retied his line and whipped it back out to sea. Only when he sat down on his little seat, took out a lunchbox and unwrapped a sandwich did she stop watching him.

She sat back down on the wall for a second and wondered what would happen next. Maybe she'd plummet into the sea and get hypothermia. Or maybe psycho-man would creep up behind her and bash her on the head with his stone. Or maybe she'd be overcome by a vegetarian fury and creep up on him instead and kick him off the end of the jetty. Maybe she'd do something even braver than that – like steal a boat and sail to Scandinavia.

It began to amuse her. It was like that film *Sliding Doors*, where the tube doors closed on Gwyneth Paltrow. In one version of the story, she caught the train, met a lovely bloke called James and got home to find her boyfriend, Gerry, in bed with another woman. In the second version, she missed the train and ended up getting mugged.

Ellie had choices, didn't she? Loads of them. Today, she'd expected to go to school, yet ended up at the harbour. Later, she'd go home and her parents would ask about her day and she could lie or tell the truth. Which course of action she chose would make an entirely different set of events occur.

That's why Tom was mad at her – she could choose, and he couldn't. She could agree to be his witness and say she saw nothing, or she could refuse. Maybe he was right and the police *would* question her again. They might even force her to go to court, but she didn't have to open her mouth and say anything. How could they make her? What could they do?

She got up from the wall, determined. Here she was feeling sorry for herself, when all the time she had this amazing ability to decide what happened next. Well, she wasn't giving up looking for the gatecrasher then, because he'd texted her five times, which meant he was keen, and over there was the tourist information office, and how many pubs could there be?

If she didn't find him, time would have passed and then she'd get the bus home. If she did find him, she'd swish her hair about and lick her lips slowly and say, *Well, hi, fancy meeting you here*. Boys fell for that stuff.

Eighteen

Ellie opened the door of the Queen's Head slowly and was immediately hit by the warm stink of food and beer. She felt primitive coming in from the mist, as if she was a wild girl and warmth and shelter meant little to her. She was a girl who invited boys to graveyards and dared them to jump in rivers. She was a girl who boldly entered the information office and demanded to know where every pub in the vicinity of the harbour was. The man had even let her borrow his pen so that she could mark them on the map with red ink.

If he was in here, she would shimmy up behind him, her hand on her hip like the world owed her something, and she'd fix her eyes on him until he felt an irresistible pull at his heart. She'd make him turn round simply by looking at his back.

The woman behind the bar frowned as Ellie approached. She was wearing a name badge that said SUE, MANAGER.

'I can't serve you without ID,' she said.

'It's OK, I don't want a drink. I'm looking for someone who might work here. A boy.'

The woman laughed. 'Are you now? Well, only two lads work for me – Mikey or Jacko. Which one are you after?'

She knew it wasn't Jacko, because he was the boy in the car the other day. Ellie found herself grinning.

'It's Mikey I want.'

'I thought you might say that.' The woman pointed beyond the bar to a carpeted dining area. 'There he is, right at the back.'

He was standing at a table with a group of elderly women smiling up at him. He looked solid and confident, entirely unlike any boy at school. Adrenalin flooded her body as she watched him.

'He the one?'

'Yes, that's him.'

The woman tutted. 'Bringing his love life to work again, is he? I'll be having words with Mister McKenzie.'

'McKenzie?'

'Yes, love, and if you're his new girlfriend you can wait till he's on his lunch break, which will be in precisely five minutes. And since you're very evidently not eighteen, could you please step away from the bar.'

Mikey *McKenzie*? But that meant . . .

The name affected her physically. She felt light-headed and nauseous.

'Take a seat in the family lounge, please, and I'll tell him you're here.'

She lurched to the seats the woman pointed to and sat down. She wanted to get to the door, to get away, but if she moved that far, something might break. Nobody took any notice of her – the customers in the other seats were chatting to each other, or staring blankly at the TV screen. Her world had shifted and nobody knew it but her.

The manager came back. 'He's on his way, and you can tell him from me that if he spends one minute longer than his regulation half-hour with you, he can consider himself sacked.'

She smiled to show she didn't really mean it, but Ellie didn't smile back. She couldn't. She could barely breathe.

He came over slowly, with a strange reluctant walk. He said, 'What are you doing here?'

She squinted at him, as if the mist was in the bar, as if she'd brought it in with her. She could see the resemblance now – the same dark hair and eyes. Why hadn't she seen it before? It was all so obvious and terrible – he was Karyn McKenzie's brother.

He sat down, frowning. 'How did you know where I worked?'

'You said a pub by the harbour.'

'I didn't say which one.'

'Well, I was just passing this one and thought I'd check it out.'

'Just passing?'

She felt such an idiot. She'd been out in the mist and got hold of some stupid fantasy that he'd be pleased to see her, that she meant something to him. Her face was burning with shame as she stood up. 'You know what? I'm going to go.'

'What's the matter?'

'Nothing.'

He shook his head. 'Something is.'

162

How could he read her better than anyone she knew? Better than her own brother?

'I'm fine. I had an argument with someone, that's all.'

'You want to talk about it?'

'Not really.'

'I'm a good listener.'

Her heart lurched. That was sweet. Maybe he didn't know who she was after all. Maybe it was all some amazing coincidence that meant they were destined to be together for ever.

But then she noticed his name badge. 'So, you're called Tyler?'

He looked down at himself and frowned. 'It's not my real name.'

Tom said Karyn McKenzie was a liar. Obviously the whole family was, since everything about this boy was fake. He'd targeted the party, rather than stumbled across it, he'd deliberately chatted her up because he knew who she was. Even now, as he looked her up and down, his eyes warm and flirtatious, it was only an act.

'You look nice,' he said. 'Windswept, but pretty.'

She didn't even blush, didn't say something dumb, like, *Oh no, I don't*, because she knew he didn't mean it, he was trying to manipulate her.

'I'm going now,' she said. 'I'll see you around.'

'You'll see me around? You came all this way and now you're going?'

'I'm sorry. It was a stupid idea.'

'It wasn't. Don't go, I've got a break now. Let me get my jacket and we can sit outside.'

163

'It's cold out there.'

'Then we'll have to sit very close together.'

He smiled, and she couldn't help it, she smiled back. She was pathetic. Even when she knew he was trying to trick her, she still liked him. She was like some brainless girl in a horror movie, the kind of girl you scream at from the sofa because she can't see that she should leave *right now* or she'll be turned into mince.

'I'll just be a minute,' he said. 'Don't go away.'

She stood outside the main door, running the choices through her head. She could get the bus back into town and never see him again. Or she could stay and find out what he was up to.

The McKenzies were liars, which meant Tom was telling the truth. And if Tom was telling the truth, then she needed to put aside her stupid doubts about what happened that night and help him, as any sister should.

If she asked Mikey the right questions, if she flirted and got him to let his guard down, she might find out stuff which could get the case thrown out of court. She'd end up a hero and Dad and Tom would be grateful for ever.

She took a breath and switched on a smile. It was too good an opportunity to miss.

Nineteen

Something had changed in her by the time he came back with his jacket, because she took his hand, actually took his hand, and led him across the car park to the sea wall.

'There's a bench over there,' she said. 'Come on.'

The tide was out and a stretch of sand had opened up. Mikey looked in both directions, up and down the beach, but apart from a bloke with a dog, and another bloke fishing, there were no people about.

'I think we should go down,' he said. 'It'll be less windy.'

'No, let's stay here. It's a better view.'

She sat on the bench and patted the space next to her. She really was very pretty. It was like it was dawning on him, like she got prettier and prettier the longer he looked. Her skin was so smooth and she had the most amazing eyes – blue with splashes of grey in them.

He cast a quick look around. Did it matter if they sat up here? It was more exposed, but apart from Jacko, no one round here would know who she was. He yanked his hood up just to be safe and sat down.

She shuffled close and leaned in to him.

'Look at that,' she said. 'So much water just for us.'

Mikey had seen people do this plenty of times, just sitting watching the sea doing its thing – in and out. It wasn't that he didn't like the wind, or the smell of the beach or the way the waves never gave up, it was that he'd never seen the point of it. But today was different. Today he was with Ellie.

He had to do things right, treat her right. What was it his mum always said? *If you want a girl to like you, you have to listen like a woman and love like a man.* She reckoned that men hardly ever ask questions and when they do, they never listen to the answers.

He'd start with something simple, to get into the swing of things.

'So, why aren't you at school?' he said.

'I bunked it.'

'Second time in five days, eh?'

'Oh, I've got no shame.'

That sent a thrill of something through him. He wanted to touch her, especially her hair. It was loose and snapping in the wind. Seaside hair with strands of blonde among the gold. He coughed, shuffled about on the bench and adjusted his jacket, tried to concentrate.

'How did you get here?' he said. 'Did you walk or get the bus?'

'My brother gave me a lift.' A pause, then, 'You met my brother, didn't you?'

He nodded, fumbled in his pocket for his tobacco. 'Yeah, at the party. Just for a minute, near the end.'

'Ah, yes,' she said, 'the party. The one you gatecrashed.'

He pinched tobacco into a paper and rolled it, aware she was looking at him. 'You sound like a cop.'

'Which makes you the criminal.' She was so quick at answers. She glittered with cleverness.

He offered her the finished rollie. 'You want this?'

'I don't smoke.'

'Sensible.'

Still she was watching him. He lit up and took a drag, pulled it down hard. 'So,' he said, 'tell me about this argument, who was it with?'

'It's too long to tell.'

'I've got time.'

'I'd rather talk about you.'

That wasn't what was meant to happen next. What was the point of asking girls questions if they refused to answer? And what were you supposed to do when they turned it round and asked you stuff?

'Tell me a secret,' she said. 'Tell me something about you that I don't know.'

What was she expecting? A confession that he was married or gay or something? He took a drag of his cigarette, then another, before he thought of the perfect thing.

'OK,' he said. 'I don't really go to college.'

She looked surprised. 'Why did you say you did?'

'I thought you wouldn't like me if I wasn't clever. I work here full-time, but I'm learning stuff I'd never discover at college. There's a great chef and he's teaching me.'

He wasn't sure she understood how important this was and he wanted her to know. 'I've always liked those cooking programmes on the telly – you know the ones? I want to be like Jamie Oliver and run a whole kitchen. It's very complicated, takes years to learn.'

Ellie nodded as if she was really listening. She asked him how long he'd worked in the pub and what his hours were. She asked about Jacko and how long they'd known each other. He told her everything, including his dream of working in a top London restaurant. He hadn't meant to let that one out, but she was so easy to talk to, taking every word somewhere deep inside. He could have sat there all day talking. But then he remembered his mum's advice.

'You tell me a secret now,' he said.

'OK.' She leaned in close. 'Here's my secret. I'm hopeless at cooking, I can't even make cakes from packets, or follow recipes or anything, but' – and here she moved closer, her breath hot in his ear – 'I think boys who cook are very sexy, and, one day, I'd like you to show me how you do it.'

He laughed out loud. 'That's a promise.'

It was weird. At the pub she'd seemed frightened, as if she was worried he hadn't wanted to see her. But out here, it was like she was running the show. She was totally flirting with him, it was great. It was obvious she wanted something to happen between them. It gave him confidence.

'So what else do you find sexy, then?'

'Easy.' She held out a hand to count on her fingers. 'Boys who play guitar, boys who make me laugh, boys who have a nice smile and boys who never lie.'

Shit! That was a lot to live up to, especially the no-lying bit.

'Can you play guitar?' she said.

'No, but I had a drumming lesson once.'

She rolled her eyes as if that was a total let-down. Well, maybe he should try and be funny then.

'I'll tell you my little sister's favourite joke,' he said.

'Go on then.'

'OK, what do you call a sheep with no legs?'

She wrinkled her nose to think about it. He liked that. She had a smattering of freckles across the bridge of her nose that he'd never noticed before.

'I give up.'

'A cloud.'

She groaned, rather than laughed. But she leaned in to him to do it, and her hair brushed his face. He kissed the top of her head, suddenly, out of the blue. He hadn't meant to, it just happened – right there on a bench outside the pub. And although a faraway part of him knew it was a bad idea, there was a much closer, bigger part of him that wasn't going to stop. Not while she didn't move away, not while his kisses climbed down her hair to her neck and one of his hands crept inside her coat to pull her closer.

'You're beautiful,' he whispered.

She went very still, then slowly pulled away. She looked startled. He felt a bit surprised too – as if he'd said he loved her, which he never had to any girl. It was one of his rules.

169

Her eyes flickered. 'Beautiful?'

'Totally.'

'What about my scar?'

'I like it.'

She looked down at herself. 'What about my legs? I've got horrible legs.'

'No, you've got beautiful legs.' To prove it he got off the bench and inspected both ankles, cupping each foot in turn.

'My shoes might be dirty.'

She was wearing her school skirt and tights, like before. It filled him with longing and fear to be down there, close to her feet, close to her ankles, her knees, her thighs.

She took a handful of his jacket and pulled it gently, so he had to look up.

'Maybe you should come and sit back down?'

But he couldn't move. He was an animal, wild and hungry. He let his tongue hang out, did that panting thing dogs did, hoping for a smile. He rubbed his head against her thigh like he wanted stroking.

But she didn't stroke him. In fact, she went a bit quiet and moved along the bench and looked at her mobile.

'Don't you need to go soon?' she said. 'Won't you get sacked or something?'

It was very complicated, the way she went from flirting to cool, but he knew she liked him, however much she was avoiding it now.

'I want to see you again,' he said. 'Will you meet me after my shift? I finish at ten.'

'I'm busy tonight.'

Of course, she was only sixteen and it was a weekday evening – what was he thinking?

'I get a half-day on Saturday,' he said. 'I'll meet you in the afternoon, we'll do something.'

She stood up, made a big show of adjusting her bag on her shoulder, then folded her arms at him. 'What will we do?'

He should've thought before he opened his big mouth. It had to be quality with a girl like her. Not a pub or a club, but somewhere amazing – hot-air ballooning, or a trip in a space ship. It also had to be somewhere far away from everywhere.

'I know. I'll borrow my mate's car and we'll do that wild swim thing. You remember telling me about some place where the waves are really massive?'

She frowned at him, like that was the worst idea in the world. But he was burning with it. It was what he wanted to do more than anything else. Just for a bit. For a day. A half-day. An hour. To be alone with her.

Seconds went past. Ellie chewed her lip and stared down at the beach. The bloke with the dog was still there and the dog was yapping because the bloke was holding a ball a fraction out of its reach. Ellie watched them. Out of the corner of his eye, Mikey watched her.

This was deep for her. She was only in Year Eleven and he was two years older and knew stuff about the world. It was his job to make her feel OK.

'Nothing can happen unless you want it to,' he said.

Which wasn't strictly true – just look at Karyn. But it would be true for Ellie. Eventually she'd give stuff away about her brother, and he wasn't going to hurt her while he looked for it. They'd hang out, kiss some more. No harm done.

'Ellie, come out with me, come on. What are you scared of?'

'Not of you.' She whipped round, her eyes shining. 'All right, let's do it then.'

It was like she was accepting a dare.

Twenty

All sensible websites suggest that you meet a potentially dangerous stranger in a crowded place, and that you tell a family member or a friend what you are doing. And here Ellie was, Saturday lunchtime, about to break the rules. In less than two hours, Mikey McKenzie would arrive at her house, and no one knew he was coming and no one but her would be in.

RSN, he texted.

He was right, it was going to be *real soon now*.

Ellie threw the phone onto her bed as if it was hot, then opened her bedroom window and looked out at the storm, at the dark clouds and fat splashing rain. She leaned on her elbows and watched. A cat dived for cover, cracks in the lawn sucked water into their grooves and all the trees sighed.

She gave revising a try, lay on her bed with geography books and tried to care about the movement of people from rural to urban areas following the industrial revolution. But thinking of big stuff made her feel small, and when she felt small, she stopped caring about revising and GCSEs and what happened next. It was easy to break any taboo when nothing mattered, so she picked up her phone and texted, *TAU*. It was true, she was thinking about him. He was pretty much all she'd been thinking about since Monday at the harbour.

His text came whizzing back: *XOXOXO*.

A series of hugs and kisses.

She needed food. Diets didn't count in a crisis.

Her parents were sitting holding hands at the kitchen table. Cups of coffee and empty plates in front of them. They looked up and smiled as she walked in. It was lovely, like a normal family again.

'Hungry?' Mum said, pushing her chair back. 'I've just made your dad a bacon butty. Want me to make you something?'

'No thanks.'

Ellie knew what she wanted – one of Tom's double chocolate muffins, kept in the bread bin and not to be eaten by anyone but him.

She ignored her mum's frown as she helped herself and sat down to unwrap it. 'You guys still going out?'

Her father nodded absently. 'As soon as this rain eases up.'

They all looked out of the window, at the garden sinking under the weight of water. And that was it. Extent of conversation. Ellie's journey down the stairs and into the kitchen had lightened the mood for a nanosecond. It was weird how there was nothing left to say or do that didn't relate to Tom. They fell back into grief so easily.

Eventually, Mum took a sip of her coffee, grimaced and put the cup back down. 'I can't believe it's the weekend again,' she said. 'I keep thinking any minute this will stop and we'll go back to normal.'

Dad wiped a hand across his brow. He looked tired. 'We shouldn't expect normal any more. Not if that little bitch insists on going through with this.'

That was new, that word, and the way he spat it out.

'Should you be calling her that, Dad?'

He looked at Ellie open-mouthed. 'She's in the process of ruining your brother's life!'

'It's a horrible word, that's all.'

He shook his head as if she was clearly mad and let his eyes slide back to the window.

When she was a kid, Ellie had spent every Saturday morning with Dad in the park – they'd go to the playground, feed the ducks on the lake, see if they could find decent trees for her to climb. Mum did a yoga class, Tom had football, it was only the two of them. 'Wild child,' Dad called her, and he'd pick leaves and sticks from her hair and let her choose whatever she wanted from the café for lunch. But something changed when she got to eleven, like he shrank away. She was *too big* for cuddles, *too old* for games and messing around. It was a slow retreat. But sometimes, if Ellie really thought about it, she realized he hadn't taken proper notice of her for years.

'Twenty-five miles in this weather,' Dad said, 'and when we get there, she won't even recognize us.'

'Simon,' Mum said, 'that's my mother you're talking about.'

He held up his hands. 'So shoot me!'

Ellie sighed, checked her mobile. Just over an hour to go. No new messages. 'So,' she said, 'are you coming back at the usual time?'

Her mum nodded. 'Should be.'

'Definitely,' Dad said.

'You're only going to see Gran, right? Nothing else? You're not going to the cottage to do more clearing out?'

'Why all the questions?' Dad said.

'No reason.' She pushed her plate away. She suddenly felt sick.

'You shouldn't've taken that muffin if you didn't want it,' Mum said. 'In fact, you shouldn't've taken it anyway.' She slipped the muffin into the bin, licked her fingers then slotted her chair back under the table and began to rinse the plate in the sink.

Ellie checked her phone again. 'And Tom's out all day, is he?'

Her mum gave her a sad smile. 'Might as well let him have fun while he can.'

'Golf club,' Dad said. 'He'll be indoors on the swing simulator if he's got any sense. Exactly where I'd like to be right now, in fact.'

Ellie see-sawed her fork, tilting it backwards and forwards. It left indents in the tablecloth.

Dad frowned at her. 'Are you up to something, Eleanor?'

Yes, don't leave me alone. I've done this foolish thing . . .

He said, 'You're supposed to be revising today, that's what we agreed.'

History notes were scattered on her bedroom floor, her Art project lay half finished on her desk, she hadn't even begun revising Spanish. If her father knew the extent to which she was falling behind, he'd freak. She'd probably be grounded until she was eighteen.

'So,' he said, 'what subject is it today?'

She told him Geography – the only subject she'd done any work on since Monday.

'Ah,' he said, 'ox-bow lakes.' And he patted her briefly on the hand. 'I envy you, Ellie. I wish I had something to take my mind off all this.'

Maybe she should tell him. *I've invited Mikey McKenzie to the house. You know him, sure you do, he's Karyn McKenzie's brother. I've got a plan. Trouble is, it terrifies me . . .*

'This rain isn't stopping,' Mum said from the sink. 'What shall we do?'

Dad stood up. 'Let's go. Get it over with.' He looked down at Ellie. 'Any messages for Gran?'

'Um no, not really. Tell her I'll come and see her soon. Tell her I miss her.'

He nodded, bent down and brushed the top of her head with a kiss. 'Work well then.'

Warmth flooded through her. He hadn't done that for years and years.

And now the ritual of finding things. Mum fumbled in her handbag for the car keys, which she eventually found in her coat pocket. Dad watched her in a distracted way before checking his own pockets for the keys she'd already found. He scooped up his wallet, turned on his mobile and then realized he had no idea where his glasses were. Mum, meanwhile, was convinced she'd lost her purse and had to root through her entire handbag again.

How vulnerable they seemed. How old and grey they'd be one day. *I could come with you*, Ellie wanted to say. *I'll look after you. Let me sit in the back of the car and we'll sing songs. When we get to the nursing home, Gran will give us Murray Mints and we'll take her out for a spin in her wheelchair.*

But, really, she knew how that kind of day would work out, and it didn't solve anything. At least if she stayed at home, everything would be different by the time her parents got back.

Twenty-one

When Mikey walked into the lounge, his mum switched off the vacuum cleaner to admire him. Holly and Karyn looked up from their game of Snakes and Ladders and wolf-whistled simultaneously.

He laughed. He had on his new T-shirt and favourite jeans. He'd shaved, showered and even used mouthwash. He knew he looked good and gave a male-model strut across the carpet to prove it.

'Look at my son,' Mum said. 'Look at my gorgeous boy.'

'Who's it today, then?' Karyn asked as she shook the dice and threw them on the table. ''Cos that's more effort than most of them get.'

She gave him that cheeky half-smile he'd forgotten about and he felt a bit bad then. But there was no way he could tell her about Ellie, not until he'd got all the information he needed. She wouldn't understand.

Holly reached for his hand, tucked her own into it. 'Where will you take her?'

'Don't know yet. Out and about.'

He sat at the table and watched them play. Karyn was going

down ladders as well as snakes to let Holly win. She winked at him when she clocked he'd noticed.

Mum switched the vacuum back on and they pulled their knees up so she could get to the spaces under their feet. It made Mikey feel like a kid.

'I'm going to buy some new cushions,' Mum yelled over the noise. 'They've got some nice ones in the market with embroidery on. New cushions would look lovely in here, don't you think? And maybe a rug.'

Mikey nodded in agreement, then checked the clock. Twenty minutes to go. He tapped his pocket for the car keys. He felt crap lying to Jacko, but there was no way he'd have lent him the car and agreed to postponing the golf-club recce a second time if he hadn't.

'There are things they look for,' Mum said as she switched off the vacuum and coiled the lead up. 'They look for dirt, but they also look for smells. I've had the windows open all morning and I got one of those plug-in air fresheners.'

She stood, hands on hips, pleased with herself.

'It's been like zero degrees with those windows open and she wouldn't let me shut them,' Karyn said, her eyes amused.

Mum smiled across at her. 'You're cold because you don't eat enough, and that's what's happening next – toast.'

Karyn packed the game away and got Holly some paper and pens instead. Mum made four cups of tea and buttered some toast, even spread it with jam and cut it into squares. She placed Karyn's plate gently on the table in front of her.

'It's ages since I saw you eat anything,' she said.

Karyn sighed with pleasure and picked up a square of toast. Easy as that.

She looked happier than Mikey had seen her for days. He knew why. She thought every day was going to be as cheery as this from now on. She thought Mum would save her.

It was easy to believe as they sat there together, sipping their tea and eating toast. Things had been better since Gillian's visit on Monday. Mum had sobered up and collected Holly, then phoned the social worker to apologize. Monday night, she'd sat down with the three of them and promised never to disappear like that again. 'Everything's going to be different from now on,' she said.

Over the last four days she'd spring-cleaned the hallway, the lounge and the kitchen. The whole flat was beginning to look bigger and brighter. Over the weekend she planned to work her way upstairs. Mikey knew what would happen then. She'd fill dustbin bags with old toys and clothes. She'd get ridiculous with it, start throwing things away that people still wanted. Mikey remembered his denim jacket going that way last year, and Holly weeping for hours over her football card collection. Next week, if Mum still hadn't run out of energy, she might get the local paper and look for jobs. She'd circle them, maybe cut them out and put them in a pile somewhere. And then she'd start saying stuff about how they all took her for granted, how nothing good ever happened to her. And then she'd give herself a little reward – maybe a cheap bottle of red from Ajay's over the road. 'Just the one,' she'd say.

And round and round they'd go again. It was so predictable.

'OK, Mum,' he said, 'a little test before I go. Monday morning. *Ding-dong*, there's the social worker again, all smiles, wanting to help. You've been cleaning for days and in she comes, very impressed. First question: *Why has Holly been off school?*'

'She won't ask me that.'

'She might. What will you say?'

'I'll say she was sick.'

'What was wrong with her?'

'She had a headache.'

'Kids don't get headaches.'

Mum moved the ashtray a centimetre to the left, matched the lighter with the edge of the table, making patterns. 'It's all right, I can handle it. I told you, it's going to be different now.'

'Tell them a fever and a cough, or that she kept throwing up. Not a headache. And don't smoke in front of her.'

He knew how important his mum's fags were, how they kept her calm. He knew he was being unkind.

'Stop worrying,' she said. 'It's only a support visit, nothing else. I'll sit by the window. I'll tell her I never do it with Holly around.'

'Show her the smoke alarm,' Holly said, pointing up at the ceiling with the end of her felt-tip pen.

Mikey followed her gaze. Sober for days, and a tidy flat was one thing, but a fully-installed and working smoke alarm was definitely something new.

Mum grinned at him. 'You're impressed.'

He couldn't help smiling back.

She glanced at the clock. 'Go and have fun, Mikey. Go on, you've done enough.'

He checked his mobile. No new messages, but that was OK. It was all agreed. Two-thirty at Ellie's house. He'd leave in a few minutes.

'Like my drawing?' Holly said.

She held it up for them all to see. It was Karyn, outside with her hair streaming behind her in the wind. She was holding a piece of string with a dragon on the end and a flaming sword.

'Nice picture,' Karyn said.

Holly smiled, carefully tore the page from her book and laid it on the table. 'I'm going to draw you at school next.'

'Let me keep the dragon,' Karyn laughed. 'I'll need it if you're sending me back there.'

Mikey took the plates to the kitchen, had a quick look in the fridge while he was there. It was stuffed – juice and yoghurts, cheese and milk, all sorts. Mum had even bought a pack of bacon and some sausages.

By the time he'd washed up the plates, all three of them were huddled together on the sofa watching a re-run of TopGear – some mountain climber was talking about how he got frostbite and later, after surgery, he had a very hot bath and his toe came off and he left it on the side of the sink for his wife to find. They cackled like witches at it. Mikey smiled, wanted to leave them with something. He went over and put ten quid on the table.

'Here,' he said, 'get yourselves a DVD and some sweets.'

You'd think he'd given them a fortune, the way they passed it between them.

He almost didn't want to leave. It wasn't that long ago when this would have been his idea of a perfect Saturday afternoon and he'd happily have squeezed in with them on the sofa.

'I'll be off then.'

Mum raised her cup of tea. 'Have a lovely time.'

Twenty-two

Ellie blushed, actually blushed, when she opened the door. Mikey wanted to sweep her up and kiss her, but he had to save that until they were safely away from the house.

'Ready?' he said.

She smiled apologetically. 'Not yet. I haven't made the picnic.'

'We'll get fish and chips.'

She wagged a finger at him. 'Every adventure has a picnic. Come inside, it'll only take a few minutes.'

'Why don't I wait in the car?'

She shook her head. 'There's nobody home, don't worry.'

What choice did he have?

When Ellie closed the door behind them, a dim blue light shone through the coloured glass and splashed the floor. There were paintings on the wall and a statue on a stand – a man and a woman wrapped together. Mikey touched it with a finger, surprised at how smooth it felt.

'It's not real,' Ellie said.

He pulled his hand away, embarrassed.

'It's a copy. Well, of course it's a copy. No one has a real Rodin.'

He nodded, as if that was obvious, mentally cursing himself for knowing nothing about anything.

She led him through a sitting room – sofa, chairs, display cabinet full of family photos (Ellie looking sexy with a swimming trophy) – through to the kitchen, right at the back of the house and smaller than he remembered. On the table was a chopping board, bread, various things for the picnic all spread out. The back door was open and beyond was the garden, that cool expanse of green that amazed him again with its endless lawn and trees.

A dog lay on a blanket and flapped its tail sleepily at them. It was an old dog, with grey hair round its nose. Here was something he recognized at least. He knew what to do with dogs.

'What's his name?'

'Stan, but she's a girl.'

'Does she bite?'

'Only if you're a biscuit. Stroke her if you like. No one else gives her any attention.'

Girls liked blokes who liked animals and he didn't even have to pretend. He took great care, was gentle and slow. The dog turned belly up and let him fuss her. Mikey smiled, forgetting where he was for a minute. 'She's a lovely dog.'

'She's my gran's. We've got her goldfish as well.'

He glanced up quickly. 'Is your gran here?'

'No, no, she's in a nursing home. Cup of tea while you wait, or do you want something else?'

His heart thumped. 'What have you got?'

'Wait there.'

She wasn't gone long. He heard her run down the hallway, heard a door open and shut. She came back with a bottle of wine and passed it over. She was trying to impress him.

He unscrewed the top, took a couple of gulps and passed it back. She tipped the bottle to her mouth and took the smallest of sips. She wiped her mouth with the back of her hand.

'What about this picnic then?' he said.

'It's only sandwiches.'

'Well, let's make them.'

They really had to hurry up. He wouldn't relax until they were out of here.

He started sorting through the stuff on the table – a bag of expensive lettuce, some cheese in a wooden box, tomatoes, olives. She'd been planning on some complicated sandwiches, though the fresh ingredients were going to be interesting to work with. She yanked more stuff out of the fridge – a red pepper, a handful of rocket.

'You want butter?' she said.

'Not if it's been in the fridge. You got mayonnaise?'

She passed it, along with a knife from a wooden holder on the cabinet. He sliced the bread and spread it with mayo, shredded the lettuce and cut up tomatoes. He liked her watching, knew it looked cool. He unpacked the cheese from its box and laid thin slices on the bread with the salad.

'Got any black pepper, any salt?'

She came over with the grinders and did it for him. When she twisted, her hips swung and her skirt shifted. It was pretty the way her skirt did that, like it was part of her.

He cut the sandwiches in half diagonally, wrapped them in foil and stepped back from the table with a bow.

'There you go.'

'You could be a chef,' Ellie said, 'the care you took.'

They smiled at each other.

'Shall we be off then?' he said.

She glanced at her mobile, then sat down at the table, pulled a packet of tobacco from a drawer, papers, a lighter and a small hunk of dope.

'What's that for?' he asked.

'What do think it's for?'

She hadn't a clue how to make a joint, it was obvious. She forgot to heat the dope, then when she figured it out, put way too much in and could barely handle the rolling at all. He wanted to tell her she didn't need to do this to keep him interested, but wasn't sure how to say it.

'I didn't know you smoked,' was all he managed, as she licked the paper and stuck it down.

'I don't.'

'What do you call that then?'

She looked at the joint in her hand as if it had nothing to do with her, gave a little shrug. 'I call it exceptional circumstances.'

She made a roach for it then, tearing a strip from the Rizla packet and rolling it small.

'That'll be too tight,' he said.

She unrolled it and started again. Every now and then she threw him a glance, but he pretended not to notice. He wasn't going to let her freak him out. Or the situation. He kept hearing noises even though he was sitting really still. The afternoon seemed full of them and he couldn't work out if they meant anything or not. Maybe they were regular noises that houses made – boilers and radiators and all the special objects sparkling. But maybe they meant something. Maybe they were noises that mattered, even in the distance. The noise of a car pulling up the drive or footsteps on gravel, or a key in the lock.

'So, where is everyone?' he said. He couldn't help himself, needed to check.

'At work.'

He shot her a look. That was a lie. Rich people didn't work weekends.

'And my brother's playing golf.'

Heat rose from Mikey's chest to his neck, to his face.

'Done it,' she said, wiggling the finished joint at him with a smile.

'Well, do you want to smoke it in the car?'

'No, let's have it here.' She shoved it at him. 'You do the honours.'

He sparked up, took a couple of tokes and passed it to her. She took one puff, didn't even inhale, then handed it back.

He shook his head. 'I'm not really into it, to be honest.'

She looked surprised, stubbed the whole thing out on a

saucer and picked up the wine. 'You want some more of this?'

Why weren't they leaving? Jacko's car was outside, the picnic was ready. He took the bottle, had a couple of glugs to calm himself down.

'Shall we go now?' he said.

She checked her mobile. 'How about a tour?'

'What do you mean? A tour of the house?'

'Yeah, why not?'

And she stood up, grabbed the wine bottle and simply walked out of the kitchen.

Like an estate agent with no hope of a sale, Ellie named rooms that lay behind closed doors. Cloakroom, study, bathroom, spare room. Outside her brother's room, Mikey slowed down. It was padlocked, still a crime scene. He laid his hand flat against the door. Ellie kept on walking.

They ended up in her bedroom, sitting together on her bed. There were books and revision papers spread on the desk and all over the floor, but when he tried to crack a joke about it, she ignored him. There was something cold about her, not warm like at the river, not flirty like at the harbour. It was messing with his head.

He got his tobacco out and rolled a thin one. She knelt up on the bed, opened the window and leaned out. He imagined her climbing up on the window ledge like a bird might, her arms open wide. Maybe she could fly. She seemed capable of anything today.

She said, 'Come over here if you're going to smoke.'

He knelt next to her and together they looked down at the garden, all green and leafy with its electric gate keeping it safe. You could have heard anything fall – feathers, dust. How did a place get to be so quiet?

'Don't you want to go swimming any more?' he said.

'Sure I do. We'll leave in a minute. Here.'

She handed him the wine and he took another swig. She had her finger in her mouth as she watched him. *Suck, suck, suck*, she went. He couldn't stop looking.

'What are you thinking?' she said.

'I'm not thinking anything.'

'Yeah you are, people are always thinking.'

He frowned at her. 'OK, I'm thinking you're being really strange.'

'Am I?'

'It's like you've gone away inside yourself. Why have you done that?'

'I don't know what you're talking about.'

A car spluttered in the distance, making them both jump. And that's when she yanked her T-shirt over her head and let it fall to the floor. She was wearing a bra, white lace.

'What are you doing?'

'Getting changed.'

She sauntered to the wardrobe and began to lazily flick through the hangers. He was getting turned on watching her. He could see every bone of her spine. Her shoulder blades looked like wings.

191

She held up some see-through thing and waved it at him. 'What about this one?' But she didn't put it on. He kept telling himself that this was ordinary. This was what rich girls did when they invited blokes to their bedrooms. But at the same time he knew it wasn't ordinary at all.

He said, 'Ellie, what's going on?'

She turned and stood before him. She looked so gorgeous standing there, smiling like there was light shining from inside her.

She said, 'You tell me.'

And he knew then why she was stalling, and he felt so dumb for not realizing it earlier. She'd got him to come to the house when everyone was out, tried to create a vibe with wine and dope, invited him upstairs. She wanted him to make a move on her.

He smiled, took a step towards her. 'No one's here, right?'

She turned to the door and locked it, put the key in her skirt pocket, turned back to him. 'They're all out.'

'When are they back?'

'Not yet.'

He held out his arms. 'Come here then.'

But she shook her head. And in the space between them something shifted, like the room got colder.

She said, 'I know who you are.'

'What?'

'You're Karyn's brother.'

'What are you talking about?'

She slapped the closed door with the flat of her hand. 'Don't even bother denying it.'

His heart was pounding. Standing there in her bedroom with a massive hard-on, he knew he was totally shafted.

She said, 'I'll read you your rights, shall I? You don't have to say anything. But it might harm your defence if you don't mention something that happens to be true. Like the fascinating fact that you're related to Karyn.'

'Fuck off.'

'*You* fuck off. My parents will be back soon and we've got CCTV at the gate, so it will have recorded you arriving. You've got fifteen minutes to tell me what's going on, or I'll tell them you tricked your way in, helped yourself to drink, smoked drugs in their house, then forced me upstairs and made me take my clothes off. See how easy it is for people to get themselves into compromising situations? See how bad this will look for your sister?'

'You set me up?'

Her eyes hardened. 'You did it to me first.'

She could do anything, say anything. She could say he touched her, that he made her do stuff.

'Did you think I wouldn't find out?' she said. 'Do you think I'm stupid?'

He sat down on the edge of the bed and wiped a hand across his eyes. 'How long have you known?'

'Since the pub. Your boss let it slip. But I knew all along you were only pretending to like me – all that chat at the party and then at the river. I didn't believe any of it.'

He shook his head. 'I wasn't pretending.'

Her eyes were stone. 'OK, let's get this straight. You crash my brother's party, you hit on me, then ask for my number. Why?'

'I liked you.'

'Bollocks.'

'OK, I liked you *and* I thought you might know stuff.'

'What kind of stuff?'

He shrugged. 'Something that might help my sister.'

'Why would I?'

'You were in the house when it happened. Karyn remembers you.'

She gave him a look. It was the strangest look, like a veil lifted, like what he was saying made some kind of sense. 'You didn't ask me anything at the river. You didn't mention my brother once.'

'I forgot.'

She looked puzzled. 'You forgot?'

'I was having a good time.' He was aware of how gravelly his voice was and gave a quick cough. 'Courts are crap, you know that. Your brother'll get off for sure and I wanted Karyn to know someone cared. I thought I'd get information out of you – where your brother hangs out, that kind of stuff. I wasn't ever going to hurt you.'

'You were going to hurt my brother?'

He shrugged. 'He raped my sister.'

Ellie's face closed down again. 'Karyn *wanted* him. It's not Tom's fault she changed her mind in the morning. She flirted with him all night – laughing and joking, knocking back the booze.'

'She fancied him. Haven't you ever done that?'

'I've never offered myself on a plate to a boy, then woken up and cried rape.'

'That's not what happened. I know her and she's not making this up.'

'I know my brother and neither is he.' She took a step forward. 'Why would he rape her when she was clearly going to give it to him anyway?'

Mikey's stomach gripped. He held on tight to the edge of the bed. 'I don't know, but he did.'

'Maybe your sister got so drunk she forgot she said yes – you ever thought of that?'

'He should have looked after her if she was drunk, not taken advantage.'

Ellie glared at him. 'Why did it take her twenty-four hours to go to the police?'

'I don't know! I don't know all the answers.' He ran a hand through his hair. 'She was scared, I know that. She still is.'

'Yeah, well it's not easy for any of us.'

And that's when they heard the car, a door slamming shut down there. 'That'll be my parents.' She looked at him with a strange fake smile and calmly turned round and unlocked the door. 'I'm going to introduce you. Come on.'

'What? Are you crazy?'

'Let's go and say hello. I'm sure they'd love to hear all about your plan to trick their daughter and hurt their son.'

He couldn't believe she was opening the door, was walking out onto the landing, expecting him to follow. She was only half dressed. Her parents would kill him.

'Ellie, come back!'

She swung round, her eyes furious. 'Why should I?'

And that was when someone yelled, 'Ellie, you up there?' which sounded like a threat and made her flinch, and footsteps came pounding up the stairs.

Twenty-three

Tom Parker stood at the top of the stairs in his ridiculous checked trousers and white polo shirt and folded his arms like a bouncer. 'What's going on?'

Ellie took a step back. 'What are you doing here?'

He didn't answer, looked Mikey up and down. 'You're the bloke from the party. You're the one who nicked the whisky.'

Mikey laughed, couldn't help it. Ellie had set him up brilliantly. Here was the brother, obviously part of the plan. The parents would turn up in a minute with handcuffs and ropes, closely followed by the cops.

'You think it's funny?' Tom unfolded his arms and took a step towards Mikey. 'You taking the piss?'

'Take it easy, man.'

'Or what?'

'I'm just saying, take it easy.'

Tom took another step forward. 'You've been smoking dope in my house. I could smell it when I came in.'

'Back off,' Ellie told him. 'It's nothing to do with you.'

He waved a hand at her, standing there in her bra and skirt, turned back to Mikey. 'Have you touched my sister?'

Mikey lunged forward and jabbed his fingers hard in Tom's chest. 'You want to stop accusing me of stuff?'

Tom slapped him away. 'Don't touch me.'

'Why? What're you going to do?' Mikey shoved him with the flat of his palm.

'I said don't touch me!'

Mikey could feel the bastard's heart slamming under his hand. Having him this close – the stink of his sweat, his hot breath in Mikey's face – it all came crashing back. Ellie might have a plan, but so did he – *destroy the bastard who hurt Karyn*. It's what he'd been chasing for weeks and it was finally here. He grabbed Tom Parker by his collar and rammed him into the wall behind.

'No!' Ellie said. 'Leave him alone.'

Mikey pulled back his fist and smashed it into the soft skin of Tom's mouth. His hand came away wet and blood dripped onto Tom's white shirt.

Mikey laughed at the pale white face. 'I'm going to kill you,' he said. It sounded true. The adrenalin was fantastic. He punched him again, on his nose this time. Tom moaned, a soft sound, clutching his hands to his face. Blood leaked between his fingers.

'That was from my sister,' Mikey said. 'That was from Karyn.'

Tom smeared blood from his nose with the back of his hand. 'You're Karyn's brother?'

'Like you didn't know!'

Ellie pulled at Mikey's jacket, but he shrugged her away. She'd

198

set him up and it wasn't working out – tough. He was invincible and Tom Parker was easier than he'd ever dreamed.

Mikey gave him another shove. 'You wasted yet?'

Tom shook his head, steadying himself with a hand on the wall.

'You are. You're wasted. Come on, aren't you supposed to win this? Wasn't that the idea?'

Mikey was stirring up anger. He knew it and couldn't stop. He felt a terrible thrill in his chest as Tom looked up, blood bubbling from his mouth.

'Your sister's a slut,' Tom said.

Mikey pulled back his arm to whack him again, but Tom went for the gap, brought up his knee and smashed it into Mikey's gut. He doubled over, gasping, his breath expelled in one shocking groan.

Tom yanked him up by his hair and belted a fist in his face – loud as a hammer, the bones of his knuckles burning into Mikey's eye.

'Outside,' Tom spat. Like it was school, like any of this could be controlled. His voice spinning as he shoved Mikey down the stairs.

'What are you doing?' Ellie yelled. 'Tom, don't!'

Mikey half fell, half stumbled, his elbows and knees bouncing against the banister and the wall. In the hallway he went crashing down and suddenly Tom was on him, dragging him up by his jacket and propelling him through the front door.

The air changed everything. It had stopped raining and was hot and surprising outside. Mikey couldn't see out of his eye and he was still winded, but he wasn't leaving like this, being driven towards the gate, panting for oxygen. He twisted round, grabbed

Tom Parker by his collar and forced him backwards. He felt like a magician, seeing victory turn to panic on his face.

'You're dead,' Mikey told him. 'You're so dead.'

Mikey threw a straight punch. He aimed for the nose, keeping his shoulder to his jaw. He remembered it from all the playground fights he'd ever had. It came back like some old instinct. The sound of his fist hitting skin was amazing.

And then they were locked together. Tom scrabbled at him, tried to reach his back to pummel him, but Mikey shoved his hands under Tom's armpits and clenched them behind his neck, so he couldn't bring his arms down. There was a stink of fear and adrenalin.

This guy hurt Karyn, he kept thinking. *This guy needs killing.*

It was like dancing – they were both pushing, grunting, trying to kick each other's feet away. Ellie hopped around them like a ref. She'd got a coat on now and was holding it around her and yelling at them to stop.

But Mikey wasn't giving up. He was going to ram into this guy, unlock his arms, shove him backwards, then break his nose for good.

But before he could do any of that, Tom slammed his leg up and kneed Mikey in the balls. The pain was unreal, hot agony searing up from his groin to his gut as his legs buckled.

Tom stood towering over him as Mikey lay holding his balls on the grass. He curled into himself, was vaguely aware of Tom moving away, of Ellie running after him. He opened one eye. They were at the front door. Ellie was shouting at her brother as he scrabbled around in a green recycling box on the doorstep.

'Don't,' she yelled.

But Tom shoved her off, and waved a wine bottle at Mikey.

'Look what I got.' He slapped it into his palm, flicked it backwards and forwards between his hands. 'You scared now?'

Ellie screamed. 'No, Tom, no!'

But he did it anyway. Bits of glass flew everywhere as he smashed the bottom off against the side of the house.

Mikey tried to struggle up as Tom strolled towards him. A broken bottle was like a knife. It was a whole different league. He wiped his eye with the back of his hand. 'Put it down.'

'Yeah, in your face.'

Tom was giving him psychotic eye contact as he got nearer, like he'd be in Mikey's life for ever, would follow him wherever he went. Mikey kicked himself along the ground to get away, scrabbling upright, holding his bollocks, barely able to move, let alone run.

Tom was laughing, sauntering after him. 'What's the matter? Not so brave now, eh?'

Mikey made it as far as the gate, but he was an idiot, because it was shut and now all his strength was gone. Outside, Jacko's car looked beautiful. In his pocket were the keys. Too late. He pressed himself against the gate, curled his arms round his head and waited for the pain.

But instead of the bottle, water slammed into him. It was freezing. The sudden cold spray of it drenched him immediately. Tom was next to him, both of them soaked, the bottle on the ground and Tom's nose bleeding hard as he tried to slap the water away.

Ellie was standing on the lawn with a garden hose. Sun glittered on the water, making crazy rainbows in the air.

'Turn it off,' Tom spluttered. 'What are you doing? Look at my nose!'

But Ellie trained the hose right in his face, forcing him away from the gate until he stood in the middle of the grass shaking his head, blood running from his mouth and nose in strings.

'Get in the house,' she said. 'It's finished.'

Mikey had a sudden longing to sit down, to lie down in fact. He was exhausted. It was like a car had crashed and flung them all over the fence and into the garden – glass and blood and water everywhere. But he couldn't lie down because Ellie was by him now, pressing some secret button that slid the whole gate open.

'Go home,' she said. 'Leave us alone.'

He pulled himself together enough to step through the gate. In the lane he turned to her. 'You won,' he said. 'Congratulations.'

She looked at him with dark eyes as the gate shut. He had an idea she was trying to tell him something, squeezing her voice out in a whisper, but his ears were ringing and his eye was swollen shut.

And anyway, why would he be interested in anything she had to say?

Twenty-four

Tom was leaning over the sink in the downstairs bathroom watching blood drip from his nose.

'Look at me!' He waved his hands at Ellie as if to prove something. They were bright and slippery with blood. 'Are you going to help me, or what?'

She closed the front door and went into the bathroom, passed him some tissue, then draped a towel round herself like a cape and sat on the closed toilet seat. She leaned back and closed her eyes.

'Well, you're a good nurse,' he said. 'Thanks very much.'

She tried to remember what had happened out there – Mikey's scared face as he staggered to the gate, Tom sauntering after him, blood everywhere, water slamming at them and the grass all slippery.

But before any of that, there'd been a moment, and this was what was hard to remember exactly – a moment when Tom smashed the bottle against the wall of the house and glass flew everywhere. She'd told him to stop, she'd kept saying it and he'd kept ignoring her. And he had that look on his face – the one she'd seen before, where nothing she said or did was going to make anything different.

She opened her eyes. Tom was still dabbing at himself with tissues over the sink. Their gaze met in the mirror.

He said, 'Why did you let him into the house?'

She'd thought about this outside, had planned to give some mad excuse – her upstairs revising, the back door open, Mikey forcing his way in, her half dressed and hysterical. But now Tom was asking, the words wouldn't come out of her mouth.

He got there before she could answer anyway. 'You fancy him!'

She didn't deny it. She couldn't be bothered.

It didn't take him long to piece a story together – Mikey crashed the party and chatted her up, he knocked on the door today to try his luck.

'He's taking the piss out of us,' he said. 'They planned it between them. She sent her brother round to spy on us! Can you believe it?'

Ellie didn't mention that she'd invited Mikey, that it was her who wanted the information, that her plan had horribly back-fired.

Through the window, the smell of cooking wafted at them. Somewhere, a perfectly normal family was having a perfectly normal lunch. Ellie wished she was with them.

'I don't think anything's broken,' Tom said. He studied the cuts on the back of his hand. 'You think we should take photos of this for evidence?'

'Evidence? You can't report him. He didn't attack *you* with a bottle.'

He turned to her, his eyes flashing. 'You think I should have let him hit me? You think maybe I deserved it?'

'I didn't say that.'

Tom licked blood from the edge of his mouth with his tongue. 'I wasn't going to bottle him. It's what guys do to protect themselves, to make themselves look hard. I wouldn't've done it. You should know that about me.'

She shook her head. 'I don't know anything about you.'

'What's that supposed to mean?'

He came up close, leaned down so his face was right over hers. He was so close it was difficult to see him properly. She concentrated on the blond bristle of hair on his chin and the blood beginning to leak from his nose again.

He said, 'What was he doing in your bedroom?'

'Nothing.'

'Why did you have your top off?'

'What's it got to do with you?'

He clutched her chin with his hand and swung her face up to look at him. 'Did you know he was her brother? Did you invite him round knowing who he was and tell him stuff about me?'

'Like what, Tom? What kind of stuff?' The cistern was cold and solid at the back of her head. She tried to push him away, but he held her there. 'Get off me, will you?'

'Make me.'

She shoved him, but he pushed her back harder and glared at her.

'So, let me get this right,' she hissed. 'He came round here to defend his sister, and here you are threatening yours! And you think he's the one with the problem?'

He crumpled then. It happened in slow motion. His shoulders sagged first, and then the light went out of his eyes. He looked like he suddenly couldn't remember where he was and couldn't even be bothered to try. He moved away from her, leaned against the towel rail and closed his eyes.

He said, 'You don't blag your way into someone's house and punch their lights out.' He rubbed at his nose, spreading new blood across his cheek.

Ellie felt heavy as she stood up. Her teeth ached and her knee was sore from where she'd slipped on the wet grass. 'Tom?'

'That whole family's crazy. Didn't you see him? I need you to believe it's them and not me.'

'Tom, your nose is bleeding loads.'

It was bright, startling. He tried to catch it, but it dripped through his fingers and splashed onto the tiled floor.

'Let me help.'

'I don't want your help.'

She gave him her place on the toilet seat and got him more tissues. 'Pinch it here, like this. And put your head down.'

He slumped there, holding his nose. The top of his head was shiny with water. 'It hurts,' he said. His voice was nasal and muffled.

'It'll stop soon. Here's some more tissue.'

He gave her the old ones. They were warm and heavy. She put them in the pedal bin, then washed her hands in the sink. There were dots of blood splashed over the mirror. She wiped them with her palm and they smeared pink across the glass. She'd have to clean it properly later.

She dried her hands, went to the cabinet on the wall and scooped out handfuls of cotton-wool balls – pink, white, eggshell blue – like little clouds. She rinsed out the sink and filled it with fresh water. It was good having something to do, it slowed her pulse down. *This is how the nurses must have felt in the First World War*, she thought. Facts seeped into her head as she dunked and squeezed the cotton balls.

The war started on 28 June 1914 and lasted over four years. Total dead: over eleven million. Factors that led to strong feelings of nationalism throughout Europe were . . . Were what? Ellie leaned on the sink for a moment, a wave of panic in her gut. She'd learned the factors only last week. What was happening to the inside of her head?

She knelt on the floor at Tom's feet in an effort to calm herself. She made him take the tissues from his nose. 'It's stopped,' she said. 'Now don't speak. I'm going to clean you up.'

'OK.'

'Shush, no talking.'

She wiped his mouth and around his nose with cotton wool. She dabbed at his eyebrow. He moaned gently as she touched a raw place on his cheek.

There was silence then, a tiny window of time when they looked at each other. 'I'm sorry,' he said.

Ellie felt her insides shift; a warmth for her brother stirred there.

He kept his eyes on her as she blotted at him. 'You think he does boxing?'

'Probably.'

Tom's face softened. 'He landed the first punch, Ellie. I couldn't let him get away with that. I couldn't just stand there and take it.'

She didn't understand the world of fighting, that's what the problem was. She'd been looking for subtlety, and there wasn't any – it came down to daring and bravado. Tom had the better weapon. Tom won. Maybe Mikey didn't mind about the bottle as much as she did. Maybe he didn't see it as cheating.

'He shouldn't've come here. He shouldn't've dared. You know what I mean?'

She nodded.

'I wouldn't've bottled him. I only wanted to scare him. Did you think I was going to bottle him for real?'

'I don't know.'

He smiled. 'You soaked me with that hosepipe.'

'Yeah.'

'You're a nutter.'

She sat down at his feet and watched him searching for pain with the tips of his fingers.

'Is there anything here?' He pushed out his lip with his tongue – it was swollen, as if he'd been stung.

'Just a graze.'

Tom said, 'You all right?'

'Sure.'

'You don't look it.'

Her throat contracted and her eyes filled with tears. 'What's going to happen next?'

'I'll go to court. I'll get off. We'll go back to normal.' Tom looked down at her fondly, the way he used to before any of this. 'It'll be all right.'

Twenty-five

'It's always the men. Have you noticed? Any trouble in the world and there are always men involved.'

'I'm a bloke, Mum.'

'I know that, Mikey.'

'Well, it'd be nice if you'd stop slagging us off.'

They'd been at it since they got up, and today was the formal hearing, so they'd all woken early – his sisters listening to Mum as if it was story time, while she told them about every unpleasant bloke she'd ever met. Karyn was lapping it up. If all men were bad, then she didn't have to feel so alone. Mum was getting off on it too. It was her new way of being close to Karyn.

'Should you be drinking that?' Mikey said. 'I thought we had a deal.'

She ignored him, licked her lips like a starved cat, tipped the glass and knocked another great gulp back. Mikey checked the clock – it was nearly eight. At this rate she'd be drunk before they even got to court.

'Look around the estate,' Mum said. 'At all the jobs women do

– bringing up kids, cleaning and shopping and cooking, and that's before they go out to work. Have you ever noticed how women can do more than two things at once?'

'I can do three,' Holly said. 'Look, I'm eating Coco Pops, putting my socks on and listening to you.'

'You're a genius,' Mikey told her as he leaned over and took Mum's bottle from the table.

She looked up quickly. 'Where are you going with that?'

'I'll swap you. I'll make you breakfast.'

'I don't want any breakfast.'

'You need to eat something before we go.'

He had a look at the bottle as he took it upstairs. Tio Nico sherry, £3.50 for half a litre from Ajay's. Seventeen per cent proof. She must've got it first thing, when he was waking the girls up, maybe told herself it was only milk she was going for. Anything that cheap tasted rubbish and a third of it was gone already. He rammed it in his wardrobe and went back down to the lounge. If he could get her to eat something, it would soak the worst of it up.

'Scrambled egg,' he said. 'I'll make that if you like.'

His mother blinked at him. 'Scrambled egg?'

'Yeah, you know – proper food for once. Little bit of onion, little bit of garlic. We've got bacon as well. It'll be nice.'

Mum looked confused, turned back to her glass and knocked the last bit back. 'If you want to.'

He tried not to listen as she told the girls one of her mad London stories about a bloke called Vivian who was married with three kids and forgot to mention that fact when he gave Mum a ring from the Argos catalogue and asked her to marry him.

'Humiliating,' Mum said, as the girls sympathized. 'I was only seventeen. Maybe that's what put me off men for life.'

'I like men,' Holly said.

Karyn shook her head. 'No you don't.'

'I do. They're good at cooking.'

Mikey shot her a grateful smile.

'Cooking's not the point,' Karyn growled. 'Men are like animals, Holly. Think of dogs. No, think of apes.'

'I like apes.'

'Yeah, but you wouldn't want to marry one.'

They all fell about laughing. Charming. Bloody brilliant. Even Holly was turning against him.

Gillian turned up when he was serving the eggs, and even though Mum didn't want any and Karyn would probably only pick at hers, it looked impressive. He wanted to say, *Told you I could manage*. He wanted her to notice Holly's brushed hair and clean school shirt, but all Gillian had eyes for was the bruise on his face. She came right up and peered at him like a doctor.

'I heard about this,' she said.

'It looks worse than it is.'

'Still, that's quite a shiner. Over two weeks ago, wasn't it? And you've still got all colours there.'

Mikey glared at Karyn, because she shouldn't've opened her gob. He knew she wouldn't grass who the fight was with, because they'd agreed not to tell anyone except Jacko, and she didn't even know the bit about Ellie being there. But he'd bet any money she'd told Gillian he'd lost. He wondered if the cop wrote it in her case notes – *Family lacks male role model. Eldest son a wimp.*

'I like his bruise,' Holly said. 'It's pretty.'

'Pretty stupid,' Mum cut in. 'He went out on a date and came home covered in blood. Wouldn't tell me anything about it, except the girl already had a boyfriend. You'd think he'd bother finding that out first, wouldn't you?'

He scowled at his mother. She should be thanking him for waking her up, running her bath and hiding the booze. Of course she was nervous on a day like today, but that didn't mean she could take it out on him.

'Any chance of a tea?' Gillian asked as she took off her jacket.

Blimey, even she was treating him like slave boy now. He banged the kettle about, so she'd know he wasn't a total pushover, then sent Holly off to get her coat and book bag. Emphasized *book bag*, so Gillian would know he was on to that too. Weird to see Karyn shove up on the sofa to let this woman sit down. Only a few weeks ago she didn't like her, but now she gave her a big smile and offered her a piece of toast.

'Karyn's feeling a bit nervous,' Mum told the cop. 'So it's great you could come.'

Gillian nodded sympathetically. 'I'm happy to. I'll stay with her until you get back. I can answer any questions she has and we'll get a phone call as soon as we hear how he pleads.' She turned to Karyn, patted her hand. 'You'll be first to know, all right?'

Karyn nodded. 'He's not going to say he did it though, is he?'

213

'I'm sorry, darling, but he probably won't. We'll keep positive though, eh? We can't know for sure until it's over.'

Mikey plonked her tea down – milk, no sugar, just how she liked it. 'Biscuit?' he said, because they had some.

'No, ta.' She smiled up at him. 'Are you taking Holly to school now?'

'Yeah,' he said. 'And you know what? She hasn't missed a day since we spoke.'

She nodded, looked impressed.

The school run was the best thing about the last three weeks. Everything else was utter crap, but getting up early and getting Holly in on time had become a challenge. He was good at it too. She'd only been late twice, and then only slightly late.

Holly came bouncing back in with her coat on and did the rounds of hugs and kisses.

'I'm coming back for Mum after,' Mikey told Gillian. 'I changed shifts at work and my mate's taking us in his car. The bus to Norwich takes too long.'

'I don't know what I'd do without him,' Mum said. 'Seriously, he's a diamond.'

She sounded like she meant it, which was nice.

Holly ended up next to Mikey, her hand curled into his. He liked that. 'I'll be back in fifteen,' he told them all.

'Well done, Mikey,' Gillian said.

Even Karyn gave him a fond wave.

Result! He led Holly to the door and got out of there before the balance tipped the other way again.

Twenty-six

'I can't do this.' Tom's voice was ragged and seemed to come from far away, even though he was sitting right next to Ellie in the back of the car.

Dad turned in the driver's seat. 'You can,' he said, 'and you have to.'

'Where's the barrister though?'

'He'll be here.'

'And the solicitor? He said he'd meet us in the car park.'

'I'll call him.'

Ellie closed her eyes and tried to think of something mundane like a chocolate biscuit or sitting on a sofa. It was difficult to concentrate though, and perhaps a biscuit wasn't big enough to distract her. She turned her attention to the shopping centre they'd passed on the way in instead. It was across the car park and beyond the court building and soon it would be open and people would go in and buy groceries and newspapers and other everyday things. They'd trail children and carrier bags and moan about prices. It was a comfort to know that the real world would go on in its usual way, whatever happened to her family this morning.

215

She opened her eyes and gave Tom what she hoped was a reassuring smile.

'What?' he said.

'What, what?'

'Why are you looking at me?'

'I dunno.'

'Well don't.'

'All right, Tom, just chill!'

'Ellie!' Mum turned in her seat.

'All I did was smile at him!'

'Well don't.'

Ellie slumped back down. She wished she was old. She'd swap her life to be in a life that was nearly over, so long as she didn't have to be here. *You're the primary witness*, Dad kept saying. *You need to show support.*

They'd made her wear the skirt and blouse she'd got for Granddad's funeral. The skirt was black nylon and stuck to her tights with static electricity. The blouse was dark grey. She'd studied herself in the hall mirror before getting into the car.

'I look like a nun.'

'You look perfect,' her mother had said.

They wanted holy. Not red-hot nail varnish, purple lipstick and a flaming orange mini-skirt stretched tight around the thighs. Those were not good girl's clothes.

Tom suddenly sat upright. 'Who are all those people?'

A small crowd walked through the gate. Nine or ten teenagers heading for the main door.

'Are they here for us?' His voice was edged with panic.

Ellie pressed her nose against the window. The little crowd had stopped at the bottom of the main steps. One of the girls looked at her mobile. Two of the boys sat down.

'The doors aren't open yet,' Ellie said. 'They can't go in.'

Tom peered past her. 'That girl in the blue coat,' he said, 'I know her from college. And the one next to her!'

He was panicking properly now. He looked desperate and hot and he didn't seem to care if they all saw him like this. Ellie tried to think of words that would help, but all she could think of were tight, angry words like *your fault* and *no* and . . . *stop! This is you*, she thought. *This is the real terrified you. Did you know this was you before this began?*

'Don't let yourself be intimidated by that mob,' Dad said. 'Come on, Tom, pull yourself together.'

Ellie felt a strange calm descend. If Tom couldn't cope, then maybe they could go home. Perhaps he'd actually go insane and they'd call an ambulance and then her and Mum and Dad could go for coffee and cake somewhere lovely and forget all about him. Tom took several deep breaths and blew them out again as if he was blowing smoke rings. Maybe he'd hyperventilate. Could you die from that?

'Why are they even here?' Tom said. 'Why would they bother?'

'I don't know,' Dad said. 'It's madness. Anyone can come to a public hearing, but what that rabble hope to get out of it, I don't know.'

Anyone could come? Why the hell hadn't he mentioned that

before? He said it was going to be boring, purely procedural, just barristers shuffling paperwork, over in an hour. *You won't have to speak*, he said. *We're simply going to impress the prosecution with a show of solidarity.*

'Why didn't you tell me?' she said. 'Why didn't you say it's a public hearing?'

Her dad swung round in his seat. 'I didn't think it was relevant, Eleanor, so don't you start getting hysterical. The chances of anyone turning up were almost zero.'

'Look,' Tom hissed. 'I know her as well.' Another group had come through the gate and he stabbed a finger at the window. 'She was at the house that night. She's Karyn's mate. Is she even allowed to be here?'

It was Stacey Clarke. She walked right past the car, so close her coat brushed the front bumper. She was with her friend from the day of the fight and a couple of other girls from school. They joined the first lot on the steps and they all stood there together. It felt like drumming under Ellie's skin.

She clawed at the back of her mother's seat. 'I'm not going in. I can't.'

But before her mother could respond, someone tapped on the window.

'Barry,' Dad said. 'About bloody time.'

Ellie had met the solicitor once before. He was short and blond and younger than her father. This morning he'd gelled his hair back in a school-boy slick and was wearing a suit and tie. He didn't look as if he could save them.

'Can I hop in?' he said.

He got in the back, squashing Ellie into the middle between him and Tom. *The car must be hot*, she thought. *It must stink of fear and sweat*. The windows were steamed up too. She felt claustrophobic and ashamed.

'How are we doing?' Barry said.

'Fighting fit,' Dad blustered. 'We just want to get on with it now.'

'There are a lot of people here that Tom knows,' Mum said. 'We wondered why.'

Barry dismissed the crowd on the steps with a wave of his hand. 'Ah, I wouldn't read too much into that. People often think formal hearings will be more interesting than they are. They'll be bored to tears in five minutes.'

Dad turned round in the front seat and smiled at Tom. 'You hear that? You simply need to put a legal slant on it. It helps to see through a solicitor's eyes, eh?'

Tom nodded, but he looked pale and shaken and his eyes were still locked on the crowd at the steps.

'It'll probably work in your favour,' Barry said. 'The very undramatic procedure will put them all off, so they won't bother turning up for the big one.'

He launched into a little speech then. He sounded cheery and certain as he wittered on about prosecution statements and lists of evidence and how a trial date would be set for about three months' time. The barrister was inside, he told them, talking to the judge in his chambers. Ellie imagined them both wearing dressing gowns and slippers and smoking cigars. There would be wigs on a stand and a lollopy dog on a rug.

'Right,' Barry said, 'I think that's everything. So, are we ready?'

They had to get out of the car and into the glare of the sun that splashed across the car park, they had to walk past the crowd and up the steps.

Tom ran a hand across his head, backwards and forwards. 'This is it,' he said. 'This is actually it.'

'Yep,' Dad said.

Barry nodded.

Mum turned round in her seat. 'Soon be over.'

But her eyes were a tired shade of blue and she didn't sound convinced.

Ellie wanted rain as she got out of the car. She wanted a low charcoal sky with great dark clouds blotting out the sun and thunder rumbling low above the court house. Instead, the sky was blue with a few drifting clouds the colour of old piano keys. She felt a weight settle on her shoulders and the back of her neck.

In twenty-five years this will be over, she thought. *I will be far away and no one will remember.*

Barry marched ahead with Tom and Dad, as if hurrying would solve anything. Ellie and her mum followed a few paces behind. Ellie touched her mother's sleeve to slow her down. 'I'm scared.'

Mum put an arm round her and held her close. Ellie wanted her to say, *You know what? We can't make you do this. It's not fair, you're only a kid. Why don't I take you home?*

But she said, 'Try not to let them bother you. Come on, love, Tom needs us.'

Then she took her arm away, tilted her chin at the crowd and kept right on walking towards them.

In that moment, Ellie realized no one could help her, because every member of her family had to save their strength and resolve for themselves. They were all alone in this, like four separate islands following Barry across the car park.

She felt self-conscious, as if her legs were spindles, as if her clothes were being judged, as if her body wasn't coordinated. She slowed right down, hyper-aware of every movement, every glance, every word from the group of teenagers on the steps. They had an alert energy, as if they were ready to leap. They whispered behind hands, unblinking, nudging each other. Ellie could imagine what they were saying. *That's him, yeah. That's his mum and dad, and that girl is the sister – yeah, the sister.*

Stacey pointed at Tom as he got halfway up the steps. Right at him, as if he was on a TV programme and couldn't see her.

'Do you recognize him?' she said to her friend. 'You remember him now?'

Ellie stopped completely, scanned the car park hoping for violence – tanks would be helpful, or battalions of soldiers to blast the curiosity off everyone's faces with machine guns. But there was nothing. No one to help.

OK, she'd have to pretend it wasn't her family being talked about. Most of these kids were from Tom's college – she didn't know them and they didn't know her and she'd never see them again after today and they'd get bored if she didn't react. She simply had to walk past them, it wasn't so bad. Tom was through the doors, so were Barry and Dad, and no one had lynched them. Mum was going through now, and apart from a couple of sneers, she got safely inside.

But Ellie felt as if she was stumbling, as if her shoes didn't fit and she'd fall. Her cheeks were stained with shame and she hated it. She wanted a blanket to hide under, like in the movies. As she put her foot on the first step, Stacey put her leg out, not to trip her, but to stop her.

'Hey, bitch,' she said.

'Leave me alone.'

'Don't you want to ask me how Karyn is today?'

'I just want to get past.'

'Don't you want to tell me how sorry you are again?'

Ellie stepped to one side, but Stacey moved in front of her. 'She's still refusing to see her friends, you know. She's still totally terrified.'

'Please, I have to go in.'

Stacey shook her head. 'If your paedo brother pleads not guilty today, she's gonna have to sit through a trial. How do you think she's gonna feel then?'

'I don't know.'

'You want to give it some thought?'

Someone in the crowd giggled. Why were there no adults? Why were there only kids? Stacey stared at her. 'I'm asking you again – why did you tell the cops you never saw anything?'

222

Ellie stared right back. The building in front of her swung, and still she couldn't let go of Stacey's gaze.

'Leave it,' her mate said. 'She's not worth it.'

Stacey looked Ellie up and down, as if she was checking that was true, then dismissed her with a flick of her eyes. The crowd laughed, loud jeering laughter, right at her as she ran up the rest of the steps and through the doors.

Barry had said it was court number two. She saw a sign, ran past the reception desk and up the stairs. She heard whispering behind her from people coming through the doors and following her up. But it was all right, because there, on the top landing, was her mother. Ellie ran to her, clutched at her arm and pulled herself close.

'Mum!'

'Ellie, don't grab me. I'm talking to someone, can't you see? This is Mr Grigson, Tom's barrister.'

There was reverence in her voice as she waved her hand at the barrister, as if to say, *Isn't he amazing with his black cloak and his white wig and his important bundle of paperwork?*

Mr Grigson nodded at Ellie as if he'd seen hundreds of girls like her already that morning. He didn't even say hello.

'Mum?'

'Ellie, I'm talking.'

'But Mum, I want—'

'If you need the toilet, it's there – look. Be quick though, we're about to go in.'

So, how could she say, *Mum, I want you to take care of me?*

The crowd was pressing up the stairs. Ellie couldn't bear to meet Stacey again.

'I'll just be a minute.'

Mum nodded. 'I'll save you a seat.'

Like it was a trip to the theatre, like a seat near the front would be pleasant.

Ellie dived into a cubicle and bolted it, leaned against the door and clutched her stomach to try and stop the gripping pain. She attempted to think of beautiful things – hummingbirds sipping nectar from small flowers in bright places, mountains capped with snow.

None of it worked. Because this would be so much worse in a few weeks when there'd be a jury, when Ellie's name would be called and she'd be invited to stand in the witness box and swear on a Bible and tell the truth, the whole truth, so help her God.

She vomited everything up into the toilet bowl – toast and coffee, last night's bolognese. She felt small and transparent afterwards. She wiped her mouth, flushed it all away and sat on the toilet seat shivering. She always cried when she puked, so she knew her mascara was smudged now, and that instead of looking truthful and holy she would look a total mess and no doubt get into more trouble with her parents.

She spun a wad of tissue from the toilet roll and wiped her eyes. Behind her, high up, a thin streak of sun glimmered through the window. She leaned back into it, closed her eyes and let it dazzle her face for a moment.

'Ellie Parker,' she told herself. 'You can do this. Do it for Tom. Do it for your family. Tom's your brother. He'd never do anything to hurt you.'

She washed her hands and face in the sink, rinsed her mouth and tamed her hair in the mirror. She opened the door a fraction and checked along the length of the corridor in both directions. No one was about, the landing and stairs were empty. The courtroom door was closed. Did that mean she wasn't allowed in now? No, this was another disaster! She hovered outside, unsure what to do, then decided to go back down the stairs to ask at reception. But as she got to the top stair she stopped because she heard voices and footsteps coming up and a rush of adrenalin flooded her face and chest. She recognized that voice.

Mikey McKenzie looked right at her as he turned the corner of the stairs. His eyes widened with surprise, but all he said was, 'Hello.'

Ellie nodded, couldn't speak.

He was with a woman, younger than her own mother, but definitely his mum. The whole family had the same dark hair. She hadn't dressed up, no make-up and just a tatty denim jacket over a tracksuit. The three of them stood together at the top of the stairs.

Mikey said, 'Are you going in?'

'I don't know. The doors were open and now they're shut.'

He shrugged mildly. 'The woman at the desk said to go in.'

His mother pressed her hand onto his arm and said, 'Is that the loo? I should pop in there first.'

'Sure, Mum. I'll wait for you.'

They watched her go, the door swung shut. Just the two of them now.

Ellie said, 'Does she know who I am?'

'No.'

'Will you tell her?'

'Why would I?'

'What about Karyn? Is she coming?'

He shook his head. Stupid question. Of course she wasn't. She was too scared to leave the flat, didn't everyone keep telling her that?

'Jacko's here,' he said. 'He's parking the car.'

She nodded, knew she was blushing. Voices rose and fell beyond the door.

She knew he blamed her, knew he thought she'd set him up. They stood there awkwardly, and all she could think of were pleasantries – *nice weather, how's work?*

'Your eye looks bad,' she said. 'Does it hurt?'

'Not really.'

'It's all bruised still.'

He flicked her a look. 'You should see the other guy.'

Maybe it was a joke, but neither of them smiled.

She said, 'I texted you.'

'Yeah.'

'Why didn't you answer?'

He shrugged, looked beyond her to the courtroom doors. 'I didn't see the point.'

'I had no idea Tom would come home when he did. I didn't mean that to happen.'

'Yeah, you said in your text.'

226

'You don't believe me.'

He waved a hand at the closed doors. 'This stinks, the whole thing does. What I did to you was out of order, what you did to me I probably deserved. So we're even, OK? No more texts. No more anything. Let's just forget it now.'

He held her gaze for a second. She looked away first.

'I better go in,' she said.

He nodded. 'Yeah, see you around.'

Twenty-seven

The public gallery wasn't high up like the Old Bailey on TV, just a few rows of chairs with an aisle between them. There was no whispered hush when Ellie walked in, no tutting judge surrounded by barristers to tell her off for being late, just groups of people sitting around on chairs waiting for it all to begin. Stacey and her mates were in the far corner, and although they stared as Ellie walked down the aisle and squeezed in next to her mother, no one else took much notice.

'I was beginning to give you up for lost,' Mum said, and she patted Ellie's hand, as if everything would be all right now.

It was like sitting in an airless registry office, waiting for a bad-vibe wedding. There was even an usher, some bloke flitting around with handfuls of paperwork. Tom was in the front row, the groom waiting for his bride. But the bride wasn't coming. Karyn McKenzie was at home weeping, her wedding dress in tatters, refusing to get in the limo. *I won't marry him, I won't! He's cruel and I hate him.*

Tom was scared – Ellie knew it from the way he concentrated on the floor in front of his feet, the tight pinch of his shoulders. He was wearing his new suit, chosen by Dad for its fine weave and quality stitching. But under his arms and along his spine, sweat would be gathering.

Mum leaned across and nudged her. 'The mother's just come in. I heard Barry say.'

Ellie turned her head slightly, pretending not to be that interested. Mikey's mum looked as if she was trying hard to be focused as she walked up the aisle, her head very straight, her neck straight too. Behind her came Mikey. And trailing behind him, his mate Jacko. Ellie couldn't take her eyes off them as they hunted for seats.

'She's very young,' Mum whispered. 'You reckon those two boys have different fathers?'

'They're not brothers.'

'They might be. How do you know?'

Ellie didn't even bother replying. Her heart stirred with softness for Mikey as he helped his mum to a seat and encouraged her to take off her jacket. She looked very nervous as her eyes darted about the place.

Mikey's gaze swept the room as he took his own coat off. He clocked Tom, Dad and the solicitor, their heads bent together, locked in last-minute discussions. Then he saw Ellie and it was like an invisible electric wire joined them across the room. She turned away quickly and focused her attention on the high window above the judge's bench. There was a line of grey cloud shifting across the sky. Under her chair, she crossed her feet, uncrossed them, recrossed them.

Mum nudged her again. 'Here we go. Here's the judge.'

The usher cried, 'Court rise.' And everyone stood up as the judge came in from a side door. He had a better wig than the barristers and was wearing a black and purple robe. He sat behind a long bench under a heraldic sign and everyone was told to sit down again. The usher sat below at a small desk and the barristers faced the judge with their laptops and their files of paper.

Ellie found it hard to concentrate, hard to focus. Mikey was behind her, three rows back on the other side of the aisle. The bride's side.

The barristers took it in turns to stand up and talk to the judge. They talked about statements on which the prosecution were relying and material that might benefit the defence. Legal jargon was tossed back and forth, and the crowd leaned forward, trying to make sense of it.

Was Mikey looking at her? How much of her could he see from where he was sitting? The back of her neck? Her shoulders?

On and on the barristers went, and just as people started to shuffle their feet and Ellie began to hope that Barry was right and people would get bored and go home, Tom was asked to go and stand in the dock. The crowd pressed forward in their chairs.

The dock was to the side of the barristers, a semi-partitioned area with steps up to it. When Tom stood there in his best suit, everyone could see his face. He looked paler than he had in the car, and very scared.

The judge said, 'Is your name Thomas Alexander Parker?'

'Yes, it is.' He sounded young, his voice achingly familiar.

The judge read out his date of birth and then his address. He even included the postcode. The room seemed to tilt as he read the charge out. The words *sexual assault* echoed inside Ellie's head. Tom was asked if he understood what he'd been accused of doing.

'Yes,' he said, 'I do.'

Like a vow.

'And how do you plead? Guilty or not guilty?'

Ellie could feel her own heart beating, her brain ticking, as the room slowed down. He could refuse to plead. He could plead insanity. He could say he did it.

'Not guilty.'

A babble of objections broke out across the room, as well as a spattering of applause. Some of Tom's friends must have come in, because a boy yelled, 'You tell 'em, mate!' The judge banged his little hammer and asked for quiet.

In the fuss, Ellie stole a look at Mikey.

He was staring at the floor as if he'd given up. Her whole body felt cold looking at him. Mikey loved his sister, that's why he'd tried to help her. He loved his mother too – see how he put his arm round her, see how she leaned in to him? He'd do anything for them, probably – isn't that what people in families did for each other? Isn't that what Tom was always telling her? But now Mikey would have to go home and tell Karyn that in a few short weeks, she'd have to leave the flat and come to court and talk about what happened. Her life would be taken apart and examined by strangers, and anyone could come and watch.

Not guilty.

The words repeated inside Ellie's head. Every time she blinked she saw them flare.

Twenty-eight

Mikey was making coffee in the kitchen and spying on Karyn and Jacko at the same time. He didn't want to be making coffee, he wanted to be in the car on his way to work, but Mum had bolted upstairs as soon as they'd got back from court and he knew caffeine was the best way to entice her down.

Karyn was curling her hair over and over one finger and listening intently to Jacko as he told her he'd called Tom Parker a wanker from the crown court steps.

'We all booed as he came out,' Jacko said. 'He put a coat over his head, he was so ashamed. There were loads of people on your side. Lots of your mates from school were there.'

'I should text them,' Karyn said. 'I've been a bit crap about that. Sometimes it's hard to believe everyone hasn't forgotten about me.'

'Forgotten you? No, girl, we're here for you.' Jacko rabbit-punched the air with his fists. 'Trouble is, the courts are full of bullshit. They should've left it to the masses. We'd have lynched him in the car park and hung him from a tree.'

'Bad idea,' Karyn said. 'Look what happened to Mikey when he got too close.'

Mikey scowled at her. 'What're you talking about? I landed plenty of punches.'

'You were trying to make yourself feel better.'

First she'd told Gillian about the fight, now she was mocking him in front of his best mate. He was astonished at how ungrateful she was.

'You came home looking like a horror film,' Karyn went on. 'How did that help anyone?'

She shook her head at him like a disappointed parent.

'He went solo, that's why,' Jacko said.

'Yeah, forgot to take the brains with him.' She leaned across and tapped Jacko's head with a finger, which made them both laugh.

They were really beginning to get on Mikey's nerves. Here he was making the drinks, and neither of them offered to do anything. They should be tidying up instead of sitting there. The table was crowded with stuff – ashtrays, coffee cups, plates from the scrambled egg earlier, a glass with scummy white lines from Holly's milk. The whole room smelled faintly mouldy, like something was festering. Mikey knew this would all look the same when he came home from work tonight. He also knew that something had shifted in Jacko, something he didn't quite understand. As Jacko riffed on about court, it was like he was suddenly in charge. It never used to be that way round.

'The sister nearly fainted,' Jacko said. 'She had to be led out by her mum. They sat her on a wall and fanned her with a newspaper.'

'Ellie Parker, you mean?'

'Yeah, that's it.'

'She was in the house the night it happened,' Karyn said, 'and now she's pretending not to know anything. I told you about her, didn't I, Mikey?'

Mikey nodded as he fiddled about with sugar and spoons. Ellie's name sounded very loud from where he was standing.

'I remember more and more,' Karyn said to Jacko. 'I spoke to her a few times that night. She even got me a bucket in case I was sick, but on her statement she said she was asleep the whole time.'

Jacko frowned. 'Shouldn't you tell the cops?'

'I did, but they say it's not enough – just my word against hers. And she's hardly going to grass her brother up, is she?'

'You hungry?' Mikey asked her, desperate to change the subject. 'Did you eat anything when we were gone?'

'Not really.'

Jacko shook his head at her disapprovingly, like he was the chef. 'You should eat properly,' he said. 'Mikey told me you're not looking after yourself.'

'Did he?' Karyn glared at Mikey as he stirred milk into the coffee. Great, another reason to sulk with him.

'Anyway,' Jacko said, 'as a mark of how brave you are, I bought you something.' He rummaged in the carrier bag he'd brought in from the car and pulled out a tin of Quality Street. Mikey knew they were from Lidl – he'd seen the offer, two for the price of one. He wondered what Jacko had done with the other tin.

The way Karyn grinned, you'd think he'd bought her an iPod. She looked right at Mikey with a *why don't you ever do anything nice for me?* face as she peeled the sellotape from around the edge of the tin, opened it up and stuck her face right in there to sniff.

'Smells of Christmas,' she said.

Mikey knew lots of things his sister liked – prawn cocktail crisps, white chocolate, Smarties, Pringles. Any of them would have done, so why hadn't he thought of it? He could have cooked her a whole meal in fact, beginning to end, that would have been more impressive. It made him mad to see Jacko doing all the right things, but none of the legwork. Jacko didn't have a clue what it was like living with three women. He'd like to see him try.

Karyn blinked at the chocolates and all the bright wrappers glowed back at her. She took a green triangle and offered the tin to Jacko. He took one without looking, unwrapped it and stuffed it in his mouth. Mikey hoped it was coconut.

He slopped a coffee down in front of them both. 'Don't take too long drinking that,' he told Jacko. 'We have to go in a minute.'

'Plenty of time,' Jacko said, and he reached out and took another chocolate.

Mikey had a sudden urge to see Sienna because she thought Jacko was a tosser. He went back to the kitchen and texted her. She texted straight back, *Die you creep*. Why not? He deserved it.

To make himself feel worse, he went to his outbox and skipped through the stacked-up messages he'd written to Ellie but never sent. Like heartbeats, over and over. *I miss you. Meet me. Forgive me.*

He deleted the lot.

She was on her brother's side, Karyn was right. He'd been an idiot to think otherwise.

As Mikey walked back through to the lounge, Jacko was going on about how Karyn was by herself too much, how it was bad for her and she should invite people over.

'I could've sat with you this morning,' he said. 'I wouldn't've minded.'

'I was fine. Gillian was here.'

Jacko looked confused. 'Gillian's her cop,' Mikey told him. 'Karyn thinks the sun shines out of her arse.'

Karyn shook her head. 'Don't make me sound like a prat, Mikey.'

'I'm taking this drink up to Mum,' he said. 'We'll go after that, Jacko, yeah?'

Jacko nodded, then turned straight back to Karyn. 'So,' he said, 'you think you could face leaving the flat soon, for a drive or something?'

What a wanker.

Upstairs, his mum sat on the edge of the bed with the ashtray on her lap. He put the coffee next to her on the table.

She said, 'How's Karyn?'

'Surprisingly chipper.'

'You told her he pleaded not guilty?'

'Gillian did. It's hardly a surprise though, is it?'

'I suppose not.' She took a long drag of her cigarette and blew the smoke towards the window. 'I don't know what to say to her, Mikey.'

'Don't worry about it. Jacko's filled her in.'

'I don't mean about today, I mean about everything. I've been sitting here trying to work it out.' She turned to him, something urgent in her eyes. 'I feel angry with her, and that's not right, is it? I keep thinking, *Why do we all have to go through this? Why did she let this happen?* You know, *Why did she get so drunk, why didn't she fight him off?*'

Mikey stood very still. He'd thought the very same things himself at times, but he didn't think you were supposed to say them out loud.

Mum took a last drag of her fag and ground it into the ashtray. 'I feel angry with the boy who hurt her, angry with myself for taking her to the police station, angry with her mates for dumping her. Where are they all now, eh? We haven't seen them for weeks.'

'She won't see them, that's why.'

'Well, it would be easier if she'd never said anything in the first place. She should have carried on as normal and tried to forget. It's not impossible to do that. You simply push bad things down and pretend they never happened.'

'You don't mean that, Mum.'

'Well, how is this trial any good for her, eh? I think she should go back to school and do her exams. She'll feel better if she does that, and then she'll be able to get a job and forget all this. But no, when I suggest it she shakes her head and carries on sitting

238

on that damn sofa.' She reached for the coffee, took a swig, then put it straight down again as if it tasted disgusting. 'Tell me how I'm supposed to handle it, Mikey. Tell me what I'm supposed to do.'

'You have to keep being her mum, that's all. Helping her and stuff.'

She put her head in her hands. 'It goes on for ever though. I had no idea.'

He wasn't sure if she meant the court case or looking after kids in general.

'We've got social services breathing down our necks,' she said. 'They even had the cheek to offer me a parenting course – shoving leaflets and phone numbers at me.'

He knew he had to get out of there. 'Jacko's downstairs waiting,' he said. 'I have to go now.'

She looked up at him. 'Are you getting Holly?'

'No, I'm going to work. You're getting her, remember?'

'Can you do it?'

'I've got a late shift. I swapped it so I could go to court.'

'They were supposed to sort out an after-school club. They can't even do the simplest things.' She stood up and went to the window. 'I can't drink that coffee, by the way.' Her voice had changed, hard somehow. 'I need something in it. I want you to tell me where my bottle is.'

'No, Mum.'

Her mouth was a thin line as she twisted from the window. 'Don't look at me like that, Mikey. In case you've forgotten, I am actually your mother and this is my roof you live under, so can you go and get it, please?'

'Mum, don't do this.'

She glared at him. 'I don't have to see where you've hidden it. Put a splash in the coffee and hide it away again.'

He wished he had a brother. Even an older sister would be nice. Hundreds of sisters in fact, all older than him. They could take it in turns.

'All right,' he said. 'Just one splash. A really small one.'

She looked so grateful, like some kind of desperate ghost, as he went to fetch the bottle from his room.

Twenty-nine

After saying goodbye to Karyn at the door, they walked in silence down the stairs and across the courtyard. The main gate was shut so they had to climb it. Jacko swung over easily in one clean move.

'Prat,' Mikey said, to even things up.

Jacko grinned, licked a finger and held it out, like he'd scored a point.

Everything was making Mikey angry – Karyn and Jacko hooting with laughter about something while he was upstairs wrestling the sherry bottle back from Mum; the fact that they were going to be late for work and he'd be blamed, because Jacko had a perfect track record, so how could it be his fault? Even the air, hot and dry and full of food smells, was pissing him off. He hadn't eaten anything all day. He'd wanted to get to the pub and have something before his shift started and now there wasn't time. Everything felt wrong.

'So,' Jacko said as they got in the car, 'Karyn's on form. I'd forgotten how funny she is.'

'Yeah, she's hilarious.'

Jacko frowned as he turned the key in the ignition. 'You want to tell me what the matter is?'

'Definitely not.'

'Come on, Mikey, what's wrong?'

'Nothing.'

They pulled away from the estate, past the newsagent's, the laundrette. A man was standing outside with a plastic cup of something. He didn't have a shirt on.

Jacko pointed at him. 'Bet he's put it in the washer.'

Mikey didn't think it was funny at all.

'Why did you say you'd take Karyn out for a drive?' he said.

'Why not?'

'You fancy her?'

'I was making her feel good.'

'By coming on to her? Give me a break.' Mikey shook his head, as if that was the most ridiculous thing he'd ever heard. He knew he was being a bastard, but he couldn't stop.

Jacko said, 'You need to look after her, that's all I'm saying.'

'You don't have to help, Jacko. Really, no one's asking you to.'

Jacko's face clouded over. They drove past the post office, past Lidl, towards the edge of town. 'Listen, man,' he said, 'I'm only telling you this because I've known your family for ever and I care about you. Ellie Parker's got nice tits and no one's popped her cherry, but she's sending you right off track.'

'We weren't even talking about her, we were talking about Karyn.'

'Same thing.' Jacko eyed him steadily. 'You've got to stop

sniffing round that girl. I saw the way you looked at her in court. You're losing it.'

'I'm not losing anything. She was part of the revenge plan, that's all.'

'You keep telling yourself that.'

'I will, because it's true.'

Mikey wound his window down and stuck his elbow out, furious with Jacko. He was jealous. It was simple. Ellie was a cut above and Jacko wouldn't stand a chance with her.

They drove in silence for a bit, past fields of pigs standing around in their own crap, past a farmhouse with a table outside, selling pots of jam and new potatoes. Mikey dug about in his pocket for his tobacco and made himself a rollie. He didn't offer Jacko one. He didn't seem to notice though, was humming along to some rubbish on the radio.

They were near the coast now. It was a long straight road. They passed a row of cottages with rabbits for sale, firewood, horse manure.

Mikey felt his chest clear as they got closer to the sea. The sky was cloudless. Blinding. He began to calm down.

He waggled the tobacco at Jacko. 'You want me to make you one?'

'Thanks.'

He made it nice and thick. He even lit it for him, which was a sign of something brotherly.

'Maybe we should be lifeguards,' Jacko said as he took the cigarette. 'We always wanted to do that, remember?'

It was true, they'd always fancied it when they were kids. The lifeguards had a hut on the beach and a blackboard that said, YOUR LIFEGUARD TODAY IS . . . and then the names. They always had cool names – Troy, Guy, Kurt. They had regulation red shirts and they sat around looking at girls and occasionally moving flags and yelling at kids to get off the rocks. The tide came in from two directions, so the job did have some responsibility, and there was always something to look at – the skiboarders, the surfers. Sometimes a yacht would sail by, or three RAF planes would zip ridiculously fast along the horizon, followed seconds later by their sound.

'What do you reckon, Mikey? We'll get jobs as lifeguards if the cooking doesn't work out?'

'We could do that,' Mikey agreed.

Jacko inhaled a chestful of smoke and blew it out. 'You and me, man.'

Round the corner they swung a left, and there, sitting on the grass verge, were a couple of girls – map in hand, rucksacks, walking boots, the whole thing.

'Hey,' Jacko said as they drove past. 'Let's give them a lift.'

'Let's not, they look religious.'

Jacko laughed, put the car in reverse and roared back. He pulled in to the verge and leaned across Mikey to the window. One of the girls looked up, then the other.

Jacko swung his shades on to the top of his head. Seeing his eyes seemed to make them relax; one of them smiled, the blonde one. 'Hi,' she said.

'You two lost?'

'We're fine, thanks. Just having a break.'

'You're looking at a map. You must be lost.'

'Not really.'

The dark one looked down, said something in a low voice to her friend and she looked down too, tracing her finger across the map. Mikey watched them closely. He recognized something in the way they didn't look up again. He'd seen it in Karyn before, how she could ignore something that was right in front of her and hope it would go away.

Jacko decided to give out names, obviously thought it might help. 'He's Mikey,' he said, 'and I'm Jacko.'

The blonde one smiled again. 'And together you're Michael Jackson?'

Jacko thought that was funny. The other girl did too; even Mikey found himself smiling. That was better. That was what you did with girls – you laughed at their jokes and made them relax.

'So,' Jacko said, getting his confidence up, 'you want a lift then?'

The dark one said, 'Actually, we're OK.' She stood up, hauled her rucksack onto her shoulders and held her hand out for her friend, who took it and stood up. 'Nice to meet you,' she said. 'We're going now.'

'Don't be like that,' Jacko told her. 'Come on, let us buy you a coffee. Or a beer. We work in a pub. Are you old enough for beer?'

The blonde one smiled again. 'We're old enough.' Mikey could see she was tempted. But the dark one was wary, and she seemed to be in charge.

'Leave it,' Mikey said. 'They don't want to.'

'Yeah, they do, they just need persuading.'

Jacko let the car slide away, down the lane, trailing them. They looked vulnerable walking away, easy to follow. So much to do with girls made Mikey feel guilty now – stuff on TV, porn lined up in the newsagent's, song lyrics, page three of the *Sun*. He was aware of it all in a new way, and he really didn't want to be. What was he supposed to do about any of it?

Jacko called out of the window to them. 'Come on, ladies. Don't ignore us.'

They were both pretty. Both nice girls.

'Can you go away now?' the dark one said.

Jacko tutted at her. 'Be nice to us. We only want to give you a ride.'

She turned to him, her eyes flashing. 'A ride? Piss off, you're not even funny.'

'You were laughing just now.'

'Come on,' Mikey told him, 'let's go, it's not worth it.'

'Yeah,' she said. 'It really isn't.'

'Don't fancy you anyway!' Jacko yelled out of the window, before roaring off, leaving them with thick black exhaust smoke.

Mikey slunk down in his seat. 'You shouldn't've done that.'

'It's your fault.'

'My fault? How?'

'You cursed us,' Jacko said, stabbing a finger at Mikey. 'You changed the rules of the universe when you fell in love with the enemy.'

Mikey slapped his hand on the dashboard. 'I'm not in love with her. We talked about this.'

'Then ask yourself why you haven't told anyone about her, not Karyn, not your mum. Why the big secret?'

'The plan didn't work, did it? Sue opened her big gob so Ellie knew who I was, then she got her psycho-brother to beat me to a pulp and now it's over. What's the point of telling Mum and Karyn that? They take the piss out of me enough as it is.'

Jacko grinned and Mikey wondered how he could see anything to smile about. 'Well, then Sue saved you from yourself.'

'I didn't need saving. I had a plan.'

'It was flawed.' Jacko turned in his seat. 'For days you've been at half mast – no girls, no drinks after work, no fun. If you're sulking 'cos you got mashed, then do something about it. We'll go back with weapons if you like. We'll take Woody and the others. We'll get bombs and guns and kick his arse for good.'

Why couldn't Jacko let it go? What an idiot. 'It's over, OK? I made a prick of myself. Ellie set me up and I'll never see her again. So leave it, will you? There's nothing to be done.'

Thirty

Ellie googled the word 'rape', but got the spelling wrong and brought up details of a sailing supplier that specialized in synthetic hemp. It made her smile for the first time in days. She changed 'rope' to 'ripe', expecting plums and tomatoes, but got some database reference manual instead, which made everything serious again. When she typed in the right word, she discovered that half of all girls experience some form of sexual abuse (from inappropriate touching to rape) before they are eighteen.

Everywhere, girls were being attacked. She made herself a jam sandwich and ate it looking out of the kitchen window.

Karyn was lying on her back, almost entirely covered by the duvet. She looked sweet, like she'd been tucked in. But when Ellie switched on the lamp . . .

No!

Ellie grabbed two packets of crisps and ate them quickly, one after the other, while she checked out the fridge and both food cupboards. Sometimes Tom hid his chocolate muffins somewhere other than the bread bin, but there was nothing. Maybe she could go out and get one? Morning had barely begun, but the bakery on the high street opened at six-thirty. She went to the hallway, pressed her ear to the front door and listened. Nothing. Even the wind, which usually whipped round the corner of the house and made the letterbox bang, was silent. She opened the door a fraction and checked along the length of the lawn in both directions. No one was about.

But there. What was that? A bird, with a splash of white on its chest, like milk on an oil slick. It swayed on the top branch of a tree in the lane and looked right at her. Was it a magpie? A jay? It cocked its head to one side and chuckled. It had little black eyes.

She waved a finger at it. 'Hello.'

It tipped its head at her and opened its wings. She was amazed by a flash of purple, a totally mad colour for a bird – like something a king would wear to bed. She watched as it lifted itself into the sky, over the top of the house and away. She could hear its cry for ages. It gave her something to hold on to, something strangely reassuring.

She ran down the front steps and across the lawn. It was brilliant – both her legs worked, she didn't get caught in a cyclone or struck by lightning, there were no crowds waiting at the gate with fists full of stones. She was making too much of it. It was totally obvious. In other countries there were wars. Right now, in some part of the world, someone was being burned alive in the street. And here she was, full of silly doubts about her brother – too freaked out to go to court and defend him.

As she came out of the lane and turned into Acacia Avenue, she noticed how wide the sky was overhead – not the grim little strip above the lane, but a whole street full of sky.

The world was beautiful.

She noticed everything as she walked – the daisies scattered on the grass verge, how they were still in shadow, waiting for the sun before they opened, like sleeping children. How the blossom hung so heavy on the cherry trees. The aeroplane, silver and tiny, glinting up there among a few wisps of cloud. Funny, she thought, to think of all those people strapped to their seats high above her head.

It wasn't far. Only two more roads, past the church and round the corner. There was the bakery – its fluorescent strip winking – next to the charity shop, which was shut, next to the newsagent's, which was just opening. The air smelled sweet.

A bell tinged as Ellie went in. A fat woman huffed up from a stool, clutching a magazine to her chest. She looked fed up. 'Yes?'

There were iced buns and doughnuts, gingerbread men and biscuits shaped like stars covered in silver sprinkles.

'Do you have any chocolate muffins?'

The woman pointed to a tray in the window. 'We've got croissants. They've got chocolate in.'

'OK.'

The tongs the woman unhooked from a place by the till were thick with sugar. How could they be used when the day was so new?

'Just the one, is it?'

The woman was gasping from bending and straightening, from asking the question. Ellie felt bloated watching her.

'Just one, yes.'

That's what happened if you ate cake. You turned into a fat old woman. But before you got there, you turned into a girl like Alicia Johnson, who ate her packed lunch in the school toilets so no one could see how much she shovelled into her mouth.

These last weeks, Ellie had understood Alicia. But after this cake, she was going to stop cramming herself full of food. She was going to stand in solidarity with her brother and hold her head high.

'Eighty-five pence then.'

Ellie took the paper bag, collected her change and left. *Ting*. Into the street.

But there, right outside the door, was a dog. A big dog with a thuggish face and bowed legs like a cowboy. Its lead was looped through the railing, and as it strained towards her she cowered in the doorway.

Don't let it jump. Don't let it bite.

A man came out of the newsagent's, folding a paper under his arm. He laughed, pummelled the dog's flank with the flat of his hand and said, 'He won't hurt you, love.'

But when he untied the lead, the dog came sniffing – at the cake, at Ellie's crotch, at her fingers. She stood there, frozen, and the man, still smiling, said, 'He's a big old softie.'

Why didn't he think there was anything wrong with letting his dog sniff at her like that? She hurried back across the road. A car hooted. There were suddenly people everywhere – a man filling the newspaper dispenser, another man shouting up at a window.

A car alarm was going off, a woman was singing somewhere far away. But it all seemed to be in slow motion, like all the muscle had gone from the world.

A boy crashed into her. Boots, jeans, hoodie, hands in pockets. He was walking fast, away from her now, but still, she hadn't expected to see anyone. It had seemed an empty world and now it was full.

Imagine being Karyn. Imagine being out here and . . .

No, no, she didn't want to be thinking about Karyn again! Ellie tried to remember the incantation she'd learned after she got bitten in Kenya and people stared at her scar – you closed your eyes and drew strength from the universe. You imagined a white tiger on an iron mountain. A burning red phoenix, a swimming blue turtle, a green dragon in a forest.

But you can't walk down a street with your eyes shut thinking of dragons. And if you open your eyes, then you see all the crap – the fag ends and chewing gum flattened into the pavement, rubbish swirling everywhere.

My brother is innocent. There, that was a better spell. She muttered it a few times and kept her head down. It didn't work for long. Thoughts of a broken bottle got in the way. And once that leaked in, other memories followed – Tom and his friends, fresh from the pub. Karyn drunk on a bed. Three boys standing around her and Ellie saying, 'What are you doing?'

Just mucking about. Just a bit of fun.

Outside the electric gate, Ellie fumbled for the button to slide it open. At the door she fumbled for her key. Inside, she closed her eyes and leaned against the wall in the hallway. She counted to fifty, then went into the kitchen and shut the blind. She filled the kettle. There was a horrible moment when she thought there might not be coffee, but there was a fresh packet at the bottom of the fridge. She found a plate for her croissant – it was her favourite plate, decorated with anchors and white sailing boats. She made a coffee and sat at the table. The drink was hot, the first bite of croissant was sweet and good. Together, they made her cry.

Tom stood in the doorway. Ellie could feel him there and knew she should stop crying. He padded across the kitchen in his bare feet and squatted next to her.

I'm scared of you, she thought. She wiped her eyes with her sleeve and tried not to look at him. But he tipped her face to his with the flat of his hand. His cheeks were scorched, like there was a fire stoking his gut.

'Where have you been?'

'The baker's.'

'Bit early for that.'

She showed him the plate with the croissant on it. 'See?'

'Did you get me anything?'

'No.'

'Why not?' He smiled, but it didn't reach his eyes. 'Don't you like me any more?'

He wasn't kidding. He was actually saying it. It was like something under the floorboards rearing up and showing itself. She didn't know how to answer, or even if he expected her to speak.

He said, 'Freddie saw you yesterday. It was early, he reckoned, around six in the morning.'

'I went for a walk.'

'Where?'

Her heart slammed in her chest. She'd walked across town, over to the estate, with the sole purpose of looking up at the windows and seeing if she could guess where Mikey and Karyn lived.

'Nowhere. Just walking.'

A beat. Then, 'Why do I feel like you're not on my side any more?' He turned and walked slowly to the door, stood there for a second before turning back to her. 'Please don't give up on me.'

Thirty-one

The curtains billowed like sails. Sunlight flickered on the carpet. On the bed, Tom lay with his eyes shut listening to his iPod. Ellie stood on the landing watching him. He looked like a perfectly ordinary boy in a perfectly ordinary room. No padlock, no police tape, the door open wide.

Tom Alexander Parker, who she'd grown up with for years, and surely he wouldn't let anything terrible happen?

He must've felt Ellie there, because he sat up suddenly and looked right at her. He took off his headphones. 'What's up?'

'Nothing.'

'Why are you standing there staring at me? You trying to creep me out?'

'Dinner's ready, that's all. Mum said to tell you.'

Ellie kneeled at the dog's basket, stroked her muzzle, stared deep into her milky eyes, said, 'How are you, my beautiful grey nose? How's my lovely old girl?'

'Eleanor,' Dad said, 'will you please sit back down at the table and leave the dog alone?'

She sat down. Mum carried a dish of lamb chops across to the table and Tom stabbed two of them up with a fork. Mum went back to the oven and turned peas and carrots into bowls. Tom passed the chops to Dad. Mum put the vegetables on the table and Tom helped himself. Mum went back to the oven and pulled out a tray of roast potatoes, using a tea towel as a glove.

'Any mint sauce?' Dad said.

'Yes, yes, it's coming.'

'Gravy?'

'That too.'

Dad tapped his fingers on the table to get Ellie's attention. 'Are you going to help your mother, or are you just going to sit there?'

'I suppose,' Dad said, 'we have to understand she must be very damaged to make up such a story in the first place. She comes from a very under-privileged background – single mum on benefits, three kids, no prospects for any of them. No wonder the girl was attracted to Tom.'

Tom waved his lamb chop in agreement. 'She was pretty impressed with the house.'

His lips shone with grease, his fingers too. He ripped meat from the bone with his teeth as though he hadn't eaten for days.

Ellie said, 'What was the food like when you were locked up?'

'I don't want to talk about it.'

'Was it worse than school dinners?'

256

Tom glared at her. 'Did you hear me?'

'Did you get three meals a day, or only one?'

'Ellie, I'm not in the mood.'

'Did you share a cell, or were you put in isolation?'

Dad slammed his fork down. 'That's enough!' A spatter of gravy flew across the table and landed on the cloth. 'If you can't be civil, then go to your room. What the hell's got into you, Eleanor?'

'Take your plate out, please,' Mum said quietly, 'and put it in the dishwasher.'

Ellie pushed back her chair, stood up and walked out into the garden.

The grass on a warm April day smelled luxurious. Ellie lay face-down and raked her fingers through it. It reminded her of the holidays they used to have camping, how the grass by the sea tasted salty, how she and Tom would lie in the dunes and chase sand bugs with their fingers.

Mum came out and sat next to her. 'Why are you doing everything conceivably possible to annoy your brother?'

Ellie twisted onto her back, crossed her arms under her head for a pillow. 'Is Dad the love of your life?'

'Of course.' Mum frowned gently.

Behind her mother's shoulder, the house looked like a fancy cake on a pale green lawn. Sunlight reflected in the windows, like tiny fires behind every pane of glass.

'Come on, Ellie, talk to me. These last few days, you've been so quiet.'

But how do you say unspeakable things to your very own mother?

'Before you met Dad, who were you?'

'I was a secretary, you know that.' She smiled fondly at the memory. 'Dad asked me out the first time we met. I was seeing someone already, so I said no, but whenever he came to my office he'd ask again. He was very persistent. Once he waited by the lifts at the end of the day and followed me home.'

'He sounds like a stalker.'

'No, it was romantic! You're always so hard on your dad, Ellie. He was lovely to me – bought me presents, told me I was special. He said fate meant us to be together. Eventually, I gave in.'

'What happened to your boyfriend?'

'He found someone else.' She made a shrug with her hands, as if there was no alternative. 'Dad wanted me more.'

The lounge was empty. Ellie turned on the TV, put the remote on the table and settled back to watch a re-run of *Friends*. Food and TV were very comforting. Three minutes later, Dad and Tom came in.

'What's this rubbish?' Dad picked up the remote and switched channels.

'I was watching that.'

'The golf's on.'

'But I was here first.'

He gave her a tired smile. 'You've got a TV in your room, haven't you? Come on, Ellie, give us a break, there's two of us.'

258

Tom shook his head, as if to say, *What we have to put up with, eh?* Then he sat down and put his feet up on the coffee table.

Dizzy behind her eyes, sharp stabbing pains in her head, like holding her breath underwater, as she reached for the door handle. *You can do this*, she thought. *You have to face it some time*. She pushed the door open a few inches – enough to see the new laptop, new duvet, new bed sheets, new mattress. Everything the forensic people took away that night had been replaced. It was as if nothing had happened.

She shut the door and went back to her room to revise.

Tom came in without knocking. He stood in the doorway and Ellie studiously ignored him. 'You're depressed,' he announced, 'so I bought you a Creme Egg.'

He left it next to her revision books on the desk and sidled out.

Easter eggs were officially swapped the next morning. Ellie ate both of hers for breakfast. In the afternoon, the neighbours had a barbecue and invited them. Ellie didn't go. She lay on her bed with the window open, listening to laughter drift across the fence. She revised the collapse of Communism and ate three hot cross buns.

Later, she walked into her father's study.

'Ellie,' he said, 'I didn't hear you knock.'

'When you and Mum met all those years ago and you asked her out, she didn't say yes straight away, did she?'

He turned from his desk, frowning. 'What is this?'

'What would you have done if she kept saying no?'

He sighed. 'I've got things to do, Eleanor. Please shut the door on your way out.'

After underwear, Mum rolled on her tights, rolling them so slowly that Ellie knew she was distracted. After tights, she pulled on her skirt, then her new blouse from Boden, carefully doing up the buttons, as if care and tidiness would get them all through. After shoes, a chain for her neck. It had been a week since Easter and Ellie had something to say, had been trying to say it for days, but her courage was waning.

'I went to look at you and Tom in your beds this morning,' Mum said. 'I haven't done that since you were babies.' She turned to Ellie. 'Your bed was empty.'

'I went for a walk.'

A pause, then, 'You're becoming a stranger to me, Ellie.'

Mum, I have something to tell you – you better sit down.

Ellie swilled the words around her mouth. How would it feel to say them out loud?

Dad kissed one of Mum's shoulders – lovely and surprising on the stairs. 'I popped into town and got your mother an egg,' he told her, 'hand-crafted and half price from that sweet shop, look.' He showed her the box. Gold foil dazzled their faces.

'That's kind of you, Simon,' she said.

'A bit after the event, but she won't mind, will she?' He smiled. 'Whenever you're ready, we'll be off to see her, eh?'

Ellie, in the hallway looking up at them, thought, *I am wrong, I am wrong, I am wrong.*

The dog could barely flap her tail. Ellie carried her outside in the basket and set her on the lawn so she could feel the sun. She sat next to her to keep her company, gave her new names – Beauty, Poor Lamb, Sweet Girl – stroked her grey nose, told her she remembered her being a puppy when Gran first got her, all those summers running together on the beach.

The dog looked at her as if she too remembered these things – such a sweetly puzzled look that Ellie leaned in to kiss her.

'That dog's beginning to smell,' Tom said, coming up silently behind her.

Go away, Ellie thought. *I don't want you near me.*

A perfectly ordinary room – no padlock, no police tape, the door open wide. Tom was downstairs watching TV, but here was his desk and new laptop, his chair, his laundry spilling from its basket. His wallpaper was blue. So were his curtains and duvet and pillows.

Blue for a boy.

Ellie took five steps inside and touched the edge of the bed with one finger. She closed her eyes and let memories leak in.

*

'She's drunk!'

Dad's jaw clicked with fury and Ellie laughed. Mum and Tom looked on in horror, which made her laugh even harder.

Dad said, 'Breathe on me, Eleanor.'

She huffed right in his face.

He frowned. 'Apples? I don't even have any cider.'

'Punch.' Ellie demonstrated with her hands – the apples she'd chopped, the little oranges she'd peeled, the vodka she'd poured, *glug, glug*, from his best bottle, the juice from the fridge. 'Lots of juice,' she slurred, pointing a finger at Tom, 'hides the taste.'

'She should go to bed,' Tom said. 'Shouldn't she? Sleep it off.'

Ellie laughed again, arms open wide. 'Gonna carry me up?'

The room spun, like it'd got caught in the wind, as Mum unbuckled Ellie's belt, pulled down her zip and yanked off her jeans.

'Silly girl,' Mum said.

Ellie clutched at her. 'I have to tell you—'

'No talking.' Mum pulled the duvet over her. 'Try and sleep. I'll check on you in a while.'

Lights smeared the ceiling as the door shut behind her and the room whirled faster and faster.

Thirty-two

Ellie sat at the kitchen table and watched her mother whisk eggs and milk into a bowl of flour. She looked furious with it. Her hips, her waist, the wings of her shoulders through her cotton dress were all twisting and pounding at it.

'What are you making, Mum?'

'Batter for Yorkshire puddings.'

'Why are you always making stuff?'

'We've got to eat, haven't we?'

'But only like once a day or something. Does it have to be three times? Don't you get sick of it?'

Her mum stopped whisking and looked down at her with a frown. 'When you get married and have a family of your own, you can hire yourself a cook, but until then, can you keep your criticisms to yourself?'

'I wasn't saying anything bad.'

Her mum ground salt and pepper into the mix, covered the bowl with a tea towel and slid it to the back of the counter. She stood hands on hips for a minute, as if wondering what to do next, then took a bottle of wine from the rack above her head, opened it up and poured herself a very large glass.

She's scared . . . and I'm about to make everything worse . . .

'Would you like a drink before lunch?' Mum said. 'There's some Diet Coke in the fridge, unless of course you'd prefer a double vodka?'

Ellie pulled a face and Mum half smiled at her. It had been days since the drinking incident and no one was letting her forget it.

'What about a cup of tea then?' Mum said.

'No thanks.'

Ellie didn't want anything to interrupt them, though she would actually have liked a drink.

The windows were steamed up and Mum opened the back door and stood on the step with her wine glass. Cold air shivered its way into the kitchen, bringing the smell of bacon and onions from somewhere. The dog snuffled in her basket, deep in a dream. Ellie wondered when Dad and Tom were going to get home.

'I love this garden,' Mum said, and she stepped right outside. Ellie followed her and they stood on the edge of the lawn together.

Mum said, 'Sometimes I think it was a mistake moving here from London. Dad kept going on about what an opportunity it was, and being close to Gran made sense at the time. But it was this' – she gestured with her hand at the lawn, the trees, the river – 'this seduced me.'

She smiled at Ellie, and her face was so warm and open. *Say it, say it, go on. Give it to her. She'll know what to do.*

Ellie bit her lip, words stuck on her tongue.

Her mum suddenly looked up, shielding her eyes with a hand. 'Look at that. Isn't it beautiful?'

Three geese flew across the sky in a straight line. Around them the clouds were swelling and darkening. There was a smell of electricity in the air. Even the birds rushing through the sky seemed aware of it.

'See what I mean about being seduced?' Mum said. She sighed then checked her watch. 'Now, do you think Barry's expecting food? I haven't a clue. Dad's invited him round to steady our nerves, but maybe he's only expecting a glass of wine or a cup of tea. I don't want to embarrass the man by offering him lunch. What do you reckon the etiquette is?'

'I don't know, Mum. I didn't even know he was coming and I don't know anything about etiquette when it comes to lawyers.'

Her mum smiled wearily. 'No, I don't suppose you do.' She leaned against the door frame, the wine glass to her cheek, cooling her down.

'Mum, there's something I need to tell you.'

Her mother nodded, but she looked so tired. 'You can talk to me about anything.'

Standard response.

One, two, three drops of rain, heavy and fat, splashing on the path. Ellie fiddled with a button on her dress – buttoning, unbuttoning it.

'Karyn McKenzie is telling the truth.'

She could tell by the stillness and the sudden clench of her jaw that her mother had heard.

'I suggest you think very carefully before you go any further, Ellie.'

'I've thought carefully for weeks. I can't stop thinking.'

Her mum shook her head very slowly, as if it was a physical thing Ellie had flung at her, a stick that was caught in her hair.

'Tom's whole future is at stake. Don't make this worse than it already is.'

'But I keep going over and over that night in my head and more stuff comes back to me, more things fit into place. I keep thinking about Karyn and how hurt she is and how it's not fair if I don't say what I know.'

'Not fair?' Her mother turned to her; wine stained the corners of her mouth. 'Your brother's reputation is in tatters. His A-level year's been ruined, his confidence is at rock bottom. You think any of that's fair?' Her voice was tremulous, her eyes wide and fearful. 'This isn't the time for misgivings.'

'So what am I supposed to do with the stuff I keep thinking?'

'You've had every opportunity,' Mum hissed. 'You've been interviewed by the police and you've made a statement. You told the police everything that happened that night.'

Not quite. Not even the beginning.

'So, you've never doubted him, Mum?'

There was a pause. It had weight to it, like you could hold it in your hand, like a rock from the garden.

'Answer the door, Ellie.'

'What?'

'That was the door. That'll be Barry.'

266

'But this is important!'

'So we leave him standing on the doorstep, do we?' Her mother's lips were trembling as she knocked the last of the wine back. 'Go on, go away if you're not going to answer the door. And don't bother coming back until you've learned to control yourself.'

Ellie's breath came hot and quick as she ran across the lawn. She felt like she had a fever, like that time she had tonsillitis. Perhaps she was sick, properly sick, in her body as well as her head. Maybe this is what a nervous breakdown felt like – feelings spilling out of you. She sat on the bench under the walnut tree fighting back tears.

There was a boy in her school called Flynn whose parents had been woken by the police at three in the morning and told that their son had been arrested. They said there must be a mistake, he's safe in his bed. But when they checked, he was gone. He'd climbed out of his window and gone tagging. He was caught with spray cans and a load of weed in his coat pocket.

Parents don't know their children at all.

No one knows anyone, in fact. Her brother could be a rapist. Mikey could be a hero.

It was raining heavily now, splattering off the leaves above her. Even the grass, dark blue in the half-light, looked like water rippling. She pulled her knees up and hugged them, closed her eyes and tried to think of nothing.

It was only a few minutes later when Barry appeared on the lawn.

'Mind if I join you?' he said.

He had her mother's little fold-up umbrella, which he closed when he reached the shelter of the tree.

'I was given special permission to smoke in the house, but I didn't feel comfortable doing that. You OK if I smoke here?'

Ellie nodded, too stunned to say anything. He pulled a pack of Silk Cut and a Zippo from his coat pocket and sat beside her. He lit up, and together they watched the smoke curl away into the rain. Ellie's heart was beating fast.

'I've just been talking to your mum,' he said, 'and she thought it might be a good idea for me to have a little chat with you about the court case.'

Hadn't Mum told Ellie to shut up and stay away? And now she'd sent the lawyer out to talk to her. What the hell was that about?

He said, 'I think the most important thing to remember, Ellie, is that you're the expert. You were the only other person in the house when the alleged assault occurred, so you already know all the answers to any questions you'll be asked in court. That might be a useful way of looking at it, don't you think?'

She shrugged. She didn't want to hear how easy it was going to be, or how she simply needed to stick to the truth. Those things wouldn't help her at all.

'What about if I fill you in on procedure a little bit?' He tossed his fag end across the grass and twisted himself round to see her better, taking her silence as consent. He talked about her state-ment, which would be read out in court, about the witness box and how she'd have to stand in it, about the barrister and all the very easy questions he'd ask – who came back to the house, what time she went to bed, if she heard any noises in the night. As he spoke, his face faded to darkness as the sky got gloomier and the rain fell more heavily around them. It was like hearing someone talk through a fish tank. He said, 'You simply have to repeat what you said in your statement, that you heard and saw nothing suspicious. That seems pretty straightforward. You think you can manage that?'

At the other end of the garden, through the window, she could see her father in the kitchen. He was standing by the sink looking out and his mouth was moving, like someone on TV with the sound turned down. Her mum was behind him with a pacifying hand on his shoulder. If Ellie was close enough, she'd be able to see the alarm in her mother's eyes, her desperate need to make everything all right. *Let Barry deal with it*, she'd be saying. *Ellie's feeling a bit nervous. No need for you to get involved.*

She thought she'd sorted it. She thought Ellie's words were a temporary blip, that she merely needed a talk with a professional and everything would be fine.

Stamp it out, ease it down, glue it back together.

'It's hard for you,' Barry said, 'we all see that, but it's important for your brother that you help him. No one else can help him as much as you can.'

He was fiddling with his Zippo, running it up and down his trouser leg so that the little lid at the top opened, then shut again.

Ellie felt strangely calm as she turned to him. 'I told Tom that Karyn was only fifteen.'

269

To her surprise, Barry smiled. 'Is that what's been bothering you – that Karyn wasn't old enough to give consent?'

'He's going around saying he thought she was sixteen.'

Barry's face fell into something she recognized from her father when he wanted to explain a concept she might find particularly complicated. 'Ellie, people often forget things they're told, especially when it's late at night, or they've been drinking. It was noisy, the music was loud, it's not impossible he didn't even hear you.'

'He definitely did.'

'Well, he clearly has no recollection, so I think we can safely rule it out as a piece of evidence.'

'You mean, let's pretend I never said it?'

'It wouldn't stand up in court, Ellie. You'd get a grilling from the prosecution for no reason. Tom would simply say he didn't remember you telling him, and anyway, unless Karyn can prove he forced himself on her the age difference is so small between them it becomes immaterial.'

There was something in his eyes, a way of looking at her blankly through a smile, as if he was adapting what she said to suit him. She hated him suddenly.

'Karyn was really drunk,' she said. 'She was so drunk that when the boys carried her upstairs between them, she couldn't even speak. Did Tom tell you that?'

The solicitor frowned. 'Carried her?'

'And shoved her on Tom's bed.'

'Do you mean the other witnesses, Freddie and James?'

'Yeah, them. James had the stick that opens the blinds and was lifting her skirt up with it. She was completely trashed and the three of them stood around laughing and taking pictures of her on their phones.' Ellie's voice sounded loud – the rain didn't dampen it, but made it ring clear. She wondered if she could be heard from the house. 'I told them to leave her alone.'

She felt Barry tense beside her. He leaned forward and stared down at the grass, as if something amazing had appeared there.

'Freddie and James went home, but Karyn was too drunk to move, so we left her on the bed and Tom went downstairs to sleep on the sofa.'

She wanted Barry to react. She stared at him, willing him to understand that Karyn couldn't possibly have consented to what happened next. But instead, he turned to her, a tight smile on his face.

'This is obviously quite an awkward situation for me,' he said, 'so I'm going to stop you there.' He stood up, hands in pockets, a shadow between her and the house. 'I don't want to be getting information from you that could compromise your brother's position.'

'So I can't talk to you?'

'Why, was there something else?'

Her hands on her lap were startling, not quite her own, lying there so passive while her head was whirling.

'There's a lot more.'

'Ellie, you told the police you saw and heard nothing all night.'

'I didn't want to get my brother into trouble.'

He sighed deeply. 'Then I suggest you seek legal advice.'

'You mean get my own lawyer?'

'I think that would be a good idea.'

'But you asked me to talk to you. You came out here and asked me questions.'

'I'm your brother's solicitor and I can't get into any situation where it looks as if I may have advised you.'

'So, you're not going to do anything?'

'I'm going to talk to your brother. Then I'm going to advise the barrister we don't call you as a witness.'

Hot waves of fear broke in her chest. 'You mean you don't want me going to court in case I blurt all this out and Tom goes to jail?'

'I mean I'm your brother's solicitor and I have to look after his best interests. There's no way we'll call you to the stand under these circumstances.'

She nodded dumbly.

'I'm going inside now, Ellie.'

She wanted to stop him, to force him to listen to the rest of it. But she didn't move. What was the point? Instead, she watched him stride back across the grass, go through the French doors and wipe his feet on the mat.

Let's just forget it, Mikey had said. *No more texts, no more anything.*

Help me, Mikey, she wanted to say. *I'm afraid. More afraid than you'd ever believe.*

And he'd take her hand and they'd fly across the rooftops and up into space and sit on some planet and watch a double sunrise or maybe a star being born or some other event that no human had ever seen, her head on his shoulder, his arm around her. And she'd tell him everything.

Her mother appeared on the step. She had her gardening shoes on and the same umbrella she'd loaned to Barry. She picked her way across the grass as if the sky was about to fall on her head.

'What did you say to him?' she said when she got close enough. 'He wants to talk to Tom alone in the study and even Dad's not allowed in.' Her eyes clutched at Ellie's. 'Did you tell him what you told me?'

'It'll be all right,' Ellie whispered.

'That's not what I asked.'

'I'm sorry, Mum, I can't do this any more.'

Her mum called, 'Where are you going?' as Ellie sprinted away. 'Come back here right now!'

Round the side of the house, through the gate and out onto the lane, kicking her way through puddles, her feet spattering mud, her legs pounding distance between her family and the world beyond them. She hadn't run for weeks. She hadn't moved for years, it felt. She would run for ever. Her limbs were strong and healthy. She felt like an animal. She ran and ran, past trees dripping with rain, past other people's houses and gardens, along the muddy lane towards the town.

Thirty-three

Mikey banged out of the door and down the stairs. Never mind the lift, stairs were quicker, racing down five flights, his heart pounding. Just before the bottom, he stopped, because there she was outside, her face pointing up to the rain. He slammed through the doors and marched up to her.

'What are you doing?'

Her dress was wet, her jeans were wet, even her eyelashes were dripping with rain. 'I had to see you.'

'You can't just text and demand I come down or you're coming up. Who do you think you are?'

'I'm sorry. I wouldn't really have come up. I don't even know which flat's yours.' She scanned the block of flats above them, shielding her eyes against the rain. 'Which one is it?'

He shook his head. 'You have to go.'

Her eyes travelled the length of the balconies, door after door. 'Does Karyn know I'm here?'

'Are you crazy?'

Ellie looked sad then, and confused. 'Please don't send me

away. You're the one who came running after me in the beginning, remember?'

That was true, and he felt a bit rubbish then. To make up for it, he pointed out the flat. He wanted her to know he didn't hate her. It wasn't about that.

'Blue door,' he said, 'with the Christmas tree outside.'

It was a dead stump of a tree, no needles, but still decorated, still covered in tinsel. It was nearly May and they'd only managed to drag it as far as the balcony. He felt foolish, like he was pointing out their chaos.

'My little sister likes it,' he said. 'She thinks it'll grow back. I'll swap it for a new one in December and hope she doesn't notice.'

Ellie looked at him, a strange, deep look. 'That's kind.'

He hadn't thought of it as being kind. It's just what you did if you wanted Holly to be happy – you pretended there was magic in the world.

'Listen,' he said. 'You have to go. Serious, I've got work in half an hour and Jacko's picking me up. My life won't be worth living if he sees you here.'

He led her round the corner, by the lift, where it was sheltered from the rain. She grabbed her hair with one hand and twisted it, wringing it out. He peeled off his jacket and offered it to her.

'Here,' he said. 'Take this, or you'll get pneumonia on the way home.'

She put it on without a word and did up the zip. She shoved her hands deep into the pockets. He hoped there weren't any scaggy tissues in there, or packets of condoms, girls' phone numbers . . .

'You're the nicest person I ever met,' she said.

She must know some total shits if she was impressed by a coat.

'Whatever,' he said. 'I'm going now.'

She put a hand on his arm. 'I have to tell you something.'

'I don't want to know.'

'Please,' she begged. 'You're the only person I can tell.'

She looked like she was tempting a bird to feed from her hand, seeing how close she could get to him. It was weird being chased.

'Two minutes,' he said.

They sat on the wall together, the lift doors in front of them. It stank of piss, but this was the best they had for now.

'So,' he said, 'did you get in another argument with someone?'

'Not really.'

'Was it your brother?'

She shook her head, looked down at her shoes.

'To be honest, if it *is* about your brother, I don't even care. Anything could be true and it wouldn't surprise me. Maybe Karyn's lying.'

'She's not.' She turned to him slowly. Fear dipped in and out of her eyes. 'I wanted to believe Tom was innocent. For weeks I wanted it. But I think he did it and I'm not going to be his witness.'

'So?'

She frowned at him, puzzled. 'That's massive! I'm supposed to stand up in court and say I didn't see or hear anything. I'm supposed to say my brother is lovely and couldn't possibly have hurt your sister. And now I'm not going to.'

It wasn't like she had video footage or anything. Plenty of other people would stand up in court and defend her brother, even if she didn't.

'It won't make any difference, Ellie.'

She let out a little sob, which shocked him. He'd thought girls like her didn't cry. Weren't brains supposed to be in charge of feelings?

'Hey,' he said. 'Hey, are you OK?'

He put an arm round her and she leaned against him for a minute. She was embarrassed, tried to hide her face from him, kept wiping below her eyes to check her mascara hadn't run.

'I'm sorry,' he said. 'I didn't mean to diss you.'

She looked up at him, her cheeks flushed. 'Why are you being nice to me now?'

'I like you.'

She started to laugh. He did too. It was great, the sound of it.

'Hey,' he said. 'You want to go somewhere? We could if you like.'

'I thought you had work?'

'Sod work. Let's get out of here.'

She nodded. 'Yes please.'

Absolute gold and unexpected.

'Where shall we go?'

She wiped her eyes with her sleeve. 'Not near my house.'

'OK.'

'And not in town.'

He knew it was wrong, knew it was slipping back into something he'd given up. But here was Ellie, telling him her brother did it. Her family were going to hate her for this. She needed him.

He looked around for inspiration. They couldn't go to the flat because of Karyn, and they couldn't go to Ellie's house because of her brother and they couldn't go into town because of everyone else. And they had to decide pretty quick. Once the rain stopped, this place would liven up and someone would come out of those lift doors and see them for sure.

'Can you get your friend's car?' she said.

He wished he could, but Jacko would be here to pick him up for work in a minute, and he didn't fancy that run-in.

'Maybe a bus,' she said. 'Where do they go from here?'

'Through town, then out to the coast.'

She looked at him as if she was working something out. 'Do they go near the bay?'

And now he knew what she was thinking. He stared at her, willing her not to change her mind, to be brave enough to go through with this.

'Pretty close,' he said. 'We could walk the last bit.'

'Because that's where my gran's cottage is.'

He tried not to look too happy. She'd told him about the cottage the day they'd gone swimming. It was near the beach and it was empty because her gran was in some nursing home. Perfect.

'Have you got a key?'

She faltered for only a second. 'There's one hidden in the garden, in case of emergencies.'

Well, this was an emergency for sure. He couldn't think of a better one. Two people locked out in the rain, who only wanted to be alone together.

She sat chewing her lip for a bit. 'My dad'll kill me if he finds out.'

'You want to stay here then?'

They looked around the place together – at the rubbish piled up near the lift, at the wet steel doors, at the drips of rust-coloured rain splashing into puddles at their feet.

She stood up and held out her hand for him, like she had that time at the pub. 'Come on.'

He half expected to hear a crowd suddenly burst out cheering.

He turned his mobile off so no one from work would bug him, and put his hood up. Ellie swung her hair in front of her face to hide from anyone walking by. They looked like a couple of criminals. It was funny. They were blazing with it, both of them jittery as they got on the bus. They sat at the back. It was quiet, too cold and wet for day trippers. Their knees touched. Mikey wondered what that meant, if Ellie even realized. He leaned in closer. She smelled of vanilla and rain.

They didn't say anything. It was impossible for him to talk with her knee against his. He was having to use all his concentration to stop himself leaning in and kissing her. Did she know this? Did she know her leg knocking against his made his whole body throb?

The bus went down the high street, past the bakery and the shops, through the estate on the other side of town and into the country. Fields appeared, cows, a few straggly sheep. Rain slammed against the windows, hot air leaked at them from heaters under the seats. Their clothes steamed, which made them laugh again.

As the coast swung into view, she nudged him. 'I saw a whale there once.'

'You never did.'

'I did. Me and my granddad used to climb over that cliff and sit on a ledge about halfway down. When the tide was in, it was amazing with all that water crashing against the rocks. We used to sit there for hours watching the boats go by. And one day we saw a whale.'

'Well, I've never seen a whale and I've lived here for years and years.'

She laughed at him softly, her eyes shining. 'Well, maybe you weren't looking in the right place.'

It was true. He used to come here sometimes with Karyn and Holly when he was a kid, but they'd just go to the beach. They'd eat pasties and doughnuts and Mum would take her shoes off. On sunny days, the place would be crawling with families, hot and salty people flinging themselves after balls, bobbing about in the water with their armbands and rubber rings. But he'd never seen a whale. He felt sad about that. It seemed strange that two people could be in the very same place and see totally different things.

The bus followed the curve of the bay and then swept back inland and up the hill.

'We're close now,' she said. 'Shall we walk from here?'

They stood on the corner and watched the bus move away. It was quiet after it had gone. It smelled different from town, like everything was wilder. The rain was lighter now, but it wasn't letting up. He was glad. She might say they had to go back if it stopped. They walked in the road. No pavement, no cars. There was something old-fashioned about it, as if they'd gone back in time.

'Look,' she said. 'Lapwings.'

Two black and white birds hung poised above the sea. He thought they were gulls, but he liked it that she knew their proper names. They watched them gliding and pitching as they walked on. Even from the top of the cliff they could hear the faraway hush and roar of the waves.

'Fancy a swim?' she said.

He laughed, hoped she wasn't serious. They'd get hypothermia down there today.

'There's a path that goes down,' she said. 'I used to stay here every school holiday with my grandparents and we'd swim every day.'

They stopped to look at the water for a bit. They stood under a tree, rain dripping around them. Out there, under the clouds, the sea was the colour of carbon. There was a strange light coming from the sky as well, like maybe a storm was coming.

'Tell me about your grandparents,' he said.

What she told him then sounded like something from a film – sunny days and picnics, games of rounders and cricket on the beach. She didn't mention Tom's name once and Mikey wondered if she was being careful, or if he never went on holiday. Maybe the grandparents were sensible enough to avoid him. They sounded nice enough.

'When we moved here last year,' she said, 'I was looking

forward to spending more time with them, but as soon as we got here, my granddad died.' She gave him a sad smile. 'Three heart attacks in a row. I didn't even know you could have that many.'

He took her hand. She didn't move it away, only looked down at their fingers laced together.

'After that, my gran went crazy,' she whispered. 'She lived with us for a while. She used to sit in a chair at the top of the stairs all night. She said if she went to bed, she'd wake up with cobwebs on her face. It infuriated my dad, so he shoved her in a nursing home. Now my mum has to drive miles if she wants a cup of tea with her own mother.'

Mikey lifted Ellie's hand to his lips and kissed it. He didn't know why he did it, but it fitted in with the sadness and the sea and the rain. He knew he'd got it right, because she gave him that look again, like he was some kind of hero.

'Come on,' she said. 'It isn't far now.'

Thirty-four

'I didn't expect it to be like this,' she said. 'It's so . . . bleak.'

There was her gran's old armchair by the side of the fireplace and Granddad's hard-backed chair by the window. There was the sofa against the opposite wall. But everything else had gone – no books or photos on the shelves, no trinkets, even the TV had disappeared.

'I thought my mum came here to get away from my dad for a bit, but she really *was* clearing the place out.'

Mikey touched her gently on the arm. 'It's cold, which doesn't help. We'll put the heating on.'

They went into the kitchen together and hunted for the boiler, which they eventually found in a cupboard. It was ancient, had some kind of pilot light that needed holding down and an ignition switch that needed pushing. Ellie stood next to Mikey while he worked it out. She liked him knowing what to do.

'Disconnected,' he said, 'which means there's probably no electricity either. I'll have a look and see if there's an oil burner or anything.'

While he searched in the hall closet, Ellie went back into the lounge, stood in front of the fireplace and rubbed her hands together, as if that would make a difference. Sadness washed over her in waves. She'd wanted it to be good, somewhere to escape to. She wanted sunlight streaming through the windows, like when she was a kid.

'Nothing,' he said as he came back in. 'Not even a candle.'

'I'm sorry. I brought you all this way and it's rubbish.'

'Don't worry.' He nudged her with his elbow. 'I like adventures.'

That was so kind; *he* was so kind. Dad or Tom would be fuming at the wasted journey and the freezing cottage. They'd be marching off down the road by now, looking for the nearest taxi rank. She felt the world loosen around her as Mikey stood there smiling.

'Well, I'm sorry anyway.' She meant for everything – the cottage, Karyn, all of it. None of it was fair. She wiped her face with her sleeve and gave him what she hoped was an upbeat smile. 'So, what shall we do now?'

He laughed. 'Wait there. I'll be back.'

He went out of the lounge, down the hallway and out the door. She heard him scrunch down the gravelled path towards the gate. She sat on her gran's chair by the empty fireplace and waited for what would happen next. He wasn't long, came back in with a pile of newspaper and some logs and sticks in a basket.

'I noticed the shed when we came in,' he said. 'I thought there might be wood.'

He ripped up sheets of paper, screwed them into balls and put them in the grate. He built a pyramid around them with twigs and stacked larger sticks around that.

She leaned forward on the chair watching him. 'How do you always know what to do?'

He grinned. 'Every bloke knows how to build a fire.'

She didn't think that was true.

Mikey got out his lighter and lit the paper. She sat next to him on the rug as the flames took hold.

'There's plenty of wood,' he said. 'We can dry our clothes as well.'

He began to unlace his trainers. She wondered if his heart was slamming as fast as hers. *All* her clothes were wet. How many were they taking off? She pulled her own trainers off and placed them next to his on the hearth. They peeled off their socks and laid them next to their shoes. She unzipped the jacket he'd lent her, knew he was looking as she carefully hung it over the chair so the heat could reach it. She watched him pull his hoodie off and spread it out on the floor. He was only wearing a vest top underneath.

'Is that a tattoo?'

A small green snake with a red tongue writhed on his shoulder as he lifted his arm to show her. She traced the tattoo with her finger and he watched her. His skin was soft and she didn't want to stop touching him. But she couldn't go on for ever, so she pulled her hand away and put it back on her lap.

They sat there looking at each other. He looked away first.

'You think there's any food hidden away?' he said.

'I doubt it.'

He smiled as if he didn't believe her. 'Show me.'

He was right. There were some potatoes in a basket at the bottom of the larder. He wrapped them in silver foil and shoved them under the fire. They played childish games while they waited for them – Noughts and Crosses and Hangman. She found a pack of cards and taught him to play Rummy and he taught her Go Fish. It was like a siege and they were hostages.

When they got bored of games, they lay next to the fire on their backs and looked at the ceiling. Spider webs shivered in each of the four corners. There were cracks all over the plaster and the paint was yellow from her grandfather's pipe. It made Ellie sad. They lay there for ages not saying a word, not touching at all. She cheered herself up by sneaking looks at him. There was something about him that made her dizzy – the dark of his hair, the brown of his eyes, the angles of him lying next to her.

This is real, she thought. *This is real*.

She wanted him to touch her. She wanted to say, *Kiss me, please, do it soon*.

But if she said that, then he'd think she was easy.

Instead she said, 'Tell me what you're thinking.'

He was thinking she'd probably never been with a boy before. He was thinking he'd never been with a girl who'd never been with anyone else. He was wondering why that was freaking him out. Lying next to her in front of the fire was stirring him up, and the longer they lay, the more he wanted to touch her. But what if he made a move and he'd mis-read the signs and she didn't want him at all? Or what if he made a move and she *did* want him, but then he was rubbish and she hated it? Whenever she was asked about her very first time she'd say, *Oh, it was shit.*

She treated her body as if it was really special. He'd noticed it at the river and again today – how she kept changing the position of a strap or pulling buttons shut or yanking her dress lower so he couldn't see bits of her. It was like she had something hidden and if you got in there, you'd be really privileged. It made him think of that line in the Spider-Man movie about power and responsibility. It was doing his head in.

'I was thinking,' he said, 'about those potatoes. You reckon they're ready?'

He dug them out with a fork while Ellie got plates from the kitchen. She came back with salt, pepper and, by some miracle, an unopened tube of cheese spread.

'Found it in the herb rack,' she said. She looked proud. Her face lit up with it.

They sat together on the carpet to eat, their plates on their knees. The potatoes were delicious.

'This was a good idea,' she said.

'Coming here, or eating?'

'Both.'

They smiled at each other. There was a sweet shyness about her that he really liked. It was as if his heart got rubbed clean looking at her, like it was possible to start again. *You're so pretty*, he wanted to say. But he didn't, because that didn't seem enough.

'I'm not sure about the cheese spread,' she said. 'It tastes like it's only a molecule away from plastic. You know, if you put a pot of margarine on the lawn, not a single insect will touch it because it doesn't recognize it as food?'

He laughed. 'How do you know that?'

'From Science.'

'I don't remember anything from school. The only lesson I liked was Food Tech and the rest was the most boring rubbish I ever had to listen to.'

'You hated it that much?'

'Don't you?'

She shrugged. 'Some things I like and the rest I put up with. Did you take any exams?'

'They put me in for five, but I only got Food Tech and ICT.'

'Did you revise?'

'Not really. There was always something going on that seemed more important. You know – with my mum and sisters and everything.'

She nodded, but didn't say anything.

'Pass your plate,' he said. 'I'll take it out if you're done.'

He might not have hundreds of GCSEs, but he could build a fire, make food, clear up, which had to be worth something.

The water hadn't been disconnected, but it came out rust-coloured and he had to run the tap for ages. He rinsed the plates, gave them a shake and put them back in the cupboard. If anyone noticed they'd been here, they might not be able to come again, and he wanted to. There was a pint glass in the cupboard and he filled it with tap water and drank it straight down. It tasted fine, even though the colour was still weird. He filled the glass again and took it in for her.

'Here,' he said.

He sat back down on the carpet and watched her drink. He liked the way her throat moved, the sound of water falling into her. He liked it so much that he leaned right over and laid his head on her shoulder.

She laughed. 'What are you doing?'

'Listening to you.'

He could feel her breath on his face.

'What do I sound like?' she whispered.

'Beautiful.'

He felt like a junkie might feel as he leaned in to kiss her.

She'd thought of it, dreamed of it, and here it was – like a slow drowning as his lips touched hers. She could feel his heart beating against her chest, could hear the pulse at her own neck thundering. It was how it should've been all along, and why had they wasted hours without touching at all?

Kissing Mikey McKenzie on the carpet in her grandparents' cottage, the world felt more intimate and more exactly right than Ellie had ever guessed it could. It was like a shape had chosen her and shifted her from ordinary to special. She'd run like an animal through the rain and gone to find him. She'd caught a bus and brought him here.

It began to get gloomy outside. It would get darker and darker and later and later. It was a long bus ride back. There was no landline or mobile signal, there were no neighbours and nobody knew they were there.

Every now and then a picture of home would leak in – her father's furious face, her mother's disappointed one, the stabbed look in Tom's eyes. The three of them would have eaten Sunday lunch with the solicitor by now. They'd be drinking coffee and talking about her, wondering where she was.

But the longer she kissed Mikey, the less important these things became.

He stroked her hair. She dared to touch his hip. There was a crazy flare under her fingers where her skin touched his. She buried herself in his neck and breathed in the boy smell of him.

'I can't get close enough to you,' she said.

He looked at her with dark eyes, his breathing like an engine. He looked like he was sinking, like he couldn't help himself as he reached to kiss her again. It made her want to laugh out loud. She did this to him. *She* did. Ellie Parker. Never, ever had she dreamed she could feel so alive.

She said, 'I haven't ever . . .' as he began to unbutton her dress, but then she gave up, because, in fact, she wanted him to unbutton it. It shocked her that this was true. How could she want this when she'd never done anything more than kiss a boy before?

He said, 'You want me to stop?'

She shook her head.

'We can just kiss,' he said. 'We don't have to do anything else.'

'I don't want to stop.'

Every girl knows if you get into a situation with a boy who has

290

had sex already, then he will want to have sex with you. He will push at your boundaries. If you say no to a boy like this, he will try and get you to change your mind.

But she wasn't saying no.

She'd broken into her grandparents' cottage and her rules were crumbling to dust. She'd known Mikey for less than eight weeks and this was only their second date.

'Are you sure?' he said.

She nodded.

Then.

He was on his knees and he held out his hand to her. She sat up and together they slid the dress from her shoulders. It was the blue dress she'd worn at the party the first time she'd spoken to him properly. That felt like years ago, like another life.

And how easy that life slipped off.

He knew he was supposed to take it slow, but all she had left was bra, jeans, knickers. Three things. He was burning with how much he wanted her. He reached out for the buckle on her belt.

'Wait,' she said.

She put her hand over his. Had he gone too far? Too fast? If this was Sienna, they'd have done the business by now and be having a fag and talking about nothing. But it was different with Ellie. He was whimpering like a dog inside, and the only way forward was to let her decide what happened next. He wanted to yank those jeans right off her. He wanted to know if her knickers matched the black lace of her bra. He wanted to tell her he probably had a condom somewhere and that everything was under control. But he didn't want to scare her.

He said, 'Am I going too fast?'

She shook her head. 'It's not that.'

'What is it then?'

'I lied to the police.'

His heart sank. Why wasn't anything ever simple? She was in front of him, confessing, and he didn't want to hear it. He wanted to kiss her.

'When I made my first statement I said I was asleep all night, and I wasn't. I'm scared that when you know how important that is, you're going to hate me.'

'I won't ever hate you.'

'I hope not.' She touched his belly. Up. Gently. Her fingers ran over the ridges of his ribcage. 'I want to help Karyn.'

'I know that.'

She said, 'So you think this is a good idea then, you and me?'

He said, 'Yes.'

Then he said, 'But only if you think so.'

She leaned in close and kissed his chin, the end of his nose, each eyelid.

She said, 'I missed you so much. I've been wanting to touch you for days.'

And he was worth something. Just like that.

Her breath on his face was salt and wood smoke and something underneath that, something sweet and pulsing. He sat very still as her kisses moved to his neck, as her right hand explored his back, all the way down his spine to his belt. If he moved, she might stop and he didn't want her to stop.

It had never crossed his mind that his body might be special too. No girl had ever taken the time to show him. Or was it that he just hadn't let them?

Whichever it was, it was like a pulse rising.

Ellie put her hand against his chest and felt his heart through his T-shirt. He was watching her and she knew she had to decide what happened next.

For the rest of her life, he'd be her first and nothing could ever change it. And if he hated her later because of what she knew about his sister and Tom, then she'd have to live with it. It was now that mattered. Right now. Right here. She watched herself move her hand down to the edge of his T-shirt.

She'd thought it would be like speaking different languages, because he was experienced and she wasn't. But she knew what she wanted and somehow she knew what to do. She dared to lift his T-shirt and he raised his arms like an obedient child and she pulled it over his head. She loved the feeling of power as he melted towards her, the way his breathing changed under her fingers.

'Do you want me to stop?' she said.

He shook his head.

They smiled at each other.

They both got it. That's what was so great. Ellie had never known it was possible for two people to want the exact same thing at the same time.

'Is this how it is for everyone?' she whispered.

'No.'

'How do you know?'

'I just do. I've never felt this with anyone before.'

'Serious?'

'Serious. That isn't a line.'

'Kiss me,' she said.

He did. Everywhere.

Afterwards, he stroked her. It made her shiver and he liked the way her eyes got serious as he stroked the bit where her leg joined her bum. All the little hairs at the top of her thigh stood up under his fingers.

'You cried,' he said.

She put her hands over her face. 'Doesn't everyone?'

'Only in songs.'

'I'm embarrassed!'

'Don't be, it's good. Other girls aren't like that.'

She peered at him from between her fingers. 'What are other girls like?'

'I dunno. That came out wrong.'

'Have you slept with lots of them?'

'Not lots.'

He tried to kiss her again. He didn't want ghosts in the room sitting around watching them. But she nudged him away and pushed herself up onto her elbows to see him properly. It was dark in the room now the fire had died down.

'I keep thinking about Karyn,' she said. 'Do you?'

'I keep thinking about your brother crashing in with a gun.'

It was a joke, but she didn't smile. 'No one knows we're here,' she said. 'We have to trust each other now, don't we?'

He pulled her down to him. She smelled great. He stroked her some more and she relaxed against him. They didn't talk.

The sound of her mobile was piercing – like a bird screaming in their ears.

'How can it be ringing? There's no signal here, there's never any signal.' She fumbled for it among a sea of clothes, her face terrified. 'Oh God, it's my mum. What shall I do?'

'Answer it, say you're busy.'

She lobbed it at him as if it was hot. 'You answer it.'

'Serious?'

'No!' She snatched it back and turned it off, then lay on the carpet and covered her head with her arms. 'She knows where I am.'

'How can she?'

'She knows what I've been doing.'

He laughed. 'She doesn't. Text her, tell her you'll call her later.'

'I forgot about home.' She sat up again and looked down at him. 'I forgot about running out, like none of it existed.'

'You ran out?'

'Kind of. Oh God! The lawyer will have spoken to Tom. Tom will have spoken to my dad. They're going to kill me when I get back.'

'Don't go. Stay here with me.'

She shook her head, dismissing him. 'Help me find my stuff.'

It was like watching a spell break. He'd wanted to kiss her again, stay the whole night through, wake up with her.

'You won't find your knickers,' he said.

'Have you got them?'

'Might have.'

'Mikey, please. I have to go.'

'Tell them you're at the cinema, say it's a late film.'

'They won't believe me.'

'Tell them you're dead, then we can stay as long as we like.'

'I can't. You might think I'm brave, but really I'm a coward. Mikey, please, I have to go and deal with this before I get too scared.'

Her knickers looked great in the palm of his hand – lacy and black. He kissed them goodbye, which made her smile.

'Sorry,' she said. 'But if my dad finds out about you too, it'll make everything a hundred times worse.'

She found her bra, did the clasp up, twisted it round and pulled the strap over her shoulders, like putting a bridle on a horse. She stuck her tongue out at him when she caught him looking, pulled on her dress, did a great wriggle as she smoothed it over her hips.

'What would your dad do if he knew?' Mikey asked.

'Kill me. Kill you. Kill himself.'

'In that order?'

'No, actually. He'd kill you first.'

He got dressed quickly while she put on her shoes, then they tidied the room together. He put water on the ashes and spread them out in the grate. She put the cushions and blankets back on the chairs and checked that everything looked the same as when they arrived. It was weird having no electricity, but still being able to see.

'Can we come here again?' he said.

'I don't know. Thursday maybe we could. I've got study leave in the afternoon. If everything's normal on Thursday, I'll meet you then.'

She had one hand on the door handle, waiting for him. She hadn't touched him since the phone rang, and as she shut the door and hid the key, it was like he'd lost something.

'That's ages away.'

'I know, but we have to be careful.'

Was this love? Because it hurt. It was like a bit of glass stuck somewhere important – his heart or his head, and it was throbbing. Already he missed her and they were only just out of the door.

'Thursday then,' he agreed.

He took her hand and laced their fingers back together as they walked down the path to the gate.

Thirty-five

The front door opened before Ellie even made it across the lawn and her mother rushed down the steps, arms open wide.

'Oh, thank God!'

She hugged her so close, Ellie could feel the sharp angles of her mother's shoulders and the curve of her ribs through her dress.

'Mum, you're hurting me.'

'I've been worried sick. We had absolutely no idea where you were.' She pressed Ellie closer for a second, then let her go, stepping back to stroke her hair and pat at her arms and face, as if checking she was real. 'We were about to call the police.'

'The police?'

'You've been gone for hours, we were desperate.'

Only now did Ellie notice her dad glowering at her from the doorstep. He looked older than he had at breakfast, thin and shabby somehow.

He said, 'Where the hell have you been?'

'I'm sorry. I went for a walk.'

'All this time? In the rain, with no coat?'

'It was stupid. I didn't think.'

'Why did you turn your phone off?'

'I ended up at the cinema, then I forgot to turn it back on when I came out.'

It sounded crap, hollow, like lines from a play. Her father leaned against the door frame and looked at her, taking her right in, from her scruffy trainers to the crumpled material of her dress. *I'm not a virgin any more*, Ellie thought as his eyes travelled up to her face. *Can you tell? Do I look different?*

He said, 'I've spent hours looking for you. Your mother's been distraught.'

'I'm sorry.'

'Your brother's up in his room, convinced he's going to jail. Do you want to explain that one to me?'

The way her father spoke so quietly was terrifying. Ellie felt tears swelling her throat.

'Do you want to let your daughter inside before you start interrogating her?' Mum put an arm round Ellie and clutched her hard. 'She's shivering out here in the cold. Why don't you go and put the kettle on or something?'

Her dad looked confused, as if Mum had suggested something so unusual and particular that it made no sense. Then he said, 'Yes, of course.'

'You could make some sandwiches as well. I expect Ellie's hungry, aren't you?'

It was wonderful having her mother suddenly fierce, as if new ways of being were possible.

'Does Dad know everything?' she asked as Mum led her up the steps. 'Does he know I spoke to you? Does he know Karyn's telling the truth?'

'Hush,' Mum said. 'It's not time for that now. Just come and listen to what he has to say.'

She led Ellie up the steps and into the house, sat her down at the kitchen table and got her a blanket, before going off to tell Tom his sister was home. Dad made hot chocolate and scattered biscuits on a plate. He put some bread in the toaster, then leaned against the sink and folded his arms.

He said, 'You can't have been in the cinema all this time.'

Ellie looked at her hands on her lap. 'Well, a few of the shops in town were open, so I looked round them for a while.'

'That doesn't take ten hours.'

'And I had to wait ages for the bus.'

'Were you on your own?'

She nodded, terrified he'd sussed her. Maybe she smelled different, maybe there was some way fathers knew when their daughters had been touched by a boy for the first time.

He frowned, turned back to his toast. 'You can't go trotting about assuming the world is a safe place to be. Anything could have happened to you.'

'I'm sorry.'

Mum came in with slippers and insisted Ellie take off her wet trainers. Tom sidled in behind her and stood in the doorway watching. His hair was messed up and his eyes were red, as if he'd been crying. Tom never cried, not ever, not when he broke his ankle, not even when he got arrested. Ellie could barely bring herself to look at him.

'Where did you go?' he said.

'Just walking.'

'All day?'

'Sort of.'

He slumped himself into the armchair in the corner. 'I told them you'd be fine. I knew you would be.'

'Well, I wasn't as confident,' Mum said. 'I was thinking all kinds of terrible things.'

Dad slapped down a plate of toast. 'Right, now we've established the runaway is safe, let's get down to business. Eleanor – apologize to your brother.'

'She doesn't have to,' Tom said, 'it's fine.'

'She absolutely does have to.' Dad sat down opposite Ellie and glared at her. 'I can't believe you tried to wriggle out of being a witness. Do you know how serious this is? Do you know the trouble you've caused?'

'I wasn't trying to wriggle out of it.'

'Your mother asks Barry to reassure you about procedure and you find it necessary to tell him you can't possibly stand up in court and say a few words in your brother's defence?'

Ellie shook her head, eyes stinging. 'It wasn't like that.'

Dad banged the table with the flat of his hand. 'After you spoke to him, that damned lawyer locked himself away with Tom for nearly an hour. I wasn't allowed into my own study, and when they came out, it had been decided not to use you as a witness.

What was the word he used, Tom? What was it he said to you?'

'He said she was wavering.'

'*Wavering*, that's it. What's that mean, Ellie? You're a bit nervous? You can't be bothered? Going to court doesn't fit in with your busy schedule?'

Ellie shot a look at Tom, over in the corner on the armchair, his legs folded under him. He looked petrified, his eyes liquid dark.

'It's difficult to explain.'

'Difficult? I'll tell you what's difficult, my girl – sitting here watching you let your brother down, that's what.' He banged the table again and all the cups shivered. 'I can't believe you're being such a coward. Where's the girl I used to know?'

'Maybe you don't know me, Dad. Maybe none of us knows each other.'

Dad stabbed his finger at her across the table. 'I've taken weeks off work. Tom's given up all hope of doing his A-levels this year. Your mother's hardly sleeping at night, worrying herself thin. I can't remember the last time any of us had a social life. And you casually tell the lawyer you don't fancy going to court very much, and we're all supposed to nod our heads and let you get away with it?'

Ellie closed her eyes to shut him out and let him rant. He told her how selfish she was, and how he was going to ground her. He didn't believe she'd been alone all day and was going to take her phone away. She was obviously being influenced by a bad crowd, he told her, because she was turning into a liar.

It was only half an hour ago that she and Mikey had run from the bus stop. The grass had rippled silver in the dark and there was rain in the air again, clouds low and broody. At the gate, Mikey's fingers had secretly swept hers.

'Give me something for courage,' she'd said. 'A piece of you to take with me.'

'What do you want?'

'What can I have?'

He'd given her his lighter, then kissed her and walked away backwards up the lane. Watching him, Ellie had been amazed at what she'd done, at who she'd become.

Then the door opened and her mum had come running down the steps. And here she was, a child again, disintegrating under her father's anger, everything strong and good about her sliding away.

'That's enough,' her mother said. 'You're upsetting her, can't you see?'

She reached across the table and cupped Ellie's chin in her hand. It was weird, like she was about to kiss her. Ellie opened her eyes, tears falling freely. How weary her mother looked.

'We want to help you,' she said. 'It all makes sense now – the business with the vodka and how quiet you've been. It's not too late and you're not in trouble. Dad's upset, that's all. We had no idea you were feeling this scared about court.'

Ellie felt ice cold. She'd told her mother she doubted Tom, hadn't she? She'd gone into the garden and said she remembered new things. She said Karyn was telling the truth. Why was that conversation being ignored?

Her mum went on, 'Listen to Dad – he's going to explain how

we're going to handle this. He's got a plan to help you. Everything's going to be all right.'

Her father leaned forward. 'We're going to start again, Ellie, and this time involve you completely. The trial isn't for ten weeks, so we've got plenty of time. First thing tomorrow morning, we're going to sack Barry. In fact, we'll sack the barrister too – let's go the whole hog.'

Ellie blinked, puzzled. 'Why would you do that?'

'You told Barry you didn't want to be a witness and if a hint of that gets out to the police, it looks pretty suspicious, doesn't it? They're going to think you know something you're not saying. You want to be hauled into court for cross-examination? No, I thought not. So, we'll get a new law firm involved and start from the top, pretend none of this conversation with Barry ever happened.'

Ellie looked at the tablecloth. This was the table where only a few hours ago they'd sat and had breakfast together as a family. There was the chopping board where her mother had cut thick slices of bread for toast. This morning. Before any of this happened.

She'd been convinced she was at the hot start of her family's destruction, that she'd grassed up Tom and betrayed them all. But it turned out Tom hadn't passed on the details to their parents. If Barry was sacked, it would all be covered up. Ellie was a scared little girl. Tom was innocent. Simple.

Her father was smiling at her now, holding her hand across the table. He used to hold her hand when they walked to the park together every Saturday. And when she got scared in movies. And when he read her books at bedtime. He'd sit by her bed and do all the voices and he wouldn't let go of her hand until she was asleep. Sometimes he used to draw cartoons of the characters and prop them by her alarm clock, so she'd find them in the morning.

His hand was warm now, and as he leaned in to stroke her cheek, he smelled so familiar.

'I'm on your side,' he said. 'We're all on the same side – Team Parker, eh?'

She nodded, tears spilling freely. 'I'm sorry.'

He stroked her hair. 'That's better.'

He said soft and wonderful things like how much he cared about her and how brave she was and how sorry he was not to have realized the pressure she'd been under. He asked for her phone and smiled as she handed it over. He'd hide it away, he said, because he wanted to protect her from herself. He told her everything was going to be all right now and she could go to bed and forget about today. Tomorrow would be a new start.

'We'll practise, Ellie – all the answers to questions you might be asked in court. When you get in from school, after you've done your homework, we'll go over it. Or we'll get up early and rehearse before breakfast, whatever suits you best. We'll think about clothes too, get you an outfit you feel comfortable in and some shoes as well. By the time the court date comes around, you're going to feel so confident that today will seem like a distant memory.'

She sipped her hot chocolate and listened to him. Mum and Tom joined in discussing the plan, full of ideas, their voices knitting together. Outside, rain battered softly against the windows. She thought briefly of Mikey, wondered if he was home yet, if he was safe, but then she pushed the thought of him away.

Everyone was smiling at her now. The blanket was soft around her shoulders, her knees curled warm beneath it, her slippered feet pulled up onto the chair. She was a little girl again, their little girl.

She must have a shower before bed. She'd use plenty of soap. She'd wash her hair, brush her teeth, rinse with mouthwash and use floss. She'd bury Mikey's lighter in the garden first thing in the morning. She'd get rid of all the evidence.

Thirty-six

Mikey knew something was wrong as soon as he walked into the lounge. Jacko was sitting in the armchair with a fag and a cup of tea, and Jacko was never there, not without Mikey. Karyn and Mum were huddled together on the sofa opposite, and all three of them looked up at Mikey as if the world had just ended and it was all his fault.

'What?' he said. 'What did I do?'

Karyn did a fake laugh. 'Like you don't know.'

Mum said, 'Let me handle this. I thought we agreed.'

Mikey clocked the wine glass on the table in front of her, the ashtray tipping with fag ends. He perched on the arm of Jacko's chair and waited. Something big was happening – his mum never took charge when she'd been drinking.

She glared at him. 'Why didn't you go to work?'

'Is that what this is about? Did I get sacked?'

'I hope so,' Karyn spat.

Mum put a hand on her arm. 'Where have you been all day, Mikey?'

'Different places. Out and about.'

'Who with?'

'Does it matter?' He turned to Jacko. 'What is this?'

Jacko shrugged, looked down at his feet.

'Will someone tell me what's going on?'

'I'll tell you,' Karyn said. 'You've got yourself a posh little girl-friend, that's what. Jacko's been filling us in.'

A pulse banged in Mikey's head. 'What are you talking about?'

'I'm talking about your latest shag – Ellie Parker.'

Like her name was a cheap thing and sleeping with her meant nothing. Like special things could be chucked out like that.

'Shut up, Karyn.'

'So it *is* true.' She shot out of her seat and flung herself at him. 'How could you? With her!'

She thumped him on the arm again and again. He had to grab her wrists to stop her, had to push her back to the sofa and shove her down.

His mother's face darkened with fury. 'Don't you dare lay a finger on your sister, Mikey.'

'Then tell her to shut up. She doesn't know what she's talking about.'

'You stupid boy!' Mum waved her hands at him as if to say, *We all know you're guilty and I don't want to hear any more about it.*

Karyn started to wail. 'How could he? He doesn't care about me at all.' Her whole face turned to tears right in front of their eyes.

Mum clutched her, whispered into her hair. 'Karyn, love, you're making me cry now. Let's find out exactly what happened before we go getting so upset.'

Mikey kicked Jacko's foot and made him look at him. For a second they were alone in a room with a couple of hysterical women and they both understood it was harsh and desperate.

'See what you've done?' Mikey said.

A look crossed Jacko's face, like maybe he was sorry. 'I didn't have a choice.'

'Bullshit.'

'I wouldn't've been the only one who saw you on that bus, Mikey. What if some random kid texted Karyn about it? Someone had to tell her properly.'

'And that was you, was it?' Mikey grabbed him by his jacket and hauled him out of the chair. 'This is my flat, do you want to get out of my flat?'

'Leave him alone,' Mum yelled.

'I don't want him here!' He jostled Jacko towards the door, heard a satisfying rip as the material of his jacket shredded under his fingers. 'Get out. Go on, get out.'

'I said *leave him alone*!' Mum roared. She stood in the middle of the lounge, hands on hips. She was swaying slightly, but she sounded like she meant business. 'Take your hands off Jacko, sit down and shut up, Mikey, because I swear if you wake Holly up and she gets brought into this, I will never forgive you.'

By the look on her face, she wasn't going to forgive him

309

anyway, but he sat down in Jacko's empty chair. At least the bastard would have to stand up.

'Jacko's our guest,' Mum said. 'He's been sitting here with us for two hours waiting for you.'

'Three,' Jacko said, 'actually.'

'Sorry,' Mum said. 'You've been good to us, Jacko. I can't thank you enough.'

'Yeah, what a great guy,' Mikey said brightly. 'Always there when you need him.'

'That's enough,' Mum said. 'At least he was thinking about Karyn in all this, which is more than I can say for you.' She looked at him like he was a total let-down and she'd been expecting this moment all her life. 'Couldn't you have kept it in your pants for once?'

What was he supposed to say to that? Shame flooded his face and there was nowhere to look except down at his feet.

'Jacko,' Mum said, 'any chance you could stick the kettle on and make Karyn some more tea?'

He nodded, went straight to the kitchen. What a suck-up. Mum poured herself another wine, emptied the bottle out and still only got half a glass. She frowned as if she couldn't believe she'd finished the lot, then knocked it back in two great gulps.

'Should you be doing that?' Mikey said.

Karyn made a face like she wanted to hit him again. 'You're such a tosser.'

'I'm only asking. Did you drink that whole bottle tonight, Mum?'

'Actually,' Mum said, 'you don't get to ask me questions. You're the one in the hot seat, not me.' She plonked her glass down. 'Now tell me about this girl. I want to know exactly what you think you're playing at.'

She folded her arms, waiting for an answer. Karyn leaned back on the sofa and looked at him too. Even Jacko stopped clattering tea things in the kitchen to listen. But there was nothing Mikey could say that would make them feel better. They'd want details, like when and where, and all he could think of was Ellie's smile, her shyness, how many crazy things she knew, and the fact that she was so good at listening that when words came out of his mouth, they made sense. And the smell of her – he'd never met anyone who smelled so entirely of themselves, even her clothes just smelled clean, not of some crappy washing powder or perfume.

'Come on,' Mum said. 'Get on with it.'

He shrugged. 'I've got nothing to say.'

'Well, I better fill everyone in then,' Karyn said. 'She's an ugly nerd.'

Mikey shook his head. 'You don't know even know her.'

'I know she's a nerd.'

'Oh for God's sake!' Mum said.

She passed her fags round, like that would calm them down. The tea came in. Mikey enjoyed the silence while it lasted.

Karyn was first to break it. 'Nice tea, Jacko, thanks.'

Mikey thought he was going to throw up, didn't even bother moving his feet when Jacko tried to find space to sit on the rug.

'So,' Mum said, 'how long's it been going on?'

'Yeah,' Karyn cut in, 'when did she first get her claws into you?'

'Don't talk about her like that.'

'I'll talk about her however I want.'

'She's not like him, she's different from the rest of her family.'

'Oh, is that right? What's so special about her then? She's not even pretty.'

'Shut up, will you?'

'No. You always think you know best, but you're wrong about this.' Karyn was almost shrieking. 'Ellie Parker's just like her brother and they're both liars.'

'She's not a liar.'

'She was in the house when it happened!'

'That doesn't make her a liar.'

'Listen to yourself, Mikey – whose side are you on?'

Fury boiled in him again. He stood up, fists curled. 'She's not even going to be a witness for her brother any more because she thinks he did it, so shut up about her, OK?'

There was a terrible silence. Nothing happened for ages. Then Karyn said very softly, 'She told you that?'

He nodded, and for a minute she watched his face as if she was trying to work something out, then she said, 'She's known for weeks and weeks and she's kept quiet all this time?'

Mikey took a last deep drag on his cigarette before stubbing it out. He needed something to get him out of this. Ellie hadn't told him not to tell Karyn, but now he saw the effect it was having on her, he wished he'd kept his mouth shut. Even his mum thought it was nuclear by the frown on her face. He needed a distraction, something that would change the whole vibe.

'Listen,' he said. 'Why don't I pop down the off-licence and get some more booze? I've got cash.' He patted his pocket to prove it. 'Do you fancy some more of that wine, Mum?'

It was a cheap trick and he knew it as soon as his mother scowled at him. She stood up suddenly. 'I'm calling Gillian.'

'What the hell for?'

'Because if this girl says her brother did it, she needs to know.'

Mikey absolutely hadn't thought of this possibility. If the cops got involved, Ellie would think he'd got the information out of her and passed it on on purpose. She'd never trust him again.

'It's the middle of the night,' he said, his mind racing. 'It's Sunday. You'll piss Gillian off if you call her now. I might have remembered it wrong anyway. I probably muddled it somehow. Let me talk to Ellie. Serious, let me talk to her first.' He went to the door. 'I'll call her now and find out exactly what she meant.'

'Don't you dare,' Karyn said. 'She lied in her witness statement, which means she's in big trouble. If you warn her, she'll change her story again.' She turned to Mum, her eyes glittering. 'Go on, phone Gillian.'

'No,' Mikey said, 'it'll make everything worse.'

Karyn flashed him a look of total hatred. 'It can't get any worse.'

'If her family freak out, it can. Let me call her and find out what's going on.'

'No.' Karyn leaped up and caught his arm. 'I want the police to go round her house and I hope it freaks them out and I hope they arrest her and she rots in jail with her brother.' Her fingers dug in like she was never letting go. 'You owe me.'

She went for it then. It was like all the rage of the last few weeks got chucked at him. Dry-eyed and fierce, she told him how he secretly blamed her for what had happened and she'd always known it, how selfish he'd been to fight Tom, how everything he did was about making himself feel better and never about her. He caved under it. He knew he should try and stay angry, but he couldn't. It fell out of him and he stood there weak and useless and not knowing anything. Listening to her, it sounded like he'd got every single thing wrong.

'Do you know what Gillian told me?' she hissed. 'She told me it's *not my fault*. She said I should be able to wear a short skirt whenever I like. She said I should be able to go to a party in my bloody bikini if I want. I should be able to dance and drink and stay up late. I should even be allowed to snog the face off Tom Parker and it doesn't mean he can do what he did.' She squeezed Mikey's arm harder, quivering with rage. 'Any time I tried to talk to you about that night, you never listened. As long as you managed to punch him on the nose, the truth didn't matter. But it's *all* that matters to me, can't you see?'

Mum shushed them then, because Holly was standing in the doorway, shivering in her pyjamas. 'Why are you fighting?'

'It's nothing,' Mum said. 'They're mucking about.'

'I heard shouting.'

'You were dreaming.'

Karyn let go of his arm and he stood there rubbing it as his mum put her phone back in her pocket and went over to Holly. She picked her up and held her, planting kisses on her hair. It was like some ancient memory of his mother, someone he hadn't seen for years.

'I'm here,' Mum said. 'Hush now, don't cry.'

They all watched, him and Karyn breathing hard like they'd been running, both of them stuck there in the middle of the lounge.

'Come on,' Mum said. 'Let's get you back to bed, sweetheart.'

Holly looked surprised. 'Are you taking me?'

'Sure, why not?'

'Can we watch TV in your room?'

'No, you've got school tomorrow.'

'Will you tell me a story?'

'No, babe, it's sleep time.'

Holly stuck her thumb in her mouth and snuggled in, hoping for a carry all the way up the stairs. Mikey could barely watch. It was usually him who took Holly upstairs when she woke up – he'd lie on the bed with her, listen to her chatter on about nothing and then watch as she slowly drifted off to sleep.

'I'll be back,' Mum said. 'Nobody go anywhere.'

The three of them were left in silence. Jacko got out his tobacco. Karyn sat down on the sofa. Mikey stood there rubbing his arm.

'I didn't mean to hurt you,' he said.

315

Karyn scowled at him. 'Don't even try and tell me that you didn't think I'd mind.'

'That's not what I'm saying.'

'What are you saying then?'

'That I didn't mean to like her, it just happened. She's a very nice person. You'd probably like her if you got to know her.'

'Ah, Mikey.' Jacko shook his head.

'What?'

'You never know when to stop, do you?'

Jacko strapped a rollie together. Karyn offered to make him a fresh tea to go with it. Mikey took the chance to go to the bathroom. He'd lock himself in and wait for things to get better. He didn't want to be alone with those two when they were being so weird.

He had a piss, then sat on the toilet seat to think. How had this happened? Earlier, when he'd dropped Ellie off, he'd thought nothing could mess with his high. And now it was ruined.

He phoned her from the bathroom, but her phone was off, so he left a message. *Call me*, he said. *It's really important.*

His mum was there when he came out, leaning against the bedroom door, waiting for him.

She said, 'Holly's asleep. Are you coming back down?'

'I'm going to bed.'

'Shouldn't we sort this out?'

She was less certain, the wine finally slowing her down. With a nudge from him, she'd go to bed and forget all about it.

He said, 'Let's leave it till tomorrow, eh?'

'What about Gillian?'

'You can't phone her now, it's late.'

She sighed, pulled out her cigarettes and offered him one. He opened the landing window and they stood there looking down at the courtyard, blowing smoke out into the dark. It had started raining again and it smelled fresh and cold out there. A baby was crying, a dog was sniffing about on the grass. A bloke, hands in pockets, whistled for it and together they went through the doors of the opposite block.

In a minute he'd try Ellie again, and if her phone was still off, he'd leave another message asking to meet tomorrow. Then, in the morning, all the normal routines would kick in – he'd get up, take Holly to school and go to work. Mum would sleep off the booze, Karyn would stop being mad at him, and when he explained to Ellie what had happened, she'd agree to come round to the flat and meet them. They'd like her. They'd drink tea together and decide what to do next.

His mum was yawning now, leaning against the window looking exhausted. She smiled wearily at him. 'I think someone finally stole your heart, didn't they, Mikey?'

He rolled his eyes. 'Go to bed, Mum.'

'I always said you weren't as tough as you made out.'

'Serious, go to bed.'

She leaned in and kissed him goodnight. 'It'll all be clear in the morning, won't it?'

'It'll be fine.'

'I've got a daughter down there who needs me, and I want to do the right thing for once.'

317

'Sleep on it. We'll talk tomorrow.'

She nodded, walked away across the landing. At her bedroom door she turned and looked at him very seriously. 'I want to be a good mum.'

'Don't worry about it.'

She laughed. 'I do though, that's the trouble.'

Thirty-seven

Mikey held the fish by the head and scraped the scales away with the edge of a spoon. 'From the tail towards the gills,' Dex said. 'Keep your strokes short and quick and work carefully around the fins – they're sharp.'

Mikey was only half listening. Most of his attention was on his phone, which he'd stuck in his jeans pocket on vibrate. He'd left three messages with his mum already and she hadn't returned any of them; he'd left at least ten with Ellie and she hadn't got back to him either. He didn't know whether to be relieved, or worried. No news was good news and all that, but if Mum woke up early and decided to ring Gillian, then anything could happen, and here he was, stuck at work.

He washed the fish under the tap, then gave it to Dex, who turned it belly up on the chopping board and slit it with a knife from its tail towards its head. Then it was blood and guts all over the place as Dex spread the fish open with his fingers and dragged the entrails out. They were bulbous and glistening as he flung them into the open bin, strangely pastel-coloured too – cream, yellow and pink, like something that belonged to summer. Dex washed the fish again, scooping his thumb up and down its insides, getting rid of the blood along its ribs and backbone and nudging off the last of the scales.

'We'll keep the head,' he said. 'Some fish you cut off behind the gills, but not this one.'

The fish looked up at them coldly as Dex explained how its eyes should be bright and round, not dehydrated or sunken. Mikey half expected it to blink, or to open its mouth and complain about having all its insides showing and nowhere to hide. Dex slapped it on the draining board and picked up the next one from a bucket at their feet.

'These aren't for the pub,' he said, 'but for me and Sue later – a little peace offering from you, Mikey. Tell her you thought of it all by yourself and tell her you're sorry.' He winked at Mikey as he handed it over. 'Here you are, keep going.'

Mikey held it at the bottom of the sink and scraped away with the spoon, the water numbing his fingers. Dex stood at his shoulder, encouraging him, explaining how a bit of thyme, a bay leaf, some lemon and salt could turn the fish into a meal. It reminded Mikey of the time he'd dug up potatoes at primary school – his surprise at discovering chips came from the ground and were once covered in dirt. Here he was, all these years later, his fingers sticky with fish scales, still learning about food.

'Is there anything you don't know, Dex?'

'Not much.'

They grinned at each other and Mikey wondered what it would

be like to have Dex as a dad – someone to be on your side, someone to show you stuff and advise you when you didn't have a clue. He wouldn't want Sue as a mum though. Here she was again, slamming into the kitchen – second time this morning and still furious.

'What are you doing in here?' she snapped, pointing a finger at Mikey.

'Gutting fish.'

'When I've got toilets that need cleaning and a bar about to open?'

'My fault,' Dex said. 'The lad wanted to prepare a feast for you, Sue, to show you how sorry he is.'

She scowled at them both, as if it was bound to be a trick.

'I encouraged him,' Dex told her. 'I thought it showed good heart.'

A shadow of a smile, which she quickly covered with a frown as she turned to Mikey. 'I hope you know you're only in a job because of my husband?'

Mikey nodded.

'And you know if you muck me around again, I'll fire you?'

He nodded again and she went for it, telling him how rude and ungrateful he was, how the previous day had been their busiest of the season and she'd had to turn customers away at the door because he hadn't bothered showing up. She asked him why he couldn't be more like Jacko, who was always reliable and cheerful and who, incidentally, had been given the morning off for good behaviour.

321

'Maybe there's a lesson for you in there, Mikey,' she said.

It struck him that Sue was the third person to shout at him in less than twelve hours and he probably should be getting used to it by now, but he wasn't. All the yelling seemed to be adding up to something that dragged him down.

Dex shot her a look. 'Give the boy a break, Sue. I'll send him through to you as soon as he's done here.'

She took a few paces towards him, hands on her hips. 'I don't know what you want to turn him into, Dex, but to me, he's a cleaner until he earns my respect. Now get rid of that fish, Mikey, and come straight out to the bar. I've got a floor that needs mopping after you've done the toilets.'

When she'd gone, there was silence. Mikey rinsed the fish under the running tap, laid it on the draining board, then washed his hands with warm water and soap. He used the scrubbing brush and took his time. Dex chopped herbs on a board. Warm mid-morning light flooded through the window and splashed the floor.

'She's angry you didn't tell her,' Dex said after a while. 'If you wanted a day off, you should have asked, that's all.'

'Something came up.'

'It always does.' Dex stopped chopping and looked at him. 'You're a clever boy, Mikey, and you could be a great chef. Don't waste your talent.'

Mikey couldn't help grinning as he dried his hands on a towel. Did Dex really believe in him that much? He wanted to please him suddenly, to make him think he was worth all the trouble.

'I'll finish the fish later if you like,' he said.

Dex looked at the fish on the draining board, the entrails in the bin, the three fish still in the bucket.

'A kind offer, but Sue has plenty to keep you busy, I think. I'll finish these off and tomorrow I'll show you how to make a stock out of the trimmings.' He patted his belly. 'I'll teach you bouillabaisse – the best French soup you ever tasted.'

They shook hands on it and Mikey had something to look forward to again, just like that.

In the toilets he called Ellie again – still no joy, and no reply from his mum either. He risked phoning Karyn, figured it'd be worth getting yelled at if he found out what was happening.

She picked up straight away. 'What do you want?'

'Just wondered how it's going?'

'Fantastic.'

She sounded like she meant it, which was worrying. 'Is Mum up?'

'Yep.'

'Can I speak to her?'

'No.'

A stab in his guts. 'Why, what's she doing?'

He strained to hear background noises, something that would tell him Mum was simply in the kitchen, stumbling about making her first coffee of the day, that Karyn was bluffing, that this would still be all right. But he heard nothing, except the sound of his sister's breathing.

'Look,' he said, 'I'm sorry for everything, OK? Just tell me what's happening.'

'Why, so you can warn your girlfriend?'

'I don't want her to be scared, that's all.'

'You think I give a toss about that?'

'She's on your side, Karyn. If you want to hate someone, hate her brother.'

'I hate them both.'

Everything tightened inside him as he pressed the phone closer, struggling to find a way to get through to her. 'Ellie wanted to believe he was innocent – that's not so weird, is it? If I did something terrible, wouldn't you help me?'

'You'd never do anything like that!'

'That's what she thought about him. He's going to hate her for grassing him up, so why do you have to make it even more difficult? Why can't you just tell me what's going on?'

It felt like minutes waiting for her to speak. Eventually she said, 'I'll get Mum to call you when Gillian's gone.'

And then she put the phone down.

Mikey rammed out of the toilets, through the bar, out of the main door and across the car park. He left Ellie a message as he walked: *Call me. Serious. Call me as soon as you get this.* He tried his mum, but she didn't pick up. He tried Karyn again. Nothing.

He should have gone over to Ellie's house after dropping Holly at school, he'd been an idiot not to. Or before school even – last night when it all kicked off. He could have climbed the gate, shinned up the drainpipe, spent the night by her side and kept her safe.

At the harbour wall he sat on a bench and tried to calm down.

OK, it was possible Karyn was winding him up and his mum was still asleep. But it was also possible that Gillian was at the flat right now, finding out all the details, organizing squad cars. Couldn't you be charged with perjury for lying to cops?

He left another message: *I'm sorry, Ellie, I'm so sorry, but I think something bad's about to happen.*

Fourth apology in twenty-four hours. He'd made such a cock-up. He'd hurt Karyn, hurt Ellie, and he hadn't meant to do either, not in a million years. He closed his eyes, tried to keep calm. If he just sat here, if he simply kept breathing, maybe it would be all right.

Thirty-eight

Good girls aren't supposed to think of a boy's velvet neck, or the tilt of his head when he smiles. They're especially not supposed to think of these things when it's their last study skills session for the non-calculator Maths exam.

Ellie blinked several times to erase all thoughts of Mikey.

'So, that's an example question,' Ms Farish said. 'Now please take up your notebooks, write down three criticisms of this method of estimation, and remember, as long as what you say is plausible and sensible, you should get the marks.'

Ellie sighed, and opened up her notebook. If she couldn't concentrate on statistics and probability, she could at least do something useful. She turned to a blank page and wrote *Revision*, then she drew a table with twelve columns and divided up the weeks until the main GCSE exams began and gave the table thirty-five rows. She'd revise for three hours every night when she got home from school. She'd eat dinner (half an hour), then she'd revise for a further two hours until bed. At weekends, she'd revise for ten hours a day and would reward herself with a DVD. She'd get seven hours' sleep a night. She tried to work out how many total hours' revision she'd given herself and how many hours' sleep she'd get, but this was a non-calculator study session and she couldn't get her head round it. Instead, at the bottom of the page she drew a green snake with a red tongue.

Beyond the classroom window, sun glittered on the playground. The edge of the playing field was just visible and the grass looked very friendly waving at her. Ellie thought of the river, just out of view. She liked the fact she couldn't see it, but that she knew its freezing sparkle would be making bright patterns on the fence.

The probability of something which is certain is one. The probability of something which is impossible is zero. Taking off her clothes and jumping into the river on that Wednesday afternoon when she should have been at school was definitely in the second category, and yet it had happened. How did mathematics explain that?

Statement: A girl and a boy jump into a river. The boy swims over to the girl and says, 'God, it's cold.'

Question: What's the probability they will kiss?'

No, she mustn't think of Mikey! She especially mustn't think of kissing him yesterday – his kisses, soft and insubstantial at first, hardly there at all, and yet enough to make her blood leap. She mustn't think of how the kisses built – becoming desperate, as if they were both searching for something.

She snapped her attention back to the classroom. Her plan was to work hard and make up for all the study sessions she'd missed, and there was no time in that regime for Mikey.

'So,' Ms Farish said, 'let's remind ourselves of different ways to represent data diagrammatically.'

Ellie wrote down, *Horizontal axis, Vertical axis*. She listened as Ms Farish described how to group data into classes. But when it came to drawing a graph, she drew a cottage instead, a fire, a boy, a zip. She wrote the words *I've never felt this with anyone before*. And bolded them, boxed them in. Wrote them again in capitals.

No one else seemed to be having trouble concentrating. She looked around at all the heads bent over tables, at all the pens feverishly scribbling. Statistically, there were kids in this room who cried themselves to sleep because of exams. They were exhausted, they had terrible headaches. They woke in the mornings feeling they'd had no sleep at all. Their eyes were itchy, their stomachs ached. These were her classmates, thirty of them, and she barely knew them at all.

What was it she'd said to her dad? *None of us knows each other*.

Question: If a room has thirty people in it, how many secrets are in the room?

Answer: Infinity.

She had a sudden and overwhelming desire to stand up and confess her own, like some kind of truth Tourette's. She'd march up to the front of the class, knock Ms Farish out of the way of the interactive whiteboard and write: *I made love with Mikey McKenzie in front of a roaring fire and I never imagined love could be so good*. Inspired by her bravery, everyone would share their secrets. Ms Farish would tell them why she left her previous school, Joseph would show them the cuts on his arms and explain his compulsion, Alicia would give her reasons for spending every lunch break in the toilets. On and on, round the whole class. Maybe she'd even get a second turn. She'd write: *My brother is guilty*. Ellie wondered if you would use a bar chart, a pie chart or a histogram to describe the data you gathered.

Outside, spring clouds bowled along, the grass continued to wave, the river flowed as it always had. She wrote a poem: *We are naked. You are tender. Your hands know exactly where to be.* She ripped it from her notebook, crumpled it into a ball and put it in her pocket. Ms Farish came over and stood at her table.

'Problems?' she said.

Ellie shook her head. Ms Farish went away. She tried aversion therapy. Every time she thought of Mikey, she pinched the soft skin on the back of her hand. Concentrating on the whiteboard now, she wrote down the words *dependent variable, independent variable* as instructed, and began to draw a graph using the data supplied. Within five minutes her hand hurt so much from pinching that she had to stop drawing. She tried to think of horrible things about Mikey, but she couldn't think of any, and in realizing there were none, she realized how much she wanted to see him again. But if she saw him, she'd have to do something about Karyn. She'd have to get a lawyer like Barry had suggested, make a new statement, get a new family to live with, because hers wouldn't want her any more.

She drew a cold shower. A shoe. A car crash. She chewed the end of her pen for a minute, then started a new list, *Being good*. It entailed revision (a lot of it), not eating anything with sugar in it, being nice to her family, dressing virtuously and not contacting Mikey. This immediately made her think of all the opposites – no revision, undressing. Calling him . . .

Yesterday, on the rug in her grandparents' cottage, she'd traced kisses along the base of Mikey's spine and told him, 'I'll always have seen you naked.'

He'd turned over to smile at her, his eyes never leaving hers as he mapped a line from her belly to her breasts. He said, 'I can feel your heart.' His fingers marked her pulse. He said, 'Now, now and now.'

How had she ever thought she'd be able to forget him?

She sank her head onto the desk. Images swam into her mind – her mum fanning herself at breakfast and saying *I can't breathe in this house*, her dad's weary smile and barely concealed irritation, the constant fear in Tom's eyes, the way her mum wouldn't meet her gaze in the car on the way to school when Ellie said, *Shouldn't we talk about what I said in the garden?*, Mikey's cigarette lighter hidden in her school bag, the knowledge of Karyn McKenzie wounded on a sofa . . .

'Ellie?' Ms Farish stood over the desk frowning. 'You all right?'

She nodded, startled. Everyone around her was gathering their stuff together and heading out of the door.

Ms Farish said, 'You can stay here if you want, Ellie, but I suggest you take the opportunity to get some fresh air and come back after lunch for part two.'

The corridors were crazy, as usual. At break time, the teachers disappeared into the staffroom for sugar and caffeine and left the kids to roam like wild buffalo. This was the time of day you were likely to get casually shoved against the lockers, to get your phone nicked, your bag rifled through, chewing gum chucked at you, your dinner money hijacked. The boys gave each other brutal and meaningless thumps. It was survival of the fittest, and the trick was to keep your head down, look no one in the eye and walk purposefully.

At least Ellie wasn't the centre of attention any more, not since Keira in Year Ten had got pregnant and the gossip machine had turned its attention to who the dad was and if Keira was keeping the baby and why hadn't she got the morning-after pill in the first place, blah, blah.

It was warm outside and quieter. Ellie walked the edge of the playground looking for somewhere to sit. Her favourite bench had been commandeered by Stacey ever since she realized it was the place Ellie liked to be. She waved at Ellie now, as she did every time she saw her.

'Hey, bitch.'

'Leave it, Stacey.'

'You leave it.'

'I'm not doing anything.'

'So you say.'

It was ridiculous that they did this every day. Maybe they'd even

miss it if one of them forgot. It was something they both understood, almost routine.

Ellie found a place to sit on the low wall by the fence and turned
her face to the sun. Vitamin D was most easily absorbed through
the eyelids and Vitamin D was the one that made you happy. She
had forty-five minutes to get there.

Thirty-nine

Mikey opened one eye to Jacko, crunching across the gravel towards him. He had his arms up, palms flat, like he was surrendering. It wasn't funny.

'I'm sorry, man,' he said when he got close. 'About last night, I mean. Serious, I didn't think it would blow up like that.'

Mikey shook his head and looked back down at the sand, at the boats marooned down there.

'I had to tell Karyn before someone else did.'

'Who are you kidding?'

'It's true. When I came to pick you up and saw you get on that bus, I knew I wouldn't be the only one who clocked it. Imagine if some random stranger told her. Imagine how that would feel.'

Mikey glared at him. 'I haven't got time for this.' He scrolled through the texts on his phone. Maybe he'd missed something from Ellie or Mum earlier. Nothing. He checked his voicemail. No new messages.

Jacko sat next to him on the bench. 'Any news?'

'Like you care.'

'I do, actually.'

Down on the beach, a little kid was running with a kite snapping on the end of a bit of string. Funny how when life was that simple, you never realized how lucky you were.

Jacko nudged Mikey's foot with his. 'So, is this an official break you're having out here?'

Mikey shuffled away, opened his phone again, texted Karyn, *Hurry up.*

Jacko said, 'Listen, man. I know this is none of my business, but I don't think you should push it with Sue. She went nuts yesterday when you didn't come in. You want to keep your job, don't you?'

Mikey texted Mum, *Call me NOW.*

Jacko sighed. 'Maybe one day we'll look back at this and laugh.'

'I doubt it.'

'You never know.'

Mikey pretended to think about that. 'No, Jacko, I really don't think that's going to happen. You know why? Because when this kicks off, Ellie's never going to speak to me again.'

'Two months ago you never knew her and she didn't speak to you anyway.'

Mikey sank his head into his hands, dizzy with how far away he and Jacko were from each other.

'Blame me if you like,' Jacko said. 'I don't mind.'

'Yeah, maybe I'll do that.'

The trill of his phone made them both start. His fingers

were clumsy. He scowled at Jacko. 'Do you mind? This is private.'

Jacko shrugged, moved away to the end of the bench and pretended not to listen. Mikey sat on the harbour wall and looked down at the boats.

'Mum?' he said. 'What's happening?'

'I can't speak for long, Mikey, we're right in the middle of things here.' She sounded sober, wide awake, oddly calm.

'You called Gillian then?'

'I wasn't going to sit around waiting to see what happened next.'

'Yeah, well, thanks for that.'

'I've got a daughter here who needs me, Mikey. I told you that last night.'

I need you too, he thought, but he didn't say it out loud. He'd brought this on himself and now he had to take it.

'So, what's the news?'

'Gillian said it's good we told her, and she phoned the detectives in charge of Karyn's case and let them know.'

'And what did they say?'

'They're going to go round and pick your friend up.'

A pulse banged in Mikey's head. 'Round where?'

'I don't know – her house, I suppose.'

'She won't be there, she'll be at school.'

'Well then, I expect they'll go there.'

'You can't send cops round the school!'

'For goodness' sake, Mikey, they only want to talk to her. It won't hurt her to tell the truth, will it?'

He cut her off, didn't want to hear any more. He turned to Jacko. 'I need the car.'

'No way.'

'You owe me.'

'I don't.'

'Come on, man, you heard that. You've got to help.'

Jacko got out his tobacco and strapped a rollie together, slowly, deliberately, as if time was something there was a lot of. Mikey tried to hold his anger down, knew he didn't stand a chance of the car if he pushed too hard.

Jacko said, 'Why do you like her so much?'

'I don't know, I just do.'

'Very descriptive.'

Mikey kicked the wall with his foot, scuffing up sand. 'What do you want me to say?'

'I want you to say why you like her.'

Jacko seriously wanted him humiliated, that was obvious. It was going against every rule, every part of the male code. But it was worth it for the car keys.

'I can't help it, it's as simple as that. I can't do anything to stop it.' He took a breath. 'Like you can't help being addicted to your car.'

Jacko frowned. 'She's like a car?'

'No, man. She's – I dunno . . .' He ran a hand through his hair, tried to think exactly what it was that Ellie did to him. It felt important to get it right. 'She shines.'

'Like a car?'

'Stop taking the piss.' He sat on the bench and looked Jacko in the eye. 'When I was growing up, I had this fantasy of a perfect girl. She never really had a face, but she had a great body and she liked everything about me.' He felt himself flush, but knew it was important to carry on. 'When I first saw Ellie, I knew it was her – she was my fantasy. I didn't want it to be true, but every time I met her it was obvious, and the funny thing was that she was better than the fantasy, like I got more stuff than I'd imagined.'

Jacko blew smoke out in a long thin line towards the harbour. 'Like what?'

He listed them on his fingers. 'She makes me laugh, she knows stuff, she listens. She surprises me, you know – like, she can be calm one minute, then totally out there the next? What else? She's drop-dead gorgeous, she's a mystery. I dunno, man, this sounds like bollocks.'

Jacko's eyes softened slightly, and Mikey dared to carry on.

'I thought I could keep away from her, but I couldn't. Whenever I wasn't with her, I'd think about her. I tried fancying other girls, and couldn't. I mean, I'd literally walk down the street and try and imagine other girls naked and it didn't do it for me, I didn't want them. And when I thought Ellie set me up for a kicking and when I didn't see her for ages and thought she didn't care, I went nuts. I didn't want to get up, or go to work or anything, and I'm sorry about that, mate, I can see how crap it was for you, but I was terrified I'd never see her again. I like her that much.'

There, he'd said it out loud and Jacko could think what he

337

wanted. But instead of yelling at him, or taking the piss, Jacko grinned. 'Thank God for that.'

'What?'

'That's the first time you've told me the truth in weeks.' He reached into his pocket and pulled out the car keys. 'Here. Don't scratch it and don't say I never do anything for you.' Their fingers touched; Jacko didn't let go of the keys. 'I'm here for you, man. I've always been here for you, it's just you stopped knowing it.'

Mikey threw an arm round him and gave him a thump on the back. It was exactly the right thing to do, he could tell by Jacko's smile. 'Tell Dex I'm sorry.'

'You're going to have to do that yourself.' Jacko nodded towards the entrance to the car park, where Dex was striding over. He looked weird outside, with his apron flapping in the wind.

'You need to come back inside,' he called. 'Both of you, now. Sue's on the warpath.'

Mikey couldn't look at him as he got close. He took off his own apron and passed it to Jacko, put the keys in his pocket.

'The car's round the back,' Jacko said, 'in the yard.'

Dex put his hands on his hips. The disappointment in his eyes was horrible. 'Where are you going, Mikey?'

'I'm really sorry.'

'If you leave again, I can't help you.'

'I know.'

'It's urgent,' Jacko said. 'I'll cover for him. You won't even notice he's gone.'

338

'No,' Dex said. 'If he goes now, that's it, there's nothing I can do.'

He had a wooden spoon in his hand, some kind of paste clinging to it in a sticky lump. And, weirdly, it was the spoon that was hard to turn away from.

Forty

It was crazy, Mikey thought, the things your body could do when you didn't want it to. The heat spreading from chest to face to eyes, blood racing, the mad adrenalin surge. Even his voice became hoarse and faltering as he saw Ellie through the school fence and called her over.

She frowned at him like maybe it was a trick, then picked up her bag and walked towards him. Just looking at her hurt.

She said, 'Aren't you supposed to be at work?'

'I bunked it. I had to speak to you.'

'Is everything OK?'

'I tried calling. I sent you loads of texts.'

'My dad took my phone.' She laced her fingers through the metal loops of the fence. She looked ashamed. He hated her family for that. None of this was her fault.

'Can you get out?'

'The bell's gone and I've got a Maths revision class.'

'It's important. Just for a few minutes?'

'I don't know.' She glanced around at the kids retreating back into school, at the teacher at the gate herding stragglers in. 'I'm trying not to get into any more trouble.'

He felt suddenly knackered. All these kids walking across the playground and back into school; soon they'd be whispering about this, nudging each other, laughing at Ellie. He felt the aching sadness of that.

'Five minutes, Ellie, please. Come and sit by the river with me. Ten minutes max, I promise.'

'You're going to hate me when you know what a coward I was last night.'

'I told you yesterday, I'll never hate you.'

She smiled. 'You always make me feel better, you know that?'

She walked to the gate, and he followed along the pavement on his side of the fence. A woman walked past with a baby twisting in her arms. Somewhere a bird sang. Everyday things. There was a teacher at the entrance, 'Come on, come on,' he yelled as the last few kids made it through. 'Move yourselves, or you're going to be late.'

Mikey shivered. He hated all this – the rules, the adults bellowing, timetables and places to be. It narrowed everything down.

Ellie tried to sidle past the guy, but he stuck his arm out, blocking her way. 'Wrong direction.'

'It's important,' Ellie said. 'And my tutor said it was OK.'

He frowned down at her. 'Do you have a permission slip?'

'He forgot to give me one.'

'Then turn round, please, and go straight to class.'

Ellie folded her arms. 'There are urgent and personal reasons why I need to leave and my tutor is fully aware of them. I'm sixteen, so it's not statutory that I remain on site and I believe you may be contravening my human rights by not allowing me out.'

Mikey was stunned. She gave the guy her name and tutor group and he simply opened the gate.

'That was cool,' Mikey said as she joined him on the pavement. 'I thought you said you weren't brave?'

'I'll be in trouble later, wait and see.' She smiled at him. 'You know, however hard I try to be good, it always goes wrong.'

They threaded hands as they crossed the bridge. It was fantastic to touch her.

'I can't be long,' she said. 'Serious, I shouldn't be. I promised myself I'd revise today.'

He didn't fancy explaining why she actually wouldn't be going back, but he managed to persuade her to step over the railings and walk with him down the grassy slope to the river. It looked dark, lots of green stuff swishing about in it and trees hanging overhead. The slope was dappled with shadow and patches of sun.

'Let's sit here for a bit,' he said.

It was hidden from the school, hidden from the road. At least if the cops came, they wouldn't see her down here.

'So,' she said. 'What's happened now?'

He reached for her hand again and clasped it, like he could take care of her in a small way, even though he was about to hurt her masses.

'You're not going to like it.'

'Just tell me.'

He shook his head, couldn't believe he was about to say this, was sure the whole town took a pause – all the cars and TVs, all the people, everything still and listening. 'I told Karyn what you said yesterday about not being a witness for your brother.'

The light left Ellie's face. 'Why did you do that?'

'I'm sorry, I didn't mean to. Jacko told her we were seeing each other and she went mad and I got mad back and it just came out.'

'Oh.'

'And that's not all. I'm sorry, but she knows you lied in your police statement.'

Ellie covered her face with her hands and collapsed backwards onto the grass. 'Oh,' she said again, but quieter this time.

He wanted to touch her, to take her hands from her face and kiss her. But he didn't know if that was the right thing to do, so instead he lay down next to her and told her the whole story, from the moment he got home last night, to the moment he took the call from his mum half an hour ago. He tried to make it less dramatic, tried to find spaces in it where it didn't sound important, but when he got to the bit about the cops wanting to haul Ellie in, there was no hiding.

'They might come to the school,' he said. 'That's why I had to find you. My mum wasn't sure if they'd go to your house or come straight here.'

Ellie lay completely still, only her belly moving up and down.

He said, 'Why aren't you saying anything?'

From behind her hands she whispered, 'You tricked me after all.'

'I didn't tell Karyn on purpose!'

'You and me at the cottage – I absolutely fell for it.'

'No, Ellie, this isn't part of some plan to get information out of you. Yesterday was real. You have to believe me.'

'I *have* to?' She sat up. She looked different, harder. 'Do you know how it feels to have no one you can trust?'

'I didn't trick you.'

'So you say. Let's look at the evidence, shall we? At the beginning you got to know me on purpose, so you could find stuff out about my brother. Then, when I discovered who you were, you did your big *Oh no, you can trust me, I really like you* speech and I fell for it. I *did* tell you stuff, and as soon as you heard it, you ran to Karyn with the details. Bit suspicious, wouldn't you say?' She narrowed her eyes at him. 'You're the world's biggest trickster.'

'You're paranoid. I could just as easily say you've been tricking me.'

'What! How did I trick you? That makes no sense.'

'Maybe you *wanted* me to tell Karyn. Maybe you didn't have the guts to tell the truth to the cops yourself, and now you can tell Mummy and Daddy that the scary boy from the housing estate forced it out of you.'

'Don't be ridiculous!'

'I might be wrong.'

'Yeah, you might be!' She stood up. 'I have to go.' She took a couple of steps up the slope, then turned back to him. 'I actually thought you liked me – isn't that mad?'

'I *do* like you. Blame me if you want, tell me I'm a total tosser, but don't tell me I don't like you. I *really* like you, Ellie.'

She smiled, a small glimmer of warmth. 'Liar.'

'Truth.'

She sank to the grass. 'Are they going to arrest me?'

'I don't know. They probably just want to talk to you.'

She buried her face in her knees. He went and sat next to her, stroked her hair, wanted her to know he was sorry.

'Don't.'

'Please, Ellie.'

'No.' She pushed him away. 'I'm thinking. Leave me alone.'

Above them, the trees were beginning to do their thing. All the leaves looked like mouths about to open.

'I've got Jacko's car,' he said. 'I could drive us somewhere.'

She didn't say anything.

'We could disappear.' It was a brilliant idea. The shit would hit the fan later – with Karyn, Mum, just about everyone in fact, and Jacko would be pissed off about the car – but it would make today easier. 'We could hide out at your grandparents' place.'

'Don't be ridiculous.'

'I've got money. We can buy food, loads of it, and go and live there for a while.'

'No.'

'Think about it, Ellie – just until the worst is over.'

'Are you insane?' She took her hands away from her face. 'It isn't going to be *over*, don't you get it? Someone's family's going to be ruined – yours or mine, that's the choice. We can't run away. This is real life, Mikey!'

She sounded like she was talking to a kid, or someone stupid from another planet. He hated that.

She lay back on the grass and covered her face with her arm. He got out his tobacco, made a rollie and lay next to her. They were quiet for ages. He wondered if she was coming up with some clever plan, or maybe she was considering the running-away idea. It'd be good holing up in that cottage. They could stay there for weeks, making fires, talking, touching.

When he'd finished smoking, he nudged her with his elbow, very gently. 'How you doing?'

'My bones hurt.'

'I'm sorry.'

'And everything's gone very bright and light, like I'm floating.'

'Maybe you're in shock.'

He leaned over and kissed her neck.

'Don't,' she said.

'Don't what?'

'Don't do that.'

'Why not?'

'Because we only met six times and now it's over.'

'Seven, and it's not over.'

She looked at him desperately. 'I don't want it to end.'

'Neither do I.' He took her hand. 'I'm sorry I told Karyn. I completely fucked up. But it doesn't have to end.'

She blinked at him. 'I think it does.'

He leaned over and kissed the tip of her nose. Very softly. Three times. She didn't stop him. He rolled her onto him and held her there. She gave him her weight, tucked her chin into his neck, so they were warm and tangled. It was sunny, maybe the warmest day of the year so far. Shadows lengthened across the grass as Monday lunchtime turned into Monday afternoon.

'What will they do to me?' she said eventually.

'Talk to you, that's all.'

'Where?'

'At the police station.'

'What will I tell them?'

'The truth.'

'I want to speak to my mum.' She rolled off, picked up her coat and bag. 'My dad won't be home from work yet.'

'I'll take you.'

'No, I'll walk. I need time to get used to the idea.'

'Ellie, you don't have to do this by yourself.'

She smiled wearily at him. 'Go back to work, Mikey, I don't want you to lose your job as well. I'll walk along the river, so no one sees me. Don't worry, I can follow it all the way home.'

He walked with her down to the path. It was cooler closer to the water. There were some ducks. A swan curved its neck down to feed. They stopped to watch.

After a few moments, Ellie took a breath and turned to him. 'Can I have a hug goodbye?'

He held out his arms and she gave him a strange half-hug. It was clumsy and sad and not what he thought was going to happen at all.

'I'm going,' she said, 'before I change my mind.'

He looked for fear in her eyes, but it seemed to have gone, replaced by a strange calm.

Forty-one

Ellie walked up from the river, through the gate and across the lawn. Her mum was kneeling on a bit of old blanket, pushing a trowel into the flowerbeds.

Tell her, tell her, you have to tell her.

She sat back on her heels when she saw Ellie. 'You're home early.' She wiped the sweat away from her forehead with her sleeve. Her gloves were all muddy and she had bits of leaf in her hair. 'Or have I lost track of time? I've been out here most of the day and it's been fantastic. Feels like summer now, wouldn't you say? Look at all these green shoots thrusting up.'

Ellie feigned interest, because this would please her mum, because it would delay things, because words were hard to find.

'Those are tulips,' Mum said, smiling, 'and those pink ones are bergenia.'

Ellie squatted on the grass. 'I need to speak to you.'

'You'll get wet sitting there.'

'It doesn't matter.'

'How was school? Was it OK?'

'It was fine. I had Maths revision.'

'Poor baby. I don't envy you that.'

She turned back to her digging. 'I've been tying things back and weeding. Look, I even planted some bulbs.'

When breaking bad news you're supposed to ask the victim to sit down so they don't bang their head when they collapse. You're supposed to provide sweet tea, a blanket and a cool hand on the forehead. But what do you do when the person refuses to listen?

'Mum, where's Tom?'

'Up in his room, I expect.'

'And Dad?'

'Norwich, trying to find a new law firm.'

Ellie took a breath. 'So, did you hear me? Can I talk to you?'

'I heard.'

But she didn't stop digging. How easy just to listen to the sharp clang of the trowel hitting stone and to watch as a soft pile of mud and weeds landed neatly in the bucket. How easy to go indoors and get some milk, eat a biscuit, watch TV.

'Can we go and sit on the bench?'

Mum frowned, pulled her coat firmly across her chest. 'Is this about yesterday?'

'Yes.'

'Can it wait until Dad gets home?'

'Not really.'

Her mum refused the bench, sat instead on the swing behind the walnut tree. Strange to see her there, like a girl, with her feet tucked under. Ellie sat on the grass and watched her pull on the ropes and lean back, her hair flying.

'I used to love swinging when I was a child,' Mum said. 'Nothing could make me dizzy.'

Ellie was aware her mouth was very dry, like she'd walked through a sandstorm. 'I've got something important to tell you.'

'I think people lose something to do with simple happiness when they grow up,' Mum said.

'Please, Mum, listen. I have to go to the police station.'

Mum scraped her feet along the ground to bring her to a stop. 'What are you talking about?'

'I'm going to make a new statement.'

'You've made a statement.'

'It was a lie.'

Mum shook her head very slowly. 'I'm calling your father.'

'Please don't.'

'You're not talking to anyone until you've spoken to him.'

'I am. The police are coming for me.'

'Coming for you? They can't just turn up and pluck little girls from their homes.'

The storm had come. It was right here, right now, and there was nothing to be done but face it. Ellie felt strangely calm, as if she'd stepped outside her own body and was looking down at herself.

'Everything was confusing that night, Mum – what happened, what I saw, what I thought was true. When Tom got arrested, I didn't want to get him in trouble, so I said I didn't see anything. I thought it would all work out.'

351

Her mum strained forward on the swing. 'It will work out. Last night, we sat round the table talking about it.'

'It's too late for that – new lawyers, shoes, clothes – it's all rubbish. Listen to me, Mum, just for a minute. Please, will you do that?'

Her mother nodded, tears filling her eyes.

'I told myself it was Karyn's fault – she was drunk, she's a liar, she's jealous of us because she lives on a rubbish estate, she's mad at Tom because he didn't want to go out with her – anything I could think of. I made her a monster and I don't even know her. I've only spoken to her twice.' Ellie looked across the lawn. A black-bird was tugging a worm out of a flowerbed. A shaft of sun hit the very top of the trees by the fence. 'It's been doing my head in trying to find ways to keep Tom innocent and I can't do it any more. I need to tell the truth now.'

Her mum had her hands over her mouth, struggling against it, maybe trying to come up with some new way of defending her son. Ellie understood. She'd done it herself for weeks.

'Mum?' Ellie whispered into the silence. 'I think that was a knock on the door.'

They both listened. It came again. It had an urgent insistence to it.

Mum grabbed her arm. 'Don't answer it.'

'I have to.'

'You don't have to do anything. Ignore them. They'll go away.'

Ellie doubted that. They were more likely to batter down the door or smash their way in through the windows. In her experience, the angrier people got, the worse it always was in the end.

'I'm going to answer it.'

The man and woman standing on the front lawn didn't have uniforms, or truncheons or handcuffs. They didn't even have a police car, just a plain white estate parked in the lane. They looked mildly surprised to see Ellie as she came round the side of the house and walked towards them, but covered it up with quick smiles.

'Hello there,' the woman said. 'Remember us? We met a few weeks ago. I'm Detective Thomas, and this is my colleague, Detective Bryce.'

The man gave her a cheery wave.

The woman said, 'We'd like to ask you a few more questions, Ellie. We'd like you to come to the station with us, if that's possible.'

But before she could answer, Tom opened the front door and came out onto the step. He was wearing a vest and running shorts and his hair was sticking up. 'What's going on?'

Ellie shook her head, desperate for him to go back in the house.

'What's happening, Ellie?'

But how could she say? If she even contemplated for a second what her speaking to the police meant to him, she'd falter. Maybe the woman detective knew this, because she took Ellie's elbow and steered her gently towards the gate. 'This way, please.'

'No,' Tom said. 'You can't just take her. Have you got a warrant?'

353

He came bounding down the steps, but the man blocked his path. 'Please stay out of this, sir. Your sister hasn't done anything wrong and we're not arresting her. There's nothing to worry about.'

Tom tried to get past him. It was horrible. Terror flared in his eyes. 'I want to speak to her.'

'I'm afraid I can't let you do that.'

'She's not under arrest, so you can't stop me.'

'Please, sir, you need to calm down. We'll sort it out very quickly and bring her safely back, I assure you.'

Ellie took a step towards him. 'Go back inside, Tom. I know what I'm doing.'

'What does that mean?'

She dared to look right at him. 'You know what it means.'

Tom shook his head at her. Then he bit his lip. He looked at his feet, then at the sky. Mum appeared behind him. She must've come through the French doors. She'd changed her coat, had her handbag with her.

Tom grabbed her. 'Stop her, Mum. Don't let her go with them.'

She put a hand on his arm. 'Tell Dad where we are. Tell him to come home and stay here with you.'

Tom's face opened in alarm. 'You're going with her?' He buckled, leaned against the door frame to steady himself. 'They haven't even got a warrant.'

'I'm aware of that.'

Tom watched her get her door keys from the hook. 'Dad'll go mad.'

'I'm sure he will.' She tried to give him a kiss goodbye, but he twisted away, yanked out his phone and stabbed at the numbers.

'I'm going to call him. I'm going to tell him what you're doing.'

Mum gazed at him sadly for a moment. 'I'm Ellie's mother, just like I'm yours,' she said.

And she buttoned her coat and walked down the steps.

Forty-two

'Are you absolutely sure my daughter's not entitled to a solicitor?'

Detective Thomas sighed. 'She's here voluntarily and so doesn't require legal representation. I thought I explained this in the car?' She folded her hands on the table. 'When my colleague comes back, he'll be very happy to show you to a waiting area, Mrs Parker. I wonder if you wouldn't be happier there?'

'No, I wouldn't.' Mum scooped up Ellie's hand and held it tight. That her mum dared to do this without consulting Dad was like a miracle of light in the middle of the dark. Tears of relief stung Ellie's eyes.

'Here,' Mum said, and pulled a tissue from her pocket, fluffed it out and gave it to Ellie.

Detective Bryce came back with coffee in plastic cups and some plain digestives spread out on a plate. 'How's it all going in here then? Everyone OK?'

He was the jovial one, the note-taker, the coffee-getter. 'Sugar, anyone? Milk?' He passed out the drinks, offered biscuits. Finally, he sat down, opened his laptop and switched it on.

Detective Thomas said, 'Right, I think we're ready to begin.' She handed Ellie a sheet of paper. 'This is your original statement. Could you read it through for me, please, and then we'll go through it point by point.'

Ellie knew the details off by heart. It had the date, the time Tom had arrived back from the pub and the names of the five people with him. Karyn McKenzie's name swam in and out of focus.

'Are there things that are incorrect?' Detective Thomas said. 'Or perhaps you've remembered something new?'

'Something new, yes.'

The detective nodded, as if that was perfectly understandable. 'Let's run through it then, shall we? You originally told us that your parents were away, and when your brother arrived home at eleven o'clock with five friends, you briefly said hello to them, then went straight upstairs to your bedroom. You saw nothing more until eleven-thirty, when you heard laughter coming from the garden and looked out of your window.' She picked up a sheet of paper in front of her. 'I quote from your statement here, Ellie: *They looked like they were having a good time out there, smoking and chatting. I noticed my brother and Karyn had their arms round each other. Karyn looked very relaxed.* Anything you want to add to that?'

Karyn McKenzie worked a finger around the inside of her mouth as if she was making a spell. Tom appeared hypnotized. Ellie stood at the window, stirring her own mouth and wondered about having that kind of power.

Detective Thomas looked up. 'Anything to add?'

'No,' Ellie whispered.

'OK, so about ten minutes later you went to bed and had no further contact with anyone until the morning. Is that still correct?'

'I did have contact.'

'Who with?'

'All of them, but Karyn first.'

'When was this?'

'I don't know, maybe an hour later. She came into my room.'

The detective frowned. 'Was she alone?'

'Yes. She was looking for the bathroom, she said she felt sick. I told her there was one downstairs, but she said there was someone in it, so I showed her the one across the landing and waited for her to come out.'

'You waited? Why did you do that?'

'She wasn't well. I wanted to check she was OK.'

Hot blood flushed Ellie's face, because although Karyn was drunk and slurring her words, Ellie also thought she might nick stuff. She hated it about herself now – that she could be worried about Dad's iPod on the bedside table and the cash lying around in her parents' room.

'She was in there for ages. Stacey came up looking for her, and the two of them stood on the landing, talking.'

'Where were you?'

'Back in my room. My door was open a bit, but they didn't know I was there.'

'And what did they talk about?'

'The boys mostly. Stacey said she liked Ben and Karyn liked Tom.

Stacey made some joke about the evening going well considering they'd only gone out to get chips, and Karyn said not to talk about food, or she might chuck up. Stacey asked why she was so wrecked and between them they counted Karyn's drinks. She'd had two in the pub and three more at the house. They said the boys were trying to get them drunk. Karyn said something like, *Well, it's working*. They both laughed at that.'

The detectives looked at each other. Ellie couldn't read the signs between them.

'And then what happened?'

'Tom came upstairs. He said the boys were getting lonely. Stacey went down to find Ben.'

'Karyn stayed with your brother?'

'Yes.'

'And did they talk?'

'They kissed.'

The detectives must think Ellie was a weirdo, spying on people kissing. But there weren't words to describe how she wanted a version of it for herself. She wanted to be dressed up and out of control on a Saturday night, allowed out to parties, able to find love in the dark.

'Was the kissing a mutual thing, Ellie? Did Karyn seem happy about it?'

'Yes, but they stopped when I opened my door. I told Tom I wanted to speak to him, and Karyn went downstairs. I told him Karyn was only fifteen and she was really drunk.'

'And what did he say?'

'He told me to chill out. He said Freddie had put two bottles of Dad's vodka in the punch and everyone was knocking it back like water.'

Mum slapped her hand to her mouth. Detective Bryce looked up from his notes. 'Are you all right, Mrs Parker?'

Mum looked as if she was going to be sick. Detective Bryce stood up and opened the window.

He said, 'If you want to step outside, Mrs Parker, I can show you to a waiting area. This must be very difficult for you.'

She shook her head. 'I'm not leaving.'

Ellie leaned across and took her hand again. 'I'm sorry, Mum, I'm so sorry. Don't stay, you don't have to . . .'

'I'm not going anywhere.'

Her hand was warm. It was good to keep holding it.

'OK, so let's go back a bit,' Detective Thomas said. 'You told your brother Karyn was only fifteen. Did he say anything to that?'

'No.'

'And what were his actual words about the punch, Ellie? Do you remember?'

'He said it was lethal and that Karyn had eaten all the fruit, which was the most alcoholic bit.'

'Did he seem upset or disturbed by how much vodka Freddie put in?'

'No, he was laughing.'

She wanted to tell this woman, *You don't know him – he rescued me from a dog once, he's funny and kind and helps me with homework*. She wanted to say, *He's lonely, he hasn't made*

proper friends with anyone since we moved from London. This is
so much more complicated than I can ever explain.

'Did you tell the girls the punch was that strong, Ellie?'

'I thought they knew.' Ellie's throat constricted with tears. 'I
often wish I *had* said something.'

'I'm sure you do.' The detective scoured the papers in front of
her. 'So, did you and Tom say anything else after that?'

'No. He went downstairs and I went back to my room.'

'And what happened then?'

Ellie tried desperately hard not to leave anything out. She told the
detective how she tried reading, but couldn't concentrate, tried
watching TV, but the music pumping up from the lounge was too
distracting. She said she texted Tom to turn it down, but he never
did. She came out of her room a couple of times and peered down
the stairs, but there was so much laughing and shouting that she
didn't dare go any further. She explained that after an hour or so,
when the laughter got ridiculously loud – up the stairs, outside her
door, lots of shushing and stumbling about – she finally intervened.

She opened her door a fraction and two of the boys, Freddie
and James, were carrying Karyn across the landing between them.
She was laughing, her hands clutching for the banister, the wall,
the light switch. But her laughter turned into a low moan as they
swung her round and edged her into Tom's bedroom.

Ellie opened the door wider, and there was Tom, coming up the
stairs.

'What are they doing?' she said.

'Why are you still awake?' He seemed embarrassed, was half smiling. 'Go back to bed, Ellie. They're just mucking about.'

And he followed them into his room and shut the door.

Mucking about? Uncertain now, Ellie went to find Stacey, because if she thought the boys were out of order, she'd charge up and yell at them. But Stacey was nowhere. Ellie went from room to room looking for her, but she'd gone and so had Ben, and so their going was probably permanent, which meant it was up to Ellie to decide what to do.

She went back up the stairs and put her ear to Tom's door. Total silence. Oh God, she was going to look a right prat barging in, but she eased the door open anyway, because her brother was in there – Tom Alexander Parker, who she'd grown up with for years – and surely he wouldn't let anything terrible happen?

Karyn lay on the bed, eyes closed. The three boys stood round her like surgeons and James had a stick in his hand – the one for opening the blinds – and he was lifting Karyn's skirt with it, like maybe if he did it with a stick it wouldn't count, and Tom and Freddie were taking photos with their phones.

'What are you doing?'

James whipped the stick behind his back, Tom stuffed his mobile in his pocket. Freddie aimed his phone at Ellie and said, 'Hello, gorgeous.' The light flashed in her eyes.

She turned to her brother. 'What's going on?'

He shook his head. 'Nothing, just a bit of fun.'

'She's out of her head.'

Freddie sputtered with laughter. 'You can say that again.'

'Then shouldn't you leave her alone?'

'She likes it. She was laughing just now.' Freddie gave Karyn a nudge with his knee. 'You've been egging us on all night, haven't you?'

Karyn's eyes fluttered open and she half smiled at him, before groaning and shutting her eyes again.

'Someone should take her home,' Ellie said. 'She doesn't look well.'

'But your brother likes her.' Freddie pulled a pretend sulky face. 'She was totally up for it and now she totally isn't.' He looked Ellie up and down. She was suddenly horribly aware that she was in her pyjamas. 'So, what do you suggest we do, little sister?'

'I suggest you leave her alone.'

Freddie's smile turned cold. He said, 'Hey, Tom, you going to let her ruin the party?'

And Tom came right up close and said, 'Why don't you fuck off, Ellie?' And he'd never said that to her before, not ever, and why did he have to do it now, in front of these boys?

Ellie said, 'Fuck off yourself.'

Freddie and James laughed at Tom like he couldn't control anything, and Tom, blushing and furious, grabbed Ellie by the wrist, hauled her out and shut the door. At first, she was grateful, like maybe he was saving her from something, but then he said, 'Stay out of it.'

She shook her head. 'Make them leave.'

'They will, soon they will.'

'Make them leave *now*.'

'Nothing's going to happen. They're drunk and a bit stoned, that's all. Everyone's had too much.'

But you haven't, she thought. *You're sober. Why are you sober?*

Still he didn't let go of her wrist. 'You're making a fool of yourself. Now go to bed.'

'Not until you make them leave.' She stood by the door and her heart was pounding so hard she swore he could hear it, and he had a look on his face like nothing she said or did was going to make any difference and there was only one way to get to the bit of him that would make anything change.

'I'm calling Dad,' she said. 'If you don't make them leave right now, I'm calling him and telling him about the booze and dope and everything.'

'The first time ever I bring anyone back and you humiliate me.' He squeezed her wrist tighter. 'You might not care about having no friends in this shit-hole of a town, but I bloody do.'

Still, she didn't budge. She tried to close down the part of her that cared what he thought. 'Get rid of them, Tom.'

Outside the police-station window, a motorbike roared into the gated yard. There were police cars and a riot van parked out there and a sky that stretched above, bright and tight and blue. The motorcyclist dismounted, took off his helmet and gloves and walked away.

Detective Thomas leaned forward. 'And did he get rid of them, Ellie?'

'He told them our parents were coming home and they had to

364

leave. They didn't believe him. Freddie said he had no balls and James told him he was a no-mark. All the way down the stairs, I heard Tom apologizing.'

Detective Bryce looked up from his laptop. Mum shuffled her feet, crossed and uncrossed her legs. The room felt suddenly cold.

Detective Thomas said, 'What happened then?'

'I went to bed.'

'Did it occur to you that Karyn shouldn't be left alone?'

'I thought she needed to sleep.'

'The drinks were strong, you've described her as being out of her head, yet you went to bed?'

'I'm sorry, I just thought . . . it was late . . .'

Mum tensed beside her. 'It wasn't Ellie's responsibility to stay with the girl.'

The detective shook her head. 'Mrs Parker, I have to ask you not to comment.'

'She's only a kid. She was doing her best. You heard her say she got rid of those boys.'

The detective smiled wearily. 'It's not those particular boys she needed to worry about though, is it, Mrs Parker?' She turned back to her paperwork. 'Now, let's get on.'

'I did get her a bucket in case she was sick,' Ellie whispered, 'and a glass of water. I took her shoes off as well and covered her with the duvet.'

The detective didn't appear to be listening. 'Where was your brother by now, Ellie?'

'Downstairs.'

365

'You didn't speak to him again?'

'Not then.'

'You did later?'

Ellie nodded.

She'd felt stupidly proud for saving Karyn. It made up for Freddie's cold smile, for the humiliation on her brother's face. Would Karyn remember and be grateful? Would they be friends at school on Monday? Would Ellie finally know someone in this town?

And then, maybe she slept, because there was a noise – like an animal in pain, that seemed to come from a dream, and she sat upright, heart thumping. Karyn was sick and needed her. Ellie stumbled out of bed and yanked the door open.

'Christ!' Tom said. 'What the hell are you doing?'

He cowered on the landing outside Karyn's room, as if Ellie had thrown a brick at his head.

'I heard a noise,' she muttered.

'You fucking terrified me!'

'Is Karyn OK?'

'She's fine. I went in to get my sleeping bag.'

'Has she been sick?'

'No, she's fine, I just told you.'

But there was something in his eyes, something desperate, and when Ellie didn't move he said, *Go to bed, just go to bed*, over and over, like maybe she would if he said it enough. She wanted to help him. Perhaps Karyn was really ill and he'd gone to check and couldn't cope. He'd been smoking after all, so wasn't the best judge. She pretended to go back to bed, listened for his footsteps on the stairs, counted to twenty and, when he'd definitely gone, opened the door again and crept out.

Karyn was lying on her back, almost entirely covered by the duvet. She looked sweet, like she'd been tucked in. But when Ellie switched on the lamp, she knew something was wrong. It was more than the spilled water darkening the carpet, more than Karyn's shoes skewed across the room, more than the sleeping bag on top of the wardrobe where it always was, so why had Tom lied about getting it? It was something to do with angles and shadows.

'I lifted up the duvet,' Ellie told Detective Thomas. 'I knew something wasn't right.'

'And what did you see?'

The shocking curl of pubic hair. Knickers ripped down. Legs at uncomfortable slants. Hair tangled like seaweed across the pillow.

'Ellie?'

'She was . . . she was undressed.'

'Karyn was naked?'

'No. Her clothes were . . . they were pulled up or down, depending . . .'

'You're going to have to be a bit more specific, I'm afraid.'

But her mum was listening, a tissue balled up in her hand. And the man at the laptop was listening, and this was Karyn, vulnerable. It would be written down and recorded and read out in court.

367

Detective Thomas tapped her pencil on the table. Detective Bryce swung on his chair. There were sweat patches under his arms.

'Her . . . her knickers were down and her skirt was up and her top was pushed up as well, and she was, she couldn't . . . She was . . .'

'What, Ellie?'

'She was doing this thing with her hands, like she was struggling to get up, but couldn't, like she was in pain. I don't think she knew . . . I mean, I don't think she . . . I don't think she consented.'

Detective Thomas shrugged. 'Consented to what? Maybe she was hot and simply tried to undress herself.'

'It wasn't that, it was different from that. Something had happened to her.'

'Perhaps you interrupted an intimate situation and she chose to feign sleep because she was embarrassed.'

'No.'

'You seem very sure.'

Because she'd given herself these same excuses for weeks and they didn't cut it. Karyn looked like she'd crashed from the sky.

The detective tapped her pencil some more, gazing at Ellie as if she was utterly bored. 'Have you had some kind of argument with your brother recently?'

'No.'

'Perhaps you're jealous of all the interest people are taking in him?'

'I'm not.'

'Do you feel left out? Would you like some attention for yourself?'

'This is ridiculous,' Mum cut in. 'You think what's happening to her brother is something she wants? Do you know how crippled our family is by this?'

'Mrs Parker,' the detective snapped, 'will you stop interrupting!'

'Please,' Ellie said, 'you have to believe me, I'm telling you the truth.'

'That's what you said last time.'

'But this time I am.'

Why weren't they taking her seriously? This had to be worth something. The truth had to count.

'Listen,' she said, trying to steady her breathing. 'There were photos. Tom doesn't know I saw them, but he took photos.'

'No,' the detective said, 'we seized his phone and laptop and there were no photos.'

'I deleted them.'

The detective leaned forward slowly, furiously, her eyes glittering. 'Let me get this right. You found photos of your brother assaulting Karyn and you deleted them?'

'I didn't want Tom sending them to Freddie . . . I didn't want them on the internet. It would be terrible . . . for Karyn, I mean, so I deleted them and overwrote the memory.'

'Describe these photos!'

Ellie was startled. 'I'm sorry, I didn't mean to . . . I wanted to help Karyn.'

'By destroying the evidence?'

'I'm sorry,' Ellie whispered into the silence.

'Please,' Mum said, 'don't talk to her like this.'

The detective slapped her hand on the table. 'Mrs Parker, if you keep interjecting, I will have you escorted from the room, do you understand?'

Mum bit her lip, nodded.

The detective turned back to Ellie. 'Now, I asked you to describe the photos. How many were there?'

'Six.'

'What were they of?'

'Karyn in different . . . in different positions, you know.'

'No, I don't know, which is why I'm asking you.'

'They were graphic . . .'

'You're going to have to do much better than that if you want me to believe you. Were there pictures of penetration?'

Ellie cringed. 'No! The first one, her skirt was a bit up, then the next one, it was a bit more up and her knickers were a bit . . . you know, down . . . and then on like that, until the last one, when she was undressed.'

'You said earlier she wasn't undressed.'

'She wasn't, not completely . . .'

'These photos don't prove a thing, do they? They probably never existed, and even if they did, Karyn could have posed for them. Why not? You said yourself she liked your brother, was flirting with him, kissing him. She posed for the pictures, had sex with him, then regretted it.'

Ellie looked out of the window at the sky. None of this was making a difference, none of it was counting for anything. She thought of Karyn in her flat, just stuck there. All these weeks in a world made up of shadows.

She took a breath, determined. 'I know you think I'm making this up now, but I'm not. I told myself my brother took a few pictures to prove something to his friends, like a dare. I didn't say anything straight away and I should have done. I'm sorry I didn't, but those pictures definitely existed.'

Detective Thomas looked at her impassively. 'You found out pretty quickly that your brother did a lot more than take pictures. He was arrested the following day and admitted having sex with Karyn. He said she consented and that he had no idea about her age. If you knew she couldn't possibly have consented, if you knew he *was* aware of her age, why didn't you tell us this when we questioned you the first time?'

'I didn't want it to be true.'

'Withholding evidence doesn't make someone innocent.'

'I know.'

'Did Tom ask you to lie?'

'No. I didn't see him again until he got bail.'

'But he knows you lied? His solicitor has a copy of your first statement and will have shown him. So presumably Tom expects you to stand up in court and continue to defend him?'

'I suppose so.'

Detective Thomas looked at her long and hard. 'Do you know someone called Mikey McKenzie?'

371

'Yes.'

'How well do you know him?'

'A bit.'

'Only a bit? Are you sure about that?'

A beat. They looked at each other.

'Ellie, I'm going to be honest with you. I've been hard on you today because when this goes to court, you'll be cross-examined by your brother's counsel, who will do everything to discredit you. I actually think you're being very brave and Karyn will be enormously grateful to you, but your evidence is not conclusive. It corroborates what Karyn has said to some extent, but it isn't key evidence, it's simply your word against your brother's. First you say one thing, then you change your mind and say something else. You tell us there was physical evidence, but you destroyed it. It looks suspicious, do you see? It's imperative you're honest with me. You can't tell us one thing and expect us to believe you, and then the next minute tell us a blatant lie. So, I'm going to ask you again about your relationship with Mikey.'

Ellie's heart was pumping hard. She hadn't thought they'd mention him. How stupid she was. Of course Karyn would have told them, of course it was all going to come out. There was nowhere left to hide.

Mum looked completely bemused. 'Can somebody tell me what's going on?'

Detective Thomas frowned at her to shush. 'Ellie,' she said, 'how well do you know Mikey McKenzie?'

'I know him very well.'

372

'I'm going to put it to you that he asked you to change your story, that between you you've concocted this new version of events.'

'That's not true.'

'I'm going to suggest that your original version was in fact true, that you heard and saw nothing all night, but that Mikey is pressurizing you, maybe even threatening you in order to help his sister. What would you say to that?'

'It's rubbish.'

'How long have you known him?'

'Nearly eight weeks.'

'Is he your boyfriend?'

'He kind of was.'

'Was?'

'He isn't now. I won't see him again.'

'But you were intimate?'

'Sort of.'

'Ellie, I need yes or no answers. I'm sorry if you feel I'm being hard on you, but the defence counsel will be a lot harder, believe me. I need to be very sure that you'll be a strong enough witness.'

Her mother tensed forward on the chair. She looked like a statue. She was barely breathing she was listening so hard.

Ellie turned to her, tears sliding down her face. 'I'm sorry you found out like this, Mum. I'm sorry I didn't tell you first.'

'We can ask Mum to leave,' Detective Thomas said, 'if it makes it more comfortable for you, Ellie. Do you want her to wait outside?'

'I want her to stay. I'm sick of secrets.'

The detective considered this for a second. 'Is that all right with you, Mrs Parker?'

She smiled sadly at Ellie, gripped her hand firmly. 'I'm staying.'

Forty-three

Karyn peered sideways at Mikey as he came out of the lift. 'Oh,' she said, 'it's you.'

She was outside! She was outside the flat and she wasn't hiding under a duvet or a pile of jumpers. She was wearing leggings and a T-shirt and she was sitting on the balcony in the spring sunshine!

Holly was next to her, both of them wearing sunglasses like a couple of Hollywood starlets. They'd got the deckchairs out and had crisps and a plate of biscuits on the floor between them.

'Hey,' Mikey said, 'how's it going?'

Karyn tilted her sunglasses to look at him properly. 'Fantastic. Like I told you earlier.'

Holly grinned up at him. 'You want some crisps? We're celebrating.'

'I'm all right, thanks. Where's Mum?'

'Inside getting a cup of tea.'

He sat on the step and got out his fags, tried to make out it was perfectly ordinary that Karyn was outside on a deckchair, her bare feet up on the railing, her toenails painted pink. When had she done that? She hadn't bothered with stuff like that for weeks. She looked pale though, like some long bout of flu had exhausted her. She was thinner too, and it surprised him he hadn't noticed that happening. Maybe it was something to do with the duvet and jumpers.

'So,' Mikey said, 'how was school today, Holly?'

'Rubbish.'

'Did you learn anything?'

She shook her head, her mouth full of crisps. He knew he was making conversation and it surprised him that he wanted to fill in the gaps, that he felt awkward with his own sisters.

'You must've learned something.'

'I didn't. We had a supply teacher and he couldn't control us.' She laughed and crisps spluttered everywhere. 'I know a secret though. Shall I tell you?'

'OK.'

'Something lives under the Christmas tree. Guess what it is?'

'Dunno, a goblin?'

'No, stupid.'

'A rat? A wolf? A bear?'

She twisted round and lifted the pot. 'Woodlice. Look, hundreds of them.' She picked one up and showed him. It uncurled on her hand and ran to the edge of her palm; she turned her hand over and it ran across the back. On and on for ever, thinking it was getting away.

'It looks like a dinosaur,' she said. 'It looks like an ankylosaurus, don't you think?'

376

'Probably.'

'It really does. Do you even know what an ankylosaurus looks like?'

'Like a woodlouse?'

She grinned at him. 'You're such an idiot.'

Mum stuck her head out. 'I thought I heard you, Mikey. You're back then?'

'Looks like it.'

'You OK?'

'Yep.'

'You want a cup of tea? I'm just making one.'

He shook his head and she frowned at him. What did that mean? *What's wrong with my tea? Karyn's outside, have you noticed? Don't upset her? Keep your big mouth shut?* All the signs were new and Mikey didn't seem able to make sense of them.

Down in the courtyard, a boy kicked a ball against the wall, and in one of the flats, someone whistled tunelessly. Holly fed crisps to the woodlice and Mikey smoked his cigarette and secretly watched Karyn turn the pages of a magazine. She was only pretending to read, he thought, faking interest in the pictures. It all felt so weird and uncomfortable.

'How long have you been outside?' he asked her eventually.

'Ages.'

'It's been nice weather, eh?'

She didn't answer and he felt himself falter, didn't know how to be with her any more.

'You know,' he said, 'maybe I want that cup of tea after all.'

Holly scrambled up. 'I'll tell Mum.'

He really didn't want to be left alone with Karyn, but Holly insisted. She pressed past him and disappeared into the flat.

Karyn turned another page.

He lit a new cigarette from the old one and inhaled, long and deep. He knew he should give talking another try, but didn't know where to begin. There were so many things he wanted to tell her – all the stuff he'd realized recently about how much she did, had always done in fact. She'd been taking Holly to school for years, collecting her too, doing the shopping and washing and keeping Mum in line. All he'd ever done was go to work, hang out with Jacko and pick up girls. Even his great scheme of becoming a chef had crumbled to nothing. The last few weeks, it was as if someone had taken his life to pieces and let him see the way it worked. And what he'd realized was that he wasn't the heroic big brother who could solve every problem and hold a family together; he was, in fact, an idiot, and of course his sister wasn't going to bother speaking to him.

He took a breath. Now or never.

'Karyn,' he said, 'I'm sorry.'

She looked over the top of her sunglasses at him.

'I wanted to help you, but I got it wrong.'

She smiled. A tiny shadow of a smile, creeping along her lips from the edge of her mouth. 'I'll think about it.'

'About what?'

'Whether to forgive you or not.' She pushed her glasses back up her nose and turned another page of her magazine.

Mum brought out the tea. She sat on a deckchair, her feet in the sun. Holly came out with a satsuma and peeled it carefully, sucked each segment dry of juice and left the empty skin on the step next to Mikey.

'It's got pips in,' she told him, 'and I don't like pips.'

Karyn smiled at her. 'You could make a bracelet out of them if there's enough. I did it at school once. You use food colouring to dye them, then string them together. Stacey's coming over later and we'll help you if you like.'

'Cool.' Holly held a piece of satsuma up to the light to examine it.

It was nice sitting there, sipping tea. Mikey felt as if he hadn't done something so simple for months. Holly fiddled about with the pips, Karyn turned pages, Mum ate a biscuit. Was that all it took to feel better about yourself – an apology? He still had no way of telling Karyn the things he felt, but it didn't seem to matter so much now. Maybe if he just sat there with her, she'd know it anyway. And maybe, later, the right words would come.

'Hey,' Mum said after a while, 'I know what I didn't tell you, Mikey. You remember that social worker who came round when no one was here?'

Holly frowned. 'Me and Karyn were here. I opened the door and everyone told me off.'

Mikey reached out and stroked her back. 'What about her?'

'She's got Holly a place in an after-school club.'

'I'm going to do football and street dancing,' Holly told him.

'At the same time?'

'No, silly. And when it's raining I'm going to make puppets.'

Karyn twisted round to look at Mikey. 'And *I'm* getting a computer.'

Mikey was tempted to ask what he was going to get, but managed to keep his mouth shut.

'It's from a charity,' Mum told him. 'They give old ones a service and hand them out again, good as new. The social worker reckons we might get a desk for the girls' room as well – I just have to write a letter and say why we need it.'

Mikey laughed. 'Remember when you got that paint for Holly?'

'For me?' Holly's whole face gleamed. 'What paint? When?'

'You were just born,' Mikey told her, 'and the council said Mum could have a budget to paint the bedroom, but they said the paint had to be white and she wanted yellow.'

Mum laughed out loud. 'Yellow *and* blue. I stood in that office and told them I wasn't leaving until they agreed. It was a ridiculous policy – everyone having white walls – what rubbish. I said, why should my kids have to stare at four plain walls, when they can have the colour of sunshine and sky in their rooms?'

Holly plonked herself on her mother's lap and gave her a hug that was so brand new and abandoned that Mikey wanted one for himself. Karyn shot him a shy smile over their heads and he felt a rush of something for them all – love? Shame? He actually felt like he might cry. It was crazy – the four of them having an OK time together for once, and here he was, choking up.

'Uh-oh,' Mum said, 'here comes trouble.'

Mikey peered over the balcony, glad of a distraction. Jacko was pulling up in his car, reversing into a space over by the bins.

'He'll get clamped there,' Mum said. 'Run and tell him, Holly. Tell him they've clamped three cars down there today.'

'I'll go,' Karyn said. 'I could do with a walk.'

She slipped on her sandals and the three of them watched as she got up from the deckchair and walked slowly, as if walking was a new thing, along the balcony to the lift door. When she pressed the button, Holly scrambled after her and took her hand. When the lift came they stepped in together.

Mum got herself a new cigarette and offered Mikey one. Their eyes met across the lighter.

'So,' he said, 'she's outside then.'

'Ever since Gillian left.'

'Amazing.'

'She's invited her mates over later as well. I think something very important happened when your friend swapped sides.'

'Swapped sides?'

Mum shrugged. 'You know what I mean.'

They looked down at Karyn together. She was leaning into the car window, talking to Jacko. Holly was walking across to the boy with the ball.

Mum said, 'Have you spoken to your friend today?'

'She rang me from a phonebox when she got out of the police station.'

'Is she OK?'

'Not really. Her brother's not allowed to live in the same house now she's a witness for the police.'

'You're worried about her?'

'She says her dad's going to go crazy when he finds out. She was going to a café with her mum to work out how to tell him.'

'At least she's got her mum with her.'

'I suppose.'

Though Mikey wasn't sure that skinny woman he'd met all those weeks ago would be any help. He took a long drag of his cigarette and exhaled slowly. Ellie had had a weird calm about her on the phone, and when she'd said goodbye, she'd made it sound like for ever. Never before had he been so hungry for someone – never so specifically, so desperately. Whenever he closed his eyes he saw her, her arms spread above her head, her legs wrapping him warm.

He wiped his face with his sleeve and took another puff on his cigarette.

His mum was staring at him.

'What?'

'If you hadn't got to know this girl, Karyn wouldn't be outside today. You think about that.'

'You're saying me knowing Ellie is a good thing?'

'I'm saying you tried to help your sister and *that's* a good thing. I'm not sure any of us would have done any different if we'd been in your little friend's shoes.'

'Yeah, well I don't think Karyn sees it like that.'

'Give her time.'

He rubbed his nose and thought about it. He looked around at the place where he lived because he didn't know the answer. There were newly-planted trees in the courtyard, thin little sticks protected by their own wire fences. He looked at the sand pit, the swing, the football area with its goal marked on the wall in red paint. The boy with the ball was still there and Holly was laughing with him about something. Mikey took a last drag of his cigarette and stubbed it out in the Christmas tree pot, picked up a stone he found and held it so it warmed in his hand.

'I lost my job, Mum.'

'Oh, Mikey!'

'I mucked them about too much.'

She shook her head as she stubbed out her own cigarette. 'Did you tell them how difficult everything's been?'

'Not exactly.'

'You should've done. It might've helped.'

'Yeah, maybe.'

'I'm really sorry about that.' She looked sorry too. 'What will you do now?'

He didn't know. It struck him how suddenly the world goes and changes. Here he was sitting on the step and he couldn't think of a single thing that was the same as the day before. Yesterday he was with Ellie and today it was over. Yesterday Tom was getting away with it, and today he wasn't. Yesterday Karyn was glued to the sofa and now she was down in the courtyard. Yesterday he had a job. He sighed and stretched his legs out. Even the weather was freakishly different – constant rain replaced by a low sun pulsing in the sky.

'Maybe I'll go down and give Holly a kick-around,' he said. 'I've been promising her one for weeks.'

'You do that,' Mum said. 'And I tell you what. Why don't I make us a proper dinner? There's some chicken pieces in the freezer and I could do potatoes and veggies like I used to. Would you like that?' She leaned over and stroked his arm.

'Thanks,' he said. 'That'd be great.'

He knew it wouldn't last for ever, knew it was only one of her cycles, but it was kind. And maybe, like a game of footie with Holly, like the sun in April, it was important to appreciate good things when they came.

Forty-four

Ellie sat on the sofa next to her mother. They'd been sitting there for so long that the room had fallen softly into darkness. Upstairs, Tom was in his bedroom packing. Dad was helping him. Ellie could hear the drag and tear of parcel tape as he sealed up boxes on the landing.

'Dad's never going to forgive me,' she whispered.

Mum squeezed her hand. 'Your father loves you.'

'That's different.'

'It's all we've got though. When it comes down to it, it's all we have to hold on to.'

It felt like a belt tightening as Dad came down the stairs. Every muscle in Ellie's body moved into tension as she watched him stack two new boxes on top of the others in the hall. It was like Tom was dead and they were clearing him out.

'Is that his Xbox?' Mum said. 'Won't Ben have things like that he can use?'

Dad snapped the lights on in the lounge and stood in the doorway, watching them blink into light. Surely he would stop being angry soon. Surely his fury would simply run out.

'Ben's at college all day,' he said, 'so Tom will be dependent on the parents' hospitality. You want your son to feel uncomfortable, asking if he might please watch TV or perhaps borrow a console to help distract him from this nightmare?'

Mum didn't answer and he shook his head at her as if that simply proved he was right. He strode off down the hallway to the downstairs bathroom. Ellie imagined him rooting through the cabinet in there, hunting down Tom's shaving gear and deodorant, his favourite hair gel.

'I suppose I should draw the curtains,' Mum said. 'It's dark outside.'

But she didn't move.

Dad came back in with Tom's toilet bag in his hand. 'How has this confession of yours helped anyone, Eleanor?' he said. 'How has it got any of us anywhere?'

'It was the truth, Dad.'

'The truth? Oh for God's sake! I have never, repeat, *never*, seen your brother this way before. Is that what you wanted?' He stabbed a finger at the ceiling. 'He's sitting up there on his bed, barely able to speak, let alone pack.'

'Should I go up?' Mum said.

'You're asking me?'

'Yes, I am.'

'You're his bloody mother – shouldn't you know?'

'I'm asking you if he *wants* me up there. If he needs me, I'll go.'

'Very noble of you.' He looked down at their hands clasped

together. It seemed to infuriate him more. 'You should've stopped her. You should've nailed her bloody feet to the floor.'

'I couldn't stop her.'

'*Couldn't?* She's a child, isn't she? Do you have no control over your children?' He scowled at her, his mouth a taut line of disapproval. Then he spun off and out, thumping furiously back up the stairs.

'Oh God,' Mum said, and she hid her face in her hands.

Ellie didn't know what to say, or what to do. 'I'm sorry,' she said. It was all she could think of.

She'd done nothing but apologize since they got back from the police station. Mum had sat everyone down in the lounge and told Dad not to interrupt, told Tom she loved him, then informed them both of the new statement Ellie had signed and of her relationship with Mikey. The accusations had gone on for hours.

Dad was climbing up into the loft now. Ellie could hear the creak of the step ladder. Maybe he was getting the Meccano down, the Lego, Tom's toy farm. All the plastic animals – the cows and horses and sheep, the rows of geese and ducks – would soon be lined up at the door.

'He's not on my side at all,' she said.

'He is. Of course he is.'

But he wasn't. She was sullied. Other. No longer his little girl. He had a new blind look, as if he might see someone he couldn't bear if he looked at her properly.

'Anyway,' Mum said, 'it's not about sides. I sat in that police station and listened to you and I wanted two things at the same time. I wanted you to stop talking, because I didn't want to hear terrible things about Tom, and I wanted you to talk all night, because I could see how much it was hurting you to hold it inside.'

She moved over to the window, slid all the pot plants back on the ledge and drew the curtains. The familiar swish was comforting.

Dad broke the spell by coming down with Tom's cricket bag and balancing it carefully on the hall table, even though the cricket season hadn't started yet and it could safely have stayed in the loft. Mum sat back down next to Ellie as he crossed the lounge to the drinks cabinet. He took no notice of either of them, poured himself a generous measure of whisky and took one, two, three gulps, swooshing each round his mouth before swallowing. He walked over to the window, reopened the curtains and looked out into the dark as if he was waiting for something. The press? TV crews? He thought this was enormous, bigger than all of them. His daughter had crossed the enemy line. She was *anti-Parker*. No longer part of the team.

'How many times did you meet the boy?'

This again. Ellie took a breath. 'Not many.'

'Where?'

'I told you – different places. We went for walks mostly.'

He turned and narrowed his eyes at her. 'Were you with him yesterday?'

She nodded. It had become imperative to tell the truth, as if any grain of goodness that was left in her life would slip away if she didn't.

'Where did you go? I don't for one minute believe you were at the cinema.'

'We went to the cottage.'

He blinked at her. 'You broke in?'

'The keys were under the pot.'

He took a step forward and glared down at Mum. 'Did you know this?'

'Ellie told me, yes.'

'And you didn't bother mentioning it?'

'In the great schemes of things, it felt rather minor.'

'*Rather minor?* Well, I'm telling you now, if that place gets ransacked or squatted it will feel rather major, I assure you!' He slammed the empty tumbler on the coffee table and turned to Ellie. 'What the hell were you doing there for so long?'

Mum squeezed her hand. This wasn't the time to share the conversation they'd had in the café after the police station.

'We cooked potatoes.'

'In the grate? Christ, girl, you could have burned the place down!'

'But she didn't,' Mum said, sitting forward, 'and surely that's the point? I don't think her friend's likely to ransack the place either.'

'Her *friend*? What's got into you?'

She shook her head at him sadly. 'I could ask you the same question.'

'What's that supposed to mean?'

She didn't answer and he scooped up his tumbler and went back to the drinks cabinet. 'You'll be taken apart in court, you know that, Eleanor? That's where this is going.'

'Should you be drinking?' Mum said. 'You have to drive the car in a minute.'

He rejected her with a wave. 'All the sordid details of your little romance will be laid out in court for everyone to see. I hope you're ready for that. I hope you've thought very carefully about it.'

'It wasn't sordid.'

He stopped pacing. 'What did you say?'

'I said it wasn't what you think.'

'Oh, is that right? What was it then, a fairytale romance? Mills and Boon? My God, girl, your brother's up there packing his bags and you sit here defending some school-girl crush!'

'Stop talking to her like that!' Mum stood up, fists clenched.

He stared at her, slack-jawed.

'This is your daughter,' she said. 'Have you forgotten? Can you for a second consider the possibility that this isn't easy for her either?'

He did consider it. Ellie saw it cross his face – something sad like a shadow. But then he dismissed it and the blind look took over again. 'I'm trying to help,' he said. 'I'm trying to help them both, isn't that obvious?'

Mum sighed. 'Come with me. Come and help me get Tom's suitcase. It's in the loft and I need you to pass it down.'

Ellie leaned back on the sofa and listened to them go upstairs. She counted breaths. Every breath, every heartbeat, was one less until maybe things stopped hurting this much. She picked at her nails, inspected her fingers. Even her hands looked unfamiliar. She didn't belong. She was the terrible stranger who'd destroyed everything warm and good.

She thought for a moment of the world outside the house. What would Mikey be doing? Was he even thinking about her? Maybe she should text him, just to let him know she was alive.

Her phone was in the bureau. Dad had dumped it there when he confiscated it yesterday. It was right at the front, not even hidden. She sat back down on the sofa with it. There were seventeen missed calls from Mikey, loads of voicemails, text upon text. It hurt to hear the desperation in his voice. It hurt that all the messages were from the night before and from earlier that morning. There was nothing new.

She wrote *I miss you*, then deleted it, put the phone in her pocket and shut her eyes.

When she opened them again, Dad stood in the doorway. He said, 'Your mum thinks I'm being too harsh.'

He walked across and sat down next to her. She wiped her eyes with her sleeve and tried not to look at him, but he tilted her face to his.

'I want to save you from being destroyed in court, that's why I'm being tough.'

This is my father. I am his child. He loves me.

'Tom's only hope is to undermine your evidence, and given that you have no physical evidence, it comes down to your word against his. Do you understand?'

She nodded. The police had said the same thing. Though they'd also said, *What you're doing is very brave and Karyn McKenzie will be very grateful.*

Dad said, 'In order to give Tom his best chance, I have to get him a brilliant barrister. And if I get him a brilliant barrister, you'll be torn apart. There's a last opportunity here, Ellie, and that's why I'm coming down hard on you. I want you to cast your mind back carefully over everything this Mikey boy said and did, and if there's anything that might be construed as overly persuasive, I want you to tell me.'

'Overly persuasive?'

Annoyance crossed his face. 'Has he threatened you?'

'No.'

'Has he blackmailed you? Has he got pictures of you on his phone for instance, or taken something of yours that you want back?'

'No.'

'Are you sure? Because if he has, we can get this whole thing turned right around. We can say he made you go to the police and told you what to say in order to protect his sister. We can say your original statement was true and this new one is false.'

She'd seen this look in her father's eyes so many times – like he knew everything, could read minds, predict the future and was absolutely right in all respects. She swallowed hard and steeled herself against it.

'He didn't threaten me, Dad. He's not blackmailing me and the new statement is true.'

He threw his hands up in despair. 'Well, there's nothing I can do for you then, is there? It's going to be your word against your brother's and I can tell you now, I won't stand by and watch him rot in jail.'

'What's going on?' Mum stood in the doorway.

Dad shot her a look of utter frustration. 'Nothing. I'm going to get the car out of the garage.'

She moved to one side to let him pass, waited for the front door to shut, then plonked herself on the sofa with a sigh. 'Am I a terrible mother?'

'No, Mum.'

'Tom might think so.'

'He doesn't.'

She smiled sadly. 'Maybe I'm just a terrible wife then.'

Her temperature had changed. She was colder since going upstairs and Ellie could feel the difference between their hands.

'Your father's been very thorough,' Mum said. 'Even in here. I didn't notice him packing those CDs away, did you?'

She nodded over at the spaces in the rack. There were gaps in the DVD collection too, rifts in the bookshelf, like teeth had been removed all over the lounge.

'Tom won't be away for long,' Ellie whispered. 'He'll come back soon.'

'Well, I hope Ben's mother doesn't think we're crazy sending him there with so many things. I hope she realizes your father simply wants him to feel secure.' Mum stroked Ellie's hand absent-mindedly. 'There isn't really an alternative, not if we want him to be nearby. He could stay in a hotel, I suppose, but what sort of life is that? He'd be lonely in a hotel, wouldn't he?'

Over and over she stroked, in the same spot with her thumb. It was uncomfortable, as if she'd rasp down to the bone.

393

'Anyway,' Mum said, 'he's getting his last few things together up there, so I'll make him some sandwiches in a minute and he can eat them in the car. I don't want them saying we sent him away hungry.'

'Mum?'

'Perhaps I should pack him some snacks for later, some crisps and things. Then it would be like he was going on a sleepover.' She smiled as if she didn't really believe it. 'I spoke to Ben's mother on the phone – did I tell you? She was very reassuring. She's a nice woman actually, I thought that when I met her at the party – we were chatting most of the night. Anyway, Dad's going to give them money, so they won't be out of pocket. It helps that they live out of town, I suppose, makes it less daunting for them. Your father thinks there may be media attention when the court case starts, and I'd hate them to feel awkward.'

'Mum, are you OK?'

She took a breath in and held it, blinked several times. 'You know, I can't help thinking that if we'd stayed in London, this wouldn't've happened.'

Ellie passed her a tissue and watched silently as she dabbed at her face.

'I'm sorry, I don't mean to get upset.' She leaned forward, gripping her stomach as if it hurt. 'He seemed so vulnerable up there, packing his things away. I looked at him and I thought, *How could he harm anyone? He's just a boy.*' She stared at the carpet, at her feet, still in her gardening shoes from earlier. Scuffed old familiar garden shoes. 'I still remember his first steps, his first words, all of it.'

Ellie passed her another tissue. 'Here.'

'He had such beautiful golden curls. You won't remember of course, you weren't born, but they were stunning.' She wiped her face roughly with the tissue. 'Oh God, I want to be stronger than this. I don't want him to see me like this when he comes down.' She turned to Ellie suddenly, as if seeing her for the first time. 'I know you love him and I know you wouldn't have done this if you didn't have to, but he's not a monster, Ellie. I don't want anyone thinking that.'

'I know.'

'He's just a scared little boy. He's *my* scared little boy.'

Ellie nodded very slowly. 'I don't want anything bad to happen to him either.'

'I know you don't.'

'Maybe I handled this all wrong, but what I said in the police station was true. It *is* what I saw, Mum, it truly is.'

She nodded, patted Ellie's hand again. 'Well, that's all right then.'

Dad marched back in. 'I'm going to start packing the car.'

'You do that,' Mum said, smiling through tears at him. 'I'll go and make some sandwiches.'

He frowned at her, but she went off to the kitchen before he could say anything, so he frowned at Ellie instead.

'You should go to your room,' he told her. 'You shouldn't be here when Tom comes down.'

'Can't I say goodbye?'

'No, you're a witness for the police. If your brother so much

395

as speaks a word to you, you could twist it and say he tried to pressurize you. He'd have his bail revoked and be back in jail quicker than I could spit.'

'I wouldn't do that.'

'Wouldn't you? I don't know what you're capable of any more.'

She crept up the stairs, holding on tight to the banister. Across the landing, Tom's door was shut. She went to the bathroom and rinsed her face, dried it at the mirror. It was the first time she'd seen herself for hours. She looked tired and older. She rubbed her face to check she was real. Yes, she was Ellie Parker, the girl who betrayed her family.

Maybe Dad was right and she *was* capable of anything.

She didn't knock, simply opened Tom's bedroom door and went in. He was sprawled on the bed, sorting through stuff in a shoebox; photos and bits of paper were scattered all over the duvet. There was a new darkness in his eyes, like something inside him had broken and spilled.

'Shut the door,' he said.

She stood with her back against it and watched him sift through photos. He glanced at several quickly, stopped at one and examined it thoroughly before passing it to her. 'Remember this?'

It was the four of them in Austria on a skiing holiday. Ellie was about ten, wearing the whole outfit – salopettes, goggles, everything. Tom was next to her. Both of them had massive grins on their faces.

'It was Christmas Eve,' he said, 'and the hotel was laying on a visit from Santa – sleigh ride, reindeer, the works. You remember?'

She nodded, passed it back. He put it on top of the suitcase, picked up a fresh handful from the box and shuffled through them.

'I didn't do it to hurt you,' she said.

He passed her another photo. 'You on a farm. That horse stood on your foot.'

It was winter again – different country, different year. She was twelve and the horse had broken three of her toes. She barely glanced at it, didn't take it from him. She had to get through this; she was determined.

'I had to say what really happened. I couldn't hold it in any more.'

'Evidently.'

'Please say it's OK.'

'You want me to say I don't mind?' His voice was low, hardly more than a whisper. 'How do you want me to answer?'

'I want you to say you understand.'

He stood up, walked over to the window and opened the curtains an inch to look out. 'You know Dad's going to hire some top-quality barrister and make you look like a liar.'

'He told me.'

'I bet he did.' He turned from the window and looked at her in such a soft and terrible way that she barely recognized him. 'The barrister will ask you really personal stuff. He'll want to know everything you did with Karyn's brother and every word that passed between you. He'll say her brother threatened you, and if you say he didn't, the barrister will say he seduced you and you're completely gullible. And if you say that's not how it was either, then you'll leave him no option but to make out you're a slut and a liar.'

'Dad said that too.'

He shook his head. 'I don't want them to do that to you.'

'Then don't let them.'

'There's only one way to stop them though, isn't there?'

She nodded.

He watched her steadily for a second, as if he was weighing it up. 'I'm not brave enough.'

She went over and hugged him. He smelled of cigarettes and her arms reached all the way round. She closed her eyes and held him, and eventually he put his arms round her too.

'I'm sorry,' he said. 'I'm so sorry.'

She held him closer. 'It's OK. Whatever you do, I'll always love you.'

The rough brush of his skin on her cheek was shocking as he buried himself in her shoulder and a great sob welled up from deep inside him.

'I'm scared,' he said. 'I'm really fucking scared!'

She held him closer as he cried, huge sobs racking through him, like a child. She was crying too now, to be with him like this. She stroked his back. They stood swaying together. Her brother, her beautiful crying brother.

The door opened. 'What the hell's going on?'

Tom pulled away, wiped his hands quickly over his face. 'Nothing. We're saying goodbye.'

Dad strode across the room. 'What have you done to him?

What did I tell you about coming in here?' He gripped Tom's shoulders and made him look at him. 'You have to be stronger than this.'

Tom winced under his scrutiny. 'I can't do it to her, Dad.'

'You can. You have to.'

He shook his head. 'You said yourself, it'll be terrible. You said they'll break her apart.'

'Nonsense, it won't be like that at all.'

'You said they'll make her stand in front of everyone and ask her really personal questions.'

Dad grimaced, turned to Ellie and pointed at the door. 'Go to your room, Eleanor.'

She didn't move. Tom stood looking from one to the other, fresh tears sliding down his face. It was as if he'd been punctured, losing air and energy. 'Really, Dad, I can't do it. I shouldn't've done any of it. It's all my fault.'

'So, you're going to plead guilty, are you?' Dad dragged him to the bed and made him sit down. 'You'll get three or four years in prison, you'll be on the sex offenders register and come out as a convicted rapist. Is that what you want?'

'No, but I don't want this either.'

Dad got a hanky from his pocket and shoved it at him. 'It's a ridiculous step to plead guilty, when the conviction rate is so low. You have every chance of getting off.'

Tom listened so hard he forgot to breathe. He listened with every fibre, like he was falling from a mountain and Dad was yelling survival instructions.

'This new statement means nothing,' Dad went on, 'not really, the police said as much. There's no physical evidence, is there? No photos or videos, or texts, only her word against yours. The incentives for you to plead guilty are non-existent.'

He talked statistics and attrition rates and made everything seem so polarized – two foolish girls, one misunderstood boy. Tom made the occasional effort to struggle against it, but the simplicity of Dad's argument was overwhelming. In court, the barrister would discredit both girls. Karyn wanted to sleep with Tom and regretted it later. Ellie was love-struck by Mikey and would do anything for him. Karyn got drunk and partied too hard. Ellie got seduced and betrayed her family.

There was a hush in the room when Dad finally ran out of words. Ellie noticed a change in herself too, as if her mind had been washed. She felt very cold and still inside.

'Eleanor?' Dad whispered into the silence. 'I told you to leave.'

She nodded goodbye to Tom and he nodded back at her, like polite strangers bidding farewell in a hotel lobby. She closed the door very gently behind her.

Forty-five

Mikey threw a stone. It missed Ellie's bedroom window, hit the drainpipe and ricocheted off into a bush. He wasn't giving up though, not until he'd spoken to her.

He found another stone and lobbed that. It clipped the edge of the window. He waited, crouching on the grass in the quiet garden. But nothing moved. Nothing happened. He rooted around, found a bigger stone and swung his arm back.

The door was yanked open.

Shit! Not Ellie, but her mum. 'What on earth are you doing?'

'Is Ellie in?'

Her mum stepped out onto the porch in her dressing gown and slippers. 'Are you throwing stones at my windows?'

'They didn't break.'

'That's hardly the point.'

'Is she in?'

'Have you heard of a telephone?'

'She doesn't pick up.'

'And what does that tell you?'

It told him Ellie was unhappy, same as he was. It told him they needed to speak.

Her mum folded her arms at him. 'How did you get in? If you climbed our gate, that's trespass.'

'I just want to see her.'

'And throwing stones at windows is criminal damage, so I suggest you leave before I call the police.'

Behind her, on the floor at the bottom of the stairs, was a black leather briefcase that gleamed. Maybe Ellie's dad had an early morning visit to the barrister planned. They had a good one, Karyn said; a famous one who never lost a case. Police, fathers, barristers – they weren't going to put him off.

He took a step back to check out the top-floor windows. 'Ellie!' he yelled.

'Stop it,' her mum hissed, 'or I'll get my husband.'

'Ellie!'

'I mean it, stop it now!'

It was a total shock when Ellie appeared in the doorway, suddenly there, behind her mother. She was in her pyjamas. She looked knackered, her eyes bruised with tiredness. He wanted to pick her up and carry her to safety.

She said, 'What are you doing here?'

'I had to see you.'

'Has something happened?'

Her mum barred the door with her arm. 'Inside!'

Ellie ignored her. 'Is Karyn OK?'

'We have to talk.'

Her mum tried to nudge her. 'Dad's only in the shower. If he comes down, there'll be hell to pay.'

Nobody's dad was scaring him off and he took a step closer to prove it. 'You haven't been at school. I waited at the gate every afternoon.'

'I missed a few days and now I've got study leave.'

'I texted you. You never texted back.'

'I'm sorry. I thought it was best.'

He shuffled his feet on the grass. 'There's something I have to tell you.'

'Something important?'

'Kind of.'

She gazed at him steadily for a second, then turned to her mum. 'Is that OK?'

Her mum glanced behind her, looked uncertain. 'What about Dad?'

Ellie smiled softly at her. 'Do you have to tell him?'

Her mum fiddled with a button on her dressing gown. 'All right, I'll make some excuse.' She nodded at Mikey. 'Make it quick.'

She wandered back up the hallway. Ellie pulled the door shut behind her and looked at him. 'What is it? What's wrong?'

But he was lost for words. When he thought about her, he remembered her at the cottage, her eyes fiery, daring to love him. But standing here in front of him, she looked defeated and sad. He hadn't imagined this.

She shouldn't be here with him. She should be up in her room with her revision notes and practice papers, watching the morning stretch across the ceiling. She shouldn't be in the garden with this strange warmth filtering through her.

'You want to walk somewhere?' he said.

She wanted to run, not walk – down to the river and under the trees. For days she'd thought of him and now he was here, so close and beautiful it hurt.

She shook her head. 'I can't.'

'That's not a reason. Tell me why not.'

What could she say? Because they might kiss again? Because if they did she might not know how to stop, or even if she wanted to? Because Karyn deserved not to be hurt any more? Because Mikey deserved to get on with his life and the best way of doing that was for her to leave him alone?

'What have they done to you, Ellie?'

Why did she love it so much when he said her name out loud? Like no one else had ever done it.

'Nothing.' She sat down on the step and hugged her knees. 'I mustn't be long.'

He sat down next to her. She didn't look at him. If she looked, she'd fall and she'd promised herself she wouldn't.

He said, 'Is your dad still giving you a hard time?'

'He's mostly going for the silent treatment now.'

'And how's your brother?'

'You want to talk about him?'

'Why not?'

Because if she talked about Tom, she might give soft parts of herself away. And she mustn't be weak. She shrugged, pretended not to care. 'He's scared mostly. I'm not allowed to see him any more, but that's what they tell me.'

'What about your mum – is she being nice?'

'Yeah, she's cool. She says reassuring things and I say them back. What about you? How's your life? You got another job yet?'

'Not yet. My mum rang up the college though and they really do have an NVQ in catering. You remember when I said about that?'

She nodded. It was the very first night, by the river.

'Anyway,' he said, 'it might come to nothing, but I got the forms and filled them in, so you never know.' He nudged her. 'I might see you there in September.'

But she wouldn't, because if he got into college she'd have to go somewhere else. Maybe there was some great-aunt no one had told her about who she could stay with? Or perhaps she'd live in her gran's cottage and do a distance learning course. She'd grow flowers, swim. Let Mikey go.

His foot came off the step and onto the grass next to her foot, and suddenly their two feet were together. *Knock, knock*, his foot touched hers and it felt like hers was on fire, as if her whole being lived where he touched.

She snatched her foot away and shuffled further along the step. 'So, what did you want to tell me?'

She kept very still as he pulled out his tobacco and put a cigarette together. 'It's about Karyn,' he said.

'What about her?'

'I didn't want you to find out by text.'

'Just tell me.'

He lit the rollie behind his cupped hand and took a long drag. He blew it out hard, then looked right at her. 'She's going back to school on Tuesday to do her Art exam.'

They looked at each other for a second. It felt like a needle had found the centre of her pain. 'The same exam as me.'

'I know.'

The two of them in the same room for the whole day, surrounded by vicious kids who'd treat the whole thing as entertainment.

'They offered her a room on her own,' he said, 'but she didn't want it. She wants to be the same as everyone else. I thought you should know, but maybe the school told you already.'

'They didn't.'

He inched closer. 'Are you OK?'

She looked away across the lawn to the gate. 'I could have the room on my own. They could give it to me instead.'

'Karyn said you'd say that.'

'Did she? Is that what she wants? That's fine, I'll ask them to do that. Or I could take the exam some other time. I'll do it next year, or something.'

'Ellie, stop doing this.'

'Stop doing what?'

'Punishing yourself.' He leaned against the door frame so he faced her. 'It was your brother who hurt Karyn, not you.'

She jumped up. 'I have to go now.'

'Is that it? You're just going to walk away?'

He sighed and stood up. She tried to take notice of everything about him as he rubbed dirt from his jeans, pocketed the tobacco and ambled down the steps. She wanted to think of him later in her room, after he was gone. She loved the easiness of his body, the swing of his hips. He turned on the grass. His eyes were brown and gold. He had long eyelashes. He clenched his teeth, a muscle working there, making his jaw tense. His eyes glimmered with something dark.

It was stupid. How could two people really like each other and not be allowed to be together? Why not? Why couldn't they? Standing there on the lawn, he felt suddenly furious. She was turning away from the one good thing to come out of this mess.

He took a step back towards her. 'Come for a walk.'

She shook her head, wouldn't look at him. 'I can't.'

'Listen, I know you think we hurt everyone by being together, but we fixed things too.'

'What did we fix?'

'Karyn's not stuck in the flat any more.'

'She wouldn't've been there in the first place if I'd said something sooner.'

That was it, that was what was making him mad. It was like she was caught in some groove of punishing herself. It was exactly what Karyn had done when she locked herself away. Ellie had taken some of the load from Karyn's shoulders, but now she was carrying it around instead. And it didn't belong to either of them – it belonged to Tom bloody Parker.

He held out his hand. 'Come with me. I'm taking you to see Karyn.'

'What? No!'

'You did something really difficult to help her and she knows that. You're so certain she hates you? Ask her yourself.'

She looked horrified. 'I can't do that.'

'Why not? What do you think she'll do?'

'I don't think she'll *do* anything, but it'll make her feel crap. It took me weeks to tell the truth. I deleted her best evidence!'

'Because you weren't sure what the truth was and you didn't want the pictures on the internet.' He was surprised how reasonable he sounded, but he was sure of this. 'Karyn's getting help – from cops, victim support – she's not on her own. You have to stand in court and grass your brother up and no one's going to help you. Even now you could change your mind, but you're not. In my book, that's brave.' He moved a step closer, 'Come on, let's go and ask Karyn what she thinks.'

She took a step back. 'My mum's calling.'

'I didn't hear anything.'

'Or maybe it was my dad.'

'Stop it, Ellie. This is me, and I can see exactly what you're doing. Punishing yourself won't help.'

'I'm not doing it on purpose!' He watched a blush creep like dye across her cheeks. 'I feel so ashamed.'

'Karyn doesn't see it like that.'

'How does she see it?'

'I guess she realizes she might have done the same thing as you, if it was the other way round.'

408

Ellie sighed. The door and the bricks of the house were glazed with sunlight. She was bathed in it.

'I wrote her a letter,' she said, 'but I never sent it. Tom's still pleading not guilty, you know that, don't you? Karyn's going to have to lay down her soul, and all that will happen is everyone will know her private life. It'll be horrible and actually, nothing will change.'

'That's not your fault. Karyn knows the score. She's always quoting statistics at me.' He took a step nearer. 'I know you think I'm a bad influence, and maybe I am, but can't we at least spend some time together?' He leaned closer, wanted her to understand that Karyn didn't mind as much as she thought. Only this morning, Karyn had sussed he was coming here and given him that mocking half-smile she was so good at. *Tell her I'll come to the wedding*, she'd said, *but I'm not being bridesmaid. And if that brother of hers is there, I can't guarantee his safety*. He couldn't tell Ellie that though, it'd freak her out – make her think he was seriously about to propose.

'Listen,' he said, 'Karyn's out of the flat loads, she has tons of support, and yes, I know your brother's pleading not guilty, and yes, the court case will be a nightmare, and yes, your dad's a tosser, and yes, my mum still drinks sherry for breakfast and hides it in the airing cupboard and hopes none of us notice. Miracles don't happen overnight, Ellie, and we don't have to fling it in Karyn's face, but maybe we can grab something good out of this while we can?'

'Well,' she said, tilting her head to one side, 'that's one way of putting it.'

He laughed. 'Come for a walk. Get changed out of those pyjamas and let's go somewhere.'

A bird cried and flapped from one tree to another. They both watched it and it changed something. She softened.

'Look,' she said, 'the sky is gold.'

It was true. The sun had risen over the rim of the gate. Pink and gold bled together; the tops of the trees washed with light.

'Come on, Ellie, just a walk. No harm done. We're on the same team, you and me.'

She frowned at him, puzzled. Light collided with the wall behind her. 'Team McKenzie?'

He smiled. 'Something like that.'

These were the things she left at home – pyjamas, slippers, dressing gown, revision, parents.

'I'm off,' she said from the doorway.

Mum and Dad turned from the breakfast table to look at her. They took her all in, from the red lips to the summer dress, from the length of exposed leg, to the new sandals.

She gave her mum a kiss on the cheek. 'See you later.'

She smiled. 'You look lovely, Ellie. Off you go.'

Dad said, 'So, it's just a walk you're going on, is it?'

'Yep. It's a beautiful day out there.'

'And how does the weather explain the lipstick?'

'Just expressing myself.'

'That's not an explanation.'

He kept on frowning. Ellie felt sad about the look that passed between her parents – strained, polite, held-in. Mum might suffer for this walk; she certainly would if Dad found out who Ellie was going with. But, later, maybe Ellie would dare to tell him, and maybe, just maybe, her mum would support her while she did it. Event by event, she'd try and whittle her dad down.

She kissed him on the top of his head to say goodbye. He looked stunned. 'Don't be all day,' he said gruffly. 'You've got plenty of revision to do.'

'Yeah, yeah, my whole future's at stake, I know.'

It came out worse than she meant it to. It came out like she didn't care. But she did. It was about balances. There were many hours in a day to revise and only a few had sunshine in them.

Sometimes, if you want something badly enough, you can make it happen. If you miss someone so desperately that it wrecks your insides, you say their name over and over until you conjure them. It's called sympathetic magic and you just have to believe in it to make it work.

Here was a whole new reality – her and Mikey, the early morning sun rising over the gate and the day becoming itself.

Her dress was circles of orange and green, bright as Ferris wheels. He wanted to whistle, but stopped himself.

Instead, he said, 'Wow, you look amazing.'

She smiled. 'My dad's still capable of a bribe, even when he isn't talking to me. The dress is a taster of what's to come if I knuckle down and get ten A-stars in my exams.'

'You're going to earn yourself a whole new wardrobe.'

'Not if I keep hanging out with you.'

She nudged him to show she didn't mean it badly, then pressed the secret button that opened the gate. They stood side by side in the lane as it slid shut behind them.

'That leads to town,' she said, pointing left, 'and that leads to somewhere else.'

They looked across the field together. The whole place was edged with trees and the sun shone on the mud and green leaves pushed their way into the air. Two crows landed as they watched, then took straight off again.

'I'm up for it, if you are,' he said.

They walked around the edge. It was furrowed and the mud had dried in the sun and was hard under their feet. They talked about Karyn a bit more and about the court case, but once they got through that, there were so many other things to talk about. She told him about her Art exam and how she was doing a project called 'Red', and she told him that now the weather was warmer she was planning on getting back to her swimming.

'You promised me a swim in the sea,' he said, 'remember?'

She raised an eyebrow. He loved it when she did that. 'Well, you promised to teach me how to cook.'

'I will.'

'All promises are good then.'

He told her about Dex being upset that Mikey hadn't confided in him, how Dex had said he could do his day release at the pub if he got on the NVQ course. He shared his theory that Jacko fancied Karyn and how it was the last thing he wanted to have a theory

412

about, and yet also how he knew it was none of his business.

As they walked, the weather chased across the field – sun, then shadow, then sun again. The trees waved in the wind, their leaves gearing up for summer.

They came to a path that led through some trees and out onto a different field. This one was bigger, stretched further. Birds reeled up from their sunbathing and twittered overhead. It was beautiful. Maybe it led to the coast. Maybe if they kept walking, they'd reach the sea.

'I don't know about you,' he said, 'but I want to keep going.'

'Yes,' she said, 'me too.'

He felt perfectly happy as he walked side by side with Ellie, their fingers occasionally brushing, electricity building between them. It was the first time for days, maybe the first time in all his life, that he didn't want to change anything.

THE END